Islamic State: England

by

John Morris

Charlotte Greene
Dorset, England

Also by John Morris

Fractured Series
Inner Sanctum
Conspiracy Theory

Star Gazer First Trilogy
The Gatekeeper and the Guardian
The Twelve Tribes
The Wrath of Gaia

Star Gazer Second Trilogy
The Centaureans

Billie Steadman Investigates:
The Man in the River

Stand Alone Novels
Islamic State: England
Domicile
The Dreamer and the Dreamed

Printed in the United Kingdom (or country of purchase)

This is a work of fiction. Names, characters, places and incidents are the product of the author's imaginations or are used fictitiously. Any resemblance to actual persons living or dead is entirely coincidental.

Published by Charlotte Greene, Dorset, England

Editor: Susan Dewey http://beeberrywoods.com/FiberEtc/

Cover: Boris Junkovic
http://www.charlotte-greene.co.uk/Agents_BorisJunkovic.htm

Acknowledgements:
Susan Dewey for a most penetrating and challenging edit. Her incisive support for helping produce a balanced manuscript was invaluable, given the possible contentious nature of the book.

Dedicated to:
A peaceful world where people from disparate society's and religions, respectfully integrate, and work together for the greater good of all.

Official author website: http://www.john-morris-author.com
Publisher website: http://www.charlotte-greene.co.uk

ISBN Print: 9781910711101
ISBN eBook: 9781910711118

Table of Contents

Main Characters

Leading Characters
Dan (Danforth) Glover, SIS (MI6) Senior Agent.
Felicity Wigglesworth, Inspector in charge of Lower Meddlington Constabulary.

Main Supporting Characters.
Constable Percy Blodwell, rural community officer.
The Director of SIS, only referred to as The Director.
Group Captain Thomas (Tom) Wigglesworth, station commander of RAF Trimingham.
Margaret, his wife, Felicity's mother.
Alison Porter, Intelligence Officer, MI6.
Stella Nicholas, neighbour of the village office.
Veronica Sadler, Intelligence Officer, MI6.
Ayesha Hussein.
Sir Jack McBride, Marshal of the Air Force, and Head of the Chiefs of Staff, UK.
Colin Talbot, the designated liaison at GCHQ.
Derek, Liaison for GCHQ Bude.
'Sinjun', Brigadier Lawrence St. John Brown, SAS.

Other Characters
Harry McKinnon, Dan's Commander and line manager.
Director Matthew Green of Peterborough Land Registry.
Chief Inspector George Lovell, Felicity's line manager.
Superintendent John Stonehouse, Lovell's boss.
Martin Edwards, Junior Agent, MI6.
Stan Parfitt, rural beat bobby for Wymondham.
Karen Wheeler, takes over from Felicity at Lower Meddlington.

Minor Characters
Cathy Collins
Her youngest son, Chris.
Her eldest son Kevin.
Kevin's friend, Neville.
Simon Walters, murdered agent.
Charlie Sidebotham and Ben Hinckley, retired policemen who assist monitor the aerodrome.
Brian, the village innkeeper.
Gwen, the head bartender.
Dick Slayton, Percy's opposite number to the east.

Chad Pickering and Phil Chandler, HM Land Registry staff who assist with property ownership.

Doug Simmons, Department Head at GCHQ.

Bernie, Head of GCHQ Bude.

Linda Snowe, NCA Director.

Alf, the villager with a Transit van.

Sid, the builder.

Detective Superintendent Terry Meads, Manchester Police.

Charity: Sylvia Cartwright and Norman Harper, run Asians in Need. They are married in Islam, but not in UK law.

Wymondham Police: Chief Inspector Walter Cartwright-Harper, Inspector Benaris Khan.

Asian Characters

Waheed Hussein, Ayesha's brother.

Mohammad, Ali, and Hussein, directors of Anglo-Asian Holding, a property management company.

Ali Bros. Solicitors, Partners Ali, Ali, and Ali.

Valinder Jahlide Ali is the businessman and director of both.

Siri and Sana, the Boko Haram suicide girls.

Places

The Village where Dan creates his base of operations is never named.

Huntley Spa Aerodrome, where flights are monitored.

Abbreviations

SIS: The Secret Intelligence Service, or MI6.

GCHQ: The heart of British Intelligence information gathering.

EDF: The English Defence Force; an extreme right wing, racist, political party that argues with fists and hobnail boots.

NCA: National Crime Agency; the British FBI [formative].

Met: The Metropolitan Police of London.

AAH: Anglo Asian Holdings [fictional].

FGM: Female Genital Mutilation.

PC: Politically Correct. Also: Police Constable.

CO: Commanding Officer, RAF.

Brum: Birmingham City.

Background Information

Islamic State: England is set in the contemporary world of today, circa 2018.

The large villages of Lower and Upper Meddlington are purely fictitious, as is Huntley Spa Aerodrome. They are located due west of Norwich, Norfolk, accessible only by local roads. The villages are thirty minutes and the airfield forty-five minutes away from the city by car on B roads.

The Village used as a base of operations is never named, and is fifteen minutes by car from Lower Meddlington. It is loosely based on Hixon, Staffordshire, a village with private airfield and trading estate.

Lower Meddlington, the larger of the two, is almost classified as a town, especially due to new housing and shopping centre.

Elements such as land registry procedures regards claims of possession of abandoned homes without ownership was heavily researched, and facts presented, however unbelievable they may appear, are in fact true under British law.

The other surprise research revealed, was just how little UK airspace is covered by Air Traffic Control, both military and civilian. Off the regular air corridors there is hardly any radar coverage, and any aeroplane flying with its transponder turned off would be very difficult to track. Strange perhaps, but true in real life.

One important discussion raised by the book is the role of Muslim women in modern England, the battle against traditional values of a male dominated culture, and especially the fight against FGM. The character named Ayesha is representative of this struggle.

Modern Muslim feminists view historical Aiesha as embodying an early Islamic idealization of women as the social and legal equal of men, valued for their contributions in both the private and public spheres. For more information please see The Battle of the Camel.

The accent when spoken is largely that of Anglians the author has known in his lifetime, supplemented by fitting phrases from other nearby parts of the country. The dialect is tuneful, if relatively slow in delivery, with a strong accent on extended vowels. One such example is the spelling 'Ooh', often said in a surprised or questioning way with facial intrigue.

Chapter 1 ~ Plane Spotting

A rural village in central Norfolk, England, late summer.

"Where on earth have you been, Christopher Collins? Your dinner's going cold. Quickly now, go and wash your hands, then come to table."

"Yes Mum." Chris's mind worked on excuses as he slowly washed his hands. His thoughts were interrupted.

"Will you hurry up, I've been keeping dinner warm, waiting for you to get home."

His mother was serving his father when he sat down to eat. "A lot of everything dear, it's been a long and strenuous day." His eyes fixed his youngest son. "Nothing for the boy until he tells us what he's been doing. Well? Out with it, and it had better be the truth this time."

Shamefaced with eyes cast down, Chris had no option but to tell the truth. He pensively mumbled, "The airfield. I was watching the airfield. A big plane came in to land, and a lot of people got out and went into a hangar."

"Is your mind away with the fairies again?" His father swiped the bread plate away from the boy's reaching hand. "I asked for the truth, so what is it?"

"But Dad, that is the truth. It was an Airbus A300."

"Utter nonsense. Nothing has flown in or out of that old aerodrome since it became an industrial park two years ago, and when the small flying club was closed."

"Well go and have a look for yourself. I bet it's still there. You'll see it from the top of the hill."

"That's enough." His father's face grew red. "I've heard enough of your tall stories. Go to your room at once, no food for you until you learn to tell the truth."

"But Dad…" Chris's words died as his father gathered his bulk and began to rise from his chair. Chris dreaded a beating and ran for the safety of his bedroom.

"This is so unfair," he muttered to himself. "I was telling the truth, and still they don't believe me."

Downstairs he heard his older brother, Kevin arrive home. "Sorry I'm late mum, but I missed the bus, it was early again."

"Never mind about that, you sit here and I'll serve. I kept this piece of meat especially for you."

"Thanks mum, you're the best. What, no Chris? Is he late again?"

"He was late, and told us some cock-and-bull story about watching passenger planes landing at the old Huntley Spa aerodrome. He refused to tell us the truth, so I sent him to his room. Now, how was sixth form today?"

Chapter 1

Breakfast the next morning was quiet. Chris seemed reclusive, so Kevin asked him, "Why were you late last night."

"I told them the truth, but they didn't believe me. A passenger plane landed, and hundreds of people got out. They went into a hanger. It was an Airbus A300, but I don't know which model."

"Shut up Chris, another of your porkies. What were you really doing?"

"I just told you. Nobody believes me. I'm saying nothing more."

Kevin tried to get more information out of his younger brother, but he remained sullenly silent. That was unusual. Typically Chris's wild imaginings became more vivid with repeated telling, but not this time.

Their mother called out from the kitchen. "The school bus is coming, you'd better hurry."

Kevin jumped up, grabbed his bag, and kissed his mother on the cheek. "I may be a little late again tonight mum."

His mother stepped away and searched his eyes with her own. "Out with it, who is she? I remember being young once myself."

Gulp. "Er, d, duh, durrr, just a friend." His mother continued to watch him with her piercing blue eyes, until he admitted, "She's just a friend from school. I sometimes carry her books home. She lives near the bus station, so it's only a small detour."

"Be careful. I know all about young girls nowadays."

"Thanks mum."

As he ran out of the door, Chris pulled his satchel over his arms and hugged his mother. "Thanks for leaving the plate out for me last night. It was cold, but great food. I didn't lie."

With that he broke away, trying to stop the tears, knowing his mother must have seen them. He ran after his brother, who was holding the school bus for him.

The weekdays passed, Chris remaining unusually silent, and always on time for evening meal. If asked, all he would say was, "I told you the truth, and you didn't believe me. End of story." Then he'd turn away, or talk about something else.

On Saturday afternoon, Kevin went to see his friend Neville, who lived half way up the hill. They were the only two of the same age in the village. The Post Office and general store closed some years before, only the pub remained, mostly as a weekend eatery for tourists.

"When I leave school, I'm going to work in the big city, somewhere there are lots of people and things to do. What about you Kev?"

"Dunno. I was thinking about going to Uni in Norwich, but haven't a clue what to study."

"What? Uni's boring, and nowadays only the rich or foreigners go there. Why not come with me to London?"

"London?"

"Yeah. It's where things happen."

"Not me. I'm going to get good qualifications and a decent job. Something professional with good pay, holidays, and where I can make a difference in life."

"You sound like my father. This morning, he suggested I train as an air traffic controller, he says it pays very well. You retire at fifty-nine, but where's the fun in being stuck up a control tower all day and night?"

Kevin was quiet for a moment, as he thought the job sounded good. Deciding to check it out himself, he changed the subject slightly. "You'll never guess what Chris came out with on Tuesday. He says there are jet planes flying into the drome. Passenger planes."

He had expected Neville to laugh, but instead he sat back with a thoughtful look on his face. "What is it Nev?"

"Nothing. Well, sometimes when I can't sleep, I hear the noise of a large jet, and it's quite close, maybe just over the ridge."

"Well I never heard nothing."

"Ah, but you wouldn't. You live in the valley. Here we get to hear some of what happens on the other side of the hill. Next time, I thought it was RAF low-flying, but I'm going to check it out. Want me to call you?"

"Only if you see something. This is one of Chris's tall tales. Forget it and get your head down. Now what's happening with you and Lizzie?"

That evening Neville couldn't sleep. Lizzie had accepted a date with him, his first, and he didn't know what to do. Distracted, and anywhere but sleepy, his mind took a while to recognise the sound of a large jet getting closer.

Within seconds his mind snapped back to his conversation with Kevin, and he sprang out of bed. He, too, wanted an answer to the question raised.

Donning his clothes quickly, he grabbed a torch, and headed up the winding trail that led between trees and bushes, to the top of The Mountain. It was a mere eighty feet high, but the only feature for miles around. The vast plains looked as if God had used a steamroller to flatten the surrounding land.

Nearing the summit, he heard the unmistakable sounds of a jet engine winding down, and ran the last few paces. Before him lay the old aerodrome, and he caught a glimpse of landing lights along the runway, before they were switched off.

It was half a mile away, across a straight, if narrow country road. What drew his attention was the passenger aircraft pulled up near one of the hangers. People were getting out; there seemed to be hundreds of them.

Chapter 1

He took snaps on his mobile phone, zooming in and out, before finding a better vantage point to his right, the east, and setting the camera to video mode. The images were not particularly good, but showed the people exiting the craft. Some were children and he recognized women wearing burkhas, because they looked like walking drapes in shadows.

Determined to see the all of it, he hardly registered the lights being turned off, as he fell asleep where he was. Just after four a.m., he was woken by the sound of a jet engine, and saw the runway lights on, the aeroplane taking off. He grabbed his mobile, but the battery was dead. Cursing, he watched as the plane left, the lights went out, and everything returned to normal. He staggered home to bed, asleep on his feet, and was up late for breakfast.

Kevin came round mid morning, and Neville showed him the pictures and video. "Damn. The little shit was telling the truth. That's a big plane, and look at those headscarves. Moms and girls, right? What does that mean?"

"That they're Muslim. They are landing in secret at the dead of night, and have not passed through customs."

"Maybe they didn't need to, they could be from another part of England."

"I guess. But why come here? It doesn't make any sense. We live in the backend of nowhere. I know. I'll give you a call tonight, if they come again. And bring your latest smart phone for when mine dies." The boys turned to planning, and imagining what was afoot.

Kevin's phone rang at five-past two. "I hear the jet. Get moving." This time it was Kevin who was half asleep, as he floundered out of bed, and donned the nearest clothes. He grabbed a bag he had prepared in advance, and was halfway out of the door, before he remembered his phone. He raced upstairs and put it in his pocket, intending to run to the top of The Mountain.

"And just where do you think you're going at this time of night?"

His mother's words brought him up short, and he turned, saying, "Chris was right. A passenger jet landed here last night, and another is about to do so. Gotta dash--get the info."

He waved with his phone, and left his mother speechless. He ran out of the house, sprinting at first, before dropping down into a sustainable running gait. As he closed on the path leading up to the highest point, he glimpsed a flashlight above him on the trail, Neville presumably.

Kevin arrived less than a minute behind his friend, who was already filming. "That's a passenger plane!"

"Yes it is. I checked the internet today, and know it is an Airbus A300 B4. It can carry about two-hundred and fifty people, depending upon internal configuration."

"They're going into that hangar, is that the same as last night?"

"Yes. Quiet, I'm counting."

Kevin was startled by a noise nearby, and stood to ward off a threat. Instead he found himself greeting his mother. "So where are the girls? The booze, the drugs?" Her yes scanned the surroundings, before aligning with the boy's direction of sight. "Oh … that's a plane. A big plane. People are getting off it. Oh my God! Chris was telling the truth."

She settled to watch, trying to understand what she was seeing. Had it been the middle of the day, she may have had a better handle on the images she saw. But she witnessed a passenger plane where none should ever be.

When all went dark, Neville stated, "Two-hundred and eighty people at least, they are cramming them in. There doesn't seem to be much luggage. Maybe they're local?"

"I dunno. That forklift is removing some large boxes, and that seems odd for a passenger plane. I'm staying here to see what happens. This time I will film it all."

"Me too," said Kevin.

Cathy Collins looked at the pair of them and said, "I need to sleep. Call me if anything happens––I'll be in the car, just down below."

"You drove here mum?"

"Yes Kev, sometimes it is better to use brains than brawn. See you in a few hours."

Cathy received the call at 4.30 a.m., just less than two hours later. She was in time to see the jet take off, and took pictures of it on her smart phone. They talked about what could be going on, bizarre imaginings without substance.

Tired to the core, Cathy Collins rose to leave. "I'll give you a lift if you come with me now. Well done, by the way."

Kevin left with his mother. He didn't think it wise she be alone in the dead of night, on a forested hill. Neville stayed, but came running up to them before they entered the family home.

"Come quickly, I just saw a coach leave, and it's heading west. Here's the video."

A glance was all she needed, and Cathy ran for the car. The teenagers scrambled in as she changed from reverse to forward, and they left. "Text your brother an apology and tell him where we are," she said as they turned onto one of only two roads out of the hamlet, headed east.

"Why not go west mum, it's the shorter route?"

Chapter 1

"Yes dear, but the slowest. That lane is dreadful, especially at night. This way we hit the main drag much sooner, where I can quickly catch up. You'll both understand, once you get your licenses."

"Okay mum, you know best. But tell me this, who are these people? What are they doing?"

"I can't say for sure. They may be illegal immigrants, refugees, freedom fighters of Islamic disposition, ne'er-do-wells, freeloaders, or frightened families fleeing oppression. I see women and children, the elderly, and I see soldiers, not cohesive family units. Your thoughts?"

Neville responded, "The men are on a jihad, they have rifles."

Kevin answered, "But the women and children? They are fleeing persecution."

"Are you sure? Maybe they are plants. What if they were sent to plead family rights, in order to bring over their 'brothers', 'uncles', and 'cousins'? All young men are of fighting age, armed with Kalashnikov's."

"No man, you're stupid. These are regular families, okay, without the men. So what?"

"Because it is the men who go to war. This is an invasion."

"So I guess you mean that all these women and children will end up being suicide bombers. Get real Nev."

"Why not?"

"Because the world is not like that. Most people are decent."

"Yes, in the West. Do you know what they do to their women?"

Cathy spoke out. "That's enough, the both of you. You have few, if any facts, so this is irrelevant. Evidence boys. Proof. You have nothing except hearsay and grand ideals of conspiracy. Where are your facts?"

The rest of the journey was spent adapting views of conspiracy theory, none of which rang true, but were not entirely hollow either.

The road was straight as an arrow, if narrow. It ran on for miles; the large fields nearby, flat as a pancake. Cathy closed to a quarter of a mile, and switched off her headlights, using only sidelights for cursory view. She was following the large seater coach directly in front.

They continued in formation for several miles, until the coach began to change speed, as if the driver were looking for somewhere particular in the dead of night. Cathy backed off, afraid their tail would be discovered.

The coach continued its unusual pattern, until it braked sharply. Somebody with a rifle got out and guided the coach to rest. Cathy killed all the lights, and on tick over, crept as near as she thought safe.

"We'll scout ahead and get good shots, mum."

"Stop! Let me switch off the interior light first ... Okay, but don't get too close." As the boys leapt into action, her heart was torn. Was she being a sensible mother? After all, this could well be a wild goose chase, or their lives could be in danger. Nevertheless, she got out her mobile, and began filming, zooming to catch what was about to happen.

Two more men got out, touting Kalashnikov's or something similar, dragging a man with wrists tied behind his back, struggling in vain. A heated exchange took place, before another man, presumably the leader, got out, pointed a handgun at the man's forehead, pressed it into the skull, and pulled the trigger.

The body began to fall forwards, as Cathy zoomed in to maximum. It would not be the most defined image, but it would be the best. No sooner had she locked on the image, than the man was flung violently backwards, and over the side of what appeared to be a bridge.

The men with guns held them to their shoulder, sights to eye line, as they checked around the coach. Finding nothing, they withdrew, and in short time, the coach headed on its way.

Cathy gave a huge sigh of relief, doubled when both young men came back to the car. They were elated; she was disturbed. She had never witnessed a murder before.

They talked for several minutes, before she edged the car, still using only sidelights, to where the coach had been. There was nothing, no bullet, no body, nothing.

Kevin said, "It was a pistol, and none of them searched for the casing, let's find it." It took a while, but they found the casing, and a lot farther away than they expected. Cathy took a tissue from her bag, and carefully wrapped it up so as not to disturb evidence or possible fingerprints.

They scanned for anything in the river, either floating, or underwater: nothing. The boys split up, taking one side of the river each, and they went as far as they could, but there was no sign of life, or death.

Returning to the car, Cathy stated, "We are going home."

"But mum, we need to follow the coach." Neville enthusiastically agreed, but Cathy put her foot firmly down on the accelerator; soon her car was headed in the opposite direction.

She explained, "We have just witnessed an execution, the first and last I ever hope to see. This is a war situation, and sometimes, especially when nobody else knows, it is better to get word back, than have that information lost through trying too hard."

"No Misses Collins, we need to know where that coach goes to."

"Yeah Mum, same for me."

"Children, quiet. Think some more. Only we three know something is going on. You want to be executed like that poor man? I do not. Get the information back to those that know what to do with it."

"But Mum…"

"Silence. This is what is happening, like it or not."

"Well at least let's call the police. The body can't be far away."

"Yes it can, actually. As soon as the river gets to Falls Reach, a tributary comes in, it gets deeper, and there's an undercurrent. A body can disappear, and wash up near the sea months later."

"I still say call the police. We got the videos."

Cathy watched the boys in the mirror, and listened as they continued to argue. She took the shorter, but more time costly route back, and stopped the car just short of Neville's home.

She turned to look at the pair, her eyes looking directly into theirs by turns. "This is how we do this. Save your pics and videos to somewhere safe. I'll have a discreet word with the local police. End of story."

"Not old plod Percy Blodwell. You cannot be serious. We need forensics, a search party of cops, divers, scouring the river. We just saw a man killed, mum."

Neville was in full agreement, until Cathy asked, "And what would be the result of that?"

"They'd find the body, mum."

"Doubtful. I've heard of several people lost to that river. What else?"

"Even if we don't find the body, Misses Collins, we draw attention to the locality. They would probably investigate the old aerodrome, and then we would get answers."

"Yeah Nev, the national media would be all over it. Nice one. We'd get our pictures, interviews on the main news channels. Cool."

Cathy reasserted her authority. "Yes they would, at least for a day or two, before the next big headline comes along, and we are forgotten about. You want media exposure. Then what will they do after all interest has died? Come on, I'm waiting …"

"You mean the airbase, the coach people … come after us."

"Yes. You got it in one. I am not going to let the pair of you sacrifice all of our lives for a few seconds' fame and glory. This stops here, stays here, and nobody else knows. And no posting anonymously on the net. Deal?"

She held her palm out eliciting high fives from both boys, even if it was not freely coming.

Cathy's life had become complicated overnight. She made a call early the next morning. "Lower Meddlington Police, I'm Police Assistant Gordon, how may we assist you?"

For no reason, except an impulsive reaction, Cathy gathered herself quickly. "I know this is stupid, and probably not a crime at all, but could you ask the beat officer to call round today?"

"What is the nature of the crime Miss?"

"Misses, Misses Cathleen Collins, he knows me well. The crime, well, my garden gnome has been stolen, and I wonder for his safety. I hear they travel all over the world, even sending postcards and holiday pictures back. Please, can you help me?"

"Let me check, Misses Collins … Yes, the beat officer is due in your village today, and I have annotated he contact you. Is there anything else we can help you with?"

"No, thank you." That's more than enough, thought Cathy as she wandered, distracted, into the kitchen. She boiled the kettle, made tea, and dozed. It seemed only minutes passed before there came a rap upon the front door.

Awakening, Cathy took a large swallow of cold tea, and opened the door. She welcomed the police officer inside, gushing with uncertainty, to make him a fresh pot of tea, returning with biscuits also.

"So, what can I do for you, Misses Collins? A missing gnome I am told."

The question came against the flow of chatty, inane conversation, and she stopped short of putting the digestive biscuit to her mouth.

Laying the biscuit down, and leaning forward she stated, "The gnome was just a ruse. I need to share a secret with somebody. I think, hope, you are the right person."

"Go on, Misses Collins, I offer you utter discretion."

"Hmm. We'll see. Let me show you something." As Percy viewed the images, Cathy explained what had happened.

Percy was an old hand, just shy of retirement. He had never had a big case, and at that current moment of his career, didn't need one. He looked up from watching the videos, inspecting the still shots, and removed his glasses. As he settled back, he asked for more tea and quietly munched a biscuit. His bushy moustache caught a few crumbs which he casually brushed aside.

In time he spoke his thoughts aloud. "These aeroplanes, this bus, the execution, I see the three streams of information, and still I cannot believe it. Why here? There's nothing hereabouts."

"Then you already have your answer, Percy. The only link is the aerodrome."

"No. All I have are unanswered questions. You are correct when you say that filing a murder complaint, thus calling in all and sundry will prejudice the case. They'll stop operating for a while, and take recriminations on those they believe to be involved; they aren't afraid to pull a trigger. I'll need to verify this with the kids when they return from school.

"Regards landing the plane, that would normally be reported to the Border Force's East Anglia Command. I am loathe to do that, at least initially, in this matter. We don't even know where the aircraft originated from. Besides, they would go in gung-ho, and I think a more cautious approach is required."

Chapter 1

"So, what's your tack?"

"On my days off, I'm a keen angler, so I propose to drop some bait, and see who bites."

"You mean you are going to release this information to the press?"

"No Cathy. I am going to file a low-key missing person's report, with the photo you took. It will percolate through the nationwide systems and databases. Let's wait and see if we get a response."

Chapter 2 ~ Missing Person

On Tuesday morning, back from the ranks of the injured, Agent Danforth Glover, SIS, was enduring a seemingly never-ending bureaucratic nightmare. His desk telephone rang, and he picked up immediately. "Hello?"

"Dan, pop into my office for a moment."

Intrigued, Dan hurried to see his line manager, Harry McKinnon. "Come in Dan, take a seat. Tell me, how is your recovery coming along?"

"Rather well. I still get the odd twinge where the bullet grazed my femur, but I'm off painkillers, and the new, harsher physio regime is helping a lot. I hope to return to the field soon."

"Good. That's exactly what I'd hoped to hear." Harry drummed his fingers on the file in front of him, before opening it and removing a picture. Passing it over he said, "You know who this is?"

The picture of a man had been enhanced, and Dan recognised him at once. "Simon Walters. He's been deep undercover in Syria for over two years. Last I heard he was in Raqqa."

The controller leaned forward conspiratorially. "He was still there on Friday."

Harry placed another picture before Dan. "This picture was taken last night, early hours. Somewhere in the wilderness of East Anglia."

"That's a bullet hole in his forehead. He was executed."

"It would appear so, and that is all we have. GCHQ picked it up as a missing persons report, filed by one Constable Percival Blodwell of Lower Meddlington Police. It would appear, he initiated the action himself. When it hit our database a flag was raised.

"You are one of our best field agents, especially where hidden clues need to be found. Leave as soon as you are ready, say within the hour, and find out what the hell is going on."

"Yes Sir! It'll be great to get back to doing some real work. I don't know how you stick all this office bullshit, it's been driving me crazy."

Back at his desk, Dan Glover finished his immediate work, cleared his desk and sat back to read the file he had been given. There was little to it. His last act before leaving was to call Lower Meddlington Police, and make an appointment with Constable Blodwell for late that afternoon.

He took a company pool car, and swung by his home to collect an overnight bag and field kit. He added a body bag just in case. Soon he was on his way, headed for the wilds of East Anglia.

Wilds? He'd never imagined anywhere so flat and lacking life. Lower Meddlington was a small town consisting of a few hundred houses with signs of a modern housing estate to the east. It was like a time warp: no modern shopping centres, no shops of national chains, just private bakeries, butchers, and general stores. The only road had a war memorial in the middle of it, the police station nearby.

He parked outside, surprised there were no yellow lines. Getting out to lock the car, Dan watched a mum, toddler by the hand, stop and chat with a shop keeper sweeping his steps. Dan momentarily wondered if this was not a better age, than the one he currently inhabited.

Several minutes later, Dan was greeted by an aged cop with rotund belly and cheerful demeanour. "Constable Blodwell at your service. How may I assist you?"

"Dan Glover, SIS. The pleasure is all mine. Is there somewhere we can talk privately, like out on the street?"

"My patrol car, but first I need to verify your ID. I presume that is acceptable."

"Of course, knock yourself out."

A few minutes later PC Blodwell handed the ID back to Dan Glover. "You check out on the database, which I knew you would, but I have learned to verify everything. Come."

They left via the rear entrance, Percy continuing to do most of the talking. "MI6 eh, I was right to be cautious. I wondered who would respond to my missing persons report. So quickly as well. This must be important. Ah here we are. Jump in the passenger side. We have much to discuss."

Percy rolled down the windows as he got in and switched the radio off. He unconsciously fluffed his moustache and said, "So why send you from MI6. I was expecting a special police unit, maybe MI5. I thought you guys only worked abroad."

"Not so, although most of my fieldwork has been in foreign lands. We work in UK in relation to international threats, and we suspect this may turn out to be one."

"Why do you say that?"

"Because the man in the picture was deep undercover in Syria on Friday. He turned up here on Monday, and was presumably executed. Not far from here, I would guess. Tell me all you know."

Percy sat back and ordered his thoughts, before speaking candidly. "I have three people who witnessed the execution. Yes, that is what it was. Here, let me show you on my phone. The quality isn't too good, but it's clear enough. Turn the sound up and you'll hear the gunshot."

Dan studied the video and related snapshots several times, but his mind began working in earnest when the copper said, "I also believe I know how he came to be in this country. Look at this video."

Dan whistled when he saw the passenger aircraft, and noted the different timestamps. Percy went on to explain everything from the beginning, closing with the words, "You'll want to meet the informants of course."

"Yes, as soon as possible."

Percy made the call. "Cathy, I'll be with you in twenty minutes, with a special guest who is most interested in what you and the boys discovered. We need to speak to all four of you, in private if possible … okay, seven-thirty it is. Call me when your husband has left for the oil platform. I presume he's still working week-on, week-off? … Good, in that case we may as well eat at the pub to kill the time."

"A problem?" Dan enquired.

"No. Mister Collins is a good man, a hard worker, but surly at times, bordering on threatening. Best he not be there. You've a place to stay?"

"No, not yet. That's the least of my worries. I'll sleep in the car if needs be."

"We have a couple of hours to kill, so let's find you somewhere to stay, and then go the village pub near our destination for a meal."

"Sounds good. Does the pub have any rooms to let? I like to be at the heart of the action, as it were."

Percy swayed back and sideways to fix Dan's eyes with his own. "Not officially. It depends upon which side of the law you come from–– modern or old school."

"I have zero interest in petit laws. Jezzz, the places I've lived, the things I have seen. I could tell you a few stories to make your teeth curl. If they are making a bit extra on the side, then good luck to them. I can pay in cash, and I mean pound notes. Make the call, this will go nowhere, my word of honour."

Percy smiled, he was beginning to like Dan Glover, which caused him to offer one more piece of advice. "Ooh, 'round these parts, well they ain't ever seen a suit of haute couture like yours."

"Jeans, tee, and trainers or Chino's, polo, and casual shoes?"

"The former would be better, most of the time. You got a car … Okay, I'll drive you round to the front, then follow me."

The old pub in Cathy's village was otherworldly, and with Percy's assistance, Dan was soon settled into their best room. It was more than adequate, with en suite bathroom, and quiet. Dan paid in advance for two nights' dinner, bed, and breakfast, before joining Percy in the bar. The place welcomed them with wooden beams, and oak panels. A short time later they were called to dinner, which was most enjoyable. Afterwards they both chose cheese instead of dessert. They were finishing up when Cathy called.

A few minutes later, they were seated around her kitchen table. "I'm Dan Glover, SIS, or MI6 to most people. I am here because of this photograph, but before I tell you why, I need a word with each of you, in turn, in private. Once I have your own perspectives, we will form a team. Let's begin. Chris, you were the first, so where can we talk?"

Cathy complained, "This sounds like interrogation…"

Her words were interrupted. "Nothing of the kind. I promise you, just a friendly chat. I need to hear this from your own lips, without interference from others."

Percy spoke in support. "This is correct practice, Ma'am. We call it one-to-one."

"Sorry, we're new at this. It's okay. Use the living room, I'll put the kettle on."

Chris was only a few minutes, and came bouncing into the kitchen. "Wow! This is so cool, having double-O seven in our home!"

He started humming the Bond theme, as Kevin was called next. Cathy also rose. "Christopher Collins, will you please desist. You are to stop this nonsense right now."

When Kevin came out he was smirking. "That guy is really good, he got me to remember something trivial that might be important."

Percy added, "That's why we do it this way, otherwise you would all already know. It can cause false memories, or conflict of testimony."

After all were interviewed, Dan took a few minutes to check his notes, regardless of the fact he had recorded each interview. His observations were about the person, and other aspects of the case, not directly related to the words spoken. He was a very good profiler.

Once satisfied, he rejoined the others at the kitchen table. Dan became proactive in debate, and managed to winkle out a few snippets of information that may, or may not, prove relevant. Percy nodded towards Dan, and assisted where he could.

As conversation began to drift, Dan regained focus. "We are a team, and I need to see the airfield. Can we all go there now, the place where you took those pictures?"

Percy said, "The top of The Mountain, yes; the aerodrome, no. It is surrounded by military style fencing, with cameras, too. We would need a very good reason to go there. I tried earlier today, and was turned away at the gate by security, uniform and all. They told me it was private property, and would not let me in without a valid reason. I could have invented something, but thought better to leave them alone. But they are hiding something. However, I did learn they have a few small jets parked at the far end of the field."

Dan rose from his sitting position and said, "Let's go."

Reaching the top of the hill, Dan immediately dug in his jeans pocket, and put a headband with eyepiece around his head. It had telescopic vision, both day and night modes. He saw a runway capable of landing far larger jets, and four pre-war hangars with thick, blast-proof walls. The other buildings were modern, and there seemed a lot of them. Nothing moved; there were no lights.

His brief surveillance complete, Dan stated, "We are done for now. If there is an airliner tonight, and presuming there will be, tomorrow morning we will establish a permanent monitoring station here. I was thinking of a small tent well to the east, and another a little way below for sustenance and sleep.

"I can bring in the equipment we need, but not the staff. Percy?"

"Well, I could take leave, although I retire in seven months, and was saving up to shorten my time. I could apply for a week…"

"Nonsense. I'll sequester your services to SIS for the duration. That okay with you?"

"Yes, but…"

"Good. Now who have we got to man or woman this twenty-four seven?" Dan stopped speaking, and looked at Cathy.

She spluttered, "Well I guess so, but I have a family to keep."

Kevin offered, "We could skip school and man it."

Cathy shut him down quickly, "Oh no you don't young man! School for you, and homework done before you even think about helping here."

Percy cut to the chase. "I know of a couple of recently retired police officers, old school like me. Good friends through the years we served together. They'd be no good at gunfights and chasing suspects, but they would be ideal for logging everything coming in, or going out of that there aerydrome. Oh, and since they are getting creaky, a hut with proper seats, not a tent. Want me to make the calls?"

It may have been the flashlights, but Dan's eyes seemed to sparkle. "That sounds damn fine, Percy. Make the calls first thing tomorrow morning, and I'll throw in a little pay, tax-free. We'll call it expenses.

" Now I'll need to have a word with the local inn, discretion being the most important aspect. Cathy, Kevin, Neville, and Chris. We usually man these positions with two people, say one needs a toilet break at precisely the wrong time. You get my drift? So we will work on what works in practice, make it up as we go along. Any problems?"

Neville was slow to speak. "I have a date with Lizzie tomorrow night. It's our first date, but I guess I can put it off."

Dan said, "Nonsense. Go, enjoy yourselves and have fun, but check back here before you go to sleep. No problem."

Dan gave them each his dedicated mobile number, included them in the operation, and made them swear total secrecy.

The group departed a short time later, most envisioning wild plans of espionage. Dan was level-headed, and after the others went on their ways, he said to the last remaining, "Percy, care to share a beer with me?

I need to understand the locality, what is normal, and not normal around this neck of the woods. I'll pay for your room if that's okay, presuming your better half doesn't object."

"I'd need to call her, yes. I'll leave a message on the home landline--on a whist drive she is, and won't be back till late.

"That hide I described was one I saw once. I'm not sure if it is still serviceable but I can check it out if you like?"

"That sounds ideal. Let's discuss this and other possible operational things when we're settled in the pub. Meanwhile, as we wander down, tell me about the locals and this area…"

"… and this here used to be the Post Office, It's one of the largest premises in the village and been empty for years. The owners went abroad I believe, Spain or somewhere warm. They did try to rent it, but who would want a shop?"

"Show me," said Dan looking about, intrigued.

Percy obliged and soon Dan had a working understanding of the size and layout of the shop and integrated living quarters.

"Percy, if what we're doing turns into a much larger investigation, which I feel it surely will, then we will need a base of operations. You said the owners tried to rent it out, and failed. Do you think it may still be available?"

"Well, Stella Nicholas lives next door there," Percy pointed at the house across a narrow access road, "and she looks after the place, cleaning and suchlike. We could pay her a visit in the morning, it's a bit late now,"

"Ideal Percy, thank you and well done. I knew you were the right man for the job. Come, time to eat and wash the day away with some local ale."

After a slightly beery night, the first in ages, Dan surfaced to the insistent ringing of his second mobile phone, the one he had dedicated to the case. The clock read 02:23 hours. "Dan, this is Nev. Get your arse up here pronto, the plane is coming in."

Dan dressed quickly and was soon sprinting towards the top of the hill, he got out his phone and set it to video recording. He was filming as soon as the airfield came in sight, and was just in time to catch the plane touching down.

Still concentrating on the video, he said, "Thanks Neville, this is great. I got the plane's number with the aid of the runway lights."

They continued to chat and film. The runway lighting died. With his eyepiece, he could make out the passengers. "Some getting out are freedom fighters, but most are civilians. I counted two hundred and eighty two in all, although some would be crew."

"Keep filming Dan, the luggage and cargo are usually next."

The luggage container was put down inside the hangar the passengers entered, before other boxes were offloaded. Dan recognised some of the crates as military in origin, but said nothing. He followed the forklifts, but came back to the personnel hanger frequently.

Dan moved slightly away to get a better view of the interior, tracking with his eyepiece, and began speaking quietly, staccato into the phone. "Three flight crew. Three militia. All taken to another building.

"Twelve militia, all carrying AK47's, taken to a different building. They appear to be new to the place. See their heads turning, taking it all in? Inside the hangar, the luggage container is being hurriedly unpacked, and it would appear names are being called. Yes, people are coming forward, collecting their belongings. Some are being seated in a Volvo coach. It is silver with a medium blue stripe down the side, cannot get the registration number at this distance. Hangar doors closing, so that's all. No, wait, the jet is being cleaned and refuelled, a maintenance crew are checking the craft over as well."

Dan continued to film until all was quiet and the lights were turned off. Neville asked, "You called the guns AK47s, we thought they were Kalashnikovs."

Dan chuckled, "They are the same thing, just different words. the AK-47 was a rifle that was developed by Mikhail Kalashnikov in 1947, hence the name. The initials AK represent Avtomat Kalashnikova, Russian for 'automatic Kalashnikov' and 47 is the year it was invented.

It is renowned for its reliability and simple operation, it was adopted by the Russian military, and has been the basis of several rifles, some of which are still in use and production to this very day.

"Wow! How do you know all this stuff"

"We are trained on the use of many weapons, and to know ones adversary, you also need to be precisely aware of what weapons they are using.

"Those things, the AK47 are a good and rugged tool, but they are not the most accurate or dependable, especially in untrained hands such as those we see."

They spoke quietly for some time, and it seemed Neville's date was a success and there would be another. Neville also impressed Dan by asking educated questions. Later, Dan took a power-nap, before sending the boy home to sleep. Dan resumed filming at four-twenty, when the lights came back on, and an SUV dropped off six people at the aircraft steps, three crew and three militia.

Supplies were being loaded into the cargo hold, before the hangar doors opened, and the luggage box returned to the plane. A few minutes later the engines came to life, and after presumed system checks, the aeroplane began to taxi towards the runway; it would take off in the direction it landed from.

Chapter 2

With the plane taxiing, Dan got his first clear view of the hangar internals, where rows of camp beds were arranged in line. There were hundreds of them, and people were grouped in busloads, complete with their baggage.

By then, the aeroplane had reached the end of the runway, and began to accelerate for takeoff. He filmed it rise into the air, and immediately the landing lights were turned off. He came back to focus on the bus pulling out of the hangar. He still could not read the number plate, so reverted to tracking the aircraft, keeping it in centre of view. It headed west climbing quickly, before turning and heading northeast.

He continued to follow it until the coach left the access road, whereupon he switched focus. The headlights were bright, obscuring most detail, but he finally got the registration number when it went past him on the road below, and spoke it into the mic. He also wrote it down. He checked the plane, and could still make out its lights. It kept a steady course until out of range.

He returned to the inn, and was soon asleep.

Chapter 3 ~ Keeping the Lid on Things

Dan's alarm woke him at seven, two hours of sleep were better than none. After ablutions and dressing, he went down and made a mug of coffee in the inn's kitchen, returning to his room to make his initial report.

Dan compiled a file on his laptop, including all video, and an operations log of what he had discovered thus far. He added a second document listing requirements, one being a telescope with night vision and a suitable video camera. He asked for one dozen magnetic transponders, that could be attached to vehicles to track them. The last was a request for a half-mile 220 Volt, all weather extension cable, or a quiet generator––just enough for a fire, lights, and a kettle, and someone to fit it. Percy had mentioned something the previous evening that sounded ideal for his needs of the moment.

He added other requests, one the official attachment of Constable Blodwell, marking it 'Top Priority'. In another document, he laid out his initial plans regards the investigation, but stopped short of drawing any conclusions. He finished by adding, "I suspect something of a much larger scale is taking place, so will make enquiries for a local base of operations. The disused old Post Office may prove ideal."

Dan's laptop, and all connections, were highly secure and encrypted. He sent the files, and made live video connection, surprised to find Harry in his office. "Good morning Dan, you don't look so good, is everything all right?"

"It's nothing. I didn't get much sleep last night, but it was well worth it. I've sent you a progress report, but need the secondment of Constable Blodwell ASAP, like by eight a.m. if possible. I've made good progress, and here's what I have so far…"

When the report concluded, Harry sat back in thought. "The jet?"

"I need it tracking. There may be more than one of them each day. What I do know is that one arrives after two a.m., and departs at precisely four-thirty. How it is avoiding civil and military tracking, I have no idea, but they must be using a ruse. Simon came in on one from Syria, and I need to track it."

"We'll get on it. Anything else?"

"No. Only what's listed in the file. Oh, and PC Blodwell."

"I'll call the Chief Constable of Norfolk Constabulary as soon as we finish. You will have your man by eight o'clock."

"Thanks Harry. I better get breakfast, today is going to be busy

Dan joined Percy for full English breakfast, and they discussed events, and the day's work ahead. At seven-fifty, Percy used the police car's radio, and logged on shift. "I'm still working with MI6, and we have a few jobs to do right now. I'll drop by the station before nine."

… "Yes, by then you will have a better understanding Sergeant. I'll speak to you in person soon. Blodwell out."

"Tetchy?"

"No, bullshit. Come, let's pay Misses Nicholas a visit. She should still hold the keys to the empty Post Office and shop."

The former postmistress was at first distrusting, and a little shaken, but Percy and Dan turned on the charm. She took the keys to the old property next door, informing them, "The owners used to pay me to clean the place, and check for damage, any problems. It wasn't much, but it helped. Here we go, down the side and in the back way."

They walked the length of the building, and coming to the end, turned right. "Is that a car park, Misses Nicholas?"

"Yes, although it was hardly ever used. Room for six vehicles, so I was told. The garden proper extends beyond it, way over to that there fence. You see it?"

"Admirable. Let's take a look inside, if you please."

As the lady unlocked the door, Dan whispered to Percy, "Ideal if we have unfamiliar vehicles, your own car included."

The building was a large, converted tithe house, with a two storey shop extension the length of one side. Percy nodded as they were ushered inside. Misses Nicholas kept gabbling, as they surveyed the premises. There were three bedrooms upstairs, plus a bathroom and large storeroom. Downstairs was a similar layout, lounge and dining rooms, kitchen to the rear, another toilet, storeroom, and shop.

Dan said, "Ideal, and almost fully-furnished too."

Percy took his cue. "Misses Nicholas, can you contact the owners. We need to rent this place, as from today. Now if possible. You will be well recompensed. My colleague here needs a base of operations. For how long we do not know."

Dan interjected, "I think a week at least, but I'll pay for the full month, up front."

Misses Nicholas appeared stunned. She knew the owners had tried to rent the building. But there had been no takers. She was all in a dither. "Gosh, just like that? I'll need to clean. Now where did I put the disinfectant, and I'll need a new broom…"

Dan gentled her. "Misses Nicholas, the call, make it if you please."

"I can't reach them, the number is discontinued. I know they had plans to emigrate and start a business in Spain. Let me make the deal."

Dan received the keys, in exchange for a three hundred pound cash deposit. Percy hand wrote a basic agreement of terms, and issued receipts. They were signed, a copy given to each. Dan was assured all services would be available by evening, including landline and internet.

They thanked Misses Nicholas, and walked back toward the inn. Dan was unusually quiet, until Percy probed, "What's up Dan?"

"Tongues are going to be wagging, if they aren't already. I … we need to keep a lid on this. Do they have a village council?"

"The Parish Council meets in the pub lounge every month or so. They make important noises, but it's just an excuse for a night out. What's on your mind?"

"Well, rather than have the locals yapping to all and sundry, probably inventing things as well. I think we should speak to all the residents tonight, say seven-thirty. What do you think?"

"Inclusion, draw them all into the scheme. Sounds good, but we'll need to plan it."

"Yes, but not too much. I'll presume the best place to hold it is the inn's restaurant."

"Yes, it's the only place large enough. Eight o'clock might be better."

"Let's have a word with the landlord. He seems an agreeable fellow. I'll need you to inform each household, including local farmers, and everyone who is regular to this village. I want them all there if possible."

Agreement was reached with **Brian the publican,** and the meeting scheduled for eight o'clock. It cost Dan fifty pounds, but it was well worth it.

"We'll call on Slugger Bates next, best to catch him early before he gets himself caught up in mischief," Percy declared.

"A trouble maker is he?"

"No, not really. He's the local man of wildlife, a poacher to be precise, but we can never catch him at it. Best let me handle him, he's harmless, but in a ferrety, weasel sort of way."

Percy rapped the door, and when it opened, he said, "Slugger, we need to have a word with you, can we come in?"

His eyes darted around furtively. "Ain't done nothing."

"I never said you had. I heard you may have a hide for rent."

"Ooh, maybe I has. It'll cost you though. Better we talk outside."

The man was awkward to deal with, but Percy persevered, and the poacher showed them a fine hide. It was a wooden structure of sectional design, which was screwed together. There was a door and a long slit of a window at eye level when seated. It was solid, and ideal.

Percy made the deal with Dan's nod of approval, and cash was exchanged. They left for the hill at once, and were joined by Slugger ten minutes later. By then, with the aid of daylight, they had determined the ideal location, and helped Slugger and his lads carry the sections uphill. Dan ensured Percy did no heavy lifting.

Once the main components were in place, Dan put a tenner in his palm, and shook Sluggers hand. "Come to the inn restaurant tonight, if you want to find out what's going on."

"You'll be hunting people from here I dare say. I may be there. Mebbe have some'ut more for thee then, depending upon what you're about. Folks round here don't take kindly to strangers."

They left at once, running behind the day's clock, but were well ahead of the overall schedule. Having the hide in place was a major bonus. As they approached Dan's car, Percy said, "I should call in."

Dan replied, "No, they will have received your secondment by now. The priority is to see the bridge, and visit that boatman you mentioned last night. I need to recover the body before anyone else does."

"The bridge it is then. The boatman lies just off the other road west, best accessed via Lower Meddlington."

The police car stopped on the bridge, and they both examined the videos. Agreement was reached, and the point located. Dan found some scraps of human remains, and bagged the exhibits for DNA match. He produced some wax marker chalk from a plastic wallet in his bag, and marked the downside of the bridge. "So I know how far to come up river. Where does this lead?"

"To the Ouse, and The Wash, eventually. It may look turgid, but there is an undercurrent that gets stronger. The body will be a lot farther north than you imagine."

Dan took several pictures, and a short video, with commentary, before they headed back to the village. Percy left immediately, and Dan reversed his car. He was about to leave, when Cathy came running over.

"Dan, thank God I caught you. I meant to give you this."

She handed over a plastic bag, with a small calibre casing inside. "We found this at the bridge. I picked it up with a tissue, longwise, so if there are prints, you should be able to get them."

Dan peered at the contents, before breaking into a wide smile, and hitting the steering wheel in pleasure. "Thanks Cathy, even without prints, the casing can tell us a great deal. You are the star!"

Thinking quickly, weighing trust versus opportunity, and needfulness, he added the scrapings of skull and brain matter, and put them with Cathy's offering, in a small, sealed bag. "Cathy, I'm going to be away for most of today. Can you keep this for now, and put it in the refrigerator. I'll arrange for someone to collect it."

"Yes, I think so."

"Thank you, I need to make a call, don't leave yet."

Dan walked out of earshot, and when his secure call ended, he quickly closed the distance between them. "Cathy, later this afternoon, someone called Timothy will knock on your door. The password is 'fluttering biodegradables'. Got that?

Cathy nodded as her brow creased, Dan continued…

"Keep the chain on the door, and call me. I will verify who he is, and then you give him the packages. Do you understand?"

"Yes. You really do all this cloak and dagger stuff? Great!"

Dan was about to tell her about the meeting that night, but thought better of it. The evidence was more important, he needed to get that back to those that could decipher the clues.

Twenty minutes later, he pulled up outside Lower Meddlington police station, and was immediately escorted to the Inspector's office. As Dan approached, he saw Percy standing to attention outside the office door. Before he could greet the man, the door opened, and a woman in uniform of rank said, "Good morning. I am Inspector Felicity Wigglesworth, Chief Police Officer of this station. Gentlemen, please come in. So, what's this all about? Agent Glover?"

Dan proffered his ID. Percy added, "I verified it personally."

"Thank you, that's on file. You did not answer my question."

Dan sat down and replied, "There's little of worth, at this stage. Other than one of our best agents was in Syria on Friday, and was assassinated near here, early on Monday morning. I need to fill in the blanks. Ma'am."

"I understand. You will share with us?"

"We may come to rely on you and this police station for support."

"Why Percy?"

"Because he filed the information that drew us here. He's old-school. He knows the locals, and has good knowledge of my main points of interest. Please place old Huntley Spar aerodrome, and the industrial trading estate, out of bounds to all officers, until I inform you otherwise. Major incidents excepted of course. Percy will deal with anything minor. This is critical to the success or failure of my mission. We must ensure they continue to operate freely, Ma'am."

"And your mission is?"

"Combating international terrorism. Something odd is happening at that airfield, and I need the time and resources to get to the bottom, to understand the all of it. Otherwise, life continues as normal, until we discover just what is going on. I'll be in regular touch. Here's my personal phone number, but don't give it out, Ma'am."

"Touché. I'll need you to sign these release forms. Here, and here. Percy, are you all right with this?"

"Never better, Ma'am."

"All right then, dismissed Constable. Agent Glover keep me posted." At that moment she pressed a button on her mobile. Dan's phone rang. She continued, "That's my number. Speak to you soon."

The men hurried away. Percy said, "She's a fine policewoman, but too good for being stuck here. She upset the wrong person, or so I hear tell. She's all modern policing, and people around here don't get that."

Chapter 3

"Time warp. I'll follow you in my car, and we'll visit the boatman. I must find the body today. You recruit the retired cops, and set up our new base of operations. I'll be back for the meeting tonight."

Chapter 4 ~ Gone Fishing

Peter 'Corky' Mortimer owned a cottage down by the river, near the road, but off the beaten track. "Peter," Percy enthused, "Good to see you. How's life treating you?" Percy tried to get a look as Peter flicked the corner of a tarpaulin over a pile of something dark. "I'd like to introduce you to a good friend of mine, Dan Glover."

The men shook hands. "Dan Glover, MI6." Peter scrutinized the ID.

Percy continued introductions. "Dan's looking for something in the river, and needs to hire you, and your boat for the day. Is that okay?"

A deal was struck, and Percy left them to get on with it. He had a lot of work to do, and reasoned that if they did not find the body, Dan would not be back in time for the start of the meeting. He headed home, as keeping his wife happy was his first concern. He would then visit the two ex policemen in turn. He called the first of them. "Charlie, you in today? … Good, mind if I drop by?"

As they prepared to embark Corky said, "So where're we headed young man? Not fishing I presume."

"Fishing, maybe. I'm looking for a body I know to be somewhere along this river, where I don't know."

Dan produced a large scale Ordinance Survey map, and pointed at a bridge upstream. "The man, whose body I must locate, was executed here around five in the morning, on Monday. That's where we go, then follow the current for as long as it takes."

"A body eh. That'll be a long ways north by now. But I guess it could have got snagged on something. We should go north."

"We go south to the bridge. Begin from the beginning. Let's be thorough, but quick about it."

Dan knew Corky was correct, but he needed to cover all unknowns. They lost thirty minutes, but to Dan it was valid. Corky returned to base and refuelled. While he was occupied, Dan called the Inspector and invited her to attend the evening meeting.

Back on the boat, they headed north and kept going.

The sun was high in the sky when Corky said, "The thing is, if this body is travelling downstream, main current, it will be much farther north. I think we can get there before nightfall. Want to give it a shot?"

"Yes. By this time the stomach will be distended, the corpse face-up. It shouldn't be hard to spot, but zigzag the wider parts of the river."

Dan kept studious watch, using a pair of sophisticated binoculars. It was later that afternoon when Corky said, "We should be getting in the right area now. The body will be around here somewhere."

Chapter 4

Dan's mobile phone rang, and he spoke to Cathy and the operative. He cleared Tim with Cathy and added, "Can you stall him a little, offer him a cup of tea or something ... Thanks."

Some minutes later Dan saw something large floating to one side. The boat broadsided a dead body, as if in hold. "That your man, Dan?"

Dan spoke to the dead body bobbing in front of them. "Oh Simon Walters, how strange to find you here."

He glanced at Corky, before adding, "He was a dear friend. Here, put on these sterile gloves, and help me get him into this body bag. Maybe that patch of grassy shore over there would work best."

They worked as a team. It was not easy until the body was on the shore and they were able to roll it into the body bag. "Mission accomplished, thank you Corky. I'll leave you a large tip, but your lips remain sealed. Understand?"

Dan called Cathy. "Yes he's still here, I'll put him on."

"Tim, I need you to stay until I get there. I found what remains of Simon ... Sure, help Percy out if you need something to do. I'll be as quick as I can. Bye."

"Corky, let's get back, and don't spare the horsepower."

"We have a speed limit, to preserve the river bank."

Dan smiled and looked at him intently. "I need to be back before dusk. My day is far from done."

"Aah. A very large tip it be then. Hang on."

They sped back, docking earlier than Dan expected. Corky helped Dan get the body into the boot of his car and shook Corky's hand. "Thanks. Your pay and your tip. Remember this is top secret, so don't breathe a word about me, or our little adventure today. Lips sealed, or you may end up like Simon. I'm running late for another appointment, so must dash. But thank you."

Dan returned to his car, and floored the throttle. The sun was setting, a glance as his watch told him it was gone seven o'clock. He arrived in the village just before eight, and found a small gathering at their new base of operations. The grass of their car park had been mown, and several cars were parked on it.

Tim came out of the back door to greet him. "Hi Dan, you found him then."

"Yes, he was a long way downstream. Open your boot and well get this transferred."

Once in Tim's SUV, he said, "You sure it's Simon?"

"Yes, certain." Dan unzipped the bag near the head, and Tim said, "That's Simon all right, confirmed."

Dan zipped the bag up and added, "Apart from manhandling the body on to the river bank, and into this, I've touched nothing. So should you. Leave it for our forensics guys and preferred mortician."

"Got yah. Cathy gave me the other stuff, so I'll head home. This place is miles from anywhere. I'll be back in a couple of days with more fuel for the generator, and whatever else you may need."

As the car receded, Percy came to join him. "Good timing Dan, you found the body I gather."

"Yes, it was a long way north. How's your day been?"

"Busy. I sent the others out the front door. Misses Nicholas is guiding them. It'll let us chat on the way. I told the wife I was on special operations, but little else. She is not expecting me home for a few days.

"My ex-colleagues were keen to help out, and will start tonight. We've each taken a bedroom in the house. Oh, here's a full set of keys for you. I presumed you would remain at the inn.

"Tim set up a small generator, which is very quiet, so the hide is ready for use. He also fitted a telescope with digital camera, says it's the bee's knees. Later, he also helped carry things from next door. Misses Nicholas is a widow, and has taken a mother hen role. Her cooking is excellent. She'll be the one to spread hopefully good gossip about us."

"Sounds like home from home. Well-done Percy. I invited your leader to attend. I think she'll appreciate the inclusion, but she is not to present anything. I haven't had time to prepare any notes, but I know what I'll say, and we keep this as short as possible. They know you, so please make the introductions. Anything else? We're almost there."

The meeting began a little late, as people ordered drinks, and children ran around within a buzz of excitement. The landlord had called in extra staff, and orders were soon filled.

Percy began, "Ladies and Gentlemen. Boys and Girls. We will not keep you long, but I know you will be wondering about this stranger in our midst, and what he and his colleagues are about.

"Rather than have idle tongues wagging, and jumping to the wrong conclusions, we decided to include you all in what is happening.

"Most of you will recognise my former colleagues, Charlie Sidebotham and Ben Hinckley. They have kindly agreed to help our team for the next few days. To the rear of the room, please stand Ma'am, is Inspector Wigglesworth, head of the local constabulary, and my boss. She is also here to learn what we are about. Thank you, Ma'am. Last, but by no means least, is Dan Glover of MI6. Dan if you please."

"Thank you Percy, all of you for attending. MI6 do work in England, on international cases. Today, I recovered the body of a dear friend, and one of our undercover agents. On Friday he was in Syria. A few hours ago, I found his body in a nearby river. He had been executed. I am here to discover how he came to be in this country, and murdered on Monday, early morning.

"All we know for certain, at this stage, is that he was on a coach that left the old aerodrome on the other side of the hill. I strongly suggest nobody goes there, or shows the slightest interest in the place, or you may also end up dead. Do I make myself clear?"

Voices murmured, shock plainly visible on many faces. Dan continued, "You will obviously talk amongst yourselves, as some are doing now. Please listen up!

"I do not want one word of this leaking from anyone in this village. Consider yourselves to be resistance fighters, like in the last war. Keep us, and yourselves, safe. If word gets out to the wrong people, then they will come here and kill all of you: every last man, woman, and child!"

Dan took his seat. The restaurant was silent. Percy waited a few moments before concluding. "What Dan told you is the truth. Say nothing to outsiders, and we will all be safe. Remember, loose lips sink ships. We will stay in case anyone wants to speak to us in person. Thank you for coming, this meeting is now concluded."

Percy sat down and grinned at Dan. "That was brief, but incisive. They won't be saying much of anything to strangers."

The jovial atmosphere of earlier had evaporated, and some people departed hurriedly for their homes. Others sat in groups, talking in low voices. Inspector Wigglesworth thanked them for inclusion, before mixing with those remaining.

Dan noticed the poacher had stayed in his seat, and went over for a word. "What is it Slugger. You got something for me?"

"My place, tomorrow morning around ten." He rose and left.

Dan's clique went through to the lounge. Felicity was with them, and ordered a Pernod with lemonade and ice. She talked and laughed with the team, and chatted with Dan. He replied in kind, and without realising it, they somehow became separated from the others.

Dan suggested a table, as he was famished and needed to eat. Felicity joined him, and ordered cucumber sandwiches. She remarked on one dish. "Oh, you have fresh salmon, I simply must come back some time to try this."

Dan said, "Let me know when you plan to come, and I could join you. I would hate for such a lovely lady to dine alone."

Felicity was about to reply, when Percy arrived, his shepherd's pie being served to table. The mood of the moment moved on, but Dan wondered if he had just asked Felicity for a date.

He thought he had. It had been a while since he had enjoyed the company of the opposite sex. Felicity was intriguing, intelligent, and attractive. Her body athletic, yet fulsome, and taller than most. He glanced up at her sparkling green eyes, framed by short, ash blonde hair. He beamed at her, before toasting both of his companions.

Chapter 5 ~ Watching and Waiting

Dan woke at seven o'clock, as was his usual, and took a mug of coffee back to this room. He filed his daily report to Harry, who did not pick up, and left a video summary for his immediate boss. He felt much fresher after a good night's sleep, and went down to enjoy breakfast, before leaving for the office.

He had been expecting to see Percy, but Charlie and Ben were sat at the breakfast table. "Here's the report from last night. The first plane landed at eight-twenty-seven, departing at precisely ten-thirty. We only just got there in time. The second plane arrived at two-nineteen, and departed at four-thirty precisely."

"Thanks Charlie. Did it go okay for you two? Any problems?"

Ben replied, "No, none at all. It was a bit boring, but we confirmed numbers, and I think I got some good images from that there telescopic camera of yours. You better check just to make sure. I presume there will be a new tape or whatever each day."

"I'll download each day, if that's what you mean. Where's Percy?"

"He relieved us at seven, and when we got back, Misses Nicholas was making breakfast. She's a good cook."

"Tell me if she gets to be a nuisance. Sometimes people can be overly helpful."

"No need, she's making us all welcome. We'll tell you if that changes, but for now, she's a boon. You should have breakfast here. It's home cooking. And think about putting her on the staff."

"Percy sorted out your pay and hours?"

"Eighty pounds per day each is fine. We'll work seven to seven through the night, as neither of us sleep that well. Talking of which, we should be getting to bed."

"Thank you both for filling the breach, I'll see you before you start tonight."

As Dan returned to his room at the inn, the landlord was hovering. "The two nights, sir. They're up. Will you be staying longer?"

"Sorry. Yes, too much on my mind. I'll be here for several more days, if that is okay?"

"Our weekly rates are cheaper."

Dan laughed. "That's fine, book me in for one week." He got out his wallet and said, "I'll have the cash later, where's the nearest ATM?"

"There's one in Lower Meddlington. But go after lunch, as it's often empty by late morning. I do take credit cards, but cash is preferred."

"Cash it is then."

Afterwards, Dan joined Percy for an hour, allowing him to attend the bathroom and top up his flask of tea at their base. He arrived back with a packed lunch, courtesy of Misses Nicholas. "She needs to go shopping for food, all and sundry. There's a small supermarket by the new housing estate. Want me to go?"

"Thanks Percy, but no. She's more interested in me, for now. I'm the unknown factor. I'll spend the time with her, but may see if Cathy is free to join us, a bit of protection if you like. Is there only one cash point in Lower Meddlington?"

"That used to be the case. There are several at the new shopping complex. I suggest you buy bread and meat on the high street, though."

"I intended to. I'll also get a few things to make this more comfortable, like an electric fire. Autumn is closing quickly."

"Yes, the weather can bring all sorts in late September…"

A few minutes after ten o'clock, Dan rapped upon Slugger's door. He answered at once, quietly closing it behind him, and ushering Dan away from the house. "The misses, well, she's all ears and chatter you know. Best sometime, men keep things to them self.

"Now what thee're about, maybe I can help. I knows these parts well. Set traps around that there aerydrome. They pays me no mind."

Slugger leaned close and whispered, "I could maybe plant some swanky gismo for yer, fer a shilling of course."

"Slugger, you are a rogue, if a likeable one. I'm not stupid, and neither am I a free cash machine. You got that?"

The poacher was slightly abashed, but re-gathered quickly to make his sale. "Well, tell me what thee wants then?"

"I need the full numbers of all three light jets at the top of the runway, I got the easy one, and a partial of the second. I also need to know where the fence is not covered by cameras."

"You're going in there?"

"No. Just an option for later. A fiver for each piece of information, ten pounds total."

"That's hardly worth me trouble, but I'll see what I can do."

"I presume you know the local farmers, especially west and northeast of here?"

"Maybe I does. Twenty quid fer each introduction."

"Ten quid, and we leave now."

"Fifteen then. Thought you wanted to know about them there aery planes."

"Yes I do. What can you tell me?"

"Well, I don't rightly know. There are four each day, 'bout six hours apart, and they take off a few hours after landing. They goes west, then northeast. Bin at it a year or so now. Which is your interest?"

"Stellar. So you've known about these flights in and out for a while, and never saw fit to mention it to anyone?"

"Well, Mebbe so. Weren't none of my business now, were it?"

"Hmmm." Dan gave Slugger a searching look. "And what about the introductions to the farmers? Time to go. Let's take my car.""

Dan arrived back just after two in the afternoon, hungry, and with more work to do. He had enjoyed Slugger's company, at times. The man had proved a means to an end. Dan reviewed his notes.

The nearest farmer had said, "Dan, I complained to the local police about the aircraft, several times, but nothing has been done. They're still at it. I was told they be light aircraft, but they sound a lot bigger."

"That's my interest, and I'll sort it out, but it may take a few weeks."

Assuring full support, Dan left for the next farm. And continued west, then northeast. The last two hadn't noticed the aircraft especially.

He returned to his room and filed an interim report, noting locations and responses. He was there only minutes, before whisking Cathy and Misses Nicholas away on a shopping expedition.

First calls were the butcher and baker. Dan went to have a word with the local Inspector. "Ah Dan, how nice of you to drop by. I was pleased to be invited last night, and it filled in several blanks for me. Thank you. I can't spare you many minutes, so what's on your mind?"

"What have you got on reports of low flying aircraft? I am aware complaints have been made to this station."

"There were a couple only, and only one was repeated. We checked them out, and the local flying club was responsible. Light aircraft, so not that much noise. We had a word with them last year, and the issue died. End of story."

"You know very well, there is no longer any flying club. It was disbanded when the airfield was taken over by the property developer."

"Not so actually. The existing club moved out, but the title and original club remains, licenced to this very day. They have three small jets if I remember correctly."

Dan thought for a moment, before smiling in reply. "Apologies Ma'am. I think I'm beginning to get an angle on this. Would it be possible for you to let me have the names and details of the directors involved, both with the flying club, holding company, trading estate, and airfield?"

"I can tell you now: Mohammad, Ali, and Hussein, though sometimes in a different order. I did a little homework after your speech last night. It was just enough by the way."

"Would you have a file copy available for me to study?"

"No, not officially without written request from your superiors. However, I might bring it with me, if say, you were to invite me to join you for dinner at that inn we were in last night. I simply must try the poached salmon."

"Let us say seven-thirty for eight?"

Chapter 5

"Delightful, talking to you that is. Until later, then. Ciao."

Dan was amused, and whistling by the time he returned to his car. He was attracted to the woman, and wondered. He began to feel a bit like the imaginary 007, for the first time in his career.

Minutes later, the women returned with armfuls of shopping, and pressed the receipts into his hand. He opened the boot and stowed the groceries, holding the rear door open for Misses Nicholas. Cathy opened the passenger door to get in, but the devil was still within him. "Stop Cathy!" he shouted.

Hurrying to the driver's seat, he looked at her and said, "I better check the ejector seat is deactivated."

She gawped at him, banged on the roof, and said, "There is no escape hatch."

"I know. It causes such a mess."

Misses Nicholas was by then chuckling in the back of the car, as Cathy caught up with the joke. "Why you, Dan Glover, I will…" No more words came, but she biffed him on the arm, before laughing.

The shopping plaza looked much like any other, and Dan drew out cash, as the women went shopping for food. He went in other directions, and bought two electric fires, two map lights, torches and batteries. He added a kettle, a small microwave oven with hotplate on top, plus notepads and biro's, and headed for the women.

They were back in the village a little while later, where the women set about the new house, and Dan took supplies up to the hide and relieved Percy.

"It's looking like six hour intervals between each take off, Dan. Landing time is a little awry, but consistent with an international schedule. I've seen two Boeing 747 - 400 for sure, and over five hundred and sixty got off each plane. Then there's a larger E-bus, probably an A-380, that carried eight-hundred passengers. It's all on video. Passenger numbers are on the notepad. I need a toilet break."

"Thanks Percy, you're off duty. I'll take watch until Charlie and Ben get here. Oh. A funny thing happened today. It seems your Inspector thinks she has a date with me tonight, here for dinner in the local restaurant. I hope you will be at the bar."

"You old dog, you. She's a fine woman actually, but not a country girl. I'll be nearby, but you won't need to call on me."

Once relieved by the retired coppers, Dan had enough time for a quick shower and shave, before greeting his dinner guest. They got on better than he expected, and had a great time. She booked her own room, but spent most of the night in his. It was a passing of ships in the night, both of them determined to follow their careers, not wiles of the flesh.

Dan asked for breakfast room service as, unbeknownst to him, did she next door. Thoughts of her got so invasive as he compiled his morning report, that he took himself off to the bathroom for a cold shower. Resolute once more, he attended astutely to his duty.

Ten minutes and more passed, and he had almost compiled his notes for the video report. He stretched, and heard a sound. Looking up he noticed a larger than A4 envelope pushed under his door. Intrigued he hurried to open it. It contained the flight details and reports he had requested from his dinner guest. He was both delighted, yet dismayed to realise she was leaving.

Dan said to himself, "No use chasing after what has gone. The new day needs to be confronted. First, I need feedback from HQ."

He sent his report, and recorded video, and rang Harry. "I need info 'H'. Anything on the plane numbers, corpse, or flight plan yet?"

There was a pause. "You've not seen the news then, perhaps just as well. Most of our resources are otherwise engaged. To answer your question, the bullet that killed Simon, was fired from an Uzi that was last placed in Libya four months ago. That bullet killed an SIS agent."

"Dexter Bennett."

"Correct."

"Harry, I need the detailed flight plan of that aircraft. There are four flights per day, two thousand people landing illegally in Britain each day, and it's been going on for perhaps one year, do the maths."

"All we have is the transponder signal from a small jet. It approached Norway, and then dipped below one-thousand, five hundred feet, and we lost it. It presumably entered Norwegian air traffic control, and landed at Stavanger airport."

"That doesn't make sense. It's a smokescreen for what they are really doing. I need to track the plane in real-time. Find out what is actually going on. I'll need access to the military grid, Harry."

"We have the protocols in place, I'll make the request right now, but you may have to go to RAF Boulmer or Scampton to get access."

"I'm near RAF Trimingham, which is an advanced head station. I may have a contact there and it's much more convenient."

He finished the call, turned on the news, and witnessed destruction in central London. "At five-thirty, yesterday afternoon, a group of fifteen terrorists stormed Harrods department store in London, and massacred hundreds of people using automatic weapons, injuring many more. Their vehicles blocked exits, and were later exploded. The death toll has reached two hundred and fifty eight, but this is likely to rise.

"Many were killed or injured by grenades and Molotov cocktails, which set the store ablaze. The Fire Brigade could not tackle the worst of the fire due to snipers, and several firemen lost their lives that way.

Chapter 5

"Special police and army units, wearing protective clothing, finally took the ground floor, and restored control. Emergency crews entered, to put out the fires and rescue those still alive, only to be met with further assault.

"It appears the main structural walls had been rigged with explosives, which were detonated. The upper floors came crashing down on those below, taking out many rescuers, and shoppers who had survived the initial attack. Specialist rescue teams are now searching the pile of rubble in the hope of finding survivors. ISIL have claimed responsibility."

Dan's job was to prevent such attacks, not be drawn in by their fallout. Switching off, he dialled a number he had not entertained calling so soon.

"Inspector Wigglesworth?"

"Dan, get off the line, I am working."

"So am I. I need to see your father this morning, you mentioned he's at RAF Trimingham, I need to speak with the Commanding Officer."

"He is the Commanding Officer. Don't you have channels?"

"Yes, but my people are preoccupied with something."

"Then you already know ISIL attacked and virtually destroyed Harrods."

"Yes I do. And that is not my concern. That is the effect. It has already happened. I am working on stopping the cause."

"Oh, so not just a one-night wonder after all. Okay, what do you want from him?"

"Tracking what are supposedly light jets, below one-thousand, five hundred feet, off the coast of Norway. There will be four each day at six hour intervals, take off from our local airstrip. Comprendre?"

"One moment, I need to make a call." The line was blanked, but left open. "Okay, dad is intrigued, and will see us late this afternoon."

"Us? I thought you were busy."

"I am, but I'm also providing you a speedy entré. You should back this up with an official request."

"Already taken care of, Ma'am. I'll see you around three?"

"Make it three-thirty, I have things I must attend to."

Dan used his time wisely, settling the team in, and asking Cathy to relieve Percy every few hours for a break. He stayed with her and walked her through what they were doing, and how to use the camera.

In addition to six coaches, he had several minibus and car registration numbers he would ask Inspector Felicity Wigglesworth to check for him. He needed to plant tracking devices on them, and needed a means to do so.

Chapter 6 ~ Low Flying

"Wing Commander Wigglesworth, my pleasure to meet you."

"And mine yours, Agent Glover. How may we assist?"

"I have a small problem that concerns national security, aeroplanes, and coaches. I believe you could assist me resolving the former issue."

"We better talk in my office. Come."

"I'll join you father. The airfield in question comes under my police jurisdiction, so I need to be kept in the loop."

Dan explained that their operation was in its infancy, but showed their results so far, handing over a prepared copy. The Wing Commander studied the information, and confirmed his understanding with questions. He looked at Dan and his daughter, and said, "This is most odd.

"So, the jumbo jet is using the transponder code of a small, personal jet plane. This continues until the coast of Norway, where it flies below normal radar detection, and the transponder signal disappears.

"Let's follow this on the wall charts." The Wing Commander pulled out an old school rubber tipped pointer. "Your airfield is here, and the planes take off in this direction. Note this is all uncontrolled airspace, a relic of the vast RAF and USAF presence in East Anglia during the war. Norwich airport eventually succeeded in increasing their controlled airspace in 2012, but not this far west.

"Follow my pointer. A likely course would be to turn here, and fly northeast along this line, which is all uncontrolled airspace to the North Sea. We monitor it, but would pay a light jet little interest, unless otherwise informed. The immediate destination, Stavanger, is close by in aeronautical terms, but the flight path is all wrong for landing there. The big clue is that the transponder is either turned off, or set to standby, before hitting Norwegian controlled airspace. I would lay a bet your aircraft did not land in Norway."

"I'm almost certain it is flying in and out of Syria, and possibly other nearby countries associated with international terrorism. Can you physically track the plane for its entire journey?"

"No. At least, not yet. Tell me what they are carrying."

Dan related what he knew, when a knock came to the door.

"Enter."

"Commander, you wanted the official request as soon as it came in."

"Thank you Corporal. Dismissed." He glanced at the document and smiled. "Now I can track the plane for you. Or rather, our systems can. We will begin according to your schedule, with the takeoff at eight-thirty hours tonight, and monitor continuously thereafter, all air traffic in and out of your local field.

Chapter 6

"You have been authorised to view the details of these flights only, which will be recorded and set aside for you personally. I suggest you pay us a visit the morning after tomorrow. Do you have a secure number?"

"Yes sir, let me tap it into your mobile."

Dan's phone rang moments later. "Admirable, that's my call. I may be able to give you final destination verbally, tomorrow, when we have tracked a few planes. I believe we are done, Agent. Felicity, you will stay a while?"

"No Father, a few minutes only, I must get back, but I'll see you for Sunday lunch."

Dan read the situation quickly. "Excuse me, and thank you Wing Commander, a pleasure to make your acquaintance."

Dan proffered his hand, and as they shook. Dan added, "Ma'am, take your time, I'll grab a coffee from the mess."

"Just follow the corridor right, it's at the end of the passage."

He turned to leave, but Felicity added, "Don't eat anything, I have a plan for the journey home."

As Dan went through the door, he heard her father say, "Is there anything you wish to tell me, Filly?"

"Don't be silly Father, we hardly know one another…" Dan closed the door.

Twenty minutes later, they were on the road headed back towards Lower Meddlington. The hourly news came over the radio. The main headline was again the strike upon Harrods, the media turning an incident into a frenzy of speculation, with little or no supporting fact.

Dan said, "Typical terrorists, strike and second strike at the rescuers. It's a common feature."

"Will you have to return?"

"I doubt it. You see, this is the effect. What I, we, are working on is preventing the cause. Three hundred militia arrived today alone, and every plane carries boxes I know to contain weapons and ammunition.

"Sometimes civilians board for departure. We suspect these to be fighters and war brides outgoing. This could have already become a daily occurrence all across the UK. The threat lies in the large numbers incoming."

"You mean we are all under threat."

"Not just yet, but we will be. This is war. The authorities do not understand how organised and wealthy these terrorists have become. They have no inkling of the devastation that could soon be unleashed upon our soil. But I do not think that is their ultimate objective. ISIL are all about controlling territory, money, and people. Gimmicks, like Harrods, are for distraction, and perhaps for getting rid of rogue elements. Those prepared to sacrifice their lives for Allah, people too stupid to realise they are doing it for ISIL."

"You talk a lot of sense. I like that. And you believe they are coming into this country at our local airfield?"

"I believe it is one of several airbases being used. Do you begin to see a bigger picture evolving? There may be ships also. Let's change the subject, as this is no way to begin a date. We are on a date aren't we?"

"I don't know. I guess so."

"You're single, I take it?"

"Yes. No regular boyfriend. But what are the chances of finding Mister Right in this backwater. What about you? You have a wife, children?"

"No, none. I had a few relationships when I was younger, but the hours, and dedication to duty gets in the way. I can arrange a date, and then be called to action, often abroad. I can be gone for days, weeks, or even months sometimes, and am not allowed social contact. So girls think I duped them, or dumped them, and I cannot tell them the real reason why. I sort of gave up. What about you?"

"Pretty similar in many respects. I had one long-term boyfriend, but we split-up after I joined the police service, and started getting moved around. That's the story of my life, as we moved often with my father, from one airbase to another. I considered becoming a specialist WPC, rape and the like, but those departments are small, with little chance of promotion. Anyway, I preferred the action out on the streets."

"You appear dedicated to your career. I admire that."

"Thank you, I am. On promotion, I got the position of shift Sergeant in Norwich city, and was good at my job. I was engaged back then, a different guy, but he could not get his head around me putting my job before him. I wasn't, but he could not see it. Near the end of shift, or on a day off, something would hit the fan, and I'd be working.

"Like you just said, it destroys personal relationships. So now, I don't bother either. Maybe if I make Chief Inspector somewhere larger, that could change, but for now, I'm just marking time."

"So that's why you wound up here. I don't think so."

"Huh. Men! When I was up for Inspector, a Chief Superintendent said he would guarantee me a position in Norwich City, under his staff, if I spent the night with him. Obviously, he wanted benefits in kind to suit his libido. I told him to fuck off and I wound up here."

"The bastard! Well done. I admire you for that. Not all men are the same."

"What's done, is done and done with. Oh, we are nearly there. I need to turn off the road soon, but this road takes you into the top of the high street. We'll dine at one of my favourite restaurants in Upper

Chapter 6

Meddlington, it's the smaller of the two towns. That new housing estate links them together. I presume you like steak."

"Love it."

The meal was a great success, and their heavy conversations of earlier, were replaced by sporty repartee and laughter. Dan ordered cheese, as Felicity chose from the sweet trolley. He left for the Gents, and paid the bill with his card.

As they finished, Felicity asked for the bill, and was informed, "The gentleman has already paid."

She was not impressed. "This was my treat. Okay. I should be taking you to your car, but because of this, you are coming back to my place for coffee, and only coffee."

Dan smiled cheekily. "Perhaps you can pay next time?"

She looked at him. "Next time. Will there be a next time?"

"I don't know, but I'll be here for a few more days yet. Weeks possibly. Let's see what happens."

Felicity lived in a detached cottage just off Lower Meddlington high street, close enough to work, without being too close. She surprised him by making Gaelic coffee, which was excellent. Their banter continued, until Dan thought it time he should be leaving.

Felicity saw him to the door, but did not open it. Instead, she locked it and tossed away the keys. She threw her arms around his neck, and her lips and tongue annulled his feeble protestations. A fiery passion enveloped them. Clothes were discarded as they precariously made their way upstairs. Neither of them got much sleep that night.

The alarm rang at six-forty five, but they lazed for a few minutes in togetherness, before they got carried away. Later, Felicity sprang out of bed and walked naked to collect her robe from the nearby chair. Dan whistled in appreciation, and she turned around, covering herself moments later in a bathrobe, and headed for the bathroom.

Dan saw the clock had moved on. He leapt out of bed, donning his clothes, and shouting, "I'm not running out on you, but I must file my daily morning report, and see to the troops."

Once dressed, he poked his head into the bathroom. "Give me a quick kiss before I leave. I'm late."

Dan was only minutes late by the time he got back to the village. He collected a coffee, and went up to his room to complete his daily, morning routine. Once showered, shaved, and report filed, he went down for breakfast, and paid the landlord in cash.

Afterwards he checked in at the old shop, where Misses Nicholas was busy cooking for Ben and Charlie. They gave a brief report, and

Dan left to catch up with Percy, who seemed in fine form. "Good morning Dan, I trust yesterday went well."

"Very well, we have the planes being monitored in real time. I should get confirmation of some destinations later this morning. Meanwhile, I need to catch up with everything here, run me through the log…"

Cathy joined them a little after ten o'clock, and all three monitored the plane taking off. Dan said, "That's an Airbus A-380-800, think eight hundred people, for that would be the number of civilians that got off."

Cathy said, "Why are they flying in families? Because that's what I see. It makes no sense."

They watched and waited, until Dan's mobile rang. Tom said, "Dan, I have a preliminary report. Raqqa, Raqqa, and Sabha, Libya, in that order. All destinations were not designated international airports."

"Thank you Commander, this is just as I feared. I'll see you tomorrow morning."

Turning to the group he said, "They are flying in from ISIL held territories. I expect we may have more incoming during the current disaster in London, a diversion, as far as I can determine."

Just then, three coaches approached, and Dan said, "I need to track these vehicles, but today I'm going to follow them. It'll give us the type of destination. I'm presuming there will be several. If I get the chance, I'll place a tracking device, but no promises."

Dan stayed with Cathy and Percy until the coaches were ready to leave, and said, "Call me when they depart. I'll be on the road ahead of them."

Cathy said, "But that's stupid, what if they turn off?"

"Then I log it for next time, and narrow the field. Or I could turn round. If you follow from behind, you will be noticed. Follow from in front, and nobody suspects you. See you later."

Dan was away, driving for a long time. At roads works with a long hold, he remonstrated outside his car, and with the coach drivers behind. He managed to bug two of the coaches, before the lights eventually changed, and he had to run back to his car.

He pulled aside a short time later and followed the untagged coach. It dropped off at an Asian community Centre in Thetford, and he stayed long enough to video people getting off and entering the building. Helpers unloaded large boxes, and took them inside. He took a chance to plant a bug.

He had trace on the other two coaches. Targeting the nearest, he caught up with it just after the coach stopped at an Asian community centre in Newmarket. Repeat in Cambridge city.

The long drive back was confounded by more road works, and thoughts of Felicity Wigglesworth. He wanted to call her to invite her to dinner. The other part of his mind wanted to forget her; it could never be between them. Nevertheless, out of uniform, she was beautiful and absorbing.

Eventually, he entered the village inn bar, ready for a pint, and to tell Percy what he had accomplished. To his surprise, Percy already had company of the female kind, his boss.

Chapter 7 ~ Project Caliphate

Dan's alarm woke them before seven the next morning. He had moved it forward because of his guest.

She looked at him with sleepy eyes and said, "We must stop doing this."

"Yes I agree, just one more kiss?"

They were late out of bed, and chasing being in different places on time. They shared breakfast, Dan learning what she liked. They were interrupted by the landlord. "Ma'am, I don't feel right about taking the money from you for your room. You never set foot in it. Please, take your money back."

"Keep it. Call it damage limitation."

"But everybody hereabouts is talking about it."

"Then limit the damage to this village."

"Ah, thank you Ma'am. That I can do."

After the landlord left, Felicity said, "You followed the coaches. The result?"

"I've transponders affixed, one to each coach, and three destinations I need checked out. Think Muslim community centres, and ISIL."

"Gimmie."

Dan handed over a prepared list containing registration numbers, destinations, names of street and building, and specific map location."

"I'm impressed, Agent Glover. This is good work. I won't be seeing you tonight, this has got to stop."

"Yes of course, I entirely agree. And anyway, it could never work out between us, the job an' all. So, dinner at eight it is then."

She stood abruptly, he respectfully following suit. She said, "You are incorrigible, Daniel Glover!"

He replied, "Danforth, Ma'am. I try to please."

She hesitated, and looked him in the eyes. "'Danforth'? That's a strange name. Explain please."

"I was raised in an orphanage, and although British, it was not in this country. We spoke English, the locals, Arabic. The Sisters that ran it gave us all Biblical names. I was the fourth of five so named Daniel, and 'Dan-fourth' stuck. Somewhere along the lines of my life, perhaps my birth registration in Malta, the 'u', was dropped. Hence Danforth. I believe Glover is my family name, but never bothered to check, Ma'am."

Dan remained standing, and at the door, she looked back and blew him a kiss. He blew one back, and she was gone.

Upstairs, Dan made his daily report, adding there would be a follow up to complete current information at midday. He joined Ben and Charlie, who were finishing breakfast, and received their duplicate log of the night.

41

Chapter 7

Misses Nicholas brought him a mug of sweet tea, and he thanked her, asking it be coffee next time. "As you wish Dan, I'll change it now."

"No, next time, better not waste this. Anyone been to see us?"

"I've had some of the locals popping in to check us out, but other than that, only the poacher yesterday afternoon. He wouldn't leave a message, but wanted to speak to you in person."

"I'll see him later. Lads, tomorrow is Saturday, do you need time off?"

Ben replied, "I'm fine. I'm not sure how long this is going on for, but I'll work through till next weekend. If we're still at it then, I'd like a couple of days off."

Charlie added, "Same here Dan. Any idea how long this will last?"

"At the moment no, but I expect the operation to move on quite soon. It depends upon what we discover."

Dan left to have a word with Percy, and checked the generator en route. It was almost out of fuel, so he topped up the tank, and took the empty jerry can to refill.

He spoke to Percy about time off. "Well, I would like to work five days per week, but I can do tomorrow. I need to take the wife to church on Sunday, and it is our custom to have a full Sunday lunch with the family and grandchildren afterwards."

"You may as well leave on Saturday evening, I'll see if I can relieve you early. Come back for seven Monday morning."

Later he spoke to Cathy, who thought that between her, Kevin and Neville, they could provide cover. Dan was the reserve. Later he collected his car, and went to see Slugger.

"Let's walk."

"What have you got for me?"

"Four of them there airy plane numbers, an' most of another. The flying club door was open ar-ter noon, and I saw two more of them little airy craft inside. They had propellers. Here, I wrote the numbers down fer yuh.

"Them there fences goes all around, but there's no cameras at the back. That's farming land. There be red dots on the back of two sheds to one side, I saw later that night. They be cameras. I'll check in daylight."

Dan took the piece of paper and gave the man a tenner. Slugger put his thumb on the note, and kept his hand out. Dan added another tenner, and Slugger was happy.

"Why do they call you Slugger?"

"I don't rightly knows, and tis none of yer business. Could be me ways of hunting, along the ground like. Quiet as a mouse, smooth as a snake."

Dan's eyes bored into Sluggers. "Well, I does like a we dram ar-ter work some time. Makes it me sen thee knows. I needs to check the brew though. Well, when the Misses' hawk-eyes ain't watching. Keeps it in the gutting shed I does. She doe go down them parts of me place."

Departing swiftly, Dan headed for RAF Trimingham.

Dan chatted to the Commander, as he was led through to their operations room. It was not all that large, and only two corporals were working at scanners.

The Commander explained, "We are a forward head unit only. Most work is now automated, but we service the legacy local group. One is RAF Neatishead, which is mainly underground, but nearer your area of operations."

Turning to a corporal he said, "Corporal Benedict, this is the man I told you about, Agent Glover of MI6. You have a panel ready for him?"

"Yes Sir, this console here is set aside for the Agent's use."

"I'll leave you to it. If you need anything, Corporal Benedict will assist you."

Dan was shown the controls, and how to speed up the tracking replay. He studied the air traffic for some time before asking, "Is there any way I can take a copy of this?"

"No sir, the computer is only compatible with military specification."

"Why does the transponder number sometimes change?"

"That's air traffic control assigning a new number regards their area of control. They call it a squawk."

Dan returned to the beginning of the feed, and used his mobile phone to video the display on fast-forward. Next to him was a real-time screen, which showed one of the transponder numbers. The aircraft was on a different course, headed for France. Intrigued, he monitored the flight for almost an hour. It landed in the wilds of southwest Belgium, near to the border with Luxembourg. Dan took a short video, before the signal stopped.

"Benedict, does the log output I have, contain all flights concerning the aircraft transponder signals I gave you?"

"No Sir, only those to or from your nearby field."

"Have any gone to other parts of England, or Europe?"

"One just now, as you can see. But as for the others, I'd have to check, once cleared by the Station Commander."

"Thanks, I'll have a word with him."

Dan had to wait a few minutes, but was soon shown inside. "Sorry to keep you waiting, Agent Glover. Military business, you know. Now, what can I do for you?"

"I would like to request details of all destinations these transponders visit. The current arrangement is to or from our local airfield only. I need to extend that to all of UK, Europe, and terrorist dominated states of the Middle East and perhaps Africa. I would also like to add these two light aircraft numbers to the list, as it appears the transponder number has matched the aircraft number to date."

"I see. This is a big step up. A terrorist threat you imply."

"Yes sir, I think we may only be seeing the tail of the dog."

"So, each new location we discover will also have to be monitored. That is a new and separate operation, and would have to be approved by the higher echelons of RAF command. The official request would need to come from your Director.

"There would need to be a regular exchange of information between your team, and the project leader. We have already established that relationship. Perhaps your request would include continuing the current state of affairs, and maintaining our personal relationship."

"I'll see to it, Sir. You have previous experience in these matters?"

"Yes, as it happens, and concerning non-military aircraft. I received a commendation, but not the promotion I had been hoping for."

"I will add this to the official request. It makes sense, and also suits all of us involved, best."

The Commander tapped the piece of paper Dan had given him, and said, "I need a peek. Rule out any wild-goose chase."

Dan waited outside the door to the control room, before being allowed inside. "This is no 'snipe hunt' Agent Glover, you have thirty seconds to look at that screen. This is off the record. Please leave as soon as you are done. This never happened."

Dan was led to the screen, which had a lot more lines on it. It was a composite of air routes taken, and transponder numbers, including the new numbers, for the preceding hours. The Commander turned his back, as if on purpose, and Dan took several pictures and a short video. Ten seconds were all he needed. "Thank you Commander, we move up several levels."

"Good. This must go through priority channels, so do not expect anything before sometime on Monday. I'll issue you with a temporary pass allowing only you, access to the control room and mess. Let's see the guard commander."

As they walked, the Wing Commander's tone changed. "You enjoyed your dinner the other evening?"

Dan knew he was fishing, in a fatherly and protective way. "Very much so. Your daughter is charming, and excellent company. I wish we could take it further, to be honest with you, but our jobs make that impossible. We talked about that on the way back, and are agreed. I will not break her heart, but I will be the perfect gentleman."

"Thank you Dan. Ah, we are here. Sergeant Frampton, please issue a 'contractor' pass to Agent Glover here. He is allowed access to the control room and mess at any time."

"Your ID Sir … Ooh, MI6, I ain't never seen one of these before. A picture for our records if you please Sir … thank you."

The Commander countersigned the pass, and bid Dan farewell. Dan stopped at a lay-by and studied the latest images. What he saw made his current operation look like a Sunday school outing. He needed to see his Director as soon as possible.

He called Norwich airport immediately, and, after several referrals, was furnished with what he required. He piloted the light jet plane he had rented, and landed fifty minutes later at London City Airport. A short time afterwards he was debriefing with Harry, awaiting the Director's call for interview.

"Jesus, Dan! If what you're showing me is validated, then this is a massive operation. They could mount a Harrods style raid every day, all over Europe."

"Yes they could, but I think that is not the intention, just a diversion. What I need to understand…"

They were interrupted as the Director called. One minute later they were admitted to her office, where Harry updated the project, and Dan filled in the pieces. "I'm going to show you a short video of their current, known operations. This is highly unofficial, but vitally important."

Dan explained exactly what she was looking at. Her stern face took on a frown of deep concern. Her subordinates expounded upon what was, and could be occurring.

"So, to confirm what we know. They have two other unofficial airstrips in England, South Yorkshire, and somewhere east of Leicester. There may be more. There are similar airfields in Belgium, Germany, and France. When it suits them, the jumbo jet transponders pass themselves off a being light aircraft. I'll need to keep this below Ministerial level, if we are to get anywhere with it. I'll action this immediately, we will call it Project…"

"Caliphate, Ma'am."

"Yes, why not indeed, Dan. Project Caliphate it is. Harry, you can stand down. I will handle this personally. Dan, stay and tell me a little more, the main points, and where you think this may be headed."

They discussed in depth as Dan spoke candidly, separating distinctly, known fact from supposition. In time, he came to repeat the question he had almost asked Harry. "The one thing I do not understand, is where all these people are going to. Thousands of them per day, for months previous. And now we know this is not the only private airstrip they are landing at, and that is for Blighty alone. It's repeating all over Europe."

Chapter 7

"We are crossing team and espionage boundaries here, and I do not like that. You need a native Arabic speaker on your team, from Syria it seems. I have two, but they are otherwise engaged. Leave it with me.

"Of course, what you actually need, is a contact inside one of these Asian community centres, they're springing up everywhere. There's even one in my neck of the woods. Dan, I need you to discover what happens to these families after they are dropped off.

"You need more resources, manpower, a change of location?"

"No Ma'am. I feel I'm at a hub, and it suits me well. I have local contacts, the police and RAF, so it's perfect. I do need you to make an official request to enlarge our operation with the RAF. Ma'am, if I may, could you add to the request that we prefer to maintain existing relationships with RAF Trimingham, and personally with the Station Commander. It is nearby, and ideal for quick, private contact, and updating on a needs of priority basis."

"You want this?"

"Yes. It is fundamentally important to operational requirements."

Dan was pleased with the result, which would not have occurred if he had requested via report. In the foyer, he returned a call. "Felicity, sorry, I was in meeting with the Director."

"You're in London?"

"Yes, I flew down here a couple of hours ago, why?"

"Nothing. I have some information for you, so drop by on Monday, I doubt you'll be back tonight."

"Actually, I should be back in the village within two-hours, say three o'clock. I'm on my way to City Airport now."

"The pilot is waiting for you?"

"No, silly. I am the pilot."

The line was silent, but he could hear Felicity breathing. In time she uttered disdainfully, "So you have a pilot's licence?"

"I'm also qualified for helicopters, Phantoms, and Harriers. Now what was that about dinner?"

"Merde alors! Come and see me in my office. Goodbye."

The connection was cut, and Dan smiled. This was turning out to be fun; fun of the female kind.

Chapter 8 ~ Tracking and Tracing

Dan entered Lower Meddlington police station a few minutes after three o'clock. Five minutes later, Felicity escorted him to her office.

"Take a seat. You've been busy it seems."

"Yes. Your father was extremely helpful, and this operation will step up. He asked about our dinner date, and I explained we were both dedicated to our duties, and that I would be a proper gentleman concerning our association."

"You better let me be the judge of that, Mister Glover. That means I'll get the third degree from Mother, but forewarned is forearmed.

"I made a few calls to local stations in Cambridge, Thetford, and Newmarket. The latter two were more helpful. They all have dedicated police officers assigned permanently to 'community relations'. That is jargon for interacting with the local Muslim population, which appears to be growing rapidly. I wonder why that is, don't you? It seems there are several new community housing projects.

"I have contact numbers for two officers. Cambridge will be in touch. I have spoken to the other two, and it appears the afternoon suits both of them better, and I will keep working on Cambridge. We should go there together. Me because I made the contacts, and am police. You, because you need to understand the bigger picture."

"Sure. Monday afternoon, it's a date. So what about tonight?"

Felicity chuckled. "You don't give up, do you? I have weekly reports to complete, monthly reports to update, and am normally late leaving on Fridays. I usually chill at home, allow the week to wash over me."

"No problem. I understand. I have work to do also. I tell you what, give me a call if you get bored. I'll probably eat late."

Felicity eyed at him with convivial circumspection. "We'll see."

Dan rose to leave, and said, "Until later, or not, then. Whichever. Have a good evening. We each need our personal space."

"Thank you. Take this with you to fill the lonely hours. It's a brief summary of what I discovered for you, today."

Dan returned to his room, and updated his log. The days were becoming complicated, and he needed information at his fingertips.

Once done, he sat back to think. Felicity had intimated there could be a lead as to where all these illegal immigrants were going: Asian community housing projects. He used the laptop to bring up a satellite view, which he compared to reports, and online research.

The communities were in established residential areas. Were the previous inhabitants being driven out somehow? Was the Asian community spreading sideways, or was a new development in play?

47

Chapter 8

Dan did not like his own possible answers to any of the questions, so did the maths himself, in longhand: 2,000 illegal immigrants per day x 3 known airports x 90 days = 540,000 people.

Dan was stunned. Over two million people per annum.

His mind moved on, assessing what could, and what might not, be happening. He spent the next hours jotting down notes of what was probable, likely, possible, and seriously fuckwitted. None of his notes gave him comfort. He needed a beer, and even considered cancelling dinner with Felicity, until the thought of her company overruled.

He was about to call her, when his mobile rang. "Dan, sorry, but there's been a fatal accident on the north road and I must attend as Senior Officer. Two children dead, I'm told. It seems three cars were involved. It's going to be messy. I'll see you tomorrow."

"Go, but thanks for letting me know. Take good care of yourself. No problem. This is what we do. See you next time, Ciao."

Felicity stared momentarily at her phone; Dan had cut the call. None of her beaus had ever said that to her before. Instead, they had all pleaded to meet later. Even if she and Dan had not quite arranged a date for that night, Dan had immediately accepted the immediacy of her job—the needs of the moment. She was impressed one moment, and interrupted the next. "Ma'am, the car's waiting."

Dan went down to the bar intent on having a beer. He glanced at the clock, and knew shift changeover was about to happen. Duty before pleasure he mused. He accompanied Ben and Charlie to relieve Percy.

After handover, Percy said, "Time to wash and change, and a pint."

"Same here, it's been a long day, a long week. But we've made astonishing progress."

"Care to share?"

"Yes Percy, over a pint or three, and then a large dinner."

Dan sat at the bar, soaking up the atmosphere of somewhere different than what he was used to. Percy was taking a bath, and packing his few belongings for tomorrow afternoon. Dan chatted, with the landlord. He insisted Dan call him Brian. "It's not my real name, and a long story, but think Magic Roundabout and you're half way there. Anyways, that's what everybody calls I. So, no date tonight?"

"No, there's been a bad smash somewhere north, two kids dead, and maybe more to follow. I don't envy her."

"So, how's your investigation going?"

Percy joined them, and somehow, talk tuned to immigrants, and Brian said, "They be taking over thee knows. Not these parts precisely, but all around. I heard tell that Greater Bedlington is now 'Asian' only."

"I agree," said Percy. "Hatton Green and Malmesbury are Muslim, and Ribblesford is as good as derelict. I think the locals were driven out. But why? It doesn't make sense. Brian, do you know…"

48

Dan listened intently, but did not say much. His mind was working on the why of it. A little later they took a table in a quiet corner and ate. "Percy, I'd like to go and visit these ghost towns and villages."

"I'd be happy to show you around, if I could be relieved."

"Come Monday, the only things we will need to track are the minibuses, plus the few delivery lorries."

"They could also be taking stuff away. We can't tell if a container is loaded or empty. The red artic from Morgan Brothers seems to be the only regular. The other trucks are haphazard, and look like rentals."

"I intend to look into that."

The long days seemed to catch up with both of them, and shortly after dinner, they went to bed. Dan felt slightly alone for the first time in ages, and sent a text message to Felicity, wishing her a good night and sweet dreams. He received another by return a minute later, and smiling, soon fell asleep.

Dan woke before the alarm and, once his morning report was concluded, considered how long to keep the operation going at the hide. Just after eight o'clock, he called the British Intelligence technology department, and spoke to Tim about cameras. Dan decided on one particular model and asked it be put aside subject to official requisition. He added this to his report rationale, then added a separate spreadsheet of information listing registration numbers and companies he needed checking out.

He added several other needs to a separate document and asked for delivery and installation for the next day, Sunday. Satisfied, he sent the communiqué with a copy to the Director as she had requested.

Dan spent the morning following minibuses from the airfield, attaching tracking devices when he could. They were dropping groups of between eight and twenty people at various community centres, others at scattered villages, where they took over empty houses. The village communities appeared to be growing. He recorded all on video.

Near midday, he followed one back to base, a rental firm in Thetford. The driver was a company man in uniform. Dan waited until he left, presumably for lunch. The minibus parked next to five others, two of which he already had the registration numbers for. It was time to put on an act. Dan went inside the office and said, "Hi, what a lovely day. I need to rent a minibus, do you have one for self-drive hire?"

"When for sir?"

"Now would be good. Our regular guy let us down at the last minute, and I have eighteen kids waiting to go to the zoo. They are a nightmare when things don't work out."

"We only have sixteen seaters available immediately, sir."

"Okay, I better take one, and we'll squeeze them in somehow. A couple could ride with the organiser, so it should not be a problem."

The girl showed Dan to several that were available, detailing the terms of rental as they went. When they reached the minibus closest to the ones he was interested in, he walked away, saying, "Can't I have one of these? They are twenty-one seaters."

"No sir. They are reserved for a client, and pre-booked, as they often have short notice requirements."

"But you have six of them, surely one won't be missed for a couple of hours."

"There are eight of them actually, and all are reserved. No can do."

"Okay. I'll take that Transit over there. Let's do the paperwork."

Dan used a false ID and driving licence, paid cash, and was gone. He did not go far, but parked up off the road, and waited. His minibus would be hard to spot unless someone was searching for it. He monitored the hire centre for over one hour, until the two other minibuses returned and parked with the six others.

When the drivers left, and the receptionist was busy, he drove behind the eight vehicles he was interested in. He placed a transponder in a secure location on each new one. He videoed the rear number plate, over speaking the transponder number, lest there be any confusion. As soon as he was done, he drew the minibus up outside reception.

The receptionist said, "I thought you drove inside."

"Sorry, yes I did, before I realised I should report to you first. You'll need to check the tank, which I just filled up. May I have a card, we may need to use you again."

"Why yes of course, sir. The kids are happy?"

"Yes, and the regular guy will collect them." Dan caused the girl to laugh, talking absolute rubbish to her. She believed him, and never thought to ask anything else. Mission accomplished.

It was after two in the afternoon, when Dan called Percy, who reported, "The red artic left here fifty-seven minutes ago, so should be in Thetford around now, if it is heading for base at Croxton."

"Thanks Percy, I'm on it." Dan caught up with the artic as it entered the yard. However, one of the trailer brake lights was not working properly, so he took a chance.

Dan pulled up by the trailer's rear, and give the lights a good kick from underneath. He walked forwards as the driver got out of his cab, Dan said, "One of your brake lights is out, I almost crashed into you."

"Not again! Damn thing." The driver hollered, "George, it's that damn brake light again." Another joined him, possibly the older brother. Dan fixed a bug behind the cab, as they proceeded to check the problem. He left the yard unnoticed; both men fiddling with the rear light cluster.

Chapter 9 ~ Tactical Surveillance

Dan relieved Percy a little after three thirty, having already written up his log, and requested more vehicle transponders. He was pleased the whole picture was now coming together, without the need for twenty-four hour cover at the hide.

Tim called him just before five o'clock. "Hi Dan, I'll be with you tomorrow afternoon with the camera you requested, and transponders. Anything else you need?"

"No that should be it for now, but I'll call you if I think of anything."

Time dragged a little, as he watched and waited. Little of note was happening, although vehicles came and went, they were now known. He filled in the logs, and checked them thoroughly, before being left with nothing to do. It was not time wasted. It allowed him to double check, plan, and think.

He heard someone approaching just after six o'clock. Dusk was settling. The door opened, and Felicity entered, the last person he had expected to see. He rose to greet her, hoping for a kiss, as his spirits lightened immediately. She dodged his advance playfully, and said, "I thought it time I checked up on British Intelligence, saw for myself what you are up to. Tell me what's going on."

Dan explained to her, as if she were a trainee, and she adapted quickly. Later he told her about his day, and his thoughts on taking the operation forwards. "Of course, I cannot define a plan until your father receives and actions my high-level request."

"Apparently, and completely unofficially, he has already actioned it, to be deleted if the request is denied. He seems to think it won't be. You know, he always wanted to make Group Captain, like his father before him. Being sent to Trimingham seemed to put a cap on that, but this new operation is at Group Captain level, so his dream may yet come true after all. I just hope they don't send somebody else in above him."

"I'll see what I can do. He seems to be a gentleman."

"Hmmm. He can be a bit of a tyrant at times, but I suppose he has his reasons."

"Yes, the job can change a man, or woman. You okay last night?"

"Yes ... No. It was awful. A car came out of a side road, smack into the middle of a car travelling fast, which skewed into another car at speed, travelling in the opposite direction. None will live. The car in the side road was driven by a foreigner, and seemed to pull out into the wrong side of the road."

"Mind if I have a look at the case file. This could be related to illegal immigrants, or the aerodrome. Have forensics check for terrorist links. It's a long shot, but may throw something up."

"Not worth it. He was Hispanic, American."

Chapter 9

"Okay, forget it. You worked late?"

"Yes, very late. Thanks for your text. It came in just before recovery vehicles arrived. I spent this morning doing the paperwork, and chasing reports from others. I'll keep you informed of developments."

They talked through her experience, until her mood seemed to lighten. "Oh! Dan, I may have a lead for you. Chief Inspector Lovell, on duty as cover, had to come out from Norwich, because of the number of deaths involved. He was my station boss when I was Sergeant there, and we always got on extremely well together, professionally that is.

"While we were marking time, waiting for others to turn up, I mentioned about the Asian community centres, and it seems Norwich now has three. There was only one in my day, a few years ago. The thing is, I know the liaison officers personally, worked with them, so maybe we should begin on my home turf, as it were."

"Definitely, agreed. Insider knowledge. Knowing how the system operates does it for me."

"I had to tell him a little about what we are up to. He was most supportive, and offered to do a station visit on Tuesday. That, effectively, gives me one day off. He will need to see you there, before we leave, so be there for nine a.m., and don't be late."

"Tuesday it is. Norwich and then the others, or can we fill in some blanks on Monday?"

"Possibly? No, doubtful given the travelling time. My time would be better spent clearing up the current mess. There are other crimes on our books you know."

"No problem. I also have a lot on my plate, and it would suit me, if my surveillance request is approved on time, to spend Monday afternoon with your father."

They heard two voices approaching, and returned to the duty of the moment, watching for nothing. Felicity said, "This seems pointless."

Dan replied, "It is for most of the time, until something happens, then it is worthwhile. I hope that by tomorrow evening, I can start scaling this down, but I could do with Percy for another week. We'll move operations back to the shop-come house I rented."

The door opened, and the pair came in. Ben said, "Dan, Ma'am, we came up a few minutes early, thinking you may have plans for this evening."

"Thank you both, but no plans as yet. We were discussing the larger operation, but good timing all the same. I'll relieve you likewise in the morning." A short debrief followed, as Felicity listened to what they were about.

Dan and Felicity wandered back to the inn, sharing small thoughts and smaller secrets. It was fun between them. Felicity headed directly for the bedroom, but Dan stole a quick shower first, setting the bath to run for her.

Back in the bar, Dan asked for a rare drink. "Brian, a large, and I mean long-glass, of Pernod with a decent Lemonade, not that stuff out of the dispenser. Make it twice as large as previous."

"Ooh. I got some Whites set aside, that do fer yer?"

"Ideal. One third Pernod, two-thirds lemonade, but on the rocks."

"A slice of lime atop. Would that be shaken or stirred, sir?"

"Stirred. We don't want it to go bang, too much lemonade involved. Brian, do you, or anyone, have any of those scented candles to put around a bathtub?"

"Bath salts, bubble bath, yes. I'll ask the girls. The same for you Dan?"

"Yes, my usual, a pint of your excellent Old Crudgy real ale, but pour it when I come back down."

As Brian stirred the concoction, Gwen hurried up to him. "Dan, I got these, and they're a bit old, but should set the scene."

"Thanks Gwen, what do I owe you?"

"They're free, but replace them before you leave."

A minute later, Dan knocked and entered his bathroom. Felicity was luxuriating in the tub, with her nose just above the waterline. He lit the candles, and set the bath salts nearby. He pulled the plug, and half draining the bath to her protests, topped up with fresh hot water. She chose to add bubble bath, and he turned out the main light.

Coming to her side he whispered, "Sit up, I need to massage your neck."

Afterwards, he eased her back down to a lying position, and with a peck on the lips, left her to enjoy the moment, knowing he had smoothed taught muscles with his ministrations.

In time she came down, they drank, ate, and drank a little more. Later, they went to bed, and were asleep minutes later, their libidos stilled by the stresses of the day.

They woke early, and were late out of bed.

Dan had set the alarm for six, knowing what might occur that morning. He arrived early for start of shift, and relieved Ben and Charlie. He remembered looking back at the girl from the door, the woman who was becoming a central feature of his thoughts, but dismissed her saying aloud, "It could never work out. Damn it!"

His internal conflict was replaced moments later, with the sounds of a jet coming in to land. It was new to their schedule, and Dan was immediately attentive. It was a cargo plane. One hundred militia disembarked, before the forklift trucks went in en mass. Dan recorded it as a military operation in the log.

Chapter 9

The plane waited near number three hangar, until the red artic arrived. Dan recognized the driver as the younger brother from the transport yard.

Felicity came to him just before ten. "Bacon butties and a flask of coffee. You shouldn't skip breakfast. I'll be gone until tomorrow, so drop by the station late Monday morning, I may have more for you."

She pecked him on the lips, and departed. Dan followed her with his eyes, until she was out of sight. Her countenance was replaced by Cathy's, hurrying up the hill.

"Sorry Dan. We were all set to leave, and then Kevin started vomiting, shaking, it was scary. We had to wait for the doctor to come out. Neville is as bad. Something that Lizzie got them to try."

"Drugs. Stupid boy."

"How do you know?"

"Because I know. He'll be fine. Give him water, simple sugars, and a little vegetable soup. By tonight, he'll be normal again. I'll do today's shift, but may need a short break later. Go, look after your boy."

"Thanks Dan, I wanted to be here for you, but I did not expect this. I'm glad his father's on the rig otherwise he would kill Kevin. I must get back. Thanks."

"Go Cathy, I'm winding this operation down. Soon there will be little point in being here. Look after your family. I'll catch you later. Now be gone."

Tim arrived after four, and they set up a movement sensitive camera on the roof of the hide. "You'll need to run the generator for two hours each day, and not more than two days without running it. But once the electric fires and cooker are not needed, the solar power pack I've fitted will be more than enough. It's already running the camera and transmitter."

"Okay Tim, I got that. I'd prefer to situate the receiver up in my hotel bedroom, as I distrust the house environment, too many people I don't know. But, neither do I want people in my bedroom, so the dining room it will have to be."

Dan looked down at his phone, knowing he had to make the call. "Hello Cathy, how's the invalid?"

"Sleeping. His natural colour has returned, he is breathing normally at last, and he seems much better. Chris is out playing with the other kids. But you have a reason for calling. You need me?"

"Sorry Cathy, but could you relieve me for ten minutes, maybe twenty? I need to be somewhere else for a short time."

"Yes, okay. I'm not doing anything much right now, but I don't want to be away long, just in case."

"Of course, I'll be as quick as I can."

Once Cathy arrived, the pair made their way to the house, and began to set up. Misses Nicholas poked her nose in a couple of times, using the pretext of making them drinks. They accepted, but Dan ushered her back to the kitchen.

Dan knew the system, but Tim showed him some new features, and they were done. "Tim, security is my worry, have you a spare lock in your SUV?"

"Yeah, I've got a padlock with three keys, want me to install it?"

"Yes please, on the outside so nobody can get in without authority. I better relieve Cathy."

"Okay Dan. I still need to tidy up the main installation, and permanently fix a better transceiver. The pub food any good?"

"Yes, very good."

"Okay, I'll stay and eat here. It means I should miss any weekend traffic hold ups. I caught a couple on the way up."

Dan ran up the hill, and relieved Cathy. She was a little twitchy, obviously concerned for her son. Dan sent her quickly on her way, adding, "I think this is the last time we will be needing you, but no guarantees. Unexpected things can happen."

"Tell me about it. I never expected to see Kevin in that state, and will ensure I never do again."

When Ben and Charlie appeared, Dan stayed to tell them about the new camera, and that this night would likely be their last night shift. "The camera is on the roof here, and running, so tonight is to double check we are not missing anything."

Ben asked with a slightly furrowed brow, "Will you still need us after that?"

"Yes, I think so. Percy is the local, rural community relations officer, and we have some things to check out. I would like to maintain a daytime presence at the house we use, and have set aside the dining room as our new office. We'll train you both over the next couple of days, once you've adjusted to day shift."

Ben's worry seemed to have eased. "So, an office job. I always fancied one of those. I'll take tomorrow off and report back on Tuesday?"

"No. Wednesday, say mid morning. I'll be busy on Tuesday, and regardless, it takes more than twenty-four hours to change your body clock around. I presume you can both use computers."

Ben nodded his head, but Charlie said, "I have tried to use them, but my eyes suffer, and sitting for so long has started my sciatica up again. I get a sympathetic twinge in the hip, hence my hobbling."

"Charlie, why on earth didn't you say something, we could have changed the job to suit you better."

Chapter 9

"Because I didn't want to let you down. It's been a thrill for me, and if you need me for a day or two, I'm available. But if it's all the same to you, I'd like to make this my last shift."

"Charlie, go now, we will be fine, won't we Ben."

Ben nodded and began to speak, but Charlie cut in. "It's not nice admitting to yourself that you are getting too old. Excuse me, I need some fresh air."

After the door closed behind Charlie, Ben said, "Damn, I should have read the signs, picked up on his casual comments, but I judged him by my own body and age. I am several years younger, and fitter, also."

"Don't blame yourself Ben, we all missed it."

"So, what about the new job?"

Dan chuckled. "You need the work?"

"A little extra is most welcome, we are not rich people. We used to live in police housing, but had to buy a new place when I retired and, well, we still have a mortgage to pay off. What about pay and hours?"

"Same pay, eight to five, say, with an hour for lunch. Five-day week. How's that sound?"

"Admirable."

Chapter 10 ~ Confronting Misogynism

Pakistani accents speaking English

"Sister, you must stop confronting father. He is the head of this household, and he is displeased with you."

"Damn you! You have zero idea what my life, my worth will be, if this arranged marriage goes through."

"Sister, it is our father's wish, and that of the Imam. It will see us grow greatly as a family."

"And my life, my future prospects are the price. I do not accept that."

"No, you will learn to be happy, and to be a good wife."

"Without a clitoris? Having my lower lips sown up so tightly together, I cannot piss properly. How about I cut off your balls, and see what remains of your manhood."

"But that is different, men…"

"No brother, it is exactly the same, sexes reversed. You are so *majnoun*. Allah gave me my body, and I intend to keep it the way of his design."

"But sister, listen, or I will have to tell father about this. You must agree, a woman's place is to serve her husband, and Allah…"

The row continued, until their mother entered and spoke sharply to the pair of them. "Waheed, what is this commotion all about?"

"Sister is still refusing to marry, mother."

"Ayesha, is this true? I thought we had discussed the matter, and you had agreed."

"To the arranged marriage yes, but not the mutilation of my body, the one Allah gave me."

"We never should have allowed you to go to that western school, it has poisoned your mind. Waheed, leave us, I will sort this out once and for all."

The door closed as Waheed left, and the mother began her rant, a cane in hand punctuating each point. "The rules of our family are such, … 'Thwack' … That your father's word must be obeyed at all times … 'Smack' … Do you want me to take you to him? … 'Kapow' … Perhaps a good beating is what you deserve. … 'Wallop' …You disgrace us … 'Thump' … We will ensure you honour your family obligations.

"The wedding is set for your eighteenth birthday, less than three weeks away, and your womanhood will need to be prepared for the special deflowering ceremony. It is a exceptional evening for every woman, the first night of marriage."

The row continued until her father was called. Ayesha was stripped to her underwear, held down by her mother and brother, other children assisting, and given fifty lashed of her father's thick leather belt. Her screams were cut off when a rag was forced into her mouth. Her tears fell freely.

Between each lash, using the full force of his arm, the father berated his daughter, threatening many fates worse than death, until she finally agreed. She had expected the lashing to stop, but her father continued, and spoke sutras, as if he were enjoying the pleasure of beating his daughter.

When it was done, she meekly agreed to do whatever her father bade, and fell to the floor in supplication.

Her father looked on with disdain. "Tomorrow you will... No, I am busy. On Tuesday morning you will be freed from the curses of womanhood. You should be grateful to Allah for his blessing. It will be a full surgery, the best. Go to your room and pray for Allah to guide you."

Up in her bedroom, she was on her knees chanting words of worship to Allah, when her mother came in. Ayesha knew she would come, and showed what her mother expected to see. Her mind was alive with other thoughts, ones hidden in the darkest recesses of her being.

Her mother started to bathe her wounded back and buttocks, while speaking continuously. "I warned you, but you paid no heed. I received several of his beatings, until I learned how to be a good wife to him. That was long ago. Let me advise you on how to be a good wife and mother..."

Her mother droned on and on, describing to the western educated and thinking Ayesha, what amounted to modern slavery. Initially her thoughts were cut off, and she screamed, as the antiseptic scoured her wounds. Later she felt numb, and could concentrate a little better. The wounds were not dressed, and she was told to sleep on her front, allowing the air to cause scabs of healing.

Ayesha lay on her bed, and thought of her elder sister, who she hardly ever saw anymore. They had been best friends, until she was married. Nowadays, she lived with her husband, and seemed to be a different person, a living caricature of their mother.

What she disliked most, as compared to the western society she believed she belonged to, was that women were slaves of men, who behaved like despots. There was no love in their family, only terror.

She slept badly, but determined to go to school the next day, Monday. It was her only chance of escape. She was still sore from the lashing, but worried if she could summon the courage to leave?

She had woken early, extremely sore and tense. Her father was already shouting at her mother, and they were only just out of bed. Her younger sister was still asleep beside her, but Ayesha listened intently. "She will go to school today, and be put under guard when she returns. I will take her, and collect her."

"But husband, the beating you gave her was severe, I think she should stay home."

"Nonsense, a beating never hurt anybody, as you should know. Do I need to give you another?"

"No, husband, it will be as you wish. I must begin breakfast, excuse me."

It seemed to Ayesha, that her parents controlled her life, regardless of her wishes. Soon, her future husband would control the rest of her life. She could never imagine cowering to a man, as her mother had just done.

While her younger sister slept, she embarked upon an audacious and dangerous plan, fearing it would never work. She hid her schoolwork, and filled her bag with clothes and a few favourite personal items.

She needed one more thing, and when her turn came to use the bathroom, she was extremely quick. As she hoped, there was a moment for her to enter her parent's bedroom. She knew where her father kept the document she needed, in a locked case in his wardrobe. She took the key from its hiding place, replacing it immediately the suitcase was open

Her passport was near the bottom of the pile, and taking it, she noticed a small stack of envelopes beneath. One had her name on it, and she opened it. Inside was a handwritten bill of sale in Arabic. She froze, dropping the paper; she been sold to the man she thought of as her father, for two thousand pounds.

A fire lit within her. These people were not her family, they had no rights over her. She put the bill of sale back in the envelope, keeping that and the passport. She checked the other envelopes, discovering all her brothers and sisters had been bought like animals.

She searched, and found a medical report. The person she had thought of as her father was sterile. She put everything else back as it was and, checking the corridor with her heart aflutter, returned to the bathroom undiscovered.

Her normal routine kicked in, when her younger sister banged on the door, complaining of being late. Ayesha played her part, as if this were a normal day, and despite grimaces of pain, managed to finish breakfast, waiting to be dropped off at school. Her father had recently insisted she transfer to a Muslim school, and she hated it.

She continued her act, and did not look back. She knew her father would be watching until she entered the school buildings. Once inside, she headed for the female toilets, and waited until morning prayers began.

She knew teachers, administrators, and security would be watchful, so she deftly made her way to the gymnasium. That was the place perverted male teachers ogled the young girls. She had been devastated when she found out, but it fitted the male Muslim psyche. A storeroom was unlocked, with a window that led to the ally at the side of the school. She had been there twice before. Smokers used it. She had tried a few puffs but disliked it intensely. Now it was her means of escape.

She slipped out of the window, closing it behind her, and ran for the back road. Once clear, she walked quickly away from school, and her known world. A bus came along and she rushed for the stop, just making it in time. She swiped her travel card, and got off at a busy shopping centre. She overdrew cash on her limited card, but had three hundred pounds in her pocket.

She wanted to sit and consider her future, her next moves, but heard a familiar voice approaching. She hid until the danger was passed, knowing a new threat could appear at any second. She had to get far away.

Her back was causing her intense pain if she moved the wrong way. She thought several wounds had reopened, and worried about blood marks showing through. Despite the pain, she hefted her bag on her back to cover any leaks, and made for a bus stop at the interchange. She had no idea where she was headed, except away.

Most buses were local, but the first intercity coach that came along said Norwich on the front. She hailed it and it stopped. She got on, and took a seat midway back. She ducked down, hiding her face until they were out in the countryside.

The enormity of her situation began to crash down on her, but she battled the impending doom of feeling worthless, by re-reading her adoption paper. It was a bill of sale such as one would prepare for an animal, yet it gave her heart to carry on.

The journey was long, several hours, but her mind had turned to the future, tentative plans of what she would do when she arrived in an unknown city.

As she planned, she fretted. She bent and ripped her bankcard to pieces, it was a means to track her. She knew her mobile phone was another, and although already turned it off, she removed the sim card, but kept it and the phone.

The bus got to Wymondham, close to her destination, where a couple of brutish, British thugs got on board. They were drunk, had shaved heads, and were looking for trouble. Ayesha ducked down and tried to become a small thing.

They spat at her as they passed, and later, started hassling her. They tried to grope her, and called her nasty names. "Best you get off dear, most folk hereabouts don't like your kind, bombing the innocent, and raping children."

"Yours is the religion of hate and bums in the air. Child rape and misogynism..."

The world Ayesha knew seemed to disintegrate. She tried to deny their words, but they stung her heart. She knew they were true. She was also a victim of Muslim men, which was why she was running away.

She implored other passengers to help, but was ignored, until the driver pulled the bus over, and threatened the two with eviction. In support, an old lady got up and, brandishing her umbrella, bawled the youths out. She said to Ayesha, "Come, sit up front with me dear, you'll be safer there. Ignore these halfwits."

Her escape to a new world was not working out as she had hoped, but at least she was free. She could do as she wished, and would not have her sexual organs mutilated the next day.

Her mind was scattering, when a voice intruded. "Now then me deary, what're you doing alone, all the way out here? Do you have a name? I'm Rosie."

She looked up at the old woman who seemed to have become her chaperone, a local by her accent. Ayesha nodded her head; words failed her.

"Where thee be going?"

Ayesha shrugged her shoulders.

The old woman said, "I see. Tell me what your problem is..." and she wittered on, seemingly forever, eventually gleaning small bits of information from Ayesha, which she associated into a larger whole.

As they approached the city, the thugs got off, and Ayesha gave a big sigh of relief. She took several deep breaths, smiled, and was able to concentrate better on what the old woman was saying. Ayesha looked directly at the old woman, and said, "Rosie, we arrive soon. I have no idea what I will do, or where I should go. Can you advise me?"

"You are looking for a free hand-out?"

"No, never. I don't know this city at all, and fear my own people will recognise me, and drag me back to forced marriage. I need to disappear from them, find work, and a place to stay. One bedroom is fine."

"I see. That puts a different complexion on things. Are you educated, do you have any skills?"

"I was studying second year A levels in Physics and Electronics. Also English Literature, because I like it. I know how to darn, sew, cook, and clean house. I don't mind being a servant, just as long as I am safe from my family."

"You mentioned an arranged marriage. I thought that was illegal?"

"Not to our people. They are so tribal. I am not like them. Today I found out I was sold as a baby, so they aren't even my real family. I have no idea where my real parents are, or even who they are." Her tears came again. Ayesha felt fragile.

Rosie said, "Surely an arranged marriage can't be that bad. You will grow to love your husband in time. It was often that way in this country, even one century ago. The rich still do it today."

"I hate them all. They are misogynists. Do you really want to hear what my life would have become, if I had not escaped?"

"Yes dear, tell me the all of it."

Ayesha spilled her heart and left nothing out. She described the kitchen table operation for extreme genital mutilation in great detail, the blunt paring knife, no anaesthetic, or aftercare. The removal of clitoris, labia major and minor, and being sewn up very tight, so she could not piss properly. And then she described the life of slavery she would endure for her future mother in law, and her husband, a fanatically devout Muslim who believed in full Sharia Law.

Rosie gaped in horror.

"Last night I refused my father's direct order to marry this beast, and received fifty lashes. My mother and siblings held me down. My back and buttocks are still extremely painful."

Rosie thought quickly, as the bus pulled into the terminal. "Come with me. You have money?"

"Yes, a little, but it will soon be gone unless I find work."

"I know someone with a room to rent, for cash. I also know of a few jobs going in local places, off the beaten track. By tomorrow, you should have a new life. Interested?"

"Oh yes. Thank you, thank you so much. I can never repay your kindness, but I will try."

They caught a local bus to a nearby village, and Rosie's home.

Chapter 11 ~ New Directions

Dan completed his morning routine, and arrived early at the office. Discovering he had not eaten, Misses Nicholas began preparing breakfast for him.

Percy arrived at a quarter to seven, ready to relieve the others, but asked for breakfast butties and a flask of tea to be sent up, as he had left before his wife woke.

Dan sat him down at the kitchen table and said, "Eat mine." Taking the projection sheet, he locked the office, and went to relieve Ben and Charlie. Misses Nicholas continued cooking full English breakfast.

Ben was on his own. "I sent Charlie back just after four, he's not well. He was on about going home, but I doubt he was up to driving."

"Shit. He's worse than I thought. His car is still parked behind the office, so he'll be sleeping."

"Don't blame yourself. You relieving me, Percy a no show."

"No, he's having breakfast, and yours is being prepared. Let's compare logs, then you can go to sleep where and when you wish."

Less than a minute passed, as the logs were in the same format, one from observation, and another from the software installed. They were identical.

Dan said, "It took me thirty minutes to do my log, you were here all night. It doesn't make sense for you to man the hide. Stay, eat, sleep, or go home, the choice is yours to make. I'll see you after ten on Wednesday."

"Thanks Dan. I'll eat and go home, sleep in my own bed. The misses will be up and out, so it should be my best sleep in ages."

Ben departed, and Percy arrived a short time later. "Percy, let me show you the overnight logs, spot any difference?"

Percy put on his glasses and made careful study. "No, they're the same. That makes a big difference. Are we moving on to a new plan?"

"Yes, although I would like to have you around for at least another week. Ma'am has already signed off on it, unless you have any objections?"

"I'm fine, Dan. Enjoying the role, and where it may lead. So today?"

"Time to wrap up. Help me carry this lot back to our new office."

"It will require two trips."

"Three. I'll need a hand with the generator. It's no longer required as the fires and cooker are gone."

"What will we do afterwards?"

"I thought we should visit some ghost villages this morning, find out what is, and is not, going on. This afternoon, I should be able to spend in an aircraft tracking station to learn more about the bigger picture. Care to join me?"

"You bet. I'd love to know what this is all about, although I already have my own thoughts about it."

Dan smiled and said, "You're probably correct, but think big, much bigger. I don't know the answers yet, but we are headed in the right direction. Please hold the telescope while I free it from the tripod."

Once everything was stored in the office, Dan showed Percy how to make a backup, and then use it to compile the log. Percy was a little unsure, so Dan said, "We'll do it together tomorrow, you working, and I watching. You'll soon get the hang of it. It's a bit like a video, but with pan and zoom facility."

Once Percy's training was completed, Dan prepared a video log to show the RAF what was happening on the ground. They heard noises upstairs, followed by someone coming down. Dan locked the office, and they went through to the kitchen. Misses Nicholas was cooking another breakfast, despite Charlie's protestations.

Dan held out his hand. "Charlie, thank you for all your help, we needed you, and you stepped up to fill that breach. Please take this envelope as a sign of our appreciation, including full payment for last night. Now go and enjoy your retirement. Ben here's one for you, thank you also.

Just then there came a rap on the rear door; it was opened to reveal Slugger glancing around furtively. He was carrying a hessian sack. "Now which of thee good gents and lady, wants a brace of plump rabbits, or a fine cock pheasant. Caught him this morning o'er by Willets Green. Lovely young bird. Feel the breast."

Heads shook, but Charlie enquired, "How much Slugger?"

"This pheasant, he be worth a lot more. But for the local law I'll deal for twenty pound. Cash, you understand."

Charlie tried to haggle, but was no match for the poacher. He ended up paying five pounds more, but the pheasant would be hung for a week, and oven-ready. Slugger concluded the trade, "That be 'perfic'. I'll gift thee the giblets an' all. A fine meal for the Lord's Day. Drop by Sunday morning. The misses goes to church. I be in the gutting shed."

As soon as slugger departed, Dan said, "Excuse me people, but I have a report to make. Say thirty minutes, Percy."

The report took a little longer to file than expected, as the Director wanted a word with him, but the clarity of sharing face to face was worth the lost time. Later, Dan found Percy studying a large-scale ordinance survey map of the greater area.

"Ah Dan. I've been doing a little homework, and thought we should take this route. What do you think?"

Percy traced a network of country roads with his finger, and Dan said, "That's fine Percy. Could we take your car, as I'd like to take pictures, video maybe, and regardless, you know these local roads. I'll show you how to fill in a mileage form to claim as expenses."

"There's no need for that Dan. I've been filling out travel vouchers for years. It's almost nine o'clock, when do you want to leave?"

"Now suits me fine."

They began what would become known as 'the grand tour'. The first village was slightly larger than their home base, and still supported a shop come Post Office. Percy went in as Dan videoed. Minutes later Percy reported, "They've seen no immigrants around here. I bought some water. Here. Onwards."

The next village was not on Percy's beat, and looked desolate. Most of the houses were boarded up, only a few showing signs of life. Dan again shot video, speaking the village name, and adding observations.

"Percy, we need local information. Drive around, I'll get road and house names and numbers. I think we should speak to a resident, if anyone's about."

They toured the village. Only two houses were definitely occupied, but no one appeared to be home. They found a similar situation at the next two villages, repeating their routine at the next: Ribblesford.

They were about to knock doors, when an elderly man rushed towards them brandishing a walking stick. He was shouting. "What you snooping at? Get out of here and don't come back."

They got out of the car, and the man slowed to look at them, continuing to close the distance, but the threat had faded. Dan set his phone to voice recording, and put it, mic facing outwards, into his top shirt pocket. He said, "Good day sir. We are here on official business, checking on the number of vacant dwellings in this area. Can you tell us what is happening?"

"Maybe, maybe not. Depends who's asking. I'll take it you're not Muslim?"

"No sir. Christian, both of us. I'm Detective Glover, and this is Constable Blodwell of Lower Meddlington Police."

Percy produced his warrant card, and the man's attitude changed at once, but he was still wary. "I still wants to know what you're abouts."

At a nod from Dan, Percy took over. "We're not interested in you sir, your business is your own affair. But there are a lot of villages hereabouts like this one. We want to know where the people went, and why. Who owns the empty houses?"

The man began to reply, but Dan asked, "Is there anywhere to talk, where I could sit down to make notes? I'm sure what you tell us will be invaluable, and it will be kept confidential."

"Well I suppose I could ask the misses to make a brew, but first, tell me your real interest."

Chapter 11

Dan took a chance, given what the old man had already said. "We are concerned about Muslim people taking over villages, such as this one…"

He had not finished speaking, when the man began a rant, leading them towards his home. "They's been here thee knows, frightening people out-er their wits. Once neighbours leave, them Muslims gangs come. They be changing the locks on houses, putting stuff inside, dumping other stuff outside, making the village a tip. I told them to go. They have no right here. I got threatened for me trouble, and now they're trying to drive us out.

"Ah, here we are, mind the step and wipe your feet. Agnes, a pot of tea, we have visitors. Police at last."

Peter and Agnes Penfold told them about how life used to be. "The village were alive back in them days, men and women hard working on the land. We was a community back then. Then them big farms came in. Over the years, the small farms was replaced by big'uns, and bigger still. There was no work. One man and the 'machinierary' did it all. There was no money for local folks. Many were forced to leave.

"The young 'uns moved abroad to find work—Norwich City and the like. Them that stayed, well the children left for city schools, and that left the old 'uns like us. Then a year or so back, those few of us left began being driven out by them there gangs of Muslim thugs."

"So who owns these empty houses, Peter? Agnes, who holds the deeds to this property?" Dan enquired.

Agnes replied, "Why, nobody. They are handed down through generations, passed on from father to son. There are no deeds for this place. Used to be a tithe cottage, but the small farms were bought up to make a big farm. They already had too many buildings, so the tithe cottages were ignored.

"The five houses set apart on the far side, see over there. Well, they used to belong to a small brick making company, but as far as I know, that went out of business just after the war. I guess the tithe lapsed."

They continued to chat for some time, discovering as much as possible about the village, but rose to depart when misses Penfold offered to make fresh tea.

Dan whispered, "Give them the station number."

Percy wrote down the details and said, "Call on this number if you have any trouble. It's the main police station line, but leave the message for me, Percy Blodwell. I'll come as soon as I am able. Good day."

They drove on to the next village, and Percy remarked, "I thought all properties had deeds."

"Not so. Outside of the homes of the wealthy in London, deeds have not been common until after the war. However, I did not envisage this scale of unregistered housing. We'll need to look into it, but it may save us a lot of travelling. Are there a lot of tithe cottages around here?"

"Yes, in the countryside at least, nearly all of them. Not in the cities and towns. When I was growing up, there were many smallholdings, farms of between twenty and one hundred acres. They were satellite to villages, which took the produce, shops selling to the local people, and some acting as regional distribution agents.

"Then the big, managed farms started to move in, and grow. You see that field over there, it's more than one thousand acres, with no hedges. In my youth, that would have been home to a dozen smallholdings, thirty or forty men, and women, milkmaids, all working the land. The villages had small industries making sacks, twine for sheaves of corn or hay.

"Now look at it. One worker and heavy machinery can maintain the one crop field, and several more. Farm cottages and hedgerows have been knocked down to make the fields as large as possible."

Dan interrupted. "It looks boring to me. So many livelihoods and communities lost to the greed of corporate farming. That in turn translates into lower prices in the nationwide supermarkets, but detracts from the quality of country life."

"I agree. The world was a much better place back then, but this is the one we live in." They were silent, both considering their thoughts, and harkening back to their boyhoods, when Percy exclaimed, "Damn it"

"What's up?"

"We've been struggling to pay off our mortgage early, and before I retire. And I just found out we could have moved into one of these empty houses, for free. No deeds, no cost. Say I were to register it with this Land Registry, then I would have the deeds, own it outright. Am I missing something here, Dan?"

"No Percy, I think that's about how it is. I'll need to check this out."

"Well I'll be damned. There's a place not far from where we live, lovely old house with grounds, that's been empty for years. If it has no owner, could I register it? What do you think?"

"Check it out first, and if it's not registered, then act promptly. But don't tell a soul. It's gotta be worth a try, you've nothing to lose, except the fee, a few hundred pounds."

The next village appeared around a bend and they set to their usual practice, Dan filming, and Percy touring. All the properties appeared to be empty, same in the next village, and then the next. They also came across a few villages that were thriving. Hatton Green had two shops, a school, and a Mosque. They spoke to various residents, but got little information. The signs were in Arabic, and the population Muslim.

They found the same in Malmesbury, and continued the grand tour.

Chapter 11

"Dan, it's already midday, and the last village, Greater Bedlington, is a few miles away. Do you want to go on, or turn back for lunch?"

"Let's finish with this last one, lunch somewhere near Norwich, and then head for RAF Trimingham."

The village was not what they were expecting. It was a hive of activity of the Muslim kind. Most of the houses appeared to be occupied, and several shops were open. The sign on the restructured church stated 'Mosque'. New sectional housing was being erected on a stretch of newly laid concrete. A relatively huge building was being erected on the village green. Percy said, "That looks like a community centre."

They came to the large village pub, which was awash with signs in Arabic. Dan read them, becoming alarmed: "School of Allah, Boys entrance, Girls entrance."

He pointed at the signs as he translated and spoke the alien tongue, then hissed, "Drive through. Get us out of here, Percy. We'll monitor by satellite. This is what they're doing, taking over."

Percy kept going, not too fast, and not too slow. Once clear, Percy accelerated, putting distance between them, and what they had just witnessed. Dan picked up the map, and guided Percy towards the main A11 road. They passed through several other Muslim villages, before reaching the main road at Wymondham.

They encountered no more villages with local residents.

They headed for Norwich City, where Percy delivered them to a pub and declared, "This is one of the best eateries in the whole of England."

Chapter 12 ~ Deeper Understandings

As luncheon concluded, Dan said, "That was a mighty fine meal, if a tad expensive for a pub. Take ten minutes to finish up. I'll pay the bill on the way out. I need to call a few people. You'll find me in the car. The keys … thanks."

Dan called the Director, and spoke his thoughts concisely. She weighed his words before responding. "So it seems to me, they are not taking over every village, at least, not yet, but only certain ones. Why is that?"

"I'll need to dig a little deeper Ma'am, and will apprise you immediately I discover the reason. I'll be on my way to RAF Trimingham in a moment."

"Keep me informed. Send a report this afternoon if you find what I suspect."

"Yes Ma'am." The line went dead. Dan called Trimingham, and spoke to the Wing Commander.

"Ah Dan, so pleased you called. Everything is in place, except for the official 'go'. The Air Commodore is on his way, and I presume he will action your request. It would be good if you arrived before him. He's travelling from RAF Boulmer via helicopter, so don't spare the horses."

"I'm already en route, less than one hour away."

As they approached their destination, Percy noticed the large Kevlar dome and said, "Is that where we're going?"

"Yes Percy, the locals call it the Trimingham golf ball."

They pulled up at the gate. Percy was signed in, and they made their way to the Commander's office.

The door opened. "Ah, Agent Glower, good timing, the Air Commodore will arrive shortly."

He looked at Percy. "Allow me to introduce Constable Blodwell of Lower Meddlington Police. He has been my right hand man during this operation. I hope it is okay if he joins us."

Percy produced his warrant card which was inspected before being returned. "I see no reason why not, if he is already a part of the team. Although I hope there will not be others."

"No sir, the fewer people who know, the better."

"Good. Please make yourselves comfortable in the Guard Room. Excuse me, but I need to finish my preparations."

Later, they grouped near the helipad, ground crew guiding the final descent. A man of power got out, and was saluted by all, including Dan and Percy. It wasn't required of civilians, but they were hoping to make a favourable impression.

Chapter 12

The Station Commander spoke. "Air Commodore, welcome to RAF Trimingham. You have been here before?"

"Once, a long time ago. Show me the problem."

"The problem was brought to light by this man, Agent Glover of MI6. He has discovered thousands of Muslims have been entering this country illegally, every day. We need to track the aircraft they use. This extends through greater Europe, the Middle East, and, we suspect, into Africa."

"You can verify this, Agent Glover?"

"Yes sir. We have identified an incursion of Muslim origin, at work right here in East Anglia. Just this morning, we began to unravel their long-term plan, but these are early days for us, we're playing catch-up. This is my dedicated assistant, Constable Blodwell, who has been monitoring the situation personally. I prepared a short video of our results so far, should you wish to see it."

"Yes, right away, Agent."

The Commander suggested, "It will be more comfortable and secure in my office. Please, I'll lead the way. Refreshments are waiting for you, Air Commodore."

Once settled, Dan showed the prepared recording to the Air Commodore, explaining in detail what was occurring. He showed several days, concluding with Sunday. "This cargo plane is new to us, and I will be interested to learn where it came from, and where it went. The others are regular, same planes, same time of day. I extrapolated the figures, and discovered over two million illegal migrants could be entering this country each year, by this means alone.

"Then there are the militia," Dan pointed out, "and the wooden boxes for guns and ammunition."

"So, another Harrods perhaps."

"With the amount of militia and weaponry that's come in just while we have been monitoring, I'd say one atrocity per day. Percy and I are currently focused on where all the people are going, and we have discovered entire villages have been taken over by Muslim civilians.

"From our research and observations, we believe similar events are occurring in all parts of the United Kingdom. We are under fifth column assault from Islamic extremists, but the how of it still has to be precisely identified. This is why we need to work directly with Station Officer Wigglesworth. He already understands and supports British Intelligence. This investigation is coming from the highest levels, Sir."

"I see. The current operation is low key, but the expansion requested is a heavy demand on our time and resources. I am empowered to assess the threat, and either undertake, or reject it. You will have my answer before I leave. First, tell me about your team, Agent."

"We are small, and dedicated, Sir. In the SIS, only my Commander, Director, and a field liaison agent have any knowledge. Locally, the villager who reported it to Constable Blodwell, and his Station Officer, Inspector Wigglesworth."

Dan was going to mention Ben and Charlie, but the Air Commodore looked away, distracted. "Wigglesworth, hmmm." His brow wrinkled in concentration, before he pronounced the name with emphasis, and looked at the Station Commander.

"Inspector Wigglesworth, the chief police officer of Lower Meddlington Constabulary, is my daughter, Sir. This is not nepotism, but chance. Her area of responsibility includes Huntley Spa aerodrome, which you have just witnessed."

"So, by leaving you in charge here, we keep a tight lid of security on this. Now the request makes sense. Wing Commander, show me what you have, and it better be good."

The Commander replied, "Thank you, Sir. That is our intention. Please, let's adjourn to the radar room and I'll show you what is going on. I took the liberty of running a preview operation, which will be deleted if this request is not approved. I wanted to either prove or disprove the threat in advance, Sir."

As they entered, Commander Wigglesworth stated, "Air Commodore, the agent has access to that console over there, which only shows civilian air traffic into, or out of the specified airfield. I believe you will be extremely interested in the display on this console over here. Please excuse us for a moment, Dan."

"The new request is to monitor anywhere these aircraft go. In British airspace, they use the transponders of small passenger jets, and fly through uncontrolled airspace. They cross the North Sea, then dive down to below civil aviation tracking, and change to the passenger aircrafts transponder, entering European airspace in their true identity.

"Here you will see that this swapping from private to commercial transponder occurs often, and across a large swathe of Europe, the Middle East, and Northern Africa. Nearly all of the destinations in Europe are small, private airfields."

"Run this model since you started."

The corporal was prepared, and the screen ran almost immediately in fast forward. Once finished, the Air Commodore looked towards heaven, and said, "That is one hell of a lot of unaccountable air traffic. All of it from the wrong parts of the world: Syria, Iraq, Afghanistan, Yemen, Somalia, and Libya!"

"All Muslim extremist countries, at least, the parts of them these aircraft are flying to and from. ISIL. We are at war."

Chapter 12

"This would explain the ease of the Paris bombings, and the Belgian link. They come and go as they wish, undetected. Please ask the agent to join us, but not the policeman."

When Dan joined them, the fast forward replay was shown again, and he was beside himself with excitement and concern. He explained the importance of some locations, and understood what was happening. Once finished, Dan said, "Sirs, may I have a copy of this? We have the hard and software to run it. For my own, and the Director's eyes only."

Silence.

The Air Commodore spoke after due consideration. "Agent, are we witnessing the Islamification of Europe?"

"I believe so, Sir. As to the how of it, that we still have to determine, but all the evidence so far collated is pointing solely in that direction."

"Good God!"

"The more information I have access to, the quicker will be the resolution, and our ability to respond to the threat."

The Air Commodore looked at Commander Wigglesworth and said, "I need to make a secure call. I'll use your office."

Tension in the room lessened as the Air Commodore departed. The Station Commander walked out of earshot, taking Dan with him. "He came up the hard way, and is not a bureaucrat. Flew in the first Gulf War, and also the Falklands. Earned his armbands the hard way. A man of action is the right person to be in charge."

They discussed matters until the Air Commodore returned. "I have provisional approval to instigate full tracking of this, and associated threats, from the Air Vice Marshall. This begins now, Acting Group Captain Wigglesworth. Show me what you can do."

The Commander's face lit with pleasure, which was soon dampened. The Air Commodore continued to speak. "This is a provisional appointment that may become permanent, if you are man enough for the job. I note you have previous experience of something similar, but not on this scale. We meet here again in ten days time, with the Air Vice Marshal, and your Director, Agent Glover. During the intervening period, you will both show me why we need to dedicate resources to this project.

"I will need a copy of the video feed shown, and grant permission for another to be made available to MI6, for the hands and eyes of Agent Glover, and his Director only."

"Thank you," Dan replied. "It will be as you wish, and a great help to us to properly assess the threat."

"If you'll excuse us, I need to speak about operational requirements with the new Group Captain."

Dan replied, "My pleasure Air Commodore, Group Captain." He flashed a half-smile at the Station Commander, and added, "We'll return to base, and I'll see you tomorrow. Thank you both."

Dan and Percy made their way to the door, and before it closed, overheard, "Now then Wigglesworth, about manning and resources, you have the projections ready?"

"Yes Sir. Let's retire to my office…"

On the return journey, Dan made several secure phone calls. One was to his Director. "Ma'am, it is much worse than we feared, but for the interim, we have the full backing of the RAF … Yes Ma'am, I'll rent a jet and be with you shortly."

Dan looked at Percy, "To Norwich airport, I'll call them to see if there is a jet available."

"They have pilots with jets standing by, like taxis?"

"No. A company there has small jets for hire, without a pilot."

Percy stared at Dan. "You'll fly it yourself?"

"Of course. Now, after you drop me off… "

Dan was with his Director less than two hours later. "So you are telling me, a network of Islamic cells are working not only within UK, but across the entirety of Europe. That they plan to take over--I find that rather hard to believe."

"The RAF believed me, when the Air Commodore saw this." Dan dangled a pen drive from his finger tips. "Have it deciphered from the military mainframe, and I need a copy of the results."

The Director placed a call. "Tim, I need you for a moment."

The results were returned in short time, one copy for each of them. The Director ran the video and was astounded. "This is what they are doing? They are everywhere."

"Yes Ma'am. I think you will be even more interested in the videos I shot this morning, the last one in particular."

Dan explained what had occurred, slowing on some, but fast-forwarding most destinations, until they came to the last one. "This explains what is happening, but not why. Why this village?"

"They are all Muslims. This is a totally Islamic village, in the wilds of Norfolk. You have any theories?"

"No, only something half-arsed. I studied the OS map, and this village is in a different Borough, and comes under Wymondham. Can you bring up satellite view of the area, other villages nearby? We can check them physically tomorrow, but this way is far more efficient."

"Yes, Wymondham you said … Here it is. Oh. This view is not current, but less than four days old."

"Anything similar nearby?"

Chapter 12

"Searching, one moment ... By Jove, yes, several. Do you think this may be about the significance of political, electoral boundaries?"

"My thoughts are heading in that direction, Ma'am. They appear to be determined to beat us at the ballot box. We already know how they can fix elections with Tower Hamlets.

"From what we discovered today, most of these properties do not have an owner, at least one recorded by the Land Registry. No Title Deeds, and most were tithe to farms or companies, long since bought out, bankrupt, or defunct."

A short discussion ensued, in which Dan told the Director everything he knew, and suspected. "I will be covering as much as I can, but this is beginning to get a bit big, even for me. I need information. I'll need to requisition other field agents to monitor the now five identified, private aerodromes in Great Britain."

"I suggest you do, but I doubt I'll find the resources required. I'll ask Alison to run support for you instead. What exactly do you need?"

"Existing properties on the list of villages (I am sending to your phone now ... sent), versus the number of houses registered with the Land Registry. I am expecting a large discrepancy, Ma'am."

"I see. It will be done, anything else?"

"Yes, we will also need to see what is happening in the towns and cities. I suspect Tower Hamlets, but worse."

"Where's this going Dan?"

"To the heart, the very fabric of our known society. I'm coming to regard this insidious infiltration as 'The Muslim Extremist Apocalypse Theory'. Everything fits."

"The Caliphate of Europe. You cannot be serious?"

"Yes, I am. All but the leaders are zombies, Ma'am."

Chapter 13 ~ Centres of the Community

Dan arrived back in Norwich just as the evening rush hour was gathering momentum. He could have called for a pick-up, hired a car, or hailed a cab. Instead, he took the bus. He felt the need to observe the local population mix. There were a lot more foreigners, mostly Muslims, than he had expected.

He was about to call Felicity, when his phone rang. "Dan, I'm just calling to confirm we are a go for tomorrow. Be at the station by nine."

"Sure, I'll be there. I was just about to call you, make a dinner date."

"Sorry Dan, my father wants me to dine in Trimingham tonight. It seems to be a special occasion. You have anything for me?"

"Felicity … No, never mind. Go. It'll be worth it."

"What do you know?"

"Nothing, except today went rather well for your father. He will need to tell you the rest himself. Dinner tomorrow perhaps?"

"Hmmm. We'll see. Men!"

The phone went dead. Dan stared at it for some time, and thoughts of her filled his mind. He wanted to call her back, leave a text, but decided to wait until later. He knew she was preoccupied with matters of the moment.

Instead, he watched the people come and go, changed buses, and got back to the village a lot later than expected. He checked the house, but it was deserted. He found Percy in the bar of the inn, and kept him company with a pint.

They made plans for the morning, and after dinner Dan went to his room. There were too many imponderables to prepare a long-term course of action. Instead, he prepared contingency plans with the focus of either establishing the threat, or disproving it.

The next morning he arrived at the house before seven o'clock, but Percy was still asleep. He got to work studying the footage from the day before, and saved the official copy. Later, Percy did the daily log of events, Dan hardly having to correct him. Afterwards, they began Percy's expenses claim sheet. Dan gave Percy a key to the office. "This door remains locked unless one of us is here."

Dan's phone rang. "Felicity, we still okay?"

"Yes Dan. Get here by nine as arranged, and we should be away soon afterwards."

When they arrived, the Chief Inspector had completed the initial phase of inspection, one that involved Inspector Wigglesworth. They went to her office, where the Inspector was with a powerful man in his late forties. "May I introduce Chief Inspector George Lovell."

Chapter 13

After formalities were completed, the Chief said, "The SIS way out here? I thought you only worked on international cases."

"We do sir, but some investigations, this one in particular, are related to UK. Much of our work is top secret."

"Ah yes of course, on a need to know basis. Is there anything you can tell me? This is quite intriguing."

The Inspector interrupted. "There is a formative official file which I will leave with you, Sir. Dan, please check it first."

She handed him a folder, but removed her private log. Dan flicked through it, reading two sections in detail. "This is fine, and about as much as I could tell you. There may be a little more over the next few days, but that's about it for now."

The Inspector took the file and handed it onwards. "Sir, for your eyes-only. Is there anything else?"

"No Felicity, get going. I know you have a lot of travelling ahead of you. I'll need an hour of your time when you get back, to finalise my visit report. The quicker you leave, the quicker you return, and I can go home."

They quickly departed, and in Norwich their meetings went well. They were able to go inside two of the three community centres, and got a feel for the general running of the places. Their physical layouts, functions, and even staff were all similar.

Once satisfied, they headed towards Cambridge, Felicity having received approval to visit the day before. They pulled into a large lay-by, the remnants of a road-widening scheme, and set to discuss the morning. Percy opened a large box on the back seat, and said, "One flask of tea, two of coffee, and three large packed meals, courtesy of Misses Nicholas."

They ate from the varied selection of sandwiches, sausage rolls, and scooped potato salad or pickles from other containers. Dan said, "I'm stuffed, and there's still tons left, what a feast.

"So to summarise, from what we have seen and been told. These self-styled Asian community centres are mainly Pakistani, and all provide similar services on similar days."

Percy added, "Yes, that's fair to say, but they are not identical. However, they vary only in local issues and slight cultural differences, meaning different roots.

"The main constants are being open from about ten in the morning for twelve hours. Morning is a drop in time, while afternoon features several events of either ethnic or British nature. For instance, traditional dress and customs, is followed by English language, and how to maintain your faith in a Christian country. These are not classes, so much as women's clubs. They are only for females. There is no male equivalent.

"The late afternoon and early evening are more of a drop in nature, although instruction for girls features highly. I would be more inclined to call it brainwashing in preparation for womanhood.

"Evenings are mainly youth club, but segregated. The boys play games, and the girls study household matters. I asked about trouble, and got little reply, except for oblique references to bullying by older Muslim boys that had left schools a few years before. I got the impression the presence of these youths was disliked, but common."

"Thank you Percy. That's what I deduced. We have a pattern as to how these places function, let's get on to the next."

In Cambridge, they were welcomed by the local community police officer. "Constable, thanks for agreeing to see me. These are my assistants, Constable Blodwell, and Advisor Glover.

"I am here to support a project for Norwich Police, dedicated to improving our community relations, and especially with regard to ethnic groups. Two of our three Muslim community centres are new, and we've had problems."

The neighbourhoods were similar to Norwich, but held a brooding air of menace. After visiting two of the Cambridge centres, they moved on to Newmarket, the community centre being central to low-rise blocks of flats. The community policeman informed them, "Many of the established residents have moved out."

Percy asked, "So new residents are moving in?"

"Yes, although I see little of them. They seem to keep themselves to themselves."

"Not like British people then."

"Oh no. These are mainly refugees from the Middle East, North Africa, and a few from Somalia, or so I've been told. This is due to Local and County Council level politics. In return, they get EU grants and subsidies."

"Sounds like they're coming in by the coach load."

"Ooh, that's interesting, and close to the bones of it. There's an international charity behind it, sanctioned by the councils, and EU. Asians in Need. It's all part of a governmental refugee crisis alleviation project, and the council is fully supportive of the initiative. The charity have local representatives hereabouts, who liaise with all parties."

"Where would we find them?"

"Now let me see, their offices are in Luton I believe, but local workers would be up at the new Cappel Moor estate."

"Where is that?"

"Across the hill from Bollington Fields, the posh part of Newmarket, and near the racecourse. There was hell on when the building proposal was announced, but guarantees were put in place, plus a promised new bypass road, so the posh community would be left alone."

Chapter 13

"What about local hoodlums, gangs, vehicles such as vans, lorries, or coaches?"

"Yes, white van man, there are several. Trucks delivering supplies, and as for buses, only those for the regular day-trips the centre frequently organises. What's this really about, Percy?"

"As Ma'am stated, we need advice, and eyes-on."

"Just as well I'm old-school, otherwise I would not have understood you. Walk with me.

"I have nineteen months and twenty-six days to survive, before retirement, and a good pension for life. You?"

"Less than seven months, but counting the days is not for me."

"You know how this country used to be. Nowadays it's hard to spot a white man on the street, or hear the English language. And I am not racist. It's a fact of life.

"The thing I noticed with the daytrip coaches was that I knew the people who went, but I didn't recognise anyone when they returned, many hours later. They weren't even Pakistani, Arabs mainly."

"Surely that has raised the alarm?"

"Nope, nothing. It seems I'm the only person, outside of these communities, to have noticed. I reported it to the Sergeant, but once the Inspector realised it was an 'Asian' issue, I was told to drop it. "

"The flats, they're owned by the residents?"

"No, they're ex-council, and now owned by a property development group, Anglo Asian Holdings. They came fully furnished, and I presume that is still a contract clause."

"Where are these people going?"

"I don't know, and I cannot officially check without approval from the Inspector. My guess is one of the new estates."

"Cappel Moor?"

"That's a good guess, Percy. I'll nose around, see what I can dig up."

"What about hoodlums?"

"This is not a place to venture late at night. And definitely not for a lone, white, young woman. I know of several ringleaders of what I will politely call 'businesses'. They are Muslim, with extensive control over this community. Regards local gangs, I had legitimate business here, if brief, but this was conducted at the gate."

"You did not go inside?"

"No. My younger self would have done so, regardless. I looked up and saw thugs gathering with hostile presence, ambling with menace towards me. The funny thing is, I was there at their request, to deliver information they wanted--community posters and the like."

"You felt physically threatened?"

"Definitely. I couldn't wait to get away."

"What happened?"

"I delivered the package, and raised a report when I got back, highlighting my concerns about intimidation, and nothing happened. I even tried to speak to the Inspector about it, but was told in no uncertain terms, to let it be."

"What do you mean?"

"He said, 'We have not got the time or resources to follow this up. If you had reasonable doubt, then you should have taken action. This is filed and closed'. He's got a degree, and is straight out of college. He understands nothing about the real job."

Percy thought for a moment, considering the risk versus advantage. "Constable."

"Jeffrey Daniels, Jeff, please."

They shook hands. "Perceval Blodwell, Percy to you. Call me the next time you have similar concerns. Here's my number."

"Wilco. Here's mine. There's more to this, isn't there?"

Percy smiled, but did not say a word. The slightest nod of head and steely look, was all Jeff received, before they rejoined the others.

Minutes afterwards, they were on the road, and drove through Bollington Fields, assuredly a classical English suburb. By contrast, Cappel Moor estate was more like a military base. There was Asian security monitoring traffic. There was one road in, and it was fronted by show homes, and apart from the English name, all writing was in Arabic. Dan took several snapshots, translating the immediate meanings, and they got the hell out of there, headed for Thetford.

A young, Pakistani constable, who appeared to be overly eager to help, greeted them. Percy began, but Dan and Felicity each took a turn, as the young officer had a knack of diverting important questions. Dan cut their meeting short, just as soon as they had toured the community centre.

They pulled up on rough ground on the outskirts of Thetford, took drinks and sandwiches as they wished, and talked informally. "Newmarket is the one that stands out for me," said Percy. "I believe we have a contact there in Jeff, the Constable we spoke to. I told him extremely little, but we exchanged numbers, and he is aware we are looking into something bigger, though he has no idea what."

"You took a chance?"

"No, not exactly Dan. I took a calculated risk, after he told me of some troubles, indicating a gang culture based there. His Inspector had zero interest, and warned him off. Jeff knows something is going on. He will make additional checks, and may say more to us later."

"Good work Percy, but what are they up too?"

"This was why he wanted to speak to me aside. Local Pakistani people get on the bus in the morning, supposedly for a day trip, of which there are many. They do not return. Instead, much later in the day, the bus arrives back with a load of Arabs. I said nothing of what we knew."

Felicity said, "You can't just move people out like that, what about furniture, household goods, personal belongings."

"From what I was told, Anglo Asian Holdings owns everything hereabouts, the flats are ex-council, and fully furnished, as in ready to be lived in. I believe that when they move out, they are only allowed to take small, personal items with them."

"But that means their new homes must also be fully furnished. We need to probe a little deeper."

Dan agreed, "Yes, see what you can delicately discover, I'll get my people on it as well."

Percy said, "Jeff is going to find out what he can. He suspects they are going to Cappel Moor, or another estate. He'll call me when he knows more."

"Great work Percy, you are a natural at this. We better head back, there's still a long way to go."

When they arrived in the station car park, Percy waited for Dan to escort the Inspector to the rear entrance. "So Felicity, are we on for dinner tonight?"

"Yes, it's overdue. I'll aim to be ready for eight, but give you a call when I'm set.

"Oh, and about my father, you chose wisely. The promotion was a great surprise, and much better coming from his own lips. Till later. Ciao."

Chapter 14 ~ Dinner Date

Dan returned to the village with Percy. He went up to his room, leaving Percy to his own devices. He thought through the day's events, and noted key points in his private journal. Later he studied OS maps online, noting the Boundary Line website showing all county, city, and town boundaries in the UK. Bollington Fields was in the same electoral ward as Cappel Moor. The new housing estate was growing, and would become larger.

He considered the implications, but would need to do more research, and discover the political make up of Thetford. He would have disregarded an electoral reason being behind the movement of ethnic minorities, except for the numbers that were entering the country, being housed in places like Cappel Moor. Surely, they were not intending to take over town and county councils. He tried to dismiss the thought, but it would not dislodge.

The phone rang at seven, and Dan answered expectantly. "Felicity, you are free?"

"Sorry Dan, another time. The Chief has asked me to dinner, and it is concerned with my present job and future promotion prospects. I would be a fool to forego the opportunity."

"I'm disappointed, but understand. Do as you must, and I wish you a good evening, and much success."

"Thanks, for the third night running. Sorry, I promise to make it up to you."

"The fourth out of five nights, but this is what we do."

"Thanks, I owe you. Oh, and I won't tell him much about today, so don't worry on that score."

"Good. Go, but tell him enough to keep him interested, we may have need of him in due course. In fact, bring him fully on board if you think it's the right call, I trust your judgement."

"Will do. I better dash, he's coming back." She blew a kiss, and the line went dead.

Dan cursed his luck, but supported her actions. He added a few more notes to his log, before heading down to join Percy for a pint, and dinner.

Some miles to the east, the Chief and Felicity entered a good restaurant, and settled down to order. Between service they spoke as friends and colleagues. "Are you happy here Felicity? It's a bit remote."

"Yes George, at least for now. It was not what I was expecting when I was promoted, but I guess I upset the wrong man."

"Ah yes, a certain Chief Superintendent, I believe."

"You know?"

Chapter 14

"I did not, until just now. There have been rumours, and complaints about him, all regards female officers. Did he offer you a deal?"

"Yes. Promotion to a very good posting, but he wanted something I would never consider giving him in return."

"A sexual service, I presume." Felicity said nothing, so he continued. "You may be pleased to know he has now been promoted, and will spend his last years on the force at headquarters."

Felicity beamed with delight. "So, he's no longer on the promotion board, the one that stuck me here."

"Correct. He has also been shifted sideways, away from daily operations. But there's more. I remember you got on very well with our Superintendent, John Stonehouse."

"Yes, the Super took me under his wing when I became sergeant, and helped me a lot, as you have done. Where's this going George?"

"Let me top up your wine first ... Our Super has been chosen to take his place, on promotion, and I am to replace him."

"Oh George, that is wonderful news. Here's to Superintendent George Lovell."

She raised her glass and they chinked in toasting. "When does this happen?"

"Oh, it'll be a while yet, probably a month or two. You know how the system operates. I've already accepted the position, but that leaves me with a problem. Who do I replace myself with?"

Felicity stared at him, then smiled. "George, are you suggesting what I think you are?"

"Felicity, you are one of our brightest, and your talents are wasted out here in the sticks. I need the support of a Chief Inspector I trust, and who can do the job, step up as required. You would be my first choice."

"Oh, but George, thank you."

"Don't thank me yet, this is what I would like. I can recommend you, and my choice will carry a lot of weight, especially with our ex-Super on the promotion board. But, we have to wait for the right time, and due process. Why I wanted to speak to you tonight, was to discover if you would like the position."

"Why yes of course. This promotion would be a dream come true, and a great stride forward in my career." Her elation turned to looking downcast. "But I can't, until we are done here."

"The second reason I invited you to dinner, was to ask how your day went. Sharing will help me balance your adherence to duty, versus your quest for promotion."

"You know I have both qualities, but I'm not the sort to give up midway through a job, just to have an extra pip on my collar. We still need to fully understand what we discovered today, extrapolate, and make checks in places our Constabulary has no right to be. If we are correct, this is more than nationwide. It is pan-European."

"What, from a few airliners landing, I don't see it."

"No? Well then, try over two thousand migrants per day, plus militia, weapons and ammo. Every day, landing here. Do the maths."

George whistled. "I make that three-quarters of a million each year."

"Our observations of the old aerodrome, make the figure for last week, add up to just over two million illegal's per annum. There are other previously unknown airfields, just like ours. How does ten million per year strike you, and all from the wrong parts of the Muslim world?"

"Hence MI6. Of course. What are they planning, taking over the Country? Impossible."

"Oh, we are beginning to believe they intend to take over and Islamify all of Europe."

"Preposterous!"

"I, we thought so, too. But our observations and enquiries lead us to a quite different conclusion. I am more concerned with where all these invaders are going, and today we got our first angle on what might be going down. It is far too early for me to share details with you, or anyone outside of the core team."

"So today, you visited Asian community centres, mostly outside of our force's jurisdiction."

"Not in an official capacity, but yes. It went rather well overall. We now know where some of these migrants are ending up, and with a strong angle on how they are doing it. And that is the limit of what I can tell you. I expect full discretion. So do not breath a word to a soul, or we will all be dead. I mean that George. You included. I'm telling you this in case we are taken out. We will need somebody to pick up the pieces, and carry on."

"Understood. I still can't get my head around the numbers, we usually talk in thousands, but millions." George shook his head.

Felicity countered, "George, do us both a favour, and see what is happening in Norwich. I don't need you to go poking your nose in, but as quietly as you can, find out if there are any new housing projects. We're interested in ones to cope with asylum seekers, or any that are projects run by Muslim organisations. In addition, check charities working with them too. "

"Okay, I'll nose around, but I know of one already, which has caused a few protests. A new housing estate, the developer is … now let me think … Ah yes, Anglo Asian Holdings. Does this help?"

Felicity was bursting with excitement inside, but kept her emotions in check. She fixed the Chief's eyes, "We heard that name today, and the charity Asians in Need. Check them both out, it may lead somewhere. We found housing associations with links to charities, local and county

Chapter 14

councils, and 'Asian' communities. That's my lot, not another word. So tell me George, how's your son doing…"

Both enjoyed the meal, and at her request, George dropped her back at the station. "Are you sure you don't want me to take you home?"

"No George, this is fine. I need to update my personal notes, before tomorrow's work begins to obfuscate my memory. Thanks for a lovely evening. Oh, and not a word to a soul."

"Accepted and actioned Ma'am. Talking of which, I would still like to put your name forward as my replacement. These things take months, but your name has to be entered at the beginning."

"Yes, please do so. I'd love to be back in the city again, and get my career back on track. Thank you George. Ciao."

She made a brief check with the desk sergeant, before going out the back way, and getting into her car. Her intention had been to go home, relax, and write up her notes. Her mind was awash with discoveries of national importance, and deeply personal significance. She decided to blot it all out, and indulge herself.

Entering the inn, she saw Dan and Percy in conversation at the bar. Brian noticed her arrival, but she put her finger to her lips. She eased herself unnoticed to the other end of the bar, and whispered to Brian. With his nod, she said loudly, "Brian, one of your long Pernods if you please, shaken and stirred. I feel a bit playful tonight."

Dan's eyes immediately snapped in her direction, and he began to rise. Brian gestured, and both Percy and Gwen motioned him to remain seated. He continued to gaze at her regardless.

The drink was delivered, and she winked at Brian, unseen by others. "Are there any gentlemen in the hostelry this eve?"

"Why no ma'am. Their ilk would'ne be of use in these parts. There be the usual roughnecks and serfs, a couple of comedians, a Shire Reeve, and a likeable rogue."

"The rogue it is then, please introduce me to him."

The mood in the bar had changed. People were no longer talking, but chuckling, all waiting expectantly to witness how this scene would play out.

As Brian guided her towards Dan, she said, "Ahha! I've met this rascal before, a most enjoyable companion, if fleeting. Thank you Brian, I'll take it from here."

A charade of Queen and Knight ensued, before Felicity said, "Enough Dan, I need to swallow some of this drink. It's been a day and a half."

Percy rose to leave them alone, but Felicity said, "Stay Percy, let's take that quiet table over there, we've much to talk about."

They talked around work, drank, chattered, and released tension. They enjoyed the moment, but soon the long day took its toll, and they all departed for bed.

The next morning, as they got ready to face the new day, Felicity debriefed, and Dan was all-attentive. "I'm not happy you told him quite so much, but then again, you didn't tell him everything."

"Dan, he won't say a word. Anyway, what would happen if a drunk driver took us out, even yesterday? We need others in the know, so that if something happens to us, they realise why, and can pick up."

"Point taken. So, did we learn anything?"

"Yes we did. You remember the name Anglo Asian Holdings? Well guess what, they are building a housing estate in Norwich. I did tell him I knew the name, and asked him to check it out discreetly. He will also look for associated charities, and council involvement. He can give us names, independent of MI6, plus local involvement."

"You beauty! Certain things from yesterday begin to take on deeper significance. I'll go to London this morning, get hands on with the flow of information. I already have somebody running significant checks."

"Good, I'll do what I can here, but I need to spend time on my own notes before facing the day ahead."

"Your office will be full of distractions, so either go home, or use ours."

"I'll breakfast with Percy, see your office, but work in my own. I can isolate it when necessary. You'll be back in time for dinner? I would like to show you our best restaurant in these parts."

"Yes, delighted. We have a date, seven-thirty for eight."

They breakfasted at the house. Felicity left for work, and Dan surveyed the office from a working point of view.

When Percy returned, Dan watched him make the daily copy of footage from their camera, and fill in the associated log. Percy then successfully updated his expenses sheet.

"Percy, we are expecting Ben around ten o'clock. After he settles in, I will go to London. Call me when he arrives, as I still have a few things to add to my daily report. Oh, and find out where we can get a filing cabinet, one of those grey metal ones with four drawers and key. This needs to become a real office."

Back in his room, Dan sent his report, adding a short list of requirements, and a long list of people and companies that needed checking out. He finished with his customary video report, containing his personal appraisal. The Director came online. "Dan, from what I've just read, your operation is growing exponentially, can't you cap it?"

"Doubtful Ma'am. I was planning to drop by this morning and talk to you about it in person."

"Cannot do. Something else has happened. A suicide bomber on the Underground, with secondary explosions designed to cause more panic and mayhem. It is bad. It was ISIL again. There are foreign elements involved, so we have been called upon.

"I need to keep you away from all this, cocooned. As you point out, we need to exterminate the cause, not be distracted by the effect. For the same reason, I am going to send Alison to you for a few days. She can operate a secure remote office via satellite. She should be with you for late lunch. Anything else?"

"Have we anyone near any of the other four airstrips?"

"No. And I don't want to involve MI5. You better do it yourself, Alison will bring the cameras and satellite links, plus the other things you requested, but you'll need to fit them yourself. I'll add a drill and toolbox. Dan, thank you and stay strong for all our sakes. I have to go."

Chapter 15 ~ Building the Team

Wednesday became a busy day for Dan, with distractions all around, filled with minutia. He felt frustrated at not making progress, but knew the building blocks for the team to function coherently had to be put in place.

Ben settled into his new role and Alison arrived earlier than expected. Dan knew her quite well, but they had never worked closely together. She was offered a room in the house, but insisted on a room at the inn. "I like to keep work and off time separate."

At times Dan felt like the local handyman, fitting an automatic door closer to their office, and an automatic lock, similar to a Yale in operation but far more secure, to the door.

A van from Lower Meddlington police arrived with several filing cabinets, extra desks and chairs, cupboards, plus a whiteboard and corkboard. Dan was soon drilling more holes in the wall. Percy explained, "These have been in storage for ages, and Ma'am said we could use them, as long as you sign for them."

Dan signed, and was asked by Misses Nicholas, "What do you want for lunch?"

"Mix and match buffet, a bit like the hamper you prepared for us yesterday, but more diverse. Add a pork pie and some baguettes."

"What?"

"Crispy French bread in long stick form, fresh. Percy, please drive her, and get sausage rolls, porkpie from the local butcher. Here's money to cover. Add it to your expenses on the in side."

They started to get ready to leave, Misses Nicholas moaning, "The fridge is not big enough, and we need a freezer."

Dan spoke over her words. "There are freezers and display fridges in the shop storeroom, plug them in and see if they work. I need to check on Alison at the inn, please excuse me."

Minutes later, Dan knocked on Alison's door. "Go away!"

"Alison, it's Dan."

The door was unlocked. "Sorry Dan, I thought it was the cleaners again, they're most disruptive."

"You're not happy here?"

"Yes I am actually, but the information I deal with is highly sensitive, and not for the eyes of housemaids. Even if I lock the door, they have master keys, and can come and go as they please. I need somewhere much more secure, and to be left alone."

"Understood, this will be resolved, quickly. Are you set up?"

"No, I took a shower to freshen up, followed by a power nap. I work long and unusual hours, so don't worry about timekeeping. Is this a briefing?"

"It may as well be. Are you solely focused on this team?"

"Virtually, just one legacy job being finished this week."

"Good, this is my priority…"

Dan briefly ran through what he needed checking, adding in the information follow-ups gleaned the day before. "Wow, I'm going to be busy for days. Dan, this is great. But, what is the greater project? I need to understand the whole, if you want me to function properly."

"Mmm. You're top down, like me. Okay. One: At least ten thousand Muslims are illegally entering the UK every day. Two: They are coming from the wrong parts of the Middle East, the Muslim world. Three: We need to understand why they are coming here. Capisce?

"In order to unravel this, my first priority is to define, via satellite, where to place cameras to monitor the four other airfields. I will need to go there and fit them myself. I have a shortlist of possible sites, but do not have the highly detailed satellite view you have live access to."

"You want to do this in one day."

"Preferred."

"Okay, leave it with me, how soon?"

"Tomorrow."

Alison's brow wrinkled. She replied, "Yes, I can do this."

"Good, let me show you exactly what I have, and then you can hone my parameters."

They worked for fifteen minutes, and had moved on to other important issues, when Dan's phone rang. "Dan, we're back and the buffet is all but ready."

"Thanks, Percy. We're on our way."

Alison looked up. "On our way, where to?"

"Buffet lunch. Pack up, log off, and come. I need you to meet the team. Well, most of them."

"Just as soon as I have secured everything, help me lock the whole lot down from those interfering maids."

The buffet was a great success, everyone finding food to their liking. Dan walked into the corridor, and made a courtesy call to Trimingham. He did not want to upset the applecart. He was also watching Alison as she began to interact with the team. When Ben said something that interested her, her manner changed immediately.

Dan finished his call, as Ben, Percy, and Alison went upstairs. Intrigued, he followed and overheard Percy say, "This back bedroom was Charlie's, but I doubt he'll ever use it again."

Dan made his presence known. "This suit you better?"

Alison replied, "Yes Dan, you set this up, didn't you. Thank you. It's a bit small, but I can make do."

Dan said, "Ben, you're now on five days per week, and I doubt you will ever need to sleep over again. Let's check out your room, it's a fair bit larger."

They did, and Alison said, "This is much better. Perfect. I'll need the transceiver satellite dish installed on the back wall, and a secure lock on the door. Add in a desk, and two secure storage cabinets, and it will be my home from home."

Alison repacked. Dan fixed the satellite dish and fitted a secure lock, as Misses Nicholas helped prepare the room. Within one hour, Alison was relocated, and set up. Dan came to her as the others left, and said, "You wanted to see a bigger picture? I can show you one, if we leave right now."

RAF Trimingham welcomed Alison with reserve, until she suggested simple enhancements to improve their surveillance, and reduce real-time monitoring by staff. She got into serious talk about the latest computer software with their most senior technician, a sergeant.

The Group Captain said, "She knows her stuff all right, and must be a big asset to you."

"That she is. She's our online information gatherer, and can access your system here, and those of other agencies, from her office. I thought it wise to personally introduce her to you and the team, as we will be working closely together, Group Captain."

"Thomas please, Tom. Except when official is required."

"Thanks Tom, please call me Dan. Alison will be dealing with the all of this on our behalf, on a daily basis. I would like her to receive an update once per day, say a morning report with video. Also if anything unusual occurs, like a transport plane landing off schedule. I would have her as dedicated liaison. Cuts out the middleman, me."

"Good thinking. The Sergeant that she is talking to right now, is an experienced operative who was sent to take over the running of this room. He has prior experience of this type of work, similar to mine."

"Let's set this up then Tom, and make it official."

Dan checked the log, and was pleased to see a stable pattern emerge for Great Britain. The results regarding Europe were less predictable in destination, but the pattern of the airplanes was repetitive. After a short discussion, he and Tom went to action their plan.

Dan spoke first. "How's it going, Alison?"

"Great. Sarge and I are getting along famously."

Tom spoke next. "Sergeant, please liaise directly with Alison, and send her a full report every morning, plus immediate instances of anything unusual--transport planes, that sort of thing."

"Yes Sir."

Chapter 15

Alison said, "I only need a video of your screens, the twenty-four elapsed hours since the last backup. You had better send me the feeds from when this went pan-European, as we seem to be a little behind."

Sarge queried, "I'll need a secure channel Ma'am, this is a military net computer."

"No problem, I already have access to it. Let me set up a secure socket we can use as a dedicated gateway to my server. It will only take a moment. Which console?"

When they got back, Dan took Alison up to the hide, showing her the physicality of what they were about. She looked through the binoculars he offered, and after studying the aerodrome, said, "Thanks. This is exactly what I needed. I've seen the bigger picture, so now I can fully relate to the details. I'll need to work for the next few hours to get everything the way I want it."

"As you do that, I'll formulate a proper list of priorities, and what we need to check. The order of importance may change over the days, but this is where we begin. The biggest threat as of this moment, comes from the aircraft, so start there."

They returned to the office, and Alison went straight to her room. Percy said, "We had another delivery from our storeroom. I think we should follow her, see if everything is Okay."

They met Alison coming down the stairs. "People have been in my room. This is not secure."

Percy said, "Ma'am. I have a key, so does Dan, you have the only other. I let my men inside, and watched them as they placed what I hope is acceptable, for now at least. I secured the door afterwards. This place is most secure, especially your room."

"I'll need to check."

They followed her, and it seemed Percy had got it about right. Alison had them move furniture around until she was happy. "Yes, this will do fine. Thank you Percy, Dan."

Alison got straight down to work. Dan and Percy caught up with Ben in the office below. They settled on a daily working routine, much of Percy's work being transferred to Ben, leaving Percy free to do what he was best at, interacting with the local community, and keeping his ear to the ground.

Ben departed just after five p.m., and Dan said, "You can go home if you want to Percy."

"I prefer to stay, at least during the week. Less nagging you know."

"No problem. Run Ben through the daily log for a few days, until you are confident he has got it. If you are not, do it yourself, and let me know. I also need to define Misses Nicholas' duties."

The neighbour bustled in twenty minutes later, asking who needed dinner. Dan made her sit down, and laid down the law. "We are extremely grateful for your help, but I, and you, need to know what you are doing.

"I would like you to provide breakfast for Percy, Alison, and I, plus probably Ben, for around eight o'clock each morning. There will also be lunch. Between breakfast and lunch, please clean and do what you do. You may only enter the two secure offices when the occupant allows. This is for your own protection. Finish after lunch, as we will all dine at the inn later.

"You are also on the payroll."

Dan handed her an envelope full of cash, and she quailed. "Dan, I don't need this! I'm supporting you, your cause."

"Thank you, and yes you are supporting us, admirably."

"No I'm not. I need something proper to do, obviously. I used to be Post Mistress of this place, and before that, confidential secretary for the manager of the local bank. I can type at over one hundred words per minute, with no mistakes."

Percy said, "That's fast."

Dan added, "Very fast. Anything else?"

"I spend most of my time online, when I am not here, and run a blog to assist older people, that has thousands of followers."

"Would those be local people?"

"Most are. Why?"

"I'd like to know why many of them left the area, and if any were—— coerced to leave by foreigners."

"Muslims you mean. Yes, some were. Want me to start a new thread?"

"Please, but keep it low key, a rant or moan thingamajig."

"Sounds like fun. I'll see to it."

"Thank you Misses Nicholas."

"Stella, please."

"We are fully staffed right now, but should things change, I will call on you first. I presume you have an idea of what we are about?"

"Yes, you are counting the number of illegal migrants and militia debarking aeroplanes that are pretending to be light aircraft, over at the old aerodrome…"

By the time she had finished, Stella had given Dan an in depth summary of their operation. Dan was horrified that Stella knew so much about their operation. He considered, and it became obvious, idle slips of the tongue over breakfast or lunch. Perhaps seeing things when cleaning. Dan felt foolish but had to react quickly. He said, "Not a word to a soul."

"My lips are sealed Dan, always have been."

"Stella, I hope you mean that. The fate of this country may hang on the silence of your tongue."

"That's why I said nout. None of my business anyways, unless you lose and the Muslims take over. I'm rooting for the team, Dan."

"Thanks Stella. Did you have any luck with the old freezer?"

"No, I need somebody strong to move it and the others to a power point. If they work, they will need moving again. You look like a strong young man. Let's go."

All the appliances appeared to work, but were in need of a good clean. Dan called Percy, and together they manhandled the items through to the shop.

Alison came to them, and looking at the display refrigerators, said, "Is one of these going begging? I could do with one in the ops room. I tend to snack a lot, not eat properly."

Stella said, "Which one?"

"Why the Pepsi one of course, I always pass the challenge."

"That may be, but I need to clean it first. Tomorrow perhaps."

"Oh, thank you so much. This place is beginning to feel like home from home."

They were about done when Dan's mobile rang. "Felicity, are we on for tonight?"

"Yes, finally. Pick me up from home at seven. Ciao."

Dan glanced at the time display and said, "Shit, I'm running late. Percy, lock up please, I gotta run."

Alison stole the moment, after his departure. "Wow! So Dan's on a date. Who is she? Come-on, spill the beans. This is so exciting."

Chapter 16 ~ Getting Set

Dan awoke in Felicity's bed, remembering a most enjoyable evening, one of the best in his life. He looked over at her sleeping form, and for the first time wondered if they did have a chance together. Almost immediately he berated himself, it could never work out. He reached over, and wrapped his arm around her, gentling her awake.

Running late, neither of them had time for breakfast. Dan said, "I'll call you for tonight," as he raced out of the door.

Smells of breakfast wafted out of the windows as Dan arrived at the office. He waited as Ben parked and they entered together. "No sign of Alison?" asked Dan.

Percy replied, "Not yet. I think she worked through the night."

Dan went up and rapped on the door. Alison opened it, and said, "I've made great progress."

Dan asked, "Have you slept?"

"No, not yet, I'll do that later, once the basics are all in place. This is what I've got so far."

Dan was amazed at the progress she had made, a full working model of the Trimingham feed since inception, with pause and mouse hover, a pop up giving flight and cargo details. "This is brilliant Alison. What about the other airfields?"

"Ah, I did those first, well, set them up at least. Now, this is not the technological stone age, so what I did was requisition four of this model drone, here on the screen. It is at the large end of mini, runs on petrol, and can hover or land vertically. It has a range of several hundred miles, but topping up the tank will be a problem.

"Each of these comes with a detachable mini-drone that's electric, and can recharge via solar panels on the wings. This would give you the ability to get close to the passengers, maybe even get facial recognition, or fly inside a hangar."

"Okay, I like this, great idea. What's the catch?"

"Somebody will need to fly them from a consol in this room: You. But first you need to put them in place, so I have chartered the jet you normally use, and it will be ready for takeoff at ten o'clock. Tim will be waiting for you at London City airport at eleven to give you the drones, plus ones for here, other things I have marked, like the tracking consol, and a proper computer with dedicated multi-screen capability."

"Good work Alison, I'll need to make my report before I leave. This is going to be tight. What about the locations?"

"Ah, I got good satellite fix of each, and have identified where the drones could be placed. They may need to be moved later, but that should not be far.

Chapter 16

"I've also identified these small airstrips, and will contact them before you get there. I'm presuming you will fly to the first from the City. Each lies within twenty miles of the target, close enough to save fuel, yet far enough away for you to not be observed."

"Alison, you are a star! I can't believe this. Thanks. We will have direct contact?"

"Yes, Tim will give you a satellite phone that can reach me on this number." She wrote it down and handed it to Dan. "It should not interfere with the aircraft, but might do, so don't use it during takeoff or landing."

"Got it. Anything else?"

"Yes, I've decided to make this an operations room. The bed needs to go, and the wardrobe. I'll need desks instead, plus secure storage. I'll sleep next door, as the inn doesn't work for me."

Dan glanced at the clock on the screen, and said, "I gotta go, will you join us for breakfast?"

"No … yes, why not, I could use a short break."

Alison joined the breakfast table a few minutes later, and brought with her a vibrant buzz, despite the fact she looked overly tired. She added food to her plate, before stopping and staring at the traditional fried bread.

She picked up one piece. It was a sodden mass of overcooked oil, fat dripping onto the plate below. "Oh my giddy aunt! You cannot be serious? Here, let me show you how it should be done. Stella, is this dripping in the frying pan?"

"Yes, I cooked the bacon in it."

"Great! I call this Irish Fried Bread, in honour of my mother, and my roots. Use lard and not cooking oil."

Alison took two slices of thick white bread, pressed one side into the hot fat of the frying pan, and set them to grill. Once golden brown, she took one piece, leaving the other for people to try. Stella cut the strange toast into four, and was surprised by the reaction: "Delicious," "Yes, so light and fluffy," "Mmm. Another please."

Misses Nicholas was unsure, but tried the last piece herself. Her eyes widened in wonder, and she said, "It seems you can teach an old dog new tricks. Much healthier too." With that, she took the plate of sodden and normal fried bread, and throwing it in the bin, cooked fresh to the new recipe.

Dan left as soon as he had eaten, and made his daily report. He added a small page of supplies, asking Tim bring them to the City airport. The Director came live online, and they spoke briefly. She finished by stating, "I've taken over sole charge of your operation. You already report directly to me, but in future you report to me only. Harry is aware, and is not expecting further contact from you, until this is over. I need you isolated. Get to the bottom of this Dan."

Dan returned to the office, and spoke briefly with all inside. The time was just before nine when he departed for Norwich airport. After pre-flight checks, he was in the air a little after ten, and touched down before eleven o'clock.

Air traffic control assigned him an apron set to one side, where Tim was waiting with an SUV. Two men got out and started loading the jet, Tim coming to Dan and saying, The Director spoke to Alison, and this is the result. This bag contains your request. Let me show you how to operate this new drone, it's state of the art."

Dan knew how to fly drones, but this was more complex, having the detachable mini-drone. He put the craft through its paces, before hovering to release, relocate, and return the mini-drone to the mother drone. The control consol was similar to a game pad, the display showing the craft under control, with the other inset top corner.

Tim pointed out some features. "This shows mobile phone connection, as with your own phone. Reception is good here, so use that if you can. The antenna below is for Wi-Fi, which I doubt you'll have, and the lowest is for direct satellite link. This always works, but is a heavy drain of power, so only use it in emergencies.

"The mini-drone is similar, and displays here when in prime focus. Both can store several days' worth of data, which you may need for the smaller drone. I set these up so that one consol controls only one drone. Normally an experienced operator would control all from the same one. You and Alison would understand this, but others may get confused. You can add other drones to the system, and define parameters using the menu, here."

"Thanks Tim, anything else?"

"Yes, the Director asked me to give you this memory stick. I've no idea what's on it, and she will send you an decryption code in due course. Be careful Dan, she seems to be relying on you to do the impossible, whatever that entails."

"Hmm. I've got a good idea."

"One last thing. One of the boxes contains a small arsenal, should you be discovered and need to fight your way out. "

When Tim left, Dan requested a take-off slot, and departed London fifteen minutes later, headed for Rochdale. Alison confirmed his landing schedule with a flying club in the nearby countryside. Dan landed, and launched the drone immediately, landing it before meeting the inhabitants.

Later, he was in Sheffield on the pretext of having his tyres checked. He paid a small fee in cash, leaving shortly afterwards, with more air in his tyres. The scenario, with differing guises, repeated in Derby and

Leicester, each drone being placed where Alison had specified, to be moved into final position later.

Dan called before takeoff, asking for a Transit van and a couple of able bodies to be in Norwich for when he touched down.

He arrived back in Norwich a little after five, tired, but happy. Less happy when he realised the able bodies were Percy and Ben. He barred their way. "Thank you, but this requires younger people, no disrespect. Please see if there are any porters, kids looking to make a buck.

A civil argument ensued, but when Dan became distracted by a call from Felicity, the oldsters started offloading. Everything was going well, until they began to remove the new, large, and heavy monitor.

Dan stopped them, and hefting one end, realised it would be a struggle for him. He hired a couple of young men to complete the job. Even they struggled with the monitor, but cleared the other items from the aircraft.

They returned to the village in convoy, and Dan sent Ben home. He went to see the two lads that had started the ball rolling, and both Kevin and Neville were pleased to assist, especially when they realised they would be paid.

Before they started work Dan said, "I want your word of honour, that you will say nothing to anyone about what you see. You are here to move furniture, and that is all you will relate, even to your parents."

They swore an oath, and began by putting smaller items aside so they could move the monitor first. They hefted it and Neville said, "Christ, what's in this. Lead?"

Dan grinned, "Yes, LED. Don't drop it. Put it down if you need a rest."

They manhandled the weight up the stairs with some difficulty, and left it on the landing. Dan checked on Alison, who was in the bath. "Oh goody, I'll be out in a minute."

"Have you slept?"

"Yes, I had six hours, and am ready to burn the midnight oil. Get rid of Charlie's bed, the one in my ops room is larger, three-quarter, and more comfortable. Take the wardrobe through as well, then we'll have room to set everything up."

Alison appeared in a bathrobe soon after and gave instructions, as she knew what the boxes contained. "I'll be a couple of minutes getting dressed, and then we're a go. Is there any coffee?"

The lads continued to carry stuff, as Percy went down to attend to drinks. He met Misses Nicholas, who had spent the afternoon cleaning the storeroom, and she took his order.

The weight of the monitor was revealed when unpacked. It was a wooden framed box, which held a large and solid metal frame. When it was assembled, the extremely large monitor was placed on top, and secured. The unit had four multi-directional trolley type wheels, which could be locked in place.

Once set aside, the lads helped Dan assemble the two flat-pack desks, and then two and three drawer cabinets on wheels that fitted underneath. With the main components assembled, Alison oversaw the restructuring of the room, which finally took on the look of an operations centre. A server, computers and smaller monitors were connected, and the job was completed when Dan and the lads put the office chairs together.

Dan said, "Kevin, Neville, please put all the packaging in the nearby, upstairs storeroom. At some point this will all need to be returned. The clock had turned seven by the time they were packing up. The ops room was coming to life, and the mood was happy.

"Mission accomplished," said Dan, and a cheer went up. He had just paid the lads, when Felicity entered the room. "So this is where you've been hiding. Wow! What is this? An operations room."

"Yes. Alison, our computer expert," Dan indicated the woman, "May I introduce you to the final member of our team, Inspector Wigglesworth, head of the local Constabulary."

They shook hands, and Alison enquired, "So, is it true you are Dan's new girlfriend?"

Felicity chuckled and replied, "That hasn't been decided, as of yet. How did you know?"

"Ma'am, we aren't called British Intelligence without good reason."

Her words elicited laughter, and a mass exodus for dinner. Most people needed to relax after a long day, but Alison returned to work.

Percy said, "I'll need to return the van tonight. I borrowed it from Alf, a neighbour, and he needs it for first thing in the morning. Also, the wife is under the weather and asked me to spend the night at home."

"Okay Percy, do that and we'll see you in the morning. Call me if there is a problem. Thanks, and good night."

Dan and Felicity dined in the lounge. At first talk was of work, but soon changed to their personal lives, what they wished for, and their dreams. Their thinking was broadly aligned: work hard, get promoted to a top job with money, a decent pension, have kids somewhere along the way, and spend retirement travelling the world.

The next morning Percy called early, "Dan, I'll need to remain at home today, sorry. Maybe for a few days. The wife is not well and I cannot leave her."

"That's fine Percy, attend to her. We'll be fine, and I hope she recovers soon."

Ben arrived for breakfast, but had little else to do. Dan spent most of the day in the ops room with Alison. With the aid of daylight, he was able to hone positioning of the drones, and got video good enough for facial recognition from the smaller drones. He made a log of each site, noting details of each aeroplane, the numbers and type of people that got off, and identified cargo boxes inwards and outgoing.

Alison had the aircraft movements as a wrap, and spent some of her time unravelling the European aspect. Once she had a handle on it, Dan said, "Can you check the geo-political boundaries of Thetford and nearby Wymondham. I need the political make up down to ward and parish level. Relate this to local council composition, and include the ethnicity and political allegiance of all elected members.

"We begin with just these two. Once that is done, correlate the results with all empty, or recently inhabited dwellings. I presume most will have been registered with the Land Agency within the last year. Before this, most were held in tithe to a factory or farm, which has long since gone--equals no property ownership."

"Understood. But I need to know the 'why', what did you discover?"

"Ah, top down, of course. This is what we found…"

Chapter 17 ~ Lost Property

Dan and Alison worked late on Thursday. Felicity called, "Dan, I need to stay in tonight, do my hair, get my head together, and have time to myself. You don't mind do you?"

"No, that's fine ... I've been wondering about us as well. Alison and I are busy-busy, working late, but making good progress. Enjoy your chill, and I'll see you tomorrow. We all need our personal space. Sweet dreams." He made kissy sounds as he rang off.

Felicity stared at the phone, the call dead. She had prepared arguments as of why she needed a quiet night in, but Dan had accepted the fact at face value. She had never met a man like him before, and wondered.

Percy was a no show on Friday also. "Dan, she's still not well, and her sister is coming over for the weekend. It's an old problem, but more severe than before, so I need to be with her. Hope that's all right?"

"Of course, Percy. Let me know when your wife is well again, and we'll begin something new. Tell me, you deal with the rural west side of Lower Meddlington, so I presume there is another who covers the east?"

"Yes, and we cover for each other when one of us is on holiday, or sick. He's covering my beat now. Why d'you ask?"

"Just a thought, we'll talk when you are available again."

Friday became another long and busy day. Alison stated, "Yesterday I lost so much time to manual searching, it was like waiting for the cows to come home. So, I set up several algorithms, and although they need honing, results are now coming in by the minute, not hours. I should have something for you by lunchtime. I can tell you this though, the majority of rural properties are tithe, and most have no traceable ownership."

"And so, the houses are filled with Muslims. Can it be that simple?"

"Curses are like chickens; they always come home to roost."

"Let me know the soonest you suspect any of your cows have come home to roost."

Alison chuckled, "I will. It's going to be fun working here with you. I'll also tell you when the chickens come home. I'm that good."

Dan looked at her quizzically, thinking of the facts, not their banter, when a penny dropped. Realising the connection, he made a call. "Percy, what's the address of that house you'd like to live in?"

After searching the address, Dan called back twenty minutes later. "Percy, bad news, the house is in tithe to the tanning factory."

"But that went out of business before the Second World War."

"Exactly! Get your arse over here pronto. Bring your credit card, and it will be yours in a few minutes."

Chapter 17

"I'll need to wait until the sister gets here, but will be with you shortly. I don't know how to thank you."

"Don't. It's been derelict for years and will need a lot of work."

After the call finished, Alison stated, "There is a similar property a few doors down, detached with large gardens, loads of space, and outbuildings. It's a dream for a city girl. It was also tithe to the same tannery."

"Put my name on it. The cost is a few hundred pounds, for a manor house. This is all lost property, and I'm making a claim."

"You'll need to complete this form, answer some personal questions, pay the fee, and they will decide if you can have title to the property. It's just up the road from your girlfriend's house."

"Thank you Alison, I know that."

"So, she is your current love then, I knew it."

"Then why do I feel like a thirteen year old caught snogging behind the bike shed?"

Dan completed the application of ownership, and they got back to work, but something nagged at the back of Dan's mind. He had just admitted, for the first time in years, that he had a girlfriend. The only way he could get his mind back to the order of the day was to accept the fact. However, he did pause on occasion to mutter, "Girlfriend," as if trying to identify with the concept.

He stopped being distracted when a cargo plane landed at one of the airfields he was monitoring. As he appended the log, Alison got a call from Sarge. "Yes, Dan's monitoring it now."

Dan launched the small drone, and flew it inside the hangar, settling it on a beam to monitor the floor. Seventy militia debarked, and a long box four feet wide was next. Other incoming crates were opened, and as he had expected, were filled with automatic weapons, explosives, and ammunition. He reasoned these were of black market origin.

Return cargo consisted mainly of food, some clothing, and several long thin boxes. Others lay open nearby and, taking a gamble, he flew the drone close to one as it departed the interior. He knew immediately it was a short-range missile and presumed the associated nearby boxes contained similar, and warheads. He got the drone out before discovery, and made a copy of the resultant footage.

In the log, he noted that each UK airbase received one cargo plane each week. A larger pattern was beginning to emerge. Just before midday Alison exclaimed, "Got it! Just one more tweak to the main algorithm, and I'll be able to rattle these off in no time."

"What have you got, Alison?"

"Okay, Wymondham occurred first, presumably because it was closer to their centre of operations, and smaller. In the country, a ward is composed of parishes. And guess what? Two-thirds are Muslim. I had to dig deep for that, as it is not common knowledge. They vote for an Islamic representative, but the problem is, they vote for any political party. Mainly Labour or Conservative, but other political flavours are also in the mix."

"I don't understand. This wasn't what I was expecting. Are they true to the party?"

"Yes, I checked that out, and the elected Muslims challenge each other in council. They appear to be fully supportive of the party line."

"Damn. I had been expecting something like a new party, the Jihad of Islam, or similar. But they appear genuine. I don't get that, with what we are seeing. What about Thetford?"

"One other point regards Wymondham. The local English Defence Force, or EDF, are strong in that town, and determined to expose a Muslim plot. They are getting nowhere, except for scaring the local, Christian population half to death.

"Thetford is more or less the same, two-thirds of elected local politicians being Muslim, and all working for an assortment of political parties. There's no overt corruption of our political system here, Dan."

"Yes there is, we've just got to decipher it. Later, I'll need you to work outwards in concentric circles, radiating from here, but first, I need you to tie this down.

"Here's the thing. In the countryside, and with most properties not being owned, but tithed to long extinct farms and factories, most property is without legal ownership, agreed?"

"Yes, that's true. I checked, and the properties in Muslim villages have all been recently lodged with the Land Registry. The thing is, this is being done through a property firm, Anglo-Asian Holdings."

"We've already come across that name in Norwich and Newmarket, they're developing new estates. Cappel Moor for one. I need you to check them out as a matter of priority. Find out everything you can about them, directors, property ownership, sub branches, or child companies. The works."

"I can tell you now, the one I just discovered is under the title Anglo-Asian Holdings, Wymondham."

"So, this company is taking over rural villages, laying claim to the houses, and filling them with migrants, probably for a rent. Then in time, the numbers accrue to be enough to take over a Ward, which in turn will only vote for the Muslim candidate."

"Yes, and they're breeding like rabbits; eight, ten kids to a family."

"I need you to relate this to the town and later, city. I believe each Ward of a town is being undermined by an influx of Muslim voters, which alters the balance of power. It does not alter the political divisions of the common people, because they remain the same as before, but now a Muslim elected. Do you follow me?"

"Yes. This is heady stuff, but I got it. So what if the Muslims pool their vote for some unknown reason?"

"That's what worries me. I need the religious demographical shift for each ward of Wymondham and Thetford, disregarding party voted for, for say the last five years? Look at Newmarket as well."

"Sure, this will take a while."

Dan answered his mobile phone. "Hello, Percy?"

"Hello Dan. The sister has arrived, so I'll be with you in about twenty minutes. These women will talk themselves to death."

Dan went down to speak to Ben, and found him helping Stella in the shop. After greetings, Ben was bullish. "Dan, I loved the action, but today, yesterday, I have done almost nothing. I feel wasted, there's no point in me being here. It's time I went home."

Dan was slightly taken aback, but realised the reason. "Sorry Ben, but with Alison here, well, she's doing all our jobs, and she's much better at it. Okay, we're done, but may I call on you in future?"

"Yes, of course."

"Great. Thanks Ben, for everything. Here, a small consideration, then we are done."

Time passed and Percy arrived, and was soon the prospective owner of his desired house. Stella called them for lunch, and they sat around the buffet table catching up. Percy mentioned ownership of his new house, and Stella said, "What? You registered it and they gave you the deeds."

"Yes, effectively. They call it a title to property nowadays. I had to answer some questions, but it proved to be simple enough. Paid a few hundred pounds for the registration, and my application has been provisionally approved."

"My, oh my. I pay no rent, my home is ex farm labourer, but nobody seems to own it. You mean I can register it as my own?"

"Yes. That seems to be the case."

"What about this house, Stella?"

"The same I shouldn't wonder. I still can't reach the owners, they may be dead, or living it up in Spain. The rest of this village will likely be the similar. How do I register my home?"

Dan was quiet for a moment. "Don't act yet. This could become rather big, quite quickly. I'll need to speak to Her Majesty's Land Registry, probably in person, and put a fast-track application process in place for all concerned hereabouts.

"Percy, Charlie mentioned a housing problem some days ago, or was it Ben? Moving out of a Police house on retirement, we should check with your colleagues as well."

"Great idea Dan, I'll get to work on it as soon as I can, run it by her Ladyship, and search out suitable properties."

"When are you likely to return to duty, Percy?"

"It depends on the misses, but if she strengthens over the weekend, I can return on Monday morning. Regardless, with her sister staying over, there should be no problem either way."

"Okay. I think we need to understand the size of the problem, so return to normal duty, but try to identify who lives in a registered property, and who does not. We'll need your opposite number to do likewise on the east."

"That's a lot of work, every single house or small farm."

"Yes. The name of occupant and official address, and who held the tithe if applicable, dated if possible."

Alison said, "It may not make much difference, but I can log all registered properties, and compare this to the electoral roll."

"That would be a great help. Okay, let's pick this up on Monday morning. I'm sure I'll be speaking with the Inspector before then."

Percy departed, and Stella began clearing up. Alison went upstairs, and Dan returned to his room to speak with his Director. He had to wait until she picked up. "Yes Dan, what is it?"

Dan explained the problem, relating a summary of what they had discovered so far that day. "It is my intention to visit the Land Registry as soon as possible. Your thoughts."

"Hmmm. Bureaucrats. I think I should go with you. This may require someone of my leverage. I'll call you back in a moment."

Dan waited, working on his log until the call came. "Dan, we have an appointment with the director for nine a.m. Monday morning. Drive down on Sunday and we'll dine at my club. It'll give us a chance to catch up fully on where this is going. My driver will collect you from your apartment a seven-thirty on Monday morning. It's only ten miles to Croydon, but the traffic will be a nightmare.

"You are on your secure phone? … Good, I'll send the encryption key for the pen drive now. Pleasant reading, for your eyes only."

"Till Sunday, Ma'am."

Using the encryption key, Dan read the files. They were the latest, current terrorist threat assessments of UK, USA, and Europe, regarding ISIL. One part struck a chord: organised human trafficking via land, air, and sea.

Dan returned to the office, and picked up monitoring the drones. Alison was preoccupied for much of the afternoon, but spoke in time. "Dan, Anglo-Asian Holdings has property all over the place. They are incredibly big, but always out of the public eye, it's most odd."

"Show me what you got."

"The directors of the main company are…"

" Mohammad, Ali, and Hussein. The Inspector told me. I needed you to verify, thank you. What else?"

Chapter 17

"These names are on the Cappel Moor estate."

"They are also the owners of the local trading estate here, airfield, and flying club, to save you checking."

"Thanks Dan. In Wymondham the directors are the same three, plus Shah. Likewise in Newmarket, the old estate is owned by those three, and somebody called Ibrahim. Thetford the same plus Al Fridi. It sounds like the latter is a local director of operations."

"That makes sense. Run checks on the extra directors."

"Already done. Ibrahim is from Syria, has British citizenship, and has worked for the company for many years. Same for Shah, except he has dual Pakistani-British citizenship, and again has worked for the company since coming here. Similar with Al Fridi."

"The new inhabitants of the old Newmarket housing estate are Syrian. A police contact there told Percy that local government, charities, and even national government are all involved, viewing this as a refugee crisis alleviation project. I'll see if Percy can get names of people from his contact. Even institutions would help."

"I'll begin with the council representative for that ward, who ..." She madly clicked keys. "Got it. Just happens to be Pakistani."

Work continued in a similar vein, until Dan's mobile phone rang. It was after seven. "Felicity, sorry, I got distracted with work. Are we on for tonight?"

"Yes Dan. I thought we could spend the night here. One of the pubs serves good food, and I fancied a drink before eating."

"That suits me fine, I have a lot to tell you, say thirty minutes at your place."

Dan slid his tablet into a brief case. "Sorry Alison, I must dash, is there anything you need?"

"No, I'll be fine, go."

"What about days off, this is Friday?"

"You must be joking. I'm working through, there's so much to do. Later I'll take a few days ... I'll need a long weekend, I've been invited to a friend's wedding. I'm a bridesmaid. My first time, so I can't miss it. The hen night begins on Thursday. You agree?"

Dan muttered as he thought aloud, "Yes in theory."

"Good, agreed. Now don't keep the lady waiting, Dan. Ba-byeee."

Chapter 18 ~ Land Registry

Dan and Felicity enjoyed a lovely evening, and on the walk back to her home, he pointed out the house he had put his name on.

"But Dan, you can't just go and claim ownership of a property."

"It seems you can, if it doesn't belong to anyone. These houses were for managers of old tannery, and have been derelict for years."

"Yes they have, but still."

"Percy took the house two doors down, apparently they always wanted to buy it, but couldn't find the owner. That's because there wasn't one. When the tannery closed these houses lay empty."

"Let's check them out in the morning. Time for a nightcap."

They returned in daylight, checking out what Dan had put his names to. The roof and brickwork were solid, if pointing required in places and a chimney rebuilding. There were broken windowpanes, but otherwise the house appeared structurally sound. Dan looked for a way in, only to find Felicity entering through the rear door. She held up a key. "I found this under a plant pot on the rear patio."

She opened the front door and gave him the key. They toured inside and discovered the remains of old furnishings; things like fabric chairs and mattresses would be scraped, but the oak dining table and sideboard could be refurbished. The rear garden seemed more like a field, and there was a strange workshop, but no garage.

Felicity threw her hands over her head and twirled. "I love this place Dan, it's massive. It has six bedrooms, although the box room could be turned into an en suite bathroom. Downstairs are a library, dining room, sitting room, and sunroom. The kitchen is massive, and off it lies a pantry and a scullery. There's even a cellar."

"The garden looks enormous, and look, there's an orchard, also massive. It's going to take a lot of work to fight back the jungle it's become." Felicity chucked a stick at him.

Locking up, they went to see the house Percy had hopefully acquired. They were not surprised to find him agog inside. "Percy, how's it looking?"

"The house is in quite good shape overall. There's some tiles to replace, and windows to fix, and that's about it. I can't believe it."

"You told the misses yet?"

"No, I daren't. What if the deal doesn't go through, there'd be hell on. If it does, then we got four bedrooms, three reception rooms, and a … What do we call it? … massive kitchen. Be too big for us, but nice to be lord of the manor. I s'pose we could treat the ground floor as a bungalow in our dotage. The grandkids could stay upstairs."

They chatted a while before Dan and Felicity returned to her home. "There may be others similar, you should check around."

Chapter 18

"Thanks Dan, I'll do that, but I like your place the best. Strange, but it felt like home. Mind you, there's one hell of a lot of work to do on it."

Felicity started a pot of coffee when they got back, and asked Dan what his plans were for the day. "I'll need to get back and work with Alison. We're making great progress. Oh, and I'll be in London on Monday. I'll drive down Sunday afternoon."

"Good, I'll be over having Sunday lunch with my parents, as usual. Now, answer me one question. Are we a couple?"

"Yes of course. I love being with you."

"Good, correct answer. So Danforth Glover, you are taking the day off, spending it with your girlfriend, and we are going to Norwich to do 'couples things'."

Dan began to protest, mentioning all the work they had to do. Felicity said, "Give me your mobile, unlocked."

Dan warily handed it over. Felicity scanned the numbers and dialled, putting it on speaker. "Hello Alison, this is Felicity. Dan wants to take me out for the day; do you need him for anything? You are on speaker, and he is listening."

"No, not at all. I have a mountain of work to do, and if he is here, he'll only give me more. Make it several days, and I'll be happy."

"Done. He'll be back next week. Thanks Alison. Ciao."

She cut the call and handed Dan his mobile back. "Looks like you are taking the weekend off. Today we go shopping for clothes, and then lunch. I'll be ready in twenty minutes. See to the coffees, there's a love."

"But, but..." Dan had already lost, and muttered under his breath. He hated shopping, and knew women took ages. He poured the coffee, and resigned himself to his fate.

The day passed extremely quickly. Dan enjoyed her company, and her no-nonsense approach to shopping. She needed shoes, skirt, and blouse, and made quick decisions, unlike every other female he had met. He even began to enjoy window-shopping with her, especially when she saw a jacket that would suit him perfectly. Even Dan liked it, although it was not his usual style.

Later, the situations reversed. "Felicity, you would look stunning in that dress. Come, try it on."

She gawped at the price, and said, "I'll never wear it, it's for posh do's."

"Well, I wear a tuxedo and bow tie occasionally, and next time I do, I would like you to be wearing that dress."

She tried the dress on, and it fitted perfectly. She looked at herself in the mirror and smoothing the fabric with her palms said, "Wow!"

Dan bought the dress for her, plus shoes and a clutch bag to match. It was fun, as again she scanned and chose quickly. They had luncheon at a classy café, and in the afternoon, visited local buildings of interest, walked in the park, and discovered a small fun fair offering rides and amusements. He bought candyfloss, and they behaved like children.

Their evening meal was Italian, and much enjoyed. Later they took in a show. Dan said, "Let's spend the night here, look, there's a hotel over there that seems okay. We can get some late drinks, a club if you fancy, and in the morning you can head off to your parents, I'll find my own way home."

A small argument ensued, but Dan got his way, and Felicity had to choose what they did next. Just then her phone rang; it was the duty sergeant, "Sorry Ma'am. There was a jewellery heist at the new supermarket come plaza a few minutes ago. One of the security guards was shot. I'll need you to attend."

"Of course, I'm on my way. I'm in Norwich, but will be there as quickly as I can."

"Oh, in that case Ma'am, stay there. We'll need a preliminary statement from the security guard, and he is en route to Norfolk and Norwich University Hospital."

"Why not Wymondham, it's much closer?"

"Because of the gunshot Ma'am. It is potentially life-threatening, but the initial prognosis was good."

"Good. I'm on my way, and will get what I can. I'll be on the scene later. What about the thieves?"

"Car chase in progress. Other units are closing in. We should trap them on Valley Road, Ma'am."

"Good, inform me as soon as anything results. Ciao."

She turned to look at Dan. "Sorry."

He stood tall, and held her firmly. Looking her in the eye he stated, "No problem. This is what we do. Go and do your job, and I will be there in the background, supporting you. I'll hail a cab to get us back to your car." He put two fingers in his mouth and whistled. "Taxi!"

Sometime later, they arrived at the hospital main A & E entrance. Dan said, "Go, see this man. I'll park the car and wait for you, but call me if you need assistance. You won't."

"Okay. Buy a ticket. The car park is Pay and Display, and they're like vultures."

Once parked, Dan locked the doors, settled back to rest his eyes, and let his thoughts linger upon the delights of the day, which were many. He could not believe how one girl could have changed his outlook on life so much, and in such a short time. He had to admit, Felicity Wigglesworth was 'a keeper'.

To distract himself, Dan rang Alison, who was still working. They chatted about work, but Alison kept trying to prise nuggets of information about his date. She got little information. "Hold on Dan, I got something coming through. Stay on the line."

Chapter 18

Dan bided his time, and could hear the keyboard clicking in the background. He was about to ask her to call back, when she said, "Got them at last. These are tricky fish to net.

"From what I just got, the directors only use one firm of lawyers, who have a conveyance and soliciting arm. You'll love the name, Ali Brothers. One of the initials are a match for the one main director of all these companies, and the other two are qualified in law. I'll get confirmation of full names later, the search is already in progress."

"That's excellent work, Alison. I'll leave you to it. Did you mean what you said earlier?"

"No silly, although you do give me a lot of work to do. Look, when a girlfriend asks her boyfriend to take her out for the day, the boyfriend does his duty. Otherwise, he is just a male friend. It went well?"

"Brilliant, and that's all I'm saying. Alison, get some sleep, goodnight."

When Felicity reappeared, Dan drove over to pick her up, and continued back to Lower Meddlington. She spent much of the journey on her mobile, but did say, "I got a few minutes with the guy. He should pull through. I had to be tough with the doctors, but the information I got is priceless. He shot footage on his mobile, which I have taken into evidence. I let his family know, but will need to visit them personally tomorrow morning. We also caught the thieves, and got the jewellery back. It's been a good result so far, but I doubt I will get any sleep. A perk of the job I guess. You okay?"

"Fine, no problem. I checked on Alison, and she's a wonder. She unlocked a key piece of information I will need to use on Monday. I'm in London, remember. Anyway, what I mean to say is, that this is annoying, but I understand. We both have difficult jobs to do, ones that call on us to do things at a moment's notice. I respect you for that. Now get back to work, and I'll get you there."

Dan stayed with Felicity at the crime scene, until it was sealed off for forensics only. They went to bed late, and got up late.

Dan was early for dinner in London with the Director. He had been to the club twice before. It was discreet, and welcomed the confidential exchange of information, something they both shared in full measure.

Before that evening, Dan had always found the Director to be predisposed to him, but bossy, nosey, and into everything. When they parted, they did so as friends, he understanding the why of it.

Dan woke at six and worked out in a corner of his apartment he had made into a gym. He showered, ordered his thoughts, and packed his briefcase with documentation he could use as weapons, if need be. Alison sent him the last. He called Percy. "How's your wife?"

"A little better, so I will be back at work today."

"Good. I'm in London and will be back later. Don't action anything we talked about yet, as things could change. "

Dan was waiting in the foyer when the director's car arrived.

He got in the back. "Good morning Dan, I hope you slept well. Good to be back in the smog, eh. Now, run me through the all of this again, from the beginning, and we'll hone our plan."

Dan and the Director talked about work for most of the trip, although she was interrupted several times concerning other matters. Just before they entered Croydon, she asked, "So how's it going with your latest girlfriend. I hear you were up late on Saturday night."

Dan was taken aback, but the Director continued, "You've been seeing her for a while now, so we checked her out. She has passed all our tests and checks. So Dan, as a mother to her son, if you want this woman, go for her. Otherwise my lips are sealed."

"Thank you Ma'am. And Alison's?"

"Why yes of course, although my information did not come from her. If your operation blossoms, as I believe it will, I'll need to put a Commander in charge. You have the credentials, but have not passed the course. I have arranged for you to be on one, all of next week. If you want to be promoted, you will attend."

"But Ma'am..."

"Stop. I need you to pass this course, no ifs, ands, or buts. Understood? I need you to officially step up to the next level.

"Now, regards this morning, this is how we will play this game. I will introduce. You lay out our needs in this order and be forceful... You will add detail as necessary and I will sit back, watching the man, looking for his tell, as the Americans say.

"Once we reach a certain point, I will ask you to step outside and then lay the law down so he understands. When we enter, set your mobile to voice recording. I have one also, but damn, these modern smart phones are much better at it. Leave the phone behind when you leave the room, and don't switch voice recording off until we are back here.

"Ah, we are here. Thank you Geoffrey. Please pull over there. Dan, are you ready to go on?"

"Yes Ma'am. Let's do this."

The director of Her Majesty's Land Registry was officious at first, bordering upon disrespectful. Dan's boss had a calming way about her, and eased the man into what they needed to discuss.

He admitted, "These ancient tithe properties are a real nightmare for us. It is difficult to prove continuity of ownership. Most applications are accepted and registered, because the company, church, or school that held the tithe, went bankrupt a century before, or ceased to exist."

Chapter 18

Dan took over. "This is our problem, Sir, and I am looking for a speedy resolution…"

He laid out what was happening to the villages in and around Lower Meddlington, in detail. He asked for a check on the property development company, Anglo-Asian Holdings. There was a pause as staff generated data.

Once completed, the real questioning began. "What is your stance on tithe property in this area?"

"If the tithe is either defunct, as in a business gone bankrupt, or, a super-farm has sold title to a property developer, then we register the property to the new owner. It is all above board."

"I disagree. Take Wymondham. These properties, entire villages, were bought by Anglo-Asian Holdings, and you gave them a transfer of ownership documents. Care to explain?"

"I assure you, we initiate most thorough checks in all instances. Barring a counter claim, the Title is passed on to new ownership. In rural areas, this is often supported by local councils and charity organisations. There remains a need for new housing to meet government targets, and these properties lie empty. Derelict."

"We need to know the details of these transfers of ownership. I also know that wards and parishes of Wymondham have been taken over by Muslim families."

"Ah. Those would be immigrant resettling projects run by local councils. Charities are involved also. There is nothing here."

"And what of British families in situ for centuries, being turfed out of their own homes, because of Mohammad, Ali, and Hussein."

"Regards forcibly removing existing tenants from their homes, that is impossible."

"No. It has already happened. Here's the name of their legal scammers." Dan placed a piece of paper face down on the desk, and asked the director to check. When the results came back they were a perfect match.

The bureaucrat looked at the paper, and then eyed Dan. "You mean, we have been conned?"

"I believe so sir."

Dan's Director spoke at that moment. "Dan, please excuse us for one moment, I need a word in private with the director."

A few minutes later she reappeared, the director of Land Registry effusive with support. "Here's your phone, Dan. Don't forget it next time, I may need to call you."

"Yes Ma'am. My mistake," he smiled courteously.

Chapter 19 ~ Peterborough

The Director dropped Dan at his apartment. "Well played in there. I got fast-track approval for all your local catchment area villages, and villagers, on proof of electoral roll registration.

"Your next appointment is for two o'clock at Peterborough office. That's the local branch that deals with East Anglia. Press them hard, but gently, the way I do."

"I understand, Ma'am."

"I'll be sending Alison to Peterborough with related facts and figures. I want no mistakes on this, Dan."

"Neither do I. Do I really have to do the course next week?"

"Only if you want to remain in command of this project. Oh, you requested more drones for your home station. You should have thought of that sooner. Tim will drop them by within the hour. Until next time."

"Ma'am."

Back at his flat, Dan spent a few minutes throwing perishables into a bin liner, and wondering if he should invite Felicity down to London the next weekend, but then, she always seemed to be on call.

He rang and was informed, "Dan, you're invited for Sunday lunch. My mother wishes to meet you. What can I say? She wants to inspect you, judge if you are a suitable husband … yes, I know it's so silly, but then, that's my mother for you. She has my best interests at heart."

"Damn!--Erm, I mean great. Okay, we can do this. I guess we need to do this, girlfriend. I'm, sitting here on my lonesome, in my London pad, wondering if I should invite you down here for a night, a weekend on the town, but you're always on call."

"Not always. It can be arranged with a few weeks' notice. Yes, that sounds good. I love London."

"I hate it, but know my way around. You okay?"

"Yes, we got the thieves' statements, but reports due from here until Christmas. The guard is off critical, and should pull through. You?"

"Good so far. Remember we spoke about putting a team in place to register all these tithe properties, well I'm on it and expect a result. I'll explain all to you later, but presume I have your interim approval?"

"Yes, of course, but I need my space tonight. I got the painters in, thank God!"

"That time of the month, eh. I could come round and give you a massage, no sex. Call me, or I'll be in the local bar."

"I know we've been careful, but a girl likes confirmation. Enjoy your drink, I'll see you next time. Thanks. Ciao."

Dan packed several bags, realising he would be away for a while. There was enough time for him to attend to personal matters. Later, Tim dropped off some stuff, and they loaded it into his car.

Chapter 19

Dan arrived early in Peterborough, expecting a repeat of earlier; he was mistaken, being treated most cordially and introduced to the boss. "Matthew Green, Director, Peterborough Land Registry. Call me Matt.

"Dan, let's cut to the chase. I have these Muslims moving in, taking over everything, everywhere, and I can do nothing about it. They have the legal proof of ownership, and we have to grant them ownership. Most of them are Muslim immigrants. It's not right, not right at all. "

"Maybe we can help, we came to the same conclusion. What about your boss in London?"

"He's a career bureaucrat with designs on becoming a top civil servant. He's in it for the money, the pension, and a Knighthood."

"Is he bent, on the take?"

"I have no proof, and I very much doubt it."

"Okay. Work with me to stem this Islamic tide of influx."

"You bet, time to share."

And share they did. Dan revealed most, but not all of a bigger picture, and the director, called in his operations manager. The names of 'Mohammad, Ali, and Hussein', seemed to reverberate around the room, between being voiced in conversation.

Just then, Alison arrived and was shown up to the meeting. "Sorry Dan, stupid road works. Hi, I'm Alison, the tech geek, where are we…"

Alison's information, backed up by verifiable fact, blew their minds, just as Dan had intended. During the elapsing hours, Alison got in direct contact with their chief technician, and Dan gave his mobile numbers to the director and his chief tech guy

A knock came to the door, and a young man hurried inside, depositing files on the director's desk. He scurried away, as if scared of his own shadow, but was asked to remain.

The director looked at the information, picking out one. "These are set aside as possible spurious claims. Danforth Glover, that would be you, Agent. What is your interest?"

"To stop the Muslims getting hold of the property. Plus, my girlfriend and I were thinking about running a bed and breakfast, to encourage tourism, and boost the local community coffers. Otherwise I have no legal claim on the property, except for the fact it has no owner."

The director stared Dan in the eye for long seconds, before concluding, "Approved. Create something."

"Sir, there is another property nearby, registered under application of Perceval Blodwell. He is the local beat copper, and this has always been their dream house. He is a central member of my team, and applied when I did. I wondered if you could sanction the title?"

"Yes I could, but what's in it for my department?"

"Look up Wymondham, you see all those villages now under control of the Muslim cartel, 'Mohammad, Ali, and Hussein'. That property developer took licence on inhabited properties, but with title deeds tithed to defunct businesses, then forced the locals out."

"Impossible!"

The clerk said, "We had numerous complaints about this, but everything seemed to be legal, from the ownership point of view."

Dan picked up immediately. "Legal ownership that is. These families had lived there for decades, generations, and were driven out of their homes by gangs of Islamic thugs, because you gave a property development company the right to the deeds of their homes, regardless of the occupancy of sitting tenant. Some had lived in the house for all of their lives. Did you check for tenants?"

"Of course, and we were informed by the independent solicitors, let me get their name…"

"Ali Brothers."

"Yes. How did you know?"

"Because we have identified them as the legal face of these criminal scammers. Their job is to prove just enough title of ownership for you to accept their claims. We need to work together to prevent this happening all over East Anglia. All future applications need checking against the electoral role. You'll find Blodwell is on that list."

"Yes, he is, let's get to it. Blodwell's application is approved."

"Can you give me the names of the large farms that were named in the Ali Brothers declaration for Wymondham area? I intend to visit them and check this out personally."

"Yes, that would be in order. I can relate them to villages, but not people living there, that is highly confidential."

"Good. I will do that tomorrow morning and let you know what I discover. Regards Lower Meddlington, we propose to use the two community policemen, Blodwell and his counterpart in the east. They will visit all the inhabitants, and ask them to enrol with Her Majesty's Land Registry. We will do this parish by parish, village by village."

"Now the memo from my boss makes sense, and we prove habitation by reference to the electoral role."

"Yes. Alison already has this, and a list of registered properties. We need the local Bobbies to show us all the unregistered houses."

"This will take weeks, but it covers everyone, thank you Dan."

"There is one more thing. I am concerned some may not play fair, try and take a neighbour's home from them or make a bogus claim. One version of your enrolment form is an online PDF I believe."

"Yes, what of it?"

"I think it best if we create a dedicated task force to resolve this issue as quickly and efficiently as possible. I propose our local beat bobby accompany one of your staff, who then makes the application via a laptop as they visit. Once verified against the electoral register you have proof of habitation. I recommend we employ the same fast track approach for Lower and Upper Meddlington as well."

"Hmmm. Our serious investigations department sometimes does similar to this. Are you sure the local police will support us?"

"Definitely. I point out, there are two officers covering different areas, so two of your staff would cover the job in half the time, be company for each other also."

There was a pause as the idea was duly considered. The clerk spoke up. "Sir, Phil Chandler and Chad Pickering would probably be ideal. They have junior positions, but are young and good with computers. I'm sure their desks can spare them."

"When do you want to begin?"

"Today, practicably, tomorrow."

The director seemed startled, and asked for a few minutes privacy. Shortly Dan was called inside, and overheard the director ask for two men to be shown up. "Agent, if I provide these men, and offer them holiday in lieu of overtime payment, that is about as far as we can go."

"We have pubs and guest houses of reasonable standard, and within easy walk of the police station. Okay, here's the deal, I'll fund bed and breakfast, throw in extra occasionally for an evening meal. How does that sound?"

"Splendid." There came a knock to the door. "Ah. This must be the lads now."

Business was completed in short time. The two young men were keen for the adventure. Dan said, "I'll meet you both at Lower Meddlington police station at six o'clock, and we'll get you settled in. Any questions?"

"Yes sir. How do we get there?"

Alison said, "The A47, but that's where I hit the roadwork's. Best detour via Downham Market, here's the route map on my screen."

Dan and Alison left a short time later, and travelled in convoy back to the village. They found Percy monitoring the five screens depicting flights. "Hello Percy, how's it going?"

"Quite well. I decided to stay here today and see if I could help out. I've updated the log since Saturday, for all five locations, but Alison warned me not to attempt to fly a drone. You return with good news?"

"Yes Percy, but first, what time does your partner in the east finish work for the day?"

"Five o'clock. He's usually back and gone before I get in."

Dan looked at the clock and said, "Close."

He called Felicity. "I'll be over a little later, and before six. I need to speak to you about work, it'll only take a minute. Percy's opposite number on the east side, he will be doing something slightly different tomorrow, is he still there?"

"Dick Slayton, yes."

"Can you tell him to wait tomorrow morning, as another will join him, a young man from the local Land Registry. I have two of them to assign ownership of property to the incumbents of tithe-less property."

"What have you been up to? No later is fine. Yes, you did mention this to me, but so soon. I'll caution him now, but this needs my approval, not yours. Remember, I run this police station, not you."

"Of course Ma'am. I'll leave you to it."

Dan and Percy caught up properly, and planned the next morning visits for their new help. Alison gave Percy two folders, one each for east and west. "Inside are the electoral role, known owned premises, and a map of parishes, including all buildings."

Glancing up, Dan noticed the clock, and departed with Percy for the station. "You staying at the village tonight?"

"Thought I may as well, those two women will drive me crazy with their incessant chatter."

"Good, I have the night off, so I'll share a beer with you later. There's just one thing I didn't tell you, your application for that house has been approved, by the director himself, and so has mine."

"Dan, that's wonderful news! I can never thank you enough."

"They were in the suspicious applications file, until the director saw the bigger picture, and showed leniency, followed by goodwill."

Percy was beside himself with happiness, and thanked Dan several times, his mind in overdrive. Dan queried, "You going to drop by and tell the misses?"

"Oh no. Well, maybe. I'll drop by and say I'm working late, plus leave the key to the new place. We'll soon know just how bad she actually is. I bet she starts cleaning tomorrow, after making a miraculous recovery. She opens all my mail you know, even when it's from the police, marked 'private and confidential'. Damn woman."

Dan pulled into the police station rear car park at a quarter to six, and reported to the desk sergeant that he was expecting company. The sergeant informed the Inspector, and he was called through. He took Percy with him.

"Inspector, how wonderful to see you again."

"Likewise, Agent. Now cut the crap Dan, what's this about?"

Dan explained, finishing with his proposal for the coming days. Percy was in full agreement, and showed the files Alison had prepared.

"Thank you Dan, Percy. Although I had been briefed on this possible course of events, this is most professional, and I will fully support it. What I like most, is the addition of these two from the Land Registry. That means one visit or call back later, wraps up the all of it. Most of all, it ensures the securing of the residents' tenure. Well done.

Chapter 19

"I'll personally brief you, after I hold a morning briefing at seven tomorrow. It will be a full briefing of all staff, so everybody knows what they are doing. Once all the outlying villages are done, we'll begin on the town. When are the lads due, Dan?"

"They should be here for six o'clock, so in a few minutes. My deal was to provide them with bed and breakfast, and while I know the pub across the road does that, I don't want them drinking late."

"Very wise. The White House at the top of the street, Percy?"

"Yes, the White House. I'll give Jenny a call, but I'm sure she'll have free rooms, and at reasonable prices also."

Arrangements were made, and the two young men arrived late, profuse with apologies. The Inspector spoke to them in private, before Percy and Dan settled them in at Jenny's B & B, and they told them where the pub and shops were.

Percy said, "Time's getting on. I'll see the wife tomorrow. Time for that pint."

Later in the village pub, they were discussing progress, when Percy said a curious thing. "What about empty houses. What do we do with them?"

"You mean whole villages?"

"No, Dan. But most villages have one or more empty houses, take our office for instance. It theoretically has unregistered owners, but they seem to be long gone. How do we log them?"

"Good question. And it would not be right for Stella, or ourselves to claim ownership. Have a word with the lads tomorrow. There must be some arrangement that can be made."

"How about 'Crown Property set aside', until a true owner can be verified."

"That sounds neat. Thank you. But there may be to be more to it."

Percy replied, after thoughtfully sipping his beer. "Entitlement of use or purchase. Like our roads. All highways belong to the Crown, but anyone can use them."

"I like your thinking, Percy. I'll have a word with Peterborough in the morning, and confirm."

Chatter resumed until Dan said, "Oh, do me a favour. Call your contact in Newmarket, and get him to discover all he can about what's on this list."

Dan passed a piece of paper. "Hopefully it will only take a few days. Also, see if he will forward copy results to Alison directly. It would cut out the middleman, you."

Chapter 20 ~ Rights of Ownership

Tuesday welcomed the beginning of Operation Ownership. Dan called Matt in Peterborough. "Land without ownership, as in abandoned property, is known as *bona vacantia*. It is a common law principle related to feudal land tenure."

"What about today. There are abandoned properties we will visit."

"What. Ah, yes. Where the land or property ceases to be owned by anyone, it escheats to become land held by the Crown in demesne. We would confirm using local records, before lodging as such."

"What does that mean in plain English."

"Sorry Dan. It means that it is held by the Crown, but does not become a part of any Crown Estate. It is held until sold."

"Thank you. You better start a property sales department. I have the feeling we will find quite a few, including our office."

"You know, we may be able to do that. I'll call the Treasury Solicitor now, and see if something suitable can be devised for this project."

The days official work began at Lower Meddlington Police Station, where both Percy and Dick chose to start at the outer boundary, and work around, and inwards. One of Percy's priorities was to attend to those at the village that had become his second home. He also went out of his jurisdiction to see Peter and Agnes Penfold, and others nearby, who were delighted with the inclusion.

Dan saw Percy, Dick, and their new assistants off. Felicity came to his side. "You mentioned you would visit the big farms today. Let's book appointments with them first, and I'll accompany you."

"But that's out of your jurisdiction."

"Some maybe, but only as Senior Police Officer. I will be acting as a police constable, and will be there to provide a legal chain of evidence. The Chief said it was in our best interests, should things come to court."

They scheduled appointments with the farms on Dan's list, and went to visit the farm managers in turn. There were not many of them.

They were only just on time for the first appointment at Lilac Farm. "Ah, Mister Gurney, thanks for seeing us at such short notice. I'm Inspector Wigglesworth, and this is my assistant, Dan Glover. I hope you don't mind me recording this. Saves confusion later."

"No, not at all, go right ahead. Now what do you want with us way out here?"

"What can you tell me about the formation of this super-farm. How did it grow?"

"Super-farm you say, I likes that. Well now, let me see. I came in about twelve years ago, when three large farms were bought out to create this one. We've just under ten thousand acres under the plough."

Dan whistled. "That's big."

"We're not as big as some, but are holding our own. You see, the key to profit is machinery and little labour. So let us say that once the combine is paid for, we buy another and larger one, and so on, until we have enough, paid for, equipment. There are maintenance and replacement issues of course, but we plan for those. Some farms lease instead. So in essence, once the expensive machinery like combine harvesters are paid off, we have money straight into the bank."

"The smaller farms could not do this?"

"Ooh no. For them, they had to hire in the machinery, plus driver. Cost a pretty penny too. And they all wanted the same machines at the same time of year. Being bigger, we're able to stagger planting, so harvest is a succession. The only vagary is the weather, but after a few years you learn to read the signs."

"So, going back in history, the large farms you bought out, they in turn were composed of smaller farms?"

"Yes, I guess so."

"You were not interested in what happened to them, didn't have any reason to keep tabs on them?"

"No, why should we? They are away in the distant past, forgotten about. Our farming methods are intensive, and demanding on time. Where's this going?"

"Do you have a list of farm workers' cottages? I presume you have some?"

"Why yes. Just over one dozen, and they are nearly all a part of the main farmstead, here. You would have passed most of them on your way in."

"Could I have a copy of your listed farm worker buildings, for our records, I'll take a picture with my phone, if that's okay?"

The manager eyed them, not quite sure what they were after, but saw no reason to lie, and he wanted to maintain good relations with the police. "Bessie, bring me the folder of our farm holdings, the one with the workers houses in it."

"Coming sir…" A woman of secretarial demeanour came through. "Here it is Jake. There's not much in it."

"All right, let's see. Here is the title deed for the 'super-farm' as you call it. This is the boundary of our land, and these are the cottages for farm workers."

Dan took photograph copies of all, before scanning the words with his eyes, as did Felicity. They both paid more attention to the title deeds, which correlated with the documentation presented. Jake appeared to be getting restless, Felicity nodded at Dan, and said, "Sorry to take the long route about this, but we had to be sure. You confirm these are all the habitable buildings this farm owns."

"Yes, fourteen of them, and they are shown here. Count them."

Felicity said, "Dan, if you please."

Dan came straight to the point; Jake was irked and needed straight answers. "The reason I am here, is because the local villages have been taken over by Muslims, all of them. Do you know why?"

"No. And they're a damned nuisance, breeding like rabbits and changing the country way of life. But what's this got to do with me?"

"One hundred years ago, and less, these village houses were nearly all in tithe to the local farms, and some to factories. The farms got progressively bigger, and they needed fewer workers, machinery took over, as you stated. Then these farms were sold, merged, and the farm buildings often destroyed to make way for land and larger fields."

"Yes, that would be about right. But I still don't see why you're interest in any of this."

"Well, the bottom line is, that with the farm mergers, and factories, schools even, going out of business, people lost track of who owned what. The villagers remained, as did the houses they lived in, except they were held in tithe to nobody."

"You mean they were not passed on as part of the estate."

"Exactly. Many deals were hand-written, stamped by a solicitor from out of the area, and the tithe housing slipped by unnoticed.

"Our problem today, is that nobody owns these tithe cottages, until interested parties knowing this, take advantage. I need to show you a document, and I will ask you in all truth, whether you have any knowledge of it. This information may be used in court."

Dan showed the letter of transfer made by Ali Bros. Solicitors, naming all village properties transferred by Lilac Farm to Anglo-Asian Holdings. Fifty-three properties had exchanged hands for an average price of £160,000. The fee payable to Lilac Farm was just over eight and a half million pounds.

Manager Gurney gawked at the piece of paper, and tried to speak, but no words were uttered. Dan said, "If this were a legitimate sale, your accounts would have records."

This gave Gurney words. "I know nothing about this, and we never received any money. You can check our bank account."

Felicity interceded. "We may do so, Mister Gurney. But there may be no need, unless this, and many similar, are taken to court. Do we have your full support?"

"Damned right you do. They've even forged my signature, and I'll be damned if I know how they got hold of that. Eight and a half million, and they scammed us out of that. I would'ne have sold regardless, what happened to the villagers?"

"They were kicked out, and their houses, homes some had lived in all their lives, were given to asylum seekers, all Muslims by the way."

Chapter 20

Mister Gurney seemed in a bad way; he muttered, "I never knew. This is a miscarriage of justice. What can be done?"

He seemed to get himself back together as they reached the car. "You'll be visiting us all I guess, the large farms. Have a word with Marty Wimpole. He said something odd to me at a market. It may have been last year, or this. Yes, late spring. He was moaning about Muslims hassling him, and I did'ne pay attention at the time. The young bull I was there to buy was just being readied for auction."

"Thanks Jake, sorry to put you through all that, but you now understand what we are up against. Please don't contact the other farms until this evening. Thanks."

As Dan drove them on to the next farm, Felicity said, "Dan, that was one hell of an insight, and we now have proof that Ali Brothers are cheating. They're, probably using the bill of sale to launder money."

"Agreed. I managed to video the all of it. Here stick my mobile on charge. We better do the lot today, but we can go a quicker next time."

"Definitely. If they're all as helpful as Jake, this will be a breeze."

Not all the farm managers were as open as Jake, but most were. All were horrified to discover they had apparently, and officially, been paid for selling property they did not realise they owned. None had received payment.

This was brought into focus when they spoke to Marty Wimpole. "I had these Muslim accountants come out here asking about old cottages. I got the impression they wanted to buy them from me, but we don't own any. All we have are the farm workers houses, and that's it."

"Was there anything else, talk of money?"

"No. What was odd though, was that as soon as I said we owned none, they said, 'Sorry, we must have made a mistake', and they left. No, wait a minute, on the way out, my secretary said they looked at our farm certificate hung on the wall, and they took a photo of it. When I heard about it, I went to challenge them, but they were driving away."

"May we see it?"

"Yes of course, let me show you."

They looked at the certificate, but saw Marty's signature on a commendation nearby. Dan held up his phone and said, "May I?"

He took a photograph, and they departed shortly afterwards. Dan said, "I'll get experts to check this signature, against the one the Land Registry hold on the bill of sale."

"This is a major scam, Dan. We should take them to court. I'm going to prepare files for the Crown Prosecution Service, and look into the money laundering aspect."

"Alison would be better at that. Don't action anything just yet. We need to see the whole picture, not scare them off or break up the team, before we understand how they work."

Nearing the end of their country gambol, and close to finishing the visits, they met with Nodger Rotes, his demeanour was as charming and as unsettling as his name.

He had an old school, broad local accent. "Now let me see there me pretty and handsome. I knows about them there old tithes. But as under manager, the bosses weren't interested. Mentioned it several times I did too, and to the regional manager—he's an accountant you know. I was driving him to the station, and mentioned it again.

"He told me this, 'What do we want with a load of old properties. The occupants can't afford to pay much in rent, and the houses are in such disrepair they'll cost a fortune in upkeep. Look at that one over there, needs a new gable end, and that one on the slant, the foundations need underpinning'."

When they drove out, Dan smacked his head and said, "I never saw that one coming. When the farms got bigger, they abandoned the tithe houses, due to the upkeep and building maintenance. Tithe was free of rent regardless. These old homes were a profit liability."

"You did good today, Danforth. One more, and then we better go back. I want to check with Percy and Dick, plus the two new lads, see how it went. I also need to try to define how long this is going to take."

"I told Matt, the director in Peterborough, about two-weeks, but less than a month should be closer to the mark."

They returned to the police station in good time, and the day's debriefing went well. Both teams had covered more ground than expected. Afterwards Felicity said, "I think you should take those few not at home every couple of days or so, early finish one day, late finish the next. It'll keep you fresher.

Percy said, "There's one village to the north where it is not worth going before six-thirty. Nobody will be there, and it's quite large."

Dick said, "Same here Ma'am, but with two villages. Even if everything goes well, it'll take a couple of visits each. Weekends would be better."

"Okay, Percy, Dick, pair up, and do these villages in one night. Work with me here. I have zero budget for overtime. So you can either start late, and finish late, or work say, Saturday, when hopefully the locals will be at home, and take Monday off instead. Comments?"

There was a hush. Dick broke the silence, "I could really use a Wednesday off, I need to go to a market, but it's in Norwich."

"Deal. Percy?"

"I'm fine Ma'am, but prefer working in the village."

"Noted. What about you two, Phil, Chad?"

Chad was the more forthcoming, "We're cool. This is great. Hardly anybody gets to do fieldwork at The Morgue, that's what we call work."

Dan asked, "Why?"

"It's an in joke. We usually deal with the estates of dead people. It gets quite complex sometimes. This is a lot of fun, thank you. We're fine with the hours, so if you want us to work every day, we're up for it."

Phil added, "Yeah. Like, it's not as if we got summut else to do. The nightlife sucks, and we're stuck here."

Felicity said, "Point noted. You'll get days off in lieu I understand."

"Yeah, but all out of hours work will be classed as standard time."

"We'll see about that. To confirm, Phil, Chad, you will each work seven days per week, and out of hours, as long as we do the overtime reckoning for you. Great, gets this finished much quicker."

Percy raised his hand and said, "For a similar deal, I'll work the same, get this done and done with."

"Same here," said Dick

Felicity looked at each of them in turn, and said, "Okay, you're on, the four of you. Tell me if or when any of you need a break. Otherwise I expect you to go for this, and break the back of it."

Everyone departed moments later, but Dan hung back. When the Inspector seated herself, Dan said, "I guess you'll be working late tonight. I could cook for you, at your home, Greek perhaps, good for settling the stomach."

"Dan, I thought to slob on the couch, but thank you. I tend not to get most symptoms of … menses, except in my guts. They are churning right now. Food is the last thing I need. It'll be over tomorrow. Well, the stomach, the curse, a day later. Mind you, this has been very light.

"Go, I am fine with this, I just need to deal with it myself. I tell you what though, if you were to make that dinner an Italian extravaganza, I will allow you to cook for me on Friday. Deal?"

"Deal." Dan turned and opened the office door, and half-stepping through, said, "Oh, and I will need help cleaning up my new house on Saturday, the Land Registry director signed off on it, and Percy's house also. You have new neighbours. Ciao."

Dan left sharply, and had only just closed the door, when something heavy thudded the wood from the inside. There was no sound of breakage, so he presumed a heavy tome of police, or female law.

Picking up the pace for leaving, he found Percy sidling beside him. "Back to the inn, Dan?"

"Yes, but I need to catch up with Alison, and I bet she's still working. It may need the both of us to get her out of there."

"I'll ride shotgun Dan. Ensure she comes with us."

Alison did join them for drinks and evening meal, but a lot later than any of them imagined. She had come up trumps, but refused to say a word until all results were in the next day.

Chapter 21 ~ Consolidation

Dan went to bed early and woke early. He enjoyed evenings at the inn, but seldom drank more than a couple of pints, although there had been rare exceptions. He completed his morning routine, adding twenty minutes weight training before his shower. He had brought a small set of dumbbells down, enough to keep his muscles in trim.

Walking into the office, he found Alison in the kitchen being served breakfast. Stella said, "Same for you, Dan?"

"Yes please, and a sausage or two if you have them."

"On its way. I made a pot of coffee for you. Tell me, how many people will be here today?"

Dan was filling the mug he always used. "From now on, just the two of us. The operation has moved on. There may be others later, but we're about it for the next few weeks."

"Good, that lets me plan ahead. Seems I won't have much to do in future. Oh, and thank you. Percy came by yesterday with a dashing young man, and I am now signed up as owner of my home. The deeds will be a few days, but it's such a relief."

"I'm pleased we could be of assistance. Percy and I each got a house as well. They were the director's and senior manager's houses of the defunct tannery. Both need one hell of a lot of work doing on them, but they are an investment."

"Let me have a key when you decide to begin cleaning. I don't mind setting too, and I have a little scooter I could use to get there and back."

"Thanks Stella, I'll call on you. Everything else okay?"

"I'll need to run to the shops today or tomorrow, as we are low on most things. These are the last two sausages."

Alison added, "I could do with going as well. Is there a supermarket here?"

"Yes, and a small plaza. You should find what you want. Let's say I run you both there just before lunchtime."

Soon after, Dan and Alison got down to work, he catching up with the aircraft log, and she working her way through a list of tasks. She was rudely interrupted when Dan shouted, "Shit!"

"What is it Dan?"

"I missed it. Maybe for weeks. "

"What?"

"These planes are occasionally switching transponder codes."

"Yes, we already know that."

"No, it's not like that, these are blips."

"What do you mean, they change them?"

"Yes, exactly that, and not because they've been told to by air traffic control. Come and check yourself."

Chapter 21

"This is weird. It's as if they switch the transponder on, then reset the code to the one they are supposed to be using."

"Precisely. And that in turn means these other codes that blip up for a split-second, also need checking."

"You'll need to follow this up with Trimingham."

"Yes, but first I need to note down all of these new codes, and that's a lot of research."

"So, the ramification is that they pretend to be different aircraft."

"Yes, and they get away with it because there is no visual confirmation. There are no eyes on, except at regular airports."

Later they went shopping, where Dan dropped the girls off on the main street and crossed the road to spend a few minutes with Felicity. She seemed chirpier and they chatted for a few minutes. He informed her, "I'll be away for most of next week. My director insists I take a course in bureaucratic bullshit, it's required for my promotion. I could do without it, but if I do not pass it, someone else will be posted in as my Commander. I want that job on this case. It will get much bigger quite soon."

"That's great news Dan, you must do well. How does promotion work at MI6?"

"Mostly it's about monitoring agents, and filling in paperwork. The key is access to information. For instance, I can access GCHQ directly, but my Commander has higher clearance. There are some requests that must be run through the Director. It will actually be most useful, as long as I can remain on the operational side of the fence. I hate office jobs."

"Seems to me you spend most of your days in an office."

"Yes, but that's different."

The intercom buzzed. "Sorry Dan, you'll need to go, I have an appointment. You still cooking Italian for me on Friday?"

"Of course. I better buy some ingredients when I take the girls to the supermarket; they'll be waiting for me by now,. Ciao."

Lunch, back at the office, was buffet style, but accompanied by vegetable soup. Stella explained, "The days grow colder as winter approaches. I thought to get a stew going, if you are Okay with beef?"

"Yes, do it."

"Mmm. Yummie with mashed spuds."

Afterwards they returned to work. One hour later, Alison jumped up with joy. "Got it! Here's the next concentric ring, covering the next twenty miles out. Have a look while I add the parish and town wards, police jurisdiction, and related electoral role."

Alison added several documents and maps, and they set to study demographics and property ownership. "You'll notice this includes Thetford and the reason I chose this width of circle."

"Excellent work, Alison. It's plain to see they are targeting medium sized towns, those with a viable town council."

"Yes, towns that contribute members to the county council."

"You mean all of these towns shown here in green, exclusively?"

"Yes. This is effectively a map of political power holdings. Regards Wymondham, the villages were required to prop up the Muslim vote. You will see that Thetford has larger villages and suburbs, a higher density of people, which they can affect more easily, especially with this housing of asylum seeker nonsense."

"I'm beginning to see a much bigger, and clearer picture now."

"I'll set the next ring to thirty miles farther out. It'll take days to generate, but it will give us the in-depth info we need to make decisions of priority. It includes Cambridge and Newmarket."

"Perfect. Add in Luton wide area, it's where the Muslim companies are based. Percy is still waiting for his informant to deliver, but he is police, so I expect the information soon. If we can unravel what they did in Thetford, and how they accomplished the takeover, it will show us their hand."

"Agreed, Dan. I'm waiting on Percy's information. I mean I could request the details officially, but that shows our interest, and word will get out to the wrong people."

"Yes it would, guaranteed. Alison, that reminds me, I think the community copper in Cambridge was okay, but not his bosses. The other in Thetford was Pakistani, and he was fluent with everything we asked of him, but I just got a bad feeling about the all of him."

"You mean, like he was a plant?"

"Yes, precisely, although I may be mistaken. His name was Constable Iqbal Mahmood. See what you can discover about him, his background, and associates. With your latest, I need to finish my daily reports, and probably speak to the Director. Anything you need?"

"No, I'm fine. I was thinking of asking Stella to join us for dinner. What do you think?"

"That's fine by me, makes the team more inclusive. She's been on her lonesome since her husband died of cancer. I'll be in my room. See you in the lounge around seven."

Dan completed his reports, and updated his personal log. He was about to send, but sat back to think. His thoughts wandered, but came to encircle a strange thing. "Why have I just bought a derelict house in the middle of nowhere?"

His alter-psyche provided an answer. "Felicity Wigglesworth."

Chapter 21

Dan jerked himself upright, and dismissed his thought. He had work to finish, and filed his report. Frustrated by his admission, he took ten minutes of hard exercise, and went for a shower. The Director had placed a video call when he returned. "Yes Ma'am."

"Dan, this is excellent work. You are honing in the boundaries I see. Can you tell me where the progression is headed?"

"Not officially. It is too early, but unofficially, they are moving into towns and large villages, ones that affect the electoral role and vote, to the west and south of our airfield. We have picked up little to the northwest, and nothing to the direct north or east."

"I'm worried about the bigger picture, these other airfields. They are coming in, in droves. We need to know where they are going, and you need to be promoted to follow the all of this."

"I will be there on Monday, Ma'am, and pass the course."

"Do you need some help, I have a folder I could send you."

"No Ma'am, I'll do it my way."

"Yes, you always do. That's what's so infuriating about you, and because you are usually correct. Tell me something?"

"It will take a few days, but we will do the next outwards ring, and that should give us their pattern. I need to assess what is happening locally around the other airfields, and would prefer feet on the ground. I could go myself, take myself away from the centre, and that's not good. We could try to work with MI5, but that usually turns into a disaster. Or we can wing it."

"What do you mean?"

"Once Alison switches to concentrate on these other cities, and we get the pattern, as compared to the one we have almost established, we'll know what to look for. I'll take Percy on a jaunt up there. He's excellent with police of his own level. The aim is to get names of individuals, companies, charities, councillors, and law firms.

"My next move is to track demographics as regards cultural balance and voting shift. We believe it will remain 'LibLabCon', but with most councillors being Muslim. That's the pattern we have established so far."

"Good. Include Luton, it's a hotbed of extremism, but seldom in the national news. Follow up with the paedophile rings, up north. This shows gang culture, tribal allegiance. You know, the ones that have hit the headlines recently: Rotherham and Bolton, Rochdale, Bradford, Sheffield, and so on. Work through them. This is where the Muslim community is in denial, and we need to know."

"Yes, and with Birmingham, Tower Hamlets, education..."

"Dan, what is it?"

"We already have Luton listed. Sorry Ma'am, I just had a thought. Education. If there's nothing else I'll get back to you."

126

"Hold. You need staff, so I'm sending Martin Edwards to you, he reminds me of yourself at a younger age. This will happen as soon as you pass the promotion course, so report to me as soon as it completes. In person."

"Ma'am, always a pleasure."

"Hmmm. If I didn't know you better, I could almost believe that. Now be off with you."

Dan pulled up the internal MI6 database and researched Martin Edwards. "Damn, he's just like I was. Thinks he knows it all."

Dan shut down in a hurry and called Alison. "We're downstairs, waiting for you."

He checked the clock: seven-twenty. He had no idea where the time had gone, but *tempus fugit*. He went downstairs and found Alison and Stella laughing at the bar, telling tales.

"Welcome Dan," said Brian. "A pint of the usual?"

"Thank you Brian. I see Stella has joined us tonight."

"Yes, and that's strange. She's usually playing cards in the snug."

"She's a regular here?"

"Of course. Comes in every night."

Dan took long drink and said, "In for a penny, in for a pound."

Brian put his elbows on the bar and looked at Dan. "I'll tell you a secret, Stella is not her given name." He flicked his eyes to a lager dispenser, 'Stella Artois'.

Dan locked eyes, and nodded with appreciation. He was shaking his head as he left the bar, wondering how little he knew of the village and its occupants. Stella proved to be fine company, but he left shortly after the meal, advising Alison to do the same.

Dan woke early the next day, his first task being to call to the Peterborough director and report. He knew that if he told the truth, court actions would swiftly follow. "I've visited all the farms you listed, and there are some inconsistencies we continue to look into. If we prove the Ali brothers' documents are false, what will you do?"

"Rescind the title of transfer, and take them to court."

"We will assist you in that respect, but we have not proven our case in law. So please leave this with us for say, one week."

"Thanks Dan, I knew we could rely upon you. How are my staff doing..."

Later, Dan spoke to Alison. "This is a bit of a curved ball, but can you check out the local schools, say Wymondham and area. See if there's been an influx of new, Pakistani children."

"Sure, but it's a bit odd. You playing baseball?"

Chapter 21

"No, cricket. Make the links: families equals children, equals schooling. I need to know where the immigrants' kids are being educated. There should be hundreds. If not, we need to go digging."

"Gotcha! Wow, that's neat. A tough cookie, but I'm on it."

Time seemed to fast-forward, as Dan discovered it was Friday afternoon, and he was running late, if only by minutes. He had left work early and got the fresh produce he needed to cook for Felicity: breads, olive oil, herbs and spices, meat, fresh fruit and vegetables, plus Chianti.

He neared the Police station just before five and pulled over to make a call. "Felicity, I'm outside and ready to begin. Cooking will take over two hours, so can you let me in?"

"I'll be here for another hour at least, so the timing should be good. I'll pop out front with the keys. Use the back door of my house."

Once in her home, Dan set to work at once, putting the wine in the fridge before making an assorted Italian cheese béchamel from a rue. He browned the diced beef, added fresh herbs and spices, onion and garlic, and plum tomatoes, then left it to simmer for a long time.

Meanwhile he made an avocado mousse, topping the sundae glasses with arranged prawns. He followed with both chocolate and lime zabaglione. Once prepared, he set them in the fridge and opened a bottle of wine. He was sitting down, waiting for the oven to preheat, when Felicity walked in. "I see you are hard at work."

"I have been working exceedingly hard. You must be tired. Like a glass of wine?"

"Yes please. Oh this smells good, what are you making?"

"Lasagne. I'm just about to layer it."

They chatted for a few minutes, before Felicity went upstairs for a soak in the bath. Dan put the completed lasagne in the oven, prepared garlic bread, and ratatouille. He set the table, added candles, and some dips. The stage was set.

The meal was a great success, Felicity loving the thought Dan had put into the meal and presentation. She intended to only eat one zabaglione, but ended up eating both, Dan finishing with cheese, biscuits, and port.

There was enough left over for a second meal, so Felicity put away as Dan washed and dried up. She made Gaelic coffee, and they relaxed to music in the living room.

They chatted a little at first, before holding hands and mellowing in the others company, they had no need of words. After a tiring week, they went up to bed early, and slept early.

Chapter 22 ~ New Beginnings

Their lovemaking the next morning was slow and tender, and they lay whispering secrets in the afterglow. The mood was shattered when Alison called. "Dan, Stella wants to know if you need her to come over."

"What? Maybe later, after lunch. I'll call you after we've had a good look at what needs doing. How's your day going?"

"I'm fine, and you are not required. Enjoy your weekend off."

Felicity reached up and gave Dan a peck on the lips. But before it could lead anywhere she skipped out of bed and said, "You make the coffee while I get ready."

"Fine, I'm still too stuffed for breakfast."

"Me, too. Let's take brunch later. That was a wonderful meal."

They wandered down to the house and went inside. By the front door lay a delivery note. "There's a secure package for me at the Post Office, sent from Peterborough. I won't be a moment."

Dan returned and opened the courier despatch. "It's from the Land Registry, confirmation I own this house. I have the Title Deeds. Now we can begin."

"Oh, let me see."

They read the pages together, and came to the last sheet, showing the property boundary. Dan stared at the map.

"What? The land extends all the way down to the river. This is amazing, a smallholding. Dan you're so clever."

"No," he chuckled. "Lucky maybe."

The following inspection was a lot more detailed than previous, and they noted things as they went through each room in turn. "The electrics are rubber insulated, it will need rewiring, but the water pipes are copper, so they're okay."

"You should add central heating as well. It'll add to the value."

After the tour, they settled in the kitchen, where Felicity wrote a list of initial things that needed doing. Dan said, "It's a shame the old, double Aga is coal fired. Gas, oil even, would be much more convenient."

"There's a main agent in Norwich, and I know they can be converted. We also have gas in this village, so it's feasible."

"Before I commit money to this project, I need a structural survey, and valuation, plus estimate after full restoration."

"Wise. No use throwing good money away on a lost cause. But I very much doubt this house is one. Let's check out the final rooms, before stepping into the jungle outside."

The attic was partly floor boarded. It had a window to the rear, and was full of junk. It was similar with the cellar, but the walls and floor were dry.

Chapter 22

The rear was overgrown, and overgrowing again. They battled their way through waist high grass with brambles rampant, avoiding hazards such as a pool. They skirted the old and crumbling concrete cover of what appeared to be a sceptic tank, and reached the workshop. Peering in through grimy windows, there was little to see.

Dan stood back to view the strange building with two wide, arched doorways. "I think this was a coach house. We'll need a locksmith out here, better add it to the list. What about you?"

"The rear of the house is southwest facing. I think we should add a large conservatory extending from the sunroom."

"I like that idea. Let's see if we can reach the river."

The way was difficult. Felicity called a halt. "We may as well be trying to hack through Sleeping Beauty's forest. I've seen what I need to. Let's head back and get mowers in."

As they retraced their steps, Dan said, "I bet Kevin and Neville would be up for a day or two's mowing, and Percy probably needs the same. Does anyone around here rent out professional size rotor scythes?"

"Yes, Joe's Mowers. He does all types and sizes. Most of these types of service industries lie along this road, between Lower and Upper Meddlington. There are a few small farms within the catchment area of the two linking roads as well. If your field is good for hay, we may be able to do a deal."

They got back and locked up. There was little purpose in staying. Felicity said, "I know of this canal-side pub that can't be reached by road. It'll take us an hour to walk there, fancy going?"

They enjoyed late lunch, and a few drinks, before heading home, but meandered along the way. They made love in a cornfield, and wallowed in the heat of the early autumn sun. "Why'd you get this house, Dan?"

"I asked myself that same question the other night. The only answer I got that made any sense was you."

"So this is our house?"

"Yes, even though it can never work out between us."

"You are wrong, Dan. It is working out between us. Let's give it some time, and you will realise I am correct. Come, it's time we made our way home. The sky clouds, and chill winds will follow."

"We need to move on."

There was something in the way Dan said those words, a look in his eyes. "Yes, I believe we do. That begins tomorrow when you meet my mother."

The rest of the weekend passed quickly. At one point, the Group Captain took Dan aside, and they talked about work. "Alison and Sarge are working on a new deception theory. These airplanes don't always use the same transponder signal--you discovered that, I believe."

"Yes I did Sir. It is a most worrying development, and it comes at the wrong time. I'm away on a promotion course next week."

"Damn. Can't you postpone it?"

"No Sir. If I do not pass this hurdle, somebody else will be put in charge of this operation."

"You better pass the course then. What's troubling you?"

"Well apart from your daughter, but in the nicest sense, Sir, could you check to see if any of the aircraft we are monitoring, have ever used an unknown transponder signal for a split second, one we do not know about. I have a list."

"There have been blips." Tom took the paper adding, " I'll check into this, it may take a few minutes, excuse me."

The Commander stepped into his office, and Dan wandered outside to call Alison. She said she was fine, but Dan decided, as was his plan, to drop by and see her in person.

He returned inside, and the Group Captain came to him promptly. "We have three such instances, two of which divert within a split-second. By that I mean, a transponder signal we are not logging."

"Yes, we need to log not only the known transponder numbers, but the ones that appear for a jot or tittle. I will need these logged as well, and that raises the question of physically identifying each aircraft.

"You think they may be swapping transponder numbers between a group of aircraft? The blip would be the real number for the craft."

"Possibly, or using a set of numbers for each one, and destination. Don't forget, the ones they squawk here on landing, belong to the light aircraft up near the hangar. I need the T's crossed and the I's dotted.

"Tom, this operation is still growing. I need a handle on Europe, and I do not trust their security services. Help us if you can."

"By that you mean tracking these unknown transponders, and satellite identification of each aircraft. If that were stated as an additional operational requirement, and given you are promoted, then you can request this directly of me. Do we understand one another?"

"Yes Tom, thank you. I'll be in touch shortly, late Friday."

They were interrupted by the approach of Misses Wigglesworth. "Now what are you two boys doing hiding in here. Talking about work no doubt, when far more important issues are at hand. I think we should have a marquee for the wedding reception, what do you say Tom?"

"It may be a bit early, Margaret."

"Nonsense, these things take ages to plan--then there's the bridal gown, and dresses for the bridesmaids..."

Dan turned to one side, and appeared to answer a call. "Sorry to spoil the party, but I've been called away, work, anti-terrorism. I hope you will excuse me."

Felicity read his ploy, and acceded. "Yes, we must go. Let me drive you to the airport."

Dan grinned. "Thank you, and thank you for a wonderful meal. I look forward to the next. But, Felicity and I are still dating and are both sorely wounded from past relationships, so please put the wedding plans on pause until much later. We are not ready, yet. Ma'am. Sir."

Once in the car, headed away, Felicity said, "I can't believe you said that to my mother. You've got some balls, Danforth Glover."

"What? Such talk is way too early for us, so I put her in her place. You saw your father grinning as I did so, didn't you?"

"Yes. I fear that will make an even bigger impression on her. She'll be ordering the wedding cake next."

As they pulled into Lower Meddlington, Felicity said, "Do you want to stay for dinner?"

"Yes I do, but I can't. I need to check on Alison. There is information for her, and then I need to pack a bag and get to London tonight, rather than an early rise tomorrow."

Felicity said, "I'll miss not having you around."

"Me too, we fit together somehow. I can't explain it."

"So my mother wasn't wrong then, just badly timed?"

"I did buy that house with you in mind, maybe a place to make our own, someday. I don't really know, and I must go."

"So, you are still running away from commitment, Dan. That's understandable, but if you want me, that has to stop." She leaned in to kiss him on the lips, and sensing his encircling arms, threw off her seatbelt and bolted out of the door. "Call me every night."

Uncharacteristically, Dan threw himself into the finer workings and understandings of bureaucracy, and came second on the course. He met his director on Friday. "Congratulations, I knew you could do it, and it seems you excelled. That's what we need here, but don't quote me.

"I herewith, promote you to Commander, responsibility, Operation Caliphate. Please sign for you new ID, and give me the old. Stay and set up your office, it shouldn't take long. I presume you won't be occupying it most of the time, and that's fine.

"Martin will come to you later next week, as something came up. He's a good kid. I say no more, except: Teach him."

"Ma'am."

"Tonight there will be a celebration in your honour, held at the club, full dress and bow tie. I know you scrub up okay, but what about your lady friend. Has she got anything suitable to wear?"

"One moment Ma'am" He tapped his phone. "Felicity, you still okay for tonight? ... Great, pack that dress we bought, you'll need to wear it tonight, with all the trimmings ... yes, I passed, but came in second to a career bureaucrat ... miss you too."

"How sweet Dan, but she better not become a threat or liability. Eight for eight-thirty I believe, dismissed."

Dan worked from his new office, calling Alison. Work was going well. Next he called the Land Registry at Peterborough and informed the director their net was growing larger. He also called Tom and officially requested satellite tracking and identification of all aircraft, sending a memo countersigned by the director.

Due to the demands of work, Felicity was running late, and one train behind schedule. Dan met her at the station and whisked her away to the club. She would need to change and prepare in the washroom.

The evening went extremely well. Dan and Felicity made a dashing couple that were well received by all. They spoke with the Director before leaving. "Well played you two, mission accomplished. You'll stay in the capital?"

"Yes, I'll show Felicity around, and we'll head back on Sunday evening. But first I need to check with my team."

"I have tickets for a box at the London Coliseum for tomorrow evening, would you like them?"

Dan nodded, but looked at Felicity. "Yes please Ma'am."

"Good, we all need a bit of culture in our lives. Enjoy the break, I have a feeling it will be your last for some time."

They returned to his apartment. "It's provided by the company. All this block is most secure."

He opened the door, and she walked in, looking around and even checking the fridge. "Is everything all right?"

"Perfect. This is a man-cave, and there hasn't been a woman in here for a long time."

"How can you tell?"

"I'm female. We know these things. A nightcap before bed?"

They enjoyed a brilliant time in London, and Felicity snuggled up to Dan on the long drive home. She was sleepy when they arrived, and they stayed the night at her house.

Monday arrived with a buzz of activity. Dan joined Felicity to catch up with Percy, Dick, Chad, and Phil.

Felicity asked, "How's it going?"

Percy spoke. "We've covered some ground all right, and worked late, but we virtually wrapped up all the outlying areas on Saturday. There are only Upper and Lower Meddlington to do. It's been a bit taxing. Not the work, but the hours. I could use another day off, but will soldier on. I presume the time in lieu can be taken later?"

"Before your retirement I presume. Yes, I'll make a note of it. Percy, you are with Dan again, but I need you today. There are a couple of minor rural issues I need you to follow up. Finish for today when they are attended to. Dick?"

"I worked yesterday to catch all those we missed earlier in the week. There weren't many, but we covered some miles. I could use a break. I'll work with the lads and local cops today, and then take my due time off."

"Hmmm. Yes, all right then. I remember you wanted a Wednesday off. Take two days beginning tomorrow. I need you to cover for Percy, so I need to stagger your time off in lieu.

"Chad, Phil, what about you?"

Phil spoke. "Ma'am, we would prefer to finish if that's okay, and then take the rest of the week off."

"Good. Here I can rotate the officers that accompany you, even have one working in advance to save time. I'll also check out the new housing estate, you have figures for that?"

"Yes Ma'am. They appear to be fully documented."

Dick said, "There are a few older houses near The Wreck that should be checked out, Ma'am."

"You'll attend to it?"

"Ma'am."

"Good. Then if there's nothing else, dismissed."

Dan accompanied Felicity back to her office. "So that's almost this station's area of jurisdiction covered. Thousands of people now own their own homes, and large families of Muslim asylum seekers do not."

"Where's this going, Dan?"

"The same applies to the bordering police areas. They all need doing, just as we have done here."

"Gosh! That's a big ask. I'll speak to the Chief later."

Chapter 23 ~ Widening the Net

"Good morning Alison, how are you?"

"I'm fine Dan, and congratulations on your promotion."

"Thanks. It won't make much difference, except for greater responsibility, and higher clearance. What's been happening?"

"I got the next thirty mile circle completed, and it follows the same pattern. I'm currently associating the usual information, parishes, electoral role, et cetera. It should only take an hour or so to complete. Except for the towns, the pattern we established appears to repeat."

"Good, I'm working on covering that angle. What of Anglo-Asian Holdings, Ali Brothers?"

"I struck lucky there as well. V. J. Ali is the business partner, the one associated with both the solicitors, and AAH. The other two brothers are actually nephews. They come from an educated background, and are residents of Luton."

"Okay. What about Mohammad and Hussein?"

"Similar to the Ali Brothers directors. Well-schooled, but renowned as heads of local gangs. Their culture is nepotistic, and all are related via greater family, and village roots in Pakistan. The fourth director is usually local to the area, and a gang lord."

"So, he has a lot of influence over the local Muslims, but his area of coercion is relatively small."

" I've put a file together for you, with full names, addresses, telephone numbers as applicable. I suggest you monitor only. I've included all I have regards interlinked and family backgrounds. They are all Pashtuns. Think northern tribes. Afghans also. It unravels like fork full of spaghetti bolognaise."

"Ah, turned but not twisted. Good work, anything on Luton?"

"Yes, but in process. I may need you to go down there, plus I think we may need Percy back with his gift of the gab regards the local police.

"His contact called me from Newmarket, after Percy referred him to me. I'm still chasing leads. He was a goldmine of information, but none of it official. Let's just say he told us what was actually going on, not the politically correct view.

"What was most interesting, was that each of the new influx, has a local leader, or should I say, ethnic overlord, who controls them, and what they do. Unofficially, the Pakistanis and Syrians are already fighting over turf, commodity, and drug supply, that sort of thing."

"It makes complete sense. I remember hearing that in Pakistan they are known as Landlords and their word is law. It would seem they may have inflicted us with their cultural governance."

"Hmm. Good summation, it sounds a lot like our feudal system."

"The other cops?"

Chapter 23

"Both the Muslim police officer in Thetford, and the other at Cambridge came up clean. The former only just scraped through his English exam, so that may be the reason for his enthusiastic evasion. I also have no record of him speaking Pashto, which the local Pakistanis do, so that would be a shot in the foot for English law enforcement, right nationality, wrong language. Try him again with an Urdu speaker in tow."

"So, we are up against tribal mentality, but on an international stage. And they are determined to inflict their culture on this country, Sharia Law. I do not like that. I think it is time we diversified, and also honed in on what we have got so far."

"Dan, that does not make any sense. Explain."

"We need to do what you are doing here, at four other airfields, and work outwards, but closing in on the greater goal.

"A second branch is to follow up on the paedophile gangs, because they are Muslim, Pakistani overlords of the local gang culture. You read the press no doubt. This information needs correlating, as I believe there are links.

"A third branch, is to look closely at hotbeds of Islamic extremism, which is why I asked you to look at Luton. There are others, Tower Hamlets, Dewsbury, Birmingham schools…"

"Wait a minute Dan, I may have something." Alison worked her computer wizardry. "Got it. You mentioned schools, and we know there are many new children. Well, there has been no correlated influx of new children in Wymondham, one or two new faces at best."

"What are you saying?"

"These children of the new inhabitants are not going to the local schools."

"Humph. I think they will be going to Muslim schools, and after Birmingham, they will not be registered schools."

"I'm already on it, needles in haystacks, right?"

"Yes, that sort of thing. We'd be better with satellite monitoring. I could try a drone for tomorrow morning. See what turns up. Alison, I have the distinct impression that this operation is going to become quite big, rather soon. To monitor everything we have talked about so far, how many staff do you need?"

"One each for the airfields, to work outwards as we have already done here. One more to follow different angles, like the paedophiles, and Luton. They all need to be internet intelligence experts."

"Can you make me a list for later this morning?"

"Yes, I'll do it now, but Ma'am will never sign off on it, you do understand."

"I think she might, at least some of it. Give me a chance here. With my new authority, it is worth taking this operation up a peg. I could do with email and phone logs, text-messaging traffic of Ali brothers, and AAH. I now have appropriate clearance for GCHQ, want to come with me, say tomorrow?"

"Absolutely. Count me in."

"You have friends there?"

"Let's just say I know one or two from college, SIS induction. I have a couple of wormholes. I am the best at what I do."

"Deal, it may be Wednesday, but I'll tell you as soon as I know. I need to speak with the Director first."

"Deal done. When you speak to her, ask if Veronica is free to assist us, she's exceptionally good."

"Veronica? I don't know of her."

"No, you wouldn't. She's semi-retired, teaching the next generation, the junior likes of me. She has nous for focus, and I do not have that skill. Well, as much as she does."

"Oh, Martin Edwards will be joining us later in the week. You know anything about him?"

"Yes Dan, a little. He seems a bright young man with a lot of potential. He's similar to you in many respects, but has a lot to learn. Good, he will be useful."

Dan set to work checking the airfield logs, and discovered a couple of new planes that landed. He noted the times, and spoke to Alison, before calling Tom, explaining what he had found.

"We'll follow up on this. We will also have some information coming through later regards the wrong transponder signals, the net is widening."

Dan finished the call and said, "Transponders, damn."

"What is it Dan?"

"With all this new information, I doubt anybody has been tracking the vehicle logs."

"I have actually. It's an automated process. I've glanced through it once or twice, but nobody has studied it."

"I better take a thorough look, can you send me the feed?"

"You already have it. Click the coach icon on your desktop."

Dan examined the log and associated map that showed the routes taken, and destinations. "So, in Newmarket they were taking residents from the old tenement blocks, and transferring them to Cappel Moor. They pick up incoming from the airfield, and deposit them back at the flats. Some are different blocks. There will be a time lag so the property can be readied. It fits what we thought.

"There are a growing number of destinations, as one area completes, at least one stage, they move on to the next. Clever. A comparatively small influx, spread in phases, so much in Thetford, change to Newmarket, Cambridge, and several other towns. I can confirm they are headed west and south. I'll put a map of East Anglia on the corkboard, and stick pins in it."

Alison smirked, "You practising voodoo now?"

"I may as well. It can't hurt. Well, us at least."

"I'll do similar, but using the computer."

"We will need to contact all of the community officers in all of these towns and cities. That's a lot of work. I'll ask Percy be released for another week, but after I have made contact, confirmed appointments, and have a proper plan in place."

Dan gathered his thoughts, examining the diverging directions the enquiry was taking. He made notes to support his report and forthcoming conversation with the Director. Rising to leave he said, "I need quiet time alone. I'll be at the inn if you need me."

Dan began his report. His main problem was finding arguments the director would respond favourably to, regards his application for more staff and resources. Having covered all aspects since he had been away, he waited for a phone call.

The call came in from RAF Trimingham. "Dan, we have just completed the first tracking of several aircraft. There are three that have used different transponder signals, briefly, before reverting to those known. The other aircraft using them are unknown to us, but match the information and timestamp you sent through earlier."

"Have you managed to trace the other destinations?"

"Yes we have. That was the delay. There are four on the continent: France, Luxembourg, Italy, and Poland. There is also one in UK, Luton."

"But that's in controlled airspace, how are they managing that?"

"The aircraft in question is a cargo plane, and satellite shows it entering a secure hangar, and it is locked in."

"Like a bonded warehouse, but including the plane. No doubt customs come along to check it later, but perhaps after specific cargo has been offloaded. Good."

"There's one more thing Dan. The Air Vice Marshall is making noises about coming down to inspect the operation on Thursday. Is your Director available to attend? It is most important. The meeting was mentioned when this operation began."

"I'll see what can be arranged. Thanks Tom. Ciao."

Dan sent through his report, requests, and waited to see if the Director would come online. He did not have to wait long.

"Dan, are you mad. We do not have the staff. And even if we did, we are far too focused on the atrocities these animals are continuing to create. My hands are tied, sorry."

"I had to ask Ma'am, you do understand. What about Veronica, is she free?"

"Alison has been speaking to you no doubt. Let me check … yes she is actually. I'll ask her to report to you, but it may take a couple of days. That's your lot."

"Thank you, Ma'am. I am planning to ask GCHQ for their support, tracking specific mobile numbers, text messages, and email accounts. I believe it may give us the breakthrough we are seeking and access to the higher thinking of the group."

"Yes, I see it here in your report. I'll support you with this, and add a helping hand since you are relatively new to them, as a Commander that is. Make your official request to Doug Simmons, he and I go back years, and I'll ask him to support you fully."

"Moving on to the properties, there are thousands of them, I never realised this was so big a task, Dan."

"Our information suggests this being repeated both south and west. There are numerous districts like the one we have almost covered, and all under different local police jurisdiction. Felicity is following this up with her line manager, and she is well thought of. She has been asked to put herself forward for promotion. Which I gather is the same job, if based in Norwich, but a larger catchment area, including her present one."

"Humph. This is starting to get too big. I had better see the Chief Constable. Then afterwards I will visit the Land Registry director in Peterborough. You also mention the Air Vice Marshal in your report, and I remember that commitment. I'll see him first, say nine-thirty a.m., Trimingham?"

"One moment Ma'am … Message passed on via the Group Captain. We should have confirmation shortly."

"Let me know as soon as possible, and before I arrange these other appointments. You will attend Trimingham, and take Alison with you. I'll keep her for the duration. I'll take the helicopter, and drop her back to your village. Ask your girlfriend to join us for lunch. I hear the pub food is very good."

Dan chuckled. "As you wish, Ma'am. Ah, I have Tom on the line, one moment please … "

Dan spoke on his second line, and then returned to the Director. "The Air Vice Marshal will arrive at nine a.m. Thursday."

"Good, early start, early finish. I suggest you arrive at GCHQ for midmorning on Wednesday, I always found that a particularly good time for a visit. Keep up the good work. Bye."

Checking the clock, Dan rang the Inspector. "Felicity, I need to speak to you at once, it's about work."

"I was about to leave for the canteen, care to join me?"

"We need to speak privately, fancy fish and chips in my car?"

Chapter 23

"Wow! You really know how to impress a girl, not! Okay, get here as soon as you can, I'll be waiting."

They spoke through mouthfuls of kebab, chips, and cola. "My Director is meeting the Air Vice Marshal at RAF Trimingham on Thursday morning. This may confirm your father's promotion.

"Later she will speak to your Chief Constable, and afterwards, has an appointment with the Land Registry in Peterborough. She'll return to the village for luncheon, and has requested your attendance."

"No doubt to discuss plans for the future."

"Yes, we have accomplished such a lot here, with the local people now owning the houses they live in, and she wants to take it everywhere north and east, to begin with."

"But that's a massive area. You're joking right?"

"I wish I were. She is going top down at this. I suggest you work bottom up. Hopefully you will meet near the middle."

"I will meet the Chief tomorrow evening for dinner in Norwich. I'm wondering if the Super and you should join us."

"Up to you, give me a call. I would bring Alison with me, she has facts and figures at her fingertips. Now what about tonight?"

"Sorry Dan, I need to catch up with me, this is a busy time."

"Understood. Same here actually, so that suits me too. Until Tuesday evening then."

Chapter 24 ~ Pieces of the Puzzle

Dan worked late from Monday afternoon, using a drone to check out the country villages around Wymondham. Of the few children on the streets, he noted all were girls. Several villages appeared to have a social centre, other large villages having one under construction.

He noticed the first signs of greater activity just before five p.m., when older girls left the community centres. From previous observations, he presumed they were being given afternoon classes in becoming good Muslim women.

Pausing only to get an idea of numbers, he flew high to cover as many villages as possible. Those with community centres showed similar results.

Some minutes later, four times the number of boys exited from the other end of the same buildings. Many crammed into minibuses, and were delivered to outlying villages. Others either played, or walked home. Dan wondered if he was witnessing segregated, academic schooling for boys only.

He parked a drone, well hidden, at each village with a community centre, holding one back for the morning. His thoughts fluid, he made a call. "How's life Percy?"

"Good, especially with a Sunday off, and an easy day today. I told the wife about the house, and as I suspected, she made a miraculous recovery. She and that sister of hers are all a mither about it. I have one small job to do, and then I'll be on my way over to you, to escape the wagging of female tongues. Hope you're around."

"Excellent. I'm still working, but finishing up, and I could use your company. Bye."

Percy arrived before Alison had finished her bath, and as Dan was preparing the log and report for the next morning. They greeted each other as would old friends, and sat to talk in the operations room. Dan accepted congratulations on his promotion. Talk turned to Felicity for a while, before Dan asked how the new house was coming along.

"We've been working on it, but a lot needs doing. I've arranged for the tiles to be replaced, and we are getting services up and running. I think the Aga will have to go."

"There's an agent in Norwich apparently, and they are converting ours to gas this week, you want the same?"

"Sounds good, I'll mention it to the misses. Ooh, and I got the lads round on Saturday and Sunday. They made great inroads into the grass. We can now walk on most of the garden, but we'll need a strimmer and hedge cutters before we're done. They cut paths so we can reach each tree in the orchard. Many are overripe with fruit, but good for home made wine. I also had them cut basic paths in your garden."

"Thanks Percy, I was going to suggest we share the cost. Felicity mentioned asking the small, local farmers to mow the field for hay, what do you think?"

"Well we've had a disagreement there, because the deeds say it belongs to us, and the misses is adamant it does not."

"That field is yours, Percy. The landholding goes all the way back to the river. We're thinking of setting a small quay for fishing and mooring a boat."

"I'm a keen angler, so a small shed down there for me. Yes, ideal."

Just then the door opened, and a figure clad in bathrobe and towel turban entered. "Hi Percy, I won't be a minute."

She was fifteen, but this allowed Percy and Dan to talk trivia and make joint plans concerning the houses: structural reports and valuations, electricians, locksmiths, and plumbers. Dan finished by saying, "The structural engineer will be here tomorrow morning, here's the key to our place. See if you can get some copies cut."

They dined at the inn, taking beers and talking first. Once the rush of catch-up exchange was complete. Dan said, "Percy, I will presume this country community policing holds valid for all areas covered by Norwich Constabulary?"

"Why yes. Normally there is only one, but ours is a large rural area, so there are two of us. Why do you ask?"

"Well, the first answer is, that we are thinking of taking what you and Dick accomplished, to all villages north and east."

"That is a lot of people, months of work, and would be much appreciated by all. The second reason?"

"There would have been the same in Wymondham."

"Of course. I met him a few times, as our routes crossed occasionally. Stan Parfitt is a year or two younger than me, but a good copper."

"I need to speak to him, any ideas?"

Percy's brows creased. "Unofficially? I could go and wait for him outside the back entrance of their nick."

"Do that, appreciated. Get a contact number, as we will need to know what he knows."

"When for?"

"Tomorrow would be good, but only if he is amenable. If he's offish, or doesn't want to know you, then don't make a big thing of it. You're good at getting police to talk, so work your magic."

Chat changed through other subjects. Percy became aware that he would be required often, and he was delighted. They did not linger that evening. Dan departed first, shortly followed to their respective beds by Percy and Alison.

They rose early on Tuesday, and Percy met Alison in the kitchen before seven a.m. She said, "We could breakfast at the inn."

Just then the backdoor opened and Stella strode in. "Oh no you will not, but you could have warned me about the early start--lucky I saw the kitchen light on. Breakfast for four it is then."

They looked at one another before clarification came. "I've not eaten either, so will cook my own breakfast, after I have cooked yours. Where's Dan, having a lie in?"

Alison replied, "I think he may already be upstairs monitoring, I'll check."

Moments later she returned. "Yes, Dan's up there, and will be busy for the next half hour at least. I'll take him up a coffee when it's ready."

Stella quipped, "I wish I were busy. Apart from cooking you breakfast, a spot of light cleaning, and preparing lunch, I have nothing to do all day."

Percy chewed over a mouthful of food before saying, "Why don't you get the old shop going again Stella? People are always moaning that they have to travel miles to get a bag of sugar, or salt for cooking. Some want a beer or Scotch in the evenings to watch TV, but there's nowhere local. Think about it. There's a Cash and Carry trade supplier on this side of Norwich, and I bet you'd make money."

Stella was silent for a long time, but muttered, "I'll think about it."

Alison went upstairs to begin her day, and moments later Dan rushed down, walking Percy to his car. "I just confirmed, only the boys are attending unregistered schools based in those few villages that have community centres. There are no girls. I know the girls attend, entering by a different entrance in the afternoons, and possibly, late mornings. I assume they are being taught how to become wives and mothers."

"It gets me that our feminist groups have zero interest in their plight, they only want to man-bash the likes of you or me. When confronted by the real misogynism happening in this country, today, they act blasé."

"I'll continue to monitor, but this appears to be the way of half a dozen villages. Other villages are building community centres, and, some are erecting temporary housing, living space that does not require planning permission. See what all you can get from Stan today."

"It's so sad our great country has come to this. I'll do my best."

Percy arrived near the rear of the Wymondham police station well before Stan would be on duty. He waited patiently and recognised the driver of one car, flashing his lights, and waving his arms. The car pulled alongside, and the driver spoke as windows wound down; "Percy? What are you doing here?"

"I need a word in private regards village life, Stan."

"We can't speak here. You've noticed as well, Muslims taking over."

"Yes, it's becoming a major concern, what can you tell me?"

"Ten minutes, and follow me. There's a lay-by east of here. Pull up close to the back of my car, and get something from the trailer. Otherwise we don't know one another."

Percy did as instructed, and bought a bacon sandwich with hot, sweet tea. Stan stood behind him in the queue, but they made no contact. Percy sat in his car, and Stan raised the boot of his car, in front, before hopping in the passenger side. "What's this all about Percy?"

"The Islamification of the English countryside."

Percy was about to say more, but Stan was immediately away on a rant. "I told 'em you know, saw it coming I did, but nobody listened to an old hand like me. I raised a report over one incident, harassment of a family, but they were driven out before it was dealt with, so it was filed as 'No Longer Valid'.

"The Muslims took over villages, and I'd visit, but they complained about me. It was my job. I was given a warning, but I did nothing wrong. However, they must have made a deal, because after that I was partially tolerated as a passing presence in those villages. Nowadays I drive around, fulfil my beat, but in some parts, there are few English villages left. I discovered a bit about how the Muslim villages operate, but it takes a lot of time. Trust is slow in coming, even from the women, who they treat as slaves. It disgusts me, Percy."

"Agreed. Did you ever try to take things higher?"

"Ooh yes, and I was almost sacked for me trouble. Old Dorothy Ford was one of two determined to stay in her home. She had been born there. She complained to me about Muslims threatening her to leave, and I raised concerns in my reports. I was told to leave it alone. How could I?

"Some days later I got a call from her grandchild, she must have given him my number. He said, 'Grandma's in hospital, they beat her up and broke her hip. She's sixty-six for Christ's sake. They hit her many times'.

"I asked how he knew, and he said, 'I left my phone on record, and got the video. They're animals. They threatened to gang raped her as well'.

"I saw her in hospital, and she was in a bad way, worse since she recovered, lost everything she did. I see her begging on the high street sometimes, and always leave a tenner and some food. It's not right."

"You reported this of course."

"Yes I did. I took days to put the full file together, including the mobile phone as registered evidence. That was aggravated assault. I made copies, and delivered them through the duty sergeant, Inspector, who is Muslim, and the Chief Inspector.

"I was told to drop the action, and I refused. I was threatened with immediate disciplinary action if I pursued the matter in any way. Percy, I'm over thirty-eight years in. In less than two I reach forty years, mandatory retirement, and receive a golden handshake, plus full pension for life. I cannot afford to give that up."

"I understand. You did the correct thing, your bosses did not. Did you make other copies?"

"Yes. I still want to bring this prosecution to court, and have Aunt Dotty, as everybody called her, given her home back."

"Does this evidence include the video?"

"Of course. You know of a means to do this?"

"I surely do. You got any more evidence against these Muslims?"

"Yes, half an attic full, but nobody wants to know."

"We do. You and I are on the same side."

"Thank God! I'm prepared to make a full statement, now. I want this heinous wrong righted."

"Full court spec, videotaped interview under caution?"

"You bet, but you better get the evidence out of my home first, and to somewhere safe. It details years of subversion and harassment by these Islamics--lunatics of Islamic persuasion."

Percy opened the car door, stood aside and phoned. "Dan, jackpot. Stan will tell us everything, and under caution. If Ma'am approves, we will meet the police van at Stan's home in twenty minutes. I need a full interview under caution for later this morning, exposing our own in Wymondham as being complicit. I'll call Ma'am now."

"No let me do it. I need a word with her. One minute." Dan called Felicity, and was suitably impressed by her instant response. He called Percy back. "Ma'am has the balls for this. Van on its way."

"Call her now, fill in the blanks and confirm destination. I'll meet you at the police station. Superb job, Percy. You better tell Stan to go home, and then you hurry back here, the Surveyor will arrive in thirty minutes."

Events of the day took on a life of their own, as Stan's testimony proved to be a damning indictment of Wymondham police area. An office and police officer were set aside to work through the evidence Stan had collected over years. There were boxes of documents, myriad files to search through. The full work would take weeks to unravel.

Felicity was all for cancelling her evening dinner date, but Dan took her to one side, and explained the longer-term importance of her gaining the right friends, influencing the right people.

"You must do this before Wymondham start trying to pull the same tricks. Get in, as deeply as you can, first. Don't forget, my Director will know, and she could mention something to the Chief Constable."

"Dan I..."

Chapter 24

"Should start getting ready. You want me along?"

"No, not this time Dan, but thanks for supporting me, being there. I need to work on him in my own way. The Super can't make it, so a small sharing tonight."

"About your own promotion, sooner would be better than later, except personally between us. You need to nominate your successor, they will like that, if you make the right choice."

"I've been thinking about that, but all the candidates are young, have degrees in 'policeology', and know zero about real life, never mind country life."

"Given the job now, with us, and where this is going, who would be your ideal choice to continue our work."

"I know of good coppers Dan, ones that would do a well here. But this place is out in the sticks. Most young Sergeants, Inspectors even looking for a change, want to get on, climb the promotion ladder, make a name for themselves. This is not where to do that.

"It would suit a time-served Inspector, one with a few years to go and seeking the quiet life until retirement. The only way it can be sold as an opportunity to a young Sergeant on promotion, is as a stepping stone, and I do not have that authority."

"Maybe, but you have friends that do. Is the post being advertised?"

"Yes, it has already been listed in the weekly force magazine. It's a small publication, mainly online, and only available to serving police officers. I'll have to wait and see who bites."

"Congratulations, that means you got your promotion."

"It is an unofficial indication only. I could be moved sideways."

"Then make a good impression tonight." Dan leant forward with his teeth bared, and pretended to take a chunk out of Felicity's arm.

Her facial slap, in process of delivery, became a hand behind his head, which was being drawn down for a kiss. Their lips met. There came a wrap at the door.

"Wait."

Chapter 25 ~ Digging Deeper

Dan was asleep, when the female voice that haunted his dreams, spoke softly to him. "Dan, I'm cold, warm me up."

Slightly surfacing, he recognised her perfume, knew her hands upon his skin, and turned over to welcome a cold thing into his embrace. She turned and they spooned together.

Early the next morning, Dan again monitored the children going to school, and checked footage from the day before. The girls attended for two hours both morning and afternoon, while the boys did a long day.

Dan called Stan, "Good morning, thanks for everything you told us, it is already in process. As I suggested yesterday, could you make a point of visiting the community centres of the Muslim villages and find out what you can? I think the boys are being schooled there, but the girls take vocational courses to become good Muslim women."

"I had already come to the same conclusion, but will try digging a bit deeper than I usually do."

"Thank you, but don't be too obvious. Let them get used to you dropping by more often, and ask seemingly harmless questions. If they get suspicious, drop the subject, or change it."

"Wilco. Dan, I was thinking the bosses would be pleased to be rid of me, and well, I wondered if I should apply to transfer to Lower Meddlington. That is, if there are any vacancies."

"That would be a good idea, then you can go through your own evidence. I'll have a word and get back to you. Bye for now."

Dan's next appointment was at GCHQ. After breakfast he informed Alison, "We leave in five-minutes for Norwich airport."

The flight took a couple of hours, but once through GCHQ security, they were escorted by a young man named Colin Talbot, and taken to the office of Doug Simmons.

"Ah, Dan Glover I presume, and this must be Alison, a pleasure to meet you in person. Please take a seat. Your Director outlined why you are here, but please tell me in your own words."

Doug proved to be shrewd and focused. Colin remained in the room, listening intently, but not participating. Dan explained the problem, referencing the flood of Islamic peoples into England and Europe. Alison assisted with further details, printouts, and a list of people they needed monitoring. The tracking of aircraft via RAF Trimingham was also detailed.

When they had presented their case, Doug said, "Hmmm. Some of these names seem familiar. Excuse me one moment while I check, it saves time in the long run."

He worked his keyboard, and stopped several times to view the results, although they could not see what had caught his interest. Doug looked up and said, "We have previously received requests for information concerning Anglo-Asian Holdings, and Ali Brothers, Solicitors. V. J. Ali is already being monitored for another agency."

Dan enquired, "MI5?"

Doug smiled, "No, Inland Revenue. We have also received a request for information from HM Land Registry."

"That will be Peterborough office, we have a joint operation underway. Is there anything you can tell us?"

"Only that Ali Brothers appear to be money manipulators, and may be money laundering. There was limited information to support tax avoidance, but not enough for Inland Revenue to pursue, so the request was put on indefinite hold.

"From what you have told me, these people and companies named on your list, are all working together. They are homing illegal immigrants, and giving them official sanction. The charity gives them a face of respectability, as do the councillors mentioned. This is a very serious matter."

"We have strong evidence to support money laundering, but it would hinder our investigation to act now."

"All right then, we'll take a look at all of them for a few days, monitor text messages, phone conversations, and email. If nothing turns up, the matter will be quickly dropped, unless you discover specifics. If we find anything, we will continue, and focus on those elements of note.

"I can offer you no more at this stage, than to pass you on to Colin here, who will monitor these events for you. We had better exchange direct contact information, and then you can talk to Colin at his desk."

"Thank you, it has been a pleasure, and I am sure you will find items of interest."

They left with Colin, who was chatty, if work orientated. "Any idea which language they may prefer?"

"Yes Colin, the ringleaders all have their family roots in the tribal hinterlands of northern Pakistan. They are Pashtuns and speak Pashto. There will likely be some Arabic as well. Anything else?"

Once business completed with Colin, Alison made contact with her friends in the building, while Dan found a discrete corner and updated his Director of recent events.

Dan had only intimated the proof they had of false documents of sale regards Ali Bros and the large farms. He did not want the Inland Revenue, and other agencies, poking their noses in, until he was ready.

They returned to the village before one o'clock, and found Percy in residence of the operations room. "I hope everything went well."

"Yes Percy, very well. What can you tell us?"

"I never got the chance yesterday, but I can confirm the Surveyor found nothing major wrong with either house, except for the wiring, which we knew about. I left a list of the findings on your kitchen table. Indication of sales value was less than half a million for you, and three hundred and fifty thousand for me. Out here, they won't sell quickly.

"Done up to full specifications, with double-glazing, central heating, the works, then half again. Add in a large conservatory, heated swimming pool, double garage, and say stables in the field, then double the current value."

"Percy, that is some result. We'll have to wait for the official surveyor's documents to come through, but at least we can both get on with more serious renovations. An electrician first I think."

"I know of a good one, an old lad whose son has taken over the business, but he still dabbles. I'll have a word. You are looking for quality workmanship, rather than strict adherence to the latest rules?"

"Absolutely. Let's leave this for later. We now have a small operation running with GCHQ, and will have to wait and see if they turn up anything. Stan is going to check out the Muslim community centres, and asked about transferring to you at Lower Meddlington. I'll ask Ma'am later."

"He'd be an asset, and could take over from me in a few months time. He also understands his evidence, and we don't. What's next?"

"I'm going to catch up with messages and information from this morning. Five minutes, and then we'll have lunch."

During the meal, Stella said, "Percy, I like the idea of reopening the shop, and I know it would make money. I'd love to give it a try, as I did help the previous people out, but I can't afford to start the business up again. Sorry."

Dan said, "Fill me in, I'm not aware of this."

He heard the proposal and deliberated, asking the occasional question. He knew Stella was capable of running the business side of it, so said, "Okay. I'll put up one thousand to get you started, and maybe another if things sell. Have a word with the butchers in town, and the bakery, see if they'll offer discount for bulk."

Percy added, "If I am based here, I could bring out fresh bread in the morning."

Dan spoke seriously. "Stella, I need you to canvass everyone in this village over the next few days, tell them what you are planning, and ask everyone what they would buy. Make it clear that things will be more expensive than the supermarket, but that it will save them more money in time and fuel. That is one of your key selling points.

"I have a feeling a licence to sell alcohol should not be a problem, but do not go putting Brain's nose out of joint. Speak to him first, he may well offer you a bulk deal, or regular sales at least. Put items of immediacy at the top of your list, you mentioned sugar and salt. Add milk, if UHT, light bulbs..."

"Dan, thank you!" Stella was alive with the prospect, finished eating quickly, and went into the shop to begin planning. The counter and most fittings were still in place and serviceable.

Once back upstairs, Dan showed Percy how to monitor the tracking devices and new drones, adding them it to his list of jobs. Dan started to follow up leads, and Alison was busy. She gave a squeal of delight. "Got them! Damn but that took some unearthing.

"The charity, Asians in Need, is run by Sylvia Cartwright, a well respected do-gooder. She is married in Islam, but not in British law. Her husband, distantly related to Muhammad through marriage, is a turncoat British citizen called Ali ben Mohammad.

"I also discovered his birth name was Norman Harper, radicalised in Luton, where he met Sylvia at college. Their only son's birth name is Walter Harper-Cartwright. He goes by the name of Haraka, nowadays."

"Good work Alison, send it to me and I'll … Begin again. You send it through to Colin as an update, additional request. Colin will need to find the private numbers of mobile phones and email addresses, before we can unlock this. Those publicised will likely be clean."

"Better I log additional mobile phones associated with the same account, it should be fairly easy to do. Then Colin will have something to work on."

Not long after they got back to work, Dan's phone rang. "Hello Felicity. What's up?"

"Dan, can you meet me in Norwich tonight, say six-thirty at the main police station. Business and pleasure, plus a free meal at a top restaurant."

"My pleasure. I presume we will not be alone."

"Correct. The new Chief Super has taken great interest in your investigation, and wants to meet all of us, including Alison. She needs to come with her laptop full of facts and figures, updated to the moment."

"Alison, we are in Norwich tonight. Get everything up to date on your laptop.

"Felicity, we may as well spend the night there, as we are at RAF Trimingham for nine a.m."

"Good, I'll make reservation for you, and I may well join you, so your room will be under my name. Alison's surname?"

"Porter. I'll need Percy here to act as cover, as we need to monitor things, and he is up to speed."

"No problem."

"I'll also need Percy for next week at least. He has a way with his peer police officers. It may be longer."

"I do need him back on the beat, Dan."

"I may just have the answer to that as well. I spoke to Stan Parfitt earlier, and he wants to transfer to your station. I told him to wait, but he'd be a shoe-in for Percy."

"He could also sort out his mess of archives."

"I could do with Percy on long term secondment."

"Under consideration.

"Dan, wear your tuxedo tonight, I think it will make the right impression. Must go, Ciao. Mwah!"

After the call finished, Dan took a moment to compartmentalise everything. "Percy, you will be here for this week and next, at least. This is what we need you to do…"

Afterwards he checked with Alison. "You need anything?"

"No, just leave me alone. I've a lot to do."

"Okay. We leave just after five, and you better wear something formal, a business suit perhaps, we'll dine posh later."

They arrived in Norwich ahead of time, and were shown to an internal waiting room. Time dragged, and the nearby vending machine produced foul liquids, none of which resembled either tea or coffee. Felicity called. "Dan, sorry, we're running late, but it's well worth it. I'll be with you in five, anything you need?"

"Two real coffees would be great, otherwise I only need you."

"Cut it out, well maybe later. In five."

Felicity joined them ten minutes later, with three coffees. "The Super will take the Office of Chief Superintendent on Monday. It seems another complaint came in against the one in situ, and the powers that be want him out of the way, quickly.

"The domino effect is that on Monday my Chief becomes acting Superintendent, and I become acting Chief Inspector. We all officially move up next month."

"Congratulations!"

"Well done!"

Felicity acceded to their felicitations of the moment, but Dan asked, "What about your replacement? Any news."

"That is strange. We had an application from a Sergeant Karen Wheeler, of Kings Lynn. She has a couple of years more service then I, but had a problem with the promotion exams, it seems. The strange part is, her application came via the Chief Constable's Office, and was approved by him. That means it will be hard for us to choose a different candidate. Fortunately there are none except for one Inspector in his early fifties, who would not be a good fit here."

"That is peculiar. See what you can dig up. And you, Alison."

Talk returned to the matter in hand, and Felicity said, "We will meet with the hierarchy in twenty minutes. Alison, the room has a computer-controlled screen. Can you show video, documents, and data in support of the presentation?"

"It'll be a bit ad hoc, but shouldn't be too bad."

"Do it. I'll get someone to set you up. Dan?"

"I'll do this chronologically, from the beginning to where we are today. I'll be brief, unless they ask for clarification. I'll need ten minutes for notes, and copy them to Alison before we go in. What's the new Chief Super's main interest?"

"Norfolk and East Anglia."

"So, Norwich leading the fight against the Islamification of the UK should be a good theme."

The meeting followed quickly, Dan projecting a larger than life persona, enhanced by his tuxedo and bow tie. He involved the attendees in the presentation, asking their opinions, and gentling them through the Islamic thinking behind what was occurring.

Engendering a crowd participation atmosphere, Dan involved them with the local, regional, and greater whole. He dropped seeds of information he knew would grow, and hopefully flourish.

He was applauded when he finished, something that almost unbalanced his equilibrium. Felicity whispered, "That was brilliant, Dan."

The new Chief Super called them to attend dinner, where they enjoyed a sumptuous feast in a nearby restaurant. Returning to HQ and the police club, the Chief later spoke privately to his inner group of Felicity, her immediate boss, and Dan.

He approved Stan's relocation to Lower Meddlington, but as a personnel requisition. He would move harshly against the Wymondham police station, and quickly.

Stonehouse sent an urgent request to the Chief Constable, asking permission to ensure the home ownership of the long-term, established villagers currently living in tithe housing, across all of Norfolk.

He was dismayed at what was occurring, and demanded that 'Aunt Dotty' be found a secure place to live, and means to support herself. Felicity said, "We will deal with it, although I will need Constable Parfitt to assist us."

After due consideration, the new Chief Superintendent, looked Dan squarely in the eye. "Here's what I propose to do. We're going to castle the keep. We lock down Norwich so our base of operations is not undermined from within. Registering the outlying villagers as owners of their property is our moat. We will work outwards.

"It will take some doing, but we will also put a block on new Muslim housing developments, now we understand how they operate. Thank you Dan, Alison. There are two in process now, and I will find means to stall them. Health and Safety is always a good ruse.

"We will also shine the spotlight on 'Asian', I hate that PC word, community centres, and send officers into what are becoming no-go zones. If residents cause us trouble, they will be arrested.

"Dan, I need your larger eyes on here. Can you support us with, say, drones? Do what you have already done with the Wymondham villages, but this time in the city. I need each community centre logged each day, and let me know if you spot signs of education. Follow the children. Find out where they go to school, because I have just been informed there are few new applications to state schools. Where are they being educated?"

"Yes, we can do this. I may need a local base of operations."

"We have a few vacant offices, some high up. You will have what you need. When can you begin?"

"Tomorrow afternoon."

"Let's say early next week, I have to be officially appointed in my new role first."

"Okay, late Tuesday afternoon, for Wednesday morning."

"Agreed."

Dan sent a request for more drones to his Director, asking she bring them with her in the morning. He would position them, record from Thursday afternoon, and be ahead of the game.

Dan escaped the expected drunkenness with Alison. He tried to take Felicity with them, but she said, "I'm in this for the long haul, and will probably be trashed by the time I get back. I don't want to do this, but this is the way they are. I've got to show my man balls if I want to kick through this glass ceiling."

He gave her a more than collegial kiss. "Come back to the hotel, and I'll look after you. Remember, lunch in the village tomorrow. Good luck."

Back at the hotel, Dan worked on several reports, and when done, got a beer from the mini-bar. Looking at the price, he put it back. He didn't need it and made coffee instead.

He sat back and contemplated the wider issues, and caught glimpses of a larger whole. He was deep in thought when Felicity stumbled into the room. "Dan…"

He hurried to catch her, and gave her water. She threw up minutes later, but looked a lot more herself when she came out of the bathroom. "I hope I never have to do that again. It was worth it though. Now I'm an insider."

Dan wiped her face with a soft flannel, gave her a little more water, and carried her to bed. She became increasingly aware of his physical presence, and said something that rocked Dan sober. "Have you ever thought about having children?"

"Yes, occasionally. Why do you ask?"

Chapter 25

"Well, confession time, but then you never bothered to ask. I am not using contraception, and we were lucky last month. You want to roll the dice, because it's the wrong time of the month. And I need you to make mad, passionate love to me, fully knowing the consequen…"

Her words were stifled by Dan's ardent lips, and it was a while until they fell into mutually contented sleep.

Chapter 26 ~ Leaders of Men

The next morning, before Felicity returned to Lower Meddlington she said, "Dan. We did it last night, the beginning of my most fertile time. You better be prepared to man-up, deal with the consequences."

Worried, but altruistically intrigued, Dan was saved from reply when Alison joined them to share breakfast. Shortly Felicity returned to lower Meddlington, while he and Alison headed east. They arrived at RAF Trimingham, and were shown through to the Station Commander.

They caught up personally with events of mutual interest, before the phone rang. "Yes, ideal."

Tom spoke, "Two helicopters requesting landing permission, about one minute apart. I'll need a moment to prepare, if you will excuse me."

Minutes later, they walked towards the landing pads, the Air Vice Marshall touching down first. The Air Commodore accompanied him, and greetings ensued. The Director, piloting her own chopper, landed moments afterwards, and after meeting Veronica, Dan officially introduced the Director to the military.

The Station Commander said, "Would you like refreshments after you long journey Ma'am, Sirs?"

The Director replied quickly. "No, I'd like to see the operation with my own eyes, meet the staff, and be appraised of the latest intelligence."

The Air Vice Marshall echoed, "Quite so. Let's get down to business. Lead on, Station Commander."

In the radar room, the Sergeant explained to the group, but spoke mainly to the Director at first. "...Then Dan observed some of the aircraft were unknown to us, and we in turn started looking for other squawks, and we found three new ones. They blip up for a split second, as if they had been previously set. I think they show when the plane is fired up."

"This led us to widen the operation to track them also, both the aeroplanes and squawks, include new destinations as discovered, and cross reference; aircraft are still being added to our observation schedule. We've also taken satellite close-ups of all planes in flight. We physically identify them, and by doing so, discovered two new ones yesterday.

"We are doing the same across all Europe, and tracking to wherever in the world these aircraft go. We've added Sudan, Chad, and Nigeria to the list, and suspect Morocco also. That flight is in the air as we speak. Here, let me show you movements for yesterday on this console."

They watched the presentation, and the Air Vice Marshall became thoughtful, asking a couple of pointed questions. Finishing his thoughts he said, "Director, I need a word with you in private, we'll use your office Tom."

The others continued to discuss the operation, until the Director rejoined them. She was looking quite pleased. "Station Commander, Air

Chapter 26

Commodore, the Air Vice Marshall is ready for you now. The rest of you, I think it is time for a cup of tea."

The Director was chatty, but apart from fully introducing Veronica, would say little on other matters. A few minutes later Tom ushered the Air Vice Marshal into the mess. "We can offer proper service, Sir."

"Nonsense. Sometimes it's good to mix with the troops, as it were, isn't that correct, Director."

"I most certainly agree. Today I will take luncheon with the team here, and discover what they are doing behind my back. It's good to pop in now and again, keeps them on their toes."

Educated banter ensued for a few minutes, before the senior man finished his drink, and rose to depart. The others left with him. Military departed first, the director closely following after giving Dan the drones he'd requested. She headed to meet the Chief Constable with Alison and Veronica in tow. Dan was left alone with the Group Captain.

"How did it go Tom?"

"Very well, I have approval to increase the operation on a needs be basis, and have been confirmed in my new position, so no more acting."

"That's brilliant news. You earned it."

"I'd never have stood a chance without your support, and don't go protesting. That is the truth of the matter."

"I'll leave you to tell Felicity, she will be delighted. She also has news of her own for you, but it is for you two, and Margaret to share, not me."

"Thank you. How's it going?"

"We are enduring as a couple, the job allowing, growing closer, and seem to be falling in love. She's one hell of a girl Tom, you must be very proud of her."

Dan drove back towards the village, but toured Norwich, leaving small, solar powered drones in pertinent locations. Percy was practicing drone manipulation when he got back, and they got to work.

It was after one when they heard a helicopter approaching, and went outside to welcome their colleagues. Felicity had already joined them, and several villagers also gathered to witness the rare event, mouths gabbling ten to the dozen.

Greetings were brief. The Director said, "I'll fill you in a bit later, but things went well. Now, let's have something to eat, I'm starved."

They took aperitifs in the restaurant, while Veronica was shown up to her room. Martin Edwards rushed in apologising for being late. He was also booked in, and shown immediately to his room.

All enjoyed the meal, the Director remarking, "That was most agreeable. I now understand why you like it out here. Put the cost on your expenses, Dan. Now, I need to see your base of operations, and then we can debrief."

The inspection was brief, and Stella was tasked to make pots of tea and coffee. Once settled in the operations room, the Director took out her notes, but spoke without looking at them.

"On my way here we detoured, and flew over many of the villages you mentioned. I now see your problem, this is a nightmare. Were this to repeat regards all old tithe housing in the country, I dread to contemplate what might ensue.

"I had a most agreeable conversation with the Air Vice Marshal, who is broadly supportive of our efforts. He is interested in the significant military intelligence that you have provided, proof of militia, weapons, ammunition, and medium range missiles.

"I, and this team, should be concerned with where these missiles could be used in UK, and what type of warhead might be employed. I am thinking particularly of dirty bombs and chemical weapons. Keep your eyes peeled for any supporting information. Let's move on.

"The Chief Constable was not a likeable man, but a dedicated servant of his force. He seemed irked that to be Chief Superintendent Stonehouse had sent a report, and request for support, on matters he knew little about. I filled in the blanks.

"Our conversation remained difficult until Alison showed him aeroplanes landing, hundreds of Muslims getting off, and later being transported. She followed this with tracking of the same aircraft, showing it had arrived directly from Raqqa in Syria. She evidenced footage of Wymondham villages, and I mentioned the locals who lived there being bullied out of their homes.

"He called Stonehouse to attend. That was perhaps a bad move on his part, as he was faced with three against one. We explained about our registering everyone in Lower Meddlington as owner of their home, and how we wished to expand the project, obviously to prevent the Islamification of more villages.

"He was wavering, when Alison produced the false bills of sale copied from the Land Registry, and she supported with the appropriate clip of a farm manager denying all knowledge.

"Stonehouse maintained pressure with the tale of Aunt Dotty, and he was tasked to complete all household registrations, as his first operation on taking up his new position.

"Alison will fill you in on other details, but the only thing not sanctioned, was to move against Wymondham police station. The Chief Constable wanted to know how badly the force was compromised before arresting them."

Attention switched focus to Peterborough. Dan asked, "How did it go with Matthew Green?"

"Extremely well, although he was taken aback at the scale of the next phase of the operation. Regardless, we have his full support, but that's because there is a bonus and recognition, for the regional office making the most new registrations.

Felicity spoke next. "This is going to make a lot of people exceptionally happy, I'm delighted. Have they offered any more staff?"

"Yes my dear, four more trainees, with the possibility of more to follow, but I doubt it. So that makes six able bodies. How will you run this, Felicity?"

"As before. I worry six young men away from home, and all together, may get up to mischief at night. So, a pair to each area, and it will probably fall to me, as acting Chief Inspector, to organise. That is a plus."

"Good, I have a few other things to mention before we wrap this up, but it won't take long. Regardless of what happens locally, the focus must remain of the bigger, nationwide threat. Dan, what is your plan?"

Dan ran them through his list of priorities, and how he would blood Martin in the field. Their immediate task was Luton, followed by eyes and transponders on vehicles attending the other airfields.

The Director said, "That's a lot of flying, Dan, and no doubt you will be visiting Europe in the near future. Time to save on hire costs. I'll requisition a small jet for use on this project, and have Tim fly it up to Norwich. You also have a pilot's licence, Veronica. That will give you all versatility."

"Yes Ma'am, but I haven't flown in years."

Dan said, "Veronica, we'll take a couple of practice flights with you in the chair. It will soon come back to you, and would prove a great relief to me."

The Director said, "Okay, we are finished here unless anyone has a question? … Good. I am ahead of schedule, so Dan, Felicity, I'd like to take a peek at this house you have claimed."

"Thank you Ma'am."

Felicity replied, "I better leave now. You'll be taking the chopper I presume."

As they landed Dan said, "Percy's house is two doors over. We own everything from the river to the road. Set down at the top of the field, just before the orchard."

"You could have a light jet runway here, but I guess the neighbours would complain. Horses for children are good, or a smallholding. But then, you will both be too busy."

Felicity met them in the orchard, and took over as tour guide. The Director poked her head in rooms, but it was clear she was not there to view the property, neither did she bother with every room. Dan had rigged up an electrical extension cable from the main supply, and they made drinks in the kitchen.

"This is impressive Dan, Felicity, and tells me of your thinking. It could become an ideal place to get away from it all. We all need our personal space you know, and someone at home. By that I mean, in both your instances, a partner that understands the duty you perform, and while that duty may never become more than your relationship and commitment to each other, it sometimes takes precedence of the moment. Finding the right person is difficult. I did not.

"It may be early days for me to say such things, but you look and behave like a couple, so you better get used to the idea."

"Thank you Ma'am, we will. But I'm sure you did not take this detour if there wasn't something else on your mind."

"Correct. The Chief Constable was most supportive of the asylum seekers cause, and hoping to offer more immigrant facilities. He mentioned moving against the illegal airports, but qualified his remarks to the contrary."

Dan said, "So, he stated what he must, and then gave reasons why this immigration should be allowed to continue unhindered.

"He called it humanitarian relief. Sounds a bit PC to me."

"My problem is that these flights are scheduled by ISIL, not the government, or a relief organisation."

"Exactly. He appeared oblivious, even after I stated the facts quite clearly. I did not pursue the point, but it disturbed me greatly. He is in with the political movers and shakers, the senior councillors, social workers, and MP's--nice for them to have the backing of the Chief Constable."

"No doubt, on retirement and a fat pension, he will be offered lucrative consultative positions, become chair of an inquiry. He's marketing his future prospects, showing he will come in on the correct political side."

Felicity added, "Yes, that is common for Chief Constables when they retire."

"Yes Felicity. One of the reasons I wanted this little chat, was to warn you of his motivations. I would advise you, and your immediate bosses, to be extremely careful when moving against the asylum projects. I strongly suggest you gather information, but do not employ more than minor delaying tactics regards any pies the Chief Constable has his fingers in."

"Understood Ma'am, I'll pass it upwards."

"Good. Now, regards GCHQ, has Colin been in touch, Dan?"

"No Ma'am, not a peep."

"He'll be working through the information provided at administrative level. I received a call late last night from Doug Simmons.

Chapter 26

He told me that the Commander of GCHQ Bude, wants to see you ASAP.

"Your requests have sparked a few red flags it appears. I suggest you go tomorrow late morning, as Tim will by then have a light jet for you. Take Alison with you… No, have Alison available to supply you with information. The two newcomers will need settling in.

"We are done, except for one last piece of advice, from a grandmother. Get a bedroom, bathroom, and the kitchen working. You will need a place to shut yourselves off, and this is ideal. Send me your report concerning your visit to Bude later, Dan. Felicity, always a pleasure."

After the Director departed, Felicity said, "What was that really all about, Dan?"

"She's a wily old stick. She was checking us out as a couple. Were you not who you are, you would be my Achilles heel. Remember, I'm adopted, raised by MI6. She's the nearest thing I have to a mother."

"Understood. I better take you back to work, and then get on with my own."

Later, Dan took time aside to research Bude, also wondering what the forthcoming meeting was all about.

GCHQ Bude was one of the most secretive arms of British central intelligence, and mainly dealt with satellite communications, and tracking. They were the only agency to be able to cover satellites in both the Atlantic and Indian Oceans. They had been used for physically identifying and tracking Taliban leaders, who were later taken out by American drones.

The terrorist link was clear to see, and he surmised the connection had to be RAF Trimingham.

Chapter 27 ~ Eyes On

Dan was awake and busy early on Friday morning. He did not present a report, having seen the Director the afternoon previous. Tim called as he was preparing to go to Norwich airport. "Hello Dan. I got an old jet ready to bring up to you, but I will need taking straight back. How does Norwich for nine a.m. sound?"

"I'll be there waiting, so arrive as early as you can. My day is going to be a long one."

"I'll be leaving shortly in that case. Anything you need up there?"

Dan requested a few more supplies, packed a small case, and departed to breakfast with the team. They were talking about work for the coming day, and he needed to make arrangements to meet in Bude.

"Alison, I need you to arrange our new jet has an apron and service facilities at Norwich airport. Refuelling after every flight, here are the details. I also need to know where to land at, or near GCHQ Bude."

Veronica insisted she take over as his PA. "Dan, I'm damn good at this, and Alison is far too busy to be distracted."

"Alison?"

"Yes please, I have too much on, and it only gets worse."

Dan was early at Norwich airport, but Tim was landing. They quickly offloaded and were soon airborne. Veronica came over comm. and said, "Dan, I've arranged an FBO, that's Fixed-Base Operator, for you at Norwich airport. They're called Lex Falconer Air Support, run by Lex himself, and provides full support services."

"Excellent, Veronica. What about Bude?"

"Your appointment is for eleven o'clock. You'll need to land at a private airfield a few miles distant. Bude will collect you when you arrive. Details..."

After dropping Tim off, Dan departed for Bude. It was a long flight, and the local airstrip granted landing clearance as he approached. He called Bude requesting collection. He landed, and departed immediately his transportation arrived.

He was introduced to the Station Commander a short while later. "Hello Dan, please call me Bernie. We only use first names here, and they may not be our real names. It's a form of security. Thanks for coming so quickly. Refreshments are on their way, and in the meantime, I thought we should have a little chat."

"My pleasure, Commander. First, I need to know which flag, or flags, alerted my operation to you."

"Dan, please, let's ease ourselves in. We both need to understand each other first, I believe. We will get to what brought you here shortly. Let me introduce some of what we do, as regards your interest..."

Chapter 27

Bernie focused mainly on identifying terrorists, the majority of whom were based in the Middle East, Afghanistan, and Pakistan. "We work closely with other international agencies, of course. The latest threat we are determining is that posed by ISIL, and this is where you come in. Tell me a little about your operation."

"We were brought in to monitor an airfield, and established two thousand illegal arrivals from Raqqa every day. Most were civilians, but several hundred were militia. They also transport weapons, ammunition, and missiles back and forth.

"We have identified four other private airfields, and Luton. I hope to check that out this afternoon, and the other airfields next week. We regard this as being the prelude to the Islamification of UK and Western Europe."

"Thank you Dan. That is all that concerns us, for now at least. I should add we are aware of RAF Trimingham's involvement, and they are using some of our resources. Switching squawks is a clever idea, as is their use of uncontrolled airspace. Never underestimate these people, Dan. How do you read what they are doing, locally I mean?"

"They are creating a Muslim majority that will vote for whom they are told to vote for. We have already witnessed the effects, town councils, county councils, all gaining more Muslim representatives, although from differing political parties. The more worrying aspect is Muslims are also dominating the local parties, and they choose who stands for MP.

"My problem is that this will take years to accomplish. I would presume that once a position of dominance is reached, they would all cross the floor and unite behind a new Muslim party. That is supposition. We have nothing on that officially."

"You think this is a wild goose chase."

"No Bernie, more of a Plan B on the back-burner. I would also state, I consider the latest rash of terrorist attacks on home soil, to be splinter groups, or Plan C. I need to determine what Plan A is."

"You are incisive Commander, and I broadly agree with you. I believe that if we co-operate, we may be able to solve that conundrum. What do you make of this?"

Bernie passed Dan a large photograph of an Arabian face. "We had it digitally enhanced, recognise him?"

"He's older, but yes. ISIL. A unit from Aleppo."

"No longer. We have been taking out their leaders, and this one is now a Commander in Raqqa. This photograph was a still from your own airfield, three nights ago. We need to know everything about this man: where he goes, who he meets, and when he leaves. Are you up for the job?"

Dan tapped the picture as he looked up. "Plan A."

Bernie said, "If there is one jihadist, there will be others. We need full disclosure of what this lot get up to in Blighty. Are we clear?"

"Crystal. Give me details of who you need watching, and we'll run facial recognition software."

"We need higher quality images. Mistakes were made in Afghanistan. An innocent family lost their father. That's why I'm prepared to offer you the latest in micro-drones. We have them on trial from U.S. intelligence. I can let you have six. They will be undetectable, once in position and are solar powered, with back-up battery."

"One dozen, and we have a deal."

"Perhaps eight."

"And what about monitoring a headquarters where all these ISIL commanders go?"

"Ah. One dozen it is. Dan this is…"

"Needs to know basis, I know. My Director, and only my closest will have knowledge. You have my word."

"Here's my direct contact number, let's swap details, and I'll introduce you to Derek, he will be your dedicated liaison here."

"Excluding myself, Alison will be our main contact with you, Veronica as second."

Derek was an amiable young man, and after a short discussion, they parted company. Dan was driven back to his light jet, where he checked in with Veronica. He headed for Luton, she scheduling private landing, apron parking, and rental car for him in advance.

As he settled to monitor the autopilot, he felt a heavy weight descend upon his shoulders. He had the support of what was becoming a great team, and had already begun to delegate. He had the backup and resources of both civilian and military at his disposal, and yet he still felt overwhelmed. He did not understand what exactly they were facing. If they--he got it wrong, it could result in the Islamification of England, and perhaps all of the United Kingdom.

His mind remained preoccupied with possibilities, until a calming memory invaded his thoughts. It was one of the last things Felicity had said to him. "Dan, let it go. You won't resolve this now, you don't have the information. Relax, and look after yourself. Prepare for the next battle."

He jerked upright, aware he was close to Luton, and needed to complete his plan. Focused, he prepared a short text to send her when he landed. 'Miss you, D xxx'.

Dan spoke to Veronica, and was guided to the hire car. He looked over the map of Luton airport and finalised his previous plans. He was ready to go, and was soon en route to his chosen destination; a part of the fence with good views of the hangar of his interest. He would need to wait twenty minutes for the cargo plane to arrive, so sent the text message to Felicity, and used the time to prepare. He practiced using the new drones, but readied a standard model for the coming mission.

The plane was a little late, but the day was still long. Waiting until the last moment, Dan sent the drone and positioned it on the top of the fuselage, overlooking the rear-offloading ramp.

The aircraft went inside the bonded hangar, and a seal was placed on the outside doors. Drone footage showed the cargo plane was turned around. It took longer than Dan expected, as if they were positioning it precisely. Almost immediately, a section of floor slid back, and people were roughly herded down steps that ran either side of a ramp.

The mix was unusual, consisting of a children's corps, and a dozen women. All travelled light, except for two-dozen militia, who carried full kit bags, with Heckler & Koch MP5 assault rifles slung on their shoulders. Dan knew the aircraft was originally from ISIL held Libya, although the last leg was from Morocco.

As the people disappeared, a small tractor unit appeared nearby, like an airport baggage car. It reversed into the plane, and was coupled to a series of cargo trolleys. Dan had to follow them, so detached the light drone from the mother unit, and parked it on top of the contents of one trolley, hoping it would not be spotted.

Dan lost contact, and feared the worst, until a slight signal reappeared, growing stronger as presumably, people came to the surface. As visual came up, he reasoned they were inside a warehouse, and the signal indicated this to be half a mile due north. He needed eyes on, and quickly departed for the locality.

The satellite map showed a main road, and track leading into what looked like a derelict motor repair yard. Dan drove on, found a suitable parking place, and worked his way through wasteland inhabited by trees, and too many brambles. In time, he neared a large, modern building hidden from the road.

There were vans and minibuses lined up outside, as if waiting for passengers and cargo. He breached the fence, and began placing transponders under each, the lead vehicle first. He had completed four out of six, when the building doors opened, and people herded towards the first minibus. He hurried to plant all the bugs, and made a dash for safety. He was momentarily exposed, but fortunately not spotted. Lying low, he took photographs of each van and number plate, and cautiously made his escape.

Dan returned to his car and reviewed footage of the small drone, repositioning it to get good internal coverage. More aware after his meeting with Bernie, he also focused on faces.

Afterwards he reviewed footage from the parent drone in the bonded hangar. Four lines of trailers, and two long trolleys with stout wooden boxes on board, were visible entering the tunnel, but none had appeared the other side. Once the cargo was offloaded, the rear ramp of the plane was raised, the underpass sealed. A small tractor moved the aircraft back, covering the access.

Dan considered the implications. The underpass was a lot of work, and not built recently. It was either an existing feature adapted from war years, or had been incorporated some while previously. Regardless, it must have been in use for several years. He asked Alison to check.

He waited as vans and minibuses took the influx of people to their destinations. A call to Alison ensured Percy was already tracking them. Once all the transients had departed, the warehouse doors were sealed, and the tractor units appeared from below. Dan recognised smuggling, and realised the returns of bringing spirits to UK from Morocco made good sense. Morocco was a wet country, alcohol plentiful, and probably a cheap copy of the expensive real thing.

As if for confirmation, the leader opened a couple of boxes, handing out bottles of whisky and cartons of cigarettes to his men. Minutes later he received a mobile call, and the doors were opened, and; a box van reversed in. The boxes were loaded on board, but they waited for a powerful looking man in a business suit to arrive, and check the cargo against the manifest. The all clear was given, and the light trucks departed.

The boss made a short call, and immediately, the doors opened to allow four SUV's inside, before being closed again. Dan noted the yard outside remained empty, except for two armed guards that had taken up station when the boss arrived.

The last two trolleys were brought up by tractor, and each was opened. The contents were thoroughly checked, but Dan recognised the substances at once: drugs. The boss used an electrical gadget to check the contents of the packages, and appeared happy. The cargo boxes were resealed, and loaded into the SUV's, with two small boxes loaded into the boss' car.

While everyone was distracted, Dan flew the drone down, and landed on the roof of the second SUV. It was a risk, but one he was monitoring. Minutes later, the convoy departed, headed in different directions at the main road. Dan retrieved the small drone, and flew it back to his car, where he put it in its case.

He remained for the final play, monitored the hangar, and waited a long time for Customs and Excise to attend. It was late afternoon when they broke the seal and entered. The Captain, Vice Captain, navigator, and Hanger Manager met them. The only others were two warehouse personnel.

The inspection was cursory, and soon paperwork was signed and the remaining cargo offloaded. After a final check, Customs departed, closely followed by the aircraft. They stopped at a nearby hangar. It was bonded, and used as an outgoing warehouse. Goods were cleared to be loaded, Customs apparently checking previously approved tickets against their log.

After Customs departed, three more people joined the flight crew, one of which Dan recognised from Bernie's list. He kept the drone in place, until refuelling and pre-flight checks were complete, and the aircraft taxied for take-off. He flew the mother drone back, and watched the cargo plane take off, knowing he had covered all bases.

After updating Bude, Dan too, taxied for take-off. He was tired and wanted an end to the day.

Chapter 28 ~ Silence For Votes

Dan spent the night with Felicity. She cooked as he wrote up his log, updated the Director, and conferred with his team. Drained, they went to bed early, and he was asleep as soon as his head touched the pillow. Felicity watched over him for a while, smoothing his hair and brow in motherly fashion, knowing his day had been a tough one.

She thought to get up and make a milk drink, but found herself rousing the next morning when he did. Their awakening proved passionate, yet gentle, love replacing hedonistic pleasures of the flesh. Breakfast was leisurely, until Dan mentioned work. Felicity rang Alison at once, putting the call on speaker. "Hi Alison, do you need Dan today?"

"No way! He's given me a week's worth of work already, and Veronica has come in to help. Well, only because there's little else for her to do out here in the sticks. Is he about?"

"You're on speaker, and he's listening."

"Good. Stay away from us, Dan. Now, what is Martin to do?"

Dan spoke for the first time. "Get him monitoring all the drones and transponders, that's becoming a full-time job. I need him up to speed. I particularly need to know where the Luton vehicles went, and I expect some to travel a long way. Martin, I need you to think about what these new people may be in UK for, because they do not fit the mould, except as suicide bombers perhaps. They carried few belongings. Work it out."

Alison replied, "I'll tell him, and show him what to do. Goodbye Dan, enjoy your weekend off. Felicity, thank you. Keep him busy."

"I intend to. Ciao."

Felicity looked menacingly at Dan. He shrugged and replied, "What can I say? An operation of this scale usually has three, four times the number of people I've got. Damn, I'm slipping into work mode. Okay, what are we doing today, sweetheart?"

"That's better. Today you're taking me shopping. The Director was correct, we need our own home habitable, and the first thing I need is a decent bed. I'll check that out when I'm working in Norwich. We need to pick up a microwave oven this morning, then at least we can cook."

"I thought we had the Aga converted last week."

"It would have been, except nobody was here to let them in. I made another appointment for ten this morning. That gives us an hour, and you five minutes to get ready. Get moving."

The weekend passed as a hectic whirl of activity, but one so different from their jobs. Kevin and Neville arrived with strimmers and hedge cutters, and made inroads into the years of overgrowth.

Dan and Felicity spent time with Percy, whose home was in the process of being rewired. Dan liked the way the man was working, and booked their home as his next job.

Chapter 28

Percy joined them later, seeking a break from his wife and her sister. "I just took Stella to the Cash and Carry and borrowed Alf's van again. She'll be chasing you for fourteen hundred quid when she sees you."

"Thanks for the heads up. I'll need to go to the cash point."

"Ma'am, Stella has completed the off sales application for sale of alcohol. Would you be able to action it, say, quite soon?"

Felicity read the form. "This is approved. I'll issue the certificate first thing on Monday, attend me then. Now let's see what the builders are up to."

A time-served plumber turned up first. He was old-school, and relished the challenge. The Aga man arrived and removed the old boiler unit for checking, and de-scaling. He completed the job by adding a nearby gas point for a modern cooker. "You see Me'dear, these Aga's are terrific in winter, but useless if you want a quick fry-up for breakfast in the middle of a hot summer. You needs a separate cooker, and maybe I just knows of a good one going for a song."

"We are interested, show me."

The Aga man returned a couple of hours later with an old cooker that had to be pre-war. "Cast iron, and as good as they come. Built to last they were in them days, not like today. Here, let me couple up and you can get a brew going."

Within the miasma of professional help and pettifoggery, Dan and Felicity found a course they could chart, and left a key outside, so tradesmen could bring their home into the twenty-first century, while retro-fitting the old equipment, and traditional fixtures and fittings.

Felicity joined her parents for Sunday lunch, where she and her father shared the joys of promotion. Dan stayed and retreated to the library to work. He found the environment to his liking.

Monday began early for both of them, and they realised that in future, they might only have weekends together. They held each other too tightly, as if afraid of losing the other. Words didn't come, their emotions getting the better of speaking aloud. Felicity pulled away. "Until next time, lover boy. Think of me, but not too much."

Her cheeky grin spilt the moment, and they went on their separate ways. Felicity left for the station, her plan to make a brief review before heading to her new job in Norwich. It took a little longer than she had hoped, but she cleared her desk, and approved Stella's application. The liquor licence was given to Percy to deliver, and he departed at once.

Meanwhile, Dan drove to the office where he debriefed with Alison. "You were correct about the smuggling, and drugs. These Paki's run the regional mafia, and are into everything. The booze and cigarettes end up via a main distribution warehouse, being sent out to small shops run by Pakistanis. Nearly all the small shops are run by Pakistanis.

"The main warehouse is in a no-go area. Even most Muslims are excluded. The vans and minibuses all belong to a 'facilitation company', as do larger vehicles: buses, lorries, and artics. The companies behind these places have four directors, three of which we already know. Veronica is compiling files on the unknown, and presumably local hood, who is named as fourth director. It's a mess Dan."

"Find out as much as you can. What about the women, the kids?"

"This opens a new can of worms. I ran facial recognition software on all of them, and most of the girls were captured by Boko Haram in Chibok village, the others are from Kummabza village, both northern Nigerian school invasions. Two of them were deposited at a terraced house in Bristol, and have not been seen since. They carried a small backpack each. I sent this through as priority to Derek, who is currently monitoring. They suspect a twin suicide bombing in the city centre, either today or tomorrow.

"Derek said they have identified most that came through, and all are related to possible terror strikes in England. They thanked you for your efforts, asked for better images, and want more."

"Good. We are getting somewhere at last. Anything on the underpass?"

"Nothing. I checked old records, rail, canal: Zilch. But I did find that during the war, the *Raf* had an air raid shelter and underground store."

"Hmmm. They must have used it, extended it. Okay.

"I wish we had more staff, but we'll have to cope. Martin, Percy, let me see your agenda for this week … Good, I'll accompany you at first, show you the ropes, Martin?"

The lad gulped and said, "You will have to, I don't have my pilots licence yet … I only need air miles, but with a qualified instructor. I have my helicopter licence though."

"Merde! I will not let this operation be hampered by lack of a piece of paper. Veronica, I need a jet pilot trainer today, and at the end of today, I expect Martin to have his qualification. You can tag along too, until you get the hang of it again. This is vitally important to the success or failure of the entire project. Do I make myself clear?"

Dan stormed off, his team shocked at the vehemence of his reaction. None had witnessed that part of his character before, and hoped never to do so again.

Some minutes later, Veronica tentatively knocked on the internal shop door, and opening it, found Dan and Stella sharing a joke. He seemed relaxed and at ease. Was the before a play of his? Feeling heartened she said, "Dan, we leave in fifteen minutes, and I will accompany you to brush up. We finish this today. I presume you and Percy will attend to the visit, while we practice flying."

"Great work. Just what I hoped for. About before, upstairs…"

She smiled and said, "I understand. Don't apologise, it's not needed, and doesn't suit you. But, you better pack your bag, Sir."

Dan and Percy spent the day in Leicester, whilst up above, Martin got his wings, and Veronica brushed up her flying skills. As Felicity had advised, Dan passed himself off as a detective, reporting to Inspector Wigglesworth for the project. It repeated as before, Percy ambling aside with the local community bobby, and gaining trust and information

During the course of the day, they were invited to speak to one other current community officer, and one recently retired. They began to get an angle on the Muslim community in Leicester, one that was well established over decades.

They were late back to the airstrip, but their transport was running even later. "What do you make of it, Percy?"

"This is a large city, Dan, generations of immigrants here, mainly Sunni, and their community roots are well established. The City, county, and local councils all seem to co-operate well with the Muslim community. But there are definitely no-go areas for non-Muslims. As the community relations officer said, 'I have a sort of pass, and by that I mean I am tolerated. These are not places for females not wearing a niqāb to be seen in, or even a couple of lads late at night. The outward appearance is that of a diverse, multicultural society that is working. I fear the obverse is the actual fact. Sharia law is rampant. Isolationism and intolerance rule the local streets' as Sunni and Shia squabble."

"Yes, but it is that word, 'appearance' that worries me most. The retired officer, the only one with nothing to lose, intimated there were unofficial Muslim schools, and that areas of the city are under Sharia law. It sounds more like separatism to me, than multiculturalism."

"Yes Dan, cultural cul-de-sacs, Muslim ghettos in the making. The city is too large for them to undermine in one go, so instead, they take over what used to be the towns that now comprise it."

"Well, at least we discovered the illegal immigrants are going to city approved, charity organised housing projects. These are being projected as pioneering schemes for the inhabitants, and yet I note, all of the new developments, are within white dominated political catchment areas. Here look on the map. They won't be satisfied, until they turn England, into the same mess of a society they fled from."

Percy studied the screen of Dan's tablet, before saying, "Were this a town, it would be Muslim by now. Given the current influx continues unabated, I reckon only a few years before Muslims dominate the city. Are they blind? And they all have large families."

"Apparently so. Remember that community centre we wanted to visit, but were denied entry? Being repainted doesn't do it for me, there was no smell of paint. I'll send a drone there and see what we find."

Dan launched a drone and the view came up on camera. There was minor work on repainting windows outside, and a distinct lack of community participation. Dan said, "This reminds me of those community centres over near Wymondham. I'm going park this drone and see what's going on. I bet it's a school for boys only."

They were interrupted by a call from the airfield supervisor. "I have a message for you. Pilot Martin Edwards is making final approach."

They realised the significance, and went to settle the bill.

Despite Martin gaining his pilot's licence, and Veronica becoming confident at flying again, Dan changed his plans, and spent the days with the away team on the ground. He clued Martin in to how Percy would walk aside, flicking his head or fingers as if to say, 'go away'.

This was Percy's skill with local peers, and he came up trumps every time. Martin learned to read the situation, and how to appear distracted by his smart phone, even if there was nothing on it. He was learning how to be an agent in the real world.

On Wednesday evening, Dan received a short phone call from Felicity. "I'm starving, but need a bath. You are bringing me takeaway tonight, so be here soon."

"You're back already?"

"No silly, just for a station visit, and to greet Karen tomorrow morning. It will be a week or more until she fills my boots, but she needs to know what she's taking on. It's standard practice. Dan, I'm hungry!"

Dan had been called, and though his duty lingered, he could work from her home. He departed, they ate, and slobbed on the settee. Dan said, "I should take a shower, but I'm desperately tired."

"Dan, all I want, need is a cuddle, and to fall asleep with your strong arms holding me. That's it."

"That's a shame, I'm horny."

"Same here, but work takes its toll." A kiss, and a hand pulling him towards her bedroom cut off their words.

Veronica had taken over collating the reports from the away team, and following up as required. Alison added to her research, offering demographics of cultural shift and drift, and a large file concerning the Pakistani grooming gangs. She was having a hard job tying all the different threads of information together, until Dan and Percy stayed late with her on Thursday.

Dan said, "Derby is similar to Leicester, too large a city to take over in one go. We were reliably informed that Nottingham, less than fifteen miles away, is similar. Together those cities are larger than Leicester. They are also in different counties, and support different MP's.

Chapter 28

"The Muslim presence is strong in areas of all three cities, and representatives of the Muslim community act as go betweens with city authorities, and often, the police. Muslim inspired, self-imposed segregation, is rampant. They are cities within a city, one where Sharia law is practiced, as are forced marriages, and female genital mutilation.

"Although classed as a city, Sheffield is like a conurbation of towns, and we visited five on Wednesday, including Rotherham, Percy."

"What we witnessed, and gleaned from local informants, was that the areas are run by gangs of Pakistani Muslims, who are into all sorts of racketeering. You name it, they're doing it, but other gangs complete, the Somali and Romanians to name but two.

"The Muslims are the largest, and dominant group. Similar prevails in Rochdale, which we visited today. I see you have the full files of the recent grooming cases, and details of some not yet made public knowledge. I can tell you, these are the tip of the iceberg. We discovered nearby Dewsbury is a hotbed of jihad insurgency.

"Everything continues as normal, until you scratch the surface, as we did. The trafficking and forced prostitution of seriously underage, white British girls is endemic, and apparently supported and promoted by social service, and local councillors. Some police were also caught in the net. This isn't the same Country I grew up in."

Percy stopped to wipe his brow, his face reddening. "This is sick, these men are paedophiles. Why are so many of them?"

Dan said, "I'll tell you why: Aisha. She was Muhammad's third wife, and they married when she was seven years old. The marriage was consummated when the child was nine, and many Muslim men want to emulate Muhammad, and gain a place at Allah's side by having a child bride. Many of today's Muslim's frown on this practice, so they take white girls 'as held in their right hand', like trophies of war. They treat them as they wish, like dogs, with Allah's blessing. Not only is it misogynism, but a victory over the white infidels: us."

Percy banged his fists on the table, barely containing his rage, but mentally regrouped to continue. "I am hopeful that a few anonymous reports will arrive at Lower Meddlington police station over the coming days, that will shed more light on what is happening in those parts."

Percy became subdued, his mind working against personal ghouls. Dan wanted to stop, but they were almost done, and the answer they sought, he believed was within reach.

Dan continued, as Percy dealt with his inner demons. "Percy did a mighty fine job. I wish I had his skill in getting police constables to talk, and share openly. We could not have done this without you, Percy."

Percy seemed to get a second wind, and responded, "Thank you, but I only did what I could. It wasn't enough."

"But a place for us all to begin. Go on, Percy." Alison chipped in.

"Veronica, as you see from our reports, we discovered similar in Rochdale and the surrounding area, Bolton especially. That is part of Greater Manchester, a large city, made up of innumerable towns. This particular layout appears to provide a base for the Muslims to take over large parts of the illegal booze, cigarette, drug, and sex trades. In this case, the seriously underage sex trade. The girls are treated as a commodity, and don't even earn money from their enforced prostitution. Sorry, but I am having a big problem with this.

"I mention this, because it gives us clues to the way they think, and that thinking is tribal. The girls are slaves, the drugs, booze, and no doubt gun, and gambling rackets are stock in trade. And we, the British people, are the targets, the enemy.

"They have zero intention of integrating, but are working to promote Islamic states within our towns and cities. This is war."

Dan said, "Agreed Percy. This is what we are witnessing, but on a larger scale. We have taken these people in, most of them worthy, and given them citizenship, equality. Their extremists respond by trying to take over our green and pleasant land, abuse our hospitality, and endeavour to turn this, our country, into an Islamic State. I have a serious problem with that, especially as no moderate Muslim stands against them. That in turn means, the Muslim community supports and empowers these extremists in our midst."

Percy said, "That is the distinct impression I got, although nobody was forthright enough to say it out loud. I heard one phrase three times, twice in Rochdale, and once in Rotherham, 'Silence for votes'.

"This represents an unwritten deal between local politicians and the Muslim community leaders. The authorities agree to turn a blind eye to all matters Muslim, in exchange for the Muslim community supporting the political party making the deal. Social Services, and the police conspire. They want to wash their hands of the whole debacle."

"Is this because of collusion, embarrassment, or entrapment?"

"All three. Embarrassment because the general Muslim community is in denial. Entrapment because these are extremely young, white girls. And collusion by the powers that have local and regional control.

"One copper explained a little deeper, you see. The local council run the social services, who follow the council line. Hence, care homes turned into grooming factories. The police are warned off checking out local smuggling operations, although I heard rumours some, including more senior officers, were being bribed. Regardless, the police dare not enter a Muslim stronghold with force. They would start a war."

"So, everyone takes a slice of the cake, gets a backhander, and all the ills are swept under the carpet. Percy, Veronica, is this all about politics regards the white British, and creating Islamic enclaves for the Muslims. Can it be that simple?"

Chapter 28

Veronica spoke first. "I believe so Dan, as in being put simply. Yes, that sums up what we are witnessing across the land. Plus, the Muslims are the first to play the racial or religious prejudice card against us. Our wet left absolve them of crimes they should be locked away for life, and have a lot to answer for. So do our money-grabbing lawyers."

Alison took up the cudgel, "But that's not all. Virtually since inception, Islam has been a battle between Sunni and Shia. Each call the other infidels, and yet that term seems to stick to us most of all, the Caucasian Christians. But the fact remains, the rich and powerful Muslims prey upon the weak and poor. Even of their own kind. They buy and sell people as a commodity, well the men do. If a woman is raped, she is found guilty of adultery, and stoned to death for her crime. The rapist is pardoned, and given a slap on the back. These people are barbaric: animals!

"I repeat, this is not about sex. It is about personal power. To me, they appear to worship the Law of Thelema, by Alistair Crowley: 'Do what thou wilt shall be the whole of the Law. Love is the law, love under will.'

"I ask you, whose will?"

During Alison's rant, Percy had been quiet, thinking at times. A pause developed and he spoke softly. "My granddaughter is eleven next week. Today I learned of another white girl, also eleven years old. She had been raped by thousands of Muslims, and not only vaginally, but orally and anally. Sometimes more than one Muslim monster at a time."

He drew out a picture of an angelic child. "Sophie," and his tears flowed, his voice stuttered. He looked up as if pleading. "How? ... How could any descent person find this child sexually attractive? ... I do not understand ... The odd paedophile perhaps, but thousands of Muslim men of all ages, impossible. This is a cultural problem. It is an ethnic problem. And it is directly related to Islam."

He tried to say more, but made mewing sounds as his face scrunched up, and his body shook. In uneven tones, he said one final thing. "This is the Devil's work, no God could be involved with such iniquity."

Dan said, as he gentled Percy to his car. "This is all about power. Controlling others. They do it because they can, and do get away with it. They even do it to other Muslims. Take Friday off."

The car started, and Dan returned to finish work quickly. When they locked up for the night, and came out the back way, Percy switched off the engine, and strolled down to meet them.

"I must finish this. Prevent it happening to Sophie--other kids. Come, time for a beer. I need to be with normal people tonight."

Chapter 29 ~ Suicide Bombers

Dan received an urgent summons, early the next morning, Friday. He only had time for a brief chat with the team over rushed breakfast, before delegated tasks and leaving.

Alison gave him a folder before he left. "Here are the full results of where the Luton vehicles went. The last item is quite unusual, the derelict, former USAF base, Lillyworth Moor. I'm running checks on it now, but Lincolnshire is at the back end of nowhere, and this place is in a remote part of that. Have fun."

Dan was in Bude by mid-Friday morning. He spent time with Derek and Bernie identifying potential threats of the human kind. Bernie said, "Keep this up Dan, those two girls, well, we got them in Bristol, saved them more like. They were supposed to blow up a shopping centre, first and second waves, but as soon as they were approached, they asked for their freedom. We learned a lot about the male Muslim mind, which I will share with you. It's all in this dossier. If you need more, you'll have to see them yourself."

"Thank you Bernie. I just need to be sure of everything."

"Perhaps that is why you are so good at what you do. But the images still need better clarity. You need more drones?"

"No, but I do need to hone focus of the ones we have deployed. They always seem to default away from facial recognition. I do not understand that."

Derek began to say something, before Bernie interrupted. "We've had these software glitches before. American programmers for you. Excuse me a moment."

Bernie stood aside and made a short call. Derek whispered, "I think they were set for topographical, and not facial recognition. That is the typical factory setting. Shush, he's coming back."

Bernie was effusive when he returned. "Sorry, the code is now being amended. Wrong setting you know. Five minutes, and the drones you have will all default to facial recognition. My time is short, so please tell me what you know about these characters."

Bernie laid a series of photographs on the table, and Dan answered as best he could. All were known terrorists. Their immediate location was the sticking point, as many appeared to be in UK, and had not departed. Bernie leaned forward and said, "Dan, I need these people found. Do your best, I know you will."

Dan retorted, "No problem Bernie, now the correct software is installed in the drones." Before offence could be taken, Dan added, "What can you tell me about the old USAF base at Lillyworth Moor?"

"Err? Let me see, Lillyworth Moor was RAF, loaned to the United States Air Force during World War Two, and is derelict."

Chapter 29

Derek raised his hand and interjected, "It's for sale actually, Bernie. Been on the market for a couple of years. Nobody wants it. It's at the back of beyond, in Lincolnshire."

Dan appeared to be listening intently, but his fingers were alive below the table: 'Message Alison: all info pronto, USAF Lillyworth Moor. Look for a Muslim buyer, transfers of militia inwards, weapons?'

Two minutes later Veronica called back. "Dan, this appears to be a jihad training establishment. Alison is still unravelling the Arabic, but this is a Muslim hothouse. Can you get eyes-on?"

Dan didn't want to get one up on Bernie, but he had to speak. "Bernie, Derek, USAF Lillyworth Moor is now under civilian management, the company that bought the property is directed by Hussein, Ali, and Mohammad. Ring any bells, gentlemen?

"I need a satellite over them now. This is of the highest threat to our democracy, until proven otherwise. I expect a feed to Alison within moments. Thank you."

Dan got up and left the table, making several short calls to Veronica, his Director, and RAF Trimingham. "Tom, I have another one for you to monitor, USAF Lillyworth Moor. I'm at GCHQ Bude now, and we're bringing the satellite into focus ... *Wilco*. More later."

They watched the repositioning satellite, as the view on screen came into focus. The scale was high-level, and showed the entirety, and surrounding farmland.

Dan said, "I make out two runways, long ones, and buildings that are not derelict, but busy. Look, those are blast-proof hangars, walls three feet thick. What are we looking at?"

Bernie coughed delicately and Derek said, "I'll zoom in on the barracks. I see signs of life."

As the satellite focused nearer to ground, so activity was visible all over the camp. They studied section by section, discovering a parade ground, assault course in use, and a battle ground with modern tanks and howitzers. They were practicing for war.

Bernie said, "Some of the Luton people went here?"

"Yes. A training ground, and the runways appear serviceable, as do the hangars. It is also a strike base. You'll come to your own conclusions, but we need twenty-four seven on the all of this, down to facial recognition level. I believe you'll find many of those you seek here."

Derek ventured to speak. "Why are they doing this?"

"What? Training personnel in the use of weapons, artillery? What springs to mind? I'll tell you what, defence of enclaves. You read the battle formations, right? Wrong, you have no idea. This is standard military drill. These are defensive layouts. Those over there, offensive. I suggest you get an expert Army tactician to analyse what they are plotting. It will give us a clue as to what they are about. And copy me in, I'm on the front line, and my team are all alone at the moment."

Bernie was about to speak, when a computerised voice stated, "Facial match, ninety-nine percent certain, Alfridi ben Absolom. Facial match, ninety-nine percent certain, Ibrahim..."

Images of faces danced across the screen, and there were a lot of matches. Bernie pulled up associated files, and Dan perceived the station changing up a gear. He turned to leave. "Gentlemen, thank you. I think you have a lot of new information to process, so I'll leave you to it. Copy us in on the results, and as soon as you get them."

Derek acknowledged Dan with a curt nod of his head. Bernie was busy on his phone. Dan excused himself, returned to his plane, and reaching for his notebook, began to write up his notes. Before planning his next move, he stated aloud, "Always work from a basis of fact, and never from half-arsed theory or speculation."

As soon as he was done, he took a break. He needed to clear his mind, and doing something different suited. He got a coffee from the local control tower office and paid his dues before staying to chat a little. He got on well with the controller and they shared several jokes before Dan finished his coffee. Looking at his watch, Dan said, "Time I was on my way, Rob. See you next time."

Dan settled into the pilot's seat, checked in with his team, updated Tom, and called the Director. She was not amused, but backed his next move to the hilt. "We, as an organisation, live off intelligence. You are correct. There are gaps of information. Tell me, why do you want to see these two girls?"

"Because they have been through the system, Ma'am, the ISIL system. Bristol police, antiterrorism, will be treating them as criminals, and I, we need information only they possess."

"Good enough. I'll send one of our translators to you. You do realise the local police will put you in a fully monitored interview room."

"Of course Ma'am. That's the game in play. Please have the translator bring two female prayer mats, and a Mecca compass."

"Nice move. Okay, I'll inform them and it will be so ... Three hours, so you may have time for lunch. Ciao."

Dan took a short nap, and waking with a clear mind, profiled the girls. He worked out several strategies to get them to talk. That was his job, and his expertise. Satisfied with his planning, he taxied for take-off, made good speed east, and was soon landing at Bristol airport.

Dan met the translator outside Bristol high security police station, and it became clear, they were both being treated with great suspicion, and were being stalled. Security wanted to take Dan's gun and mobile phone. He used the latter to make a short phone call. His Director said, "I'll call the Home Office at once."

Less than one minute later, a senior officer came rushing into the foyer. "Stand down everybody. Orders from the top, allow these people through as they are. Commander, apologies, we seldom get visitors holding so high a station. The interview room is available. Please follow the Detective Inspector."

As they walked, Dan said, "Just as well we are on the same side as them. I wonder how they are treating the two girls."

They were shown into an imposing room, where one girl cowered in a chair, trying to look small. Dan said, "I'll see both girls together, if you don't mind."

"That is not our policy, Commander."

"What part of that phone call did you not understand? This is my interview, my policy, so please bring the other girl at once. I need to study how they interact with one another. We call it profiling."

The officer was obviously unhappy, but did as instructed. Dan set his phone to voice recording, and took a chair opposite the girl. He said, "Don't be scared, we're not with that lot. We just want a little chat. You do speak English, don't you?"

"Yes, a little. Thank you."

The other girl was brought in, and they ran to hug each other. Dan gave them a moment before asking them to sit down. The interpreter was busy writing notes, and whispered, "The girls spoke in their native tongue, Hausa. They said nothing of note, except being worried about each other. I'll give you a full transcript before we leave."

Dan began in a friendly fashion. "We are not police. I am with the security service, and I want to ask you a few questions. Please relax. My name is Dan, and my colleague is a translator, called Maye. Please speak in the language that suits you best. Your names are Siri and Sana?"

The girls nodded, but were apprehensive. Dan said, "Please, we only want to talk."

He leant forward as if bowing to them, and whispered, "This room has video cameras, and they record what we say. If you have a secret to tell, whisper it to me."

Dan pulled back, stretched, and said in his normal voice, "Have you prayed today?"

The translator offered Dan a bag, and he gave a prayer mat to each girl, and sat a compass-like device on the table. "As a sign of good faith, I will allow you a few minutes for prayer. Mecca is in that direction."

Dan pointed his finger, echoing the display of the Islamic compass, and nodded at the translator, who repeated his words in Hausa.

They looked startled but smiled before going about their devotions. Dan looked directly at the cameras, smiled, and said, "The prayer mats and compass now belong to you girls, but I do not know if the police will allow you to keep them. They are now your property, regardless."

He was speaking as much for the information of the police listening in, as for the girls. The prayer break gave Dan the opportunity to speak quietly with the translator in preparation for the coming interview.

The girls returned to the table, looking a little more confidant. Dan began the interview, setting a pattern in motion. He would ask a question, one girl would reply, and the other reply afterwards. Sometimes they spoke together, or in alternating sentences. The translator always spoke Dan's words in their language, unless they waved the translation aside. As with other Nigerians Dan had known, their English proved to be very good, if African in dialect.

Dan began. "Tell me about your lives, before that night?"

"We were happy, both at school, which is wonderful for women, and we had happy families, a lovely life."

Sana spoke. "Yes it is true. My family were so proud of me, as few women are educated. I dreamt of going to university, but then the *Shai mugaye* came, and everything was destroyed."

The translator said, "That means 'Satan's evil ones' in Hausa."

Dan said, "Tell me about that night, please, I'm sorry if it brings back painful memories, but I need to understand how these people work. You are both from Chibok?"

Siri spoke first, as usual. "Yes, that night, we can never forget. We all thought we would be killed. They were mean, fired at anyone. We were herded like animals, and beaten for no reason."

Sana spoke next, adding to the story. "It was horrendous. They put us in a truck, and I looked back. They lined the men up and shot them, women too. Both my parents are dead."

Her tears came, and soothing words ensued. Dan allowed them a moment, before gently pressing forward. "I need your help. You have been with these men. Tell me what life was like with Boko Haram. I know it was most unpleasant, so speak openly."

"We grew up fast, learned about the ways of men. We were raped and beaten every day. The pretty ones like us became favourites, and we were passed from one man to another, many in the same hour. I felt defiled. It was a journey into hell, except the hell never stopped."

Sana added, "They are not Muslim, they cannot be, because they had sex with us. It is against Allah's wishes. I don't understand how they could do it to us. I learned to switch my mind off to the sex, but some girls could not cope. I hated the constant beatings. Usually there was no reason, they almost broke me. But for my sisters, I would have fallen. We were treated as slaves, chattels of war."

Dan continued to get them to talk about their experiences, often adding a few words to ease the story along. "Was there no way out?"

"Only one: death. We were taught their version of Islam, which conflicted with our own. But we had to do as they said, or be killed. Some girls were beheaded."

Sana added, "Our days were long, filled with chores, rape, and beatings. In between, they subjected us to learning their version of Islam, and we had to learn and practice that, or die.

"Then they made some sort of deal with ISIL, and they started training us to become suicide bombers. At last we had the chance to escape through death."

Dan's stomach churned as he studied their faces. They had been happy to have that choice, even though they seemed quite young. Troubled he asked, "How old are you?"

Siri said, "Fourteen, Sir. I am hoping not to see another birthday," her smile was one of martyred acceptance.

Dan looked towards Sana, who said, "I'm just fifteen and my life is already over."

Shocked but undeterred, Dan continued to probe the all of it; "How did you come to England?"

"Once we volunteered, they took a group of us up through Chad, and gave us to ISIL in Libya. They were nasty people, but we weren't there long, and were imprisoned for most of the time. The next day guards came and took a few of us. I don't know where the others went, but we were sent to a plane, and arrived in England, carrying our suicide vests, our only possession."

Sana said, "I was scared, but such a relief to be away from Shai mugaye. I was going to blow myself up, but not take too many others with me, when a strange thing happened, it was as if we were expected. The woman spoke to us in Hausa, and offered us life, but only if we surrendered to her."

Siri said, "Yes, same for me. It felt like Allah was offering to spare us, Assalaamu Álaykum."

"Yes, I felt that too. Maybe he has other plans for us."

Dan let their banter continue for a moment; they were reanimating as people, and he wanted to indulge their coming back into the world, but not too much.

He interrupted and said, "I'm thirsty, and could do with a coffee, strong, milk and sugar. Translator? Girls?"

They spoke their wishes, and Dan asked the translator to knock the door and present their request. It was a distraction, but also an offer of friendship.

Dan stretched back, clicking bones in his back and shoulders, as he showed a relaxed persona. Once the translator was in earshot he spoke, "Tell me everything you can about your flight, your time in England."

"Well, it was rather late when we left, and almost daylight, but the night got darker, and we landed somewhere. We were there for hours, and not allowed off, even for a pee. Our seats were hard, and lined both sides of the cargo plane. It was not nice. They filled up the centre with lots of carriages, packed full of stuff.

"Much of it was whisky and cigarettes, drugs as well. I feel so ashamed. Boko Haram forced us to drink, smoke things, and take drugs. I feel humiliated. I have sinned, even though I could do nothing to prevent them. We can never go home. My parents would kill me."

Sana said, "They weren't Muslims, not good ones like we are. They used those evils to loosen us up, before raping us, oh so many times. My life is worthless. No man will take us as wives. Dying is a release."

Sensing the moment slip, Dan interjected, slapping his hand on the table for effect. "They were Muslims, but then you don't know you were in Morocco, did you?"

The girls' faces looked stunned, "M... Morocco!"

"Yes indeed. What can you tell me about that, the rest of the flight..."

Dan cajoled and worked his witnesses to the best of his ability, learning their ways, and keeping a level path through the girls' highs and lows of retelling.

They came to the last item on Dan's list, the house they stayed at. The girls spoke openly about their experience, "It was a staging place, but we were reasonably well looked after. The man in charge was Muslim, but not radicalised like all those we had met since leaving our village, and we almost felt safe, and sort of enjoyed our time there. We were offered a room each, but chose to sleep together."

Siri said, "I locked the door after dinner, and put a chair under the handle. We could hear the owner moving about downstairs, and then he came up to the bathroom, and went into another room."

Sana added, "It was good sleep, although we woke often because of strange noises, usually outside. Do people in this country ever go to sleep?"

"Sometimes, but not everyone at the same time, our society is twenty four hours you know."

"Wow. I can't believe."

"What about when you both woke up the next day?"

"I will never forget it. Our room overlooked the rear garden. The sun shone down on us, warming us, as if a new life had begun. We prayed, then went down for breakfast, and the man was cooking English style, it was strange, but good to eat."

Dan smiled, and encouraged the girls to speak, knowing everything they said was being recorded by his mobile phone, as always. Inwardly, his mind focused on a map he had studied in detail. The house they had been taken to was 42 Acacia Avenue, and it faced south. The rear bedroom would never see the morning sun. The police were tearing number 42 apart, and had found nothing. It was the wrong house.

Dan leaned forward and whispered, "You went into a house, then where did you go to end up where you slept. Whisper."

As a distraction, Dan had his mobile in his hand, and was setting up his final play. Sana whispered, "We went in the front door, and were told to wait for a while. We were not allowed to do, or touch anything. Then we were given drapes to wear, and shown out the back. We walked down an alley a few houses left, and in the back way to the house on the other side."

Dan said, "Thank you. That is all I needed. One last thing before I go, do you recognise any of these people?"

Dan showed them a slideshow of the faces Bernie had sent him, and he counted by picture number, as he recorded the girls' verbal responses. He learned a lot about a few of the men pictured.

Once finished, he wished the girls well, departed quickly, and before the local plod could interrogate him. Their refreshments never did arrive.

Chapter 30 ~ A Home of Their Own

Before taking off, Dan tasked Bernie to follow up on the house switch the girls were involved with, and was soon in possession of a short video showing their movements after arrival. He chuckled. Because of the aggressive police tactics, the girls had not told about the change of house. Certainly no detective had thought to ask.

He was late back home, because he had already paid a visit to the householder and house in question, 53 Salmond Avenue. His team were already working on ownership and residents, known associates, and local police information channels.

The owner, as it turned out, said, "I was just doing a favour for my nephew, Sunil Khan. He had rescued those two poor girls you know. Frightened of their own shadows they were. They were only here two nights, and hid in one room, even though I gave them a room each. They were scared. Are you from Social Services, looking out for them?"

"Yes, I'm concerned for their welfare. May I come in?"

"Of course, I'll put the kettle on. Not often I have visitors. The young ones only come round when they want something. You'll take it British style?"

"Yes, milk and three sugars." Dan learned much about Islamic culture, and the way it was changing in recent times. There came a natural break in conversation, he gave thanks, and departed.

It was dark when Dan touched down in Norwich. He made for his car, and spent twenty minutes dictating the day's events to log. He forwarded official reports to other agencies via official channels, knowing bureaucracy would delay them.

Leaning back, he stretched and ran a memory check of all he had to do. His thoughts drifted to the next phase, and he must have nodded off, because he was jarred awake by his phone ringing. It was a special ringtone reserved for only one person.

"Felicity, I was about to call you, I just got in."

"Hmm. Where are you?"

"Norwich airport."

"Good. I'm almost done in the office, so meet me at my digs, I'm at the Glen Avon Hotel, it's west Norwich, just off…"

While Dan was waiting in the foyer, he informed both Bristol police and the Met the wrong house was being torn apart. He signed with his new credentials, and officially reported the fact via official channels.

A little later, Felicity arrived. She looked tired, and was laden down with baggage. "Here, let me carry this. Are you okay sweetheart? You look worn-out."

They showered together, and sat back to recount their tales of work. Both fell asleep in chairs, finally crawling to bed hours later.

Despite their early night, they slept late, their minds and bodies needing the convalescence of good sleep. Dan called room service for coffee, as they slowly came alive that morning. He enquired, "Breakfast? We missed dinner."

"The both of us. You fell asleep first," she said playfully.

"No I did not, I was waiting for you."

Their play brought them both fully awake, heightened by a second coffee. Felicity said, "There's a truck stop eatery just down the road. Full English breakfast, all grease and unhealthy eating, fancy a bite?"

"Count me in. A man-meal is just what I need."

They both tucked in to feast of what nutritionists and doctors would have fifty fits over, greasy, full of saturated fats, and delicious.

Felicity said, "This week is the worst, and next almost as bad. Once Karen is in situ, I can stop doing two jobs. My official promotion is set for the first of next month. I just have to survive another long week of hell. How's it going with you?"

Dan recounted days as short sentences, keeping it brief. This was catching up, not problem-sharing. He reached across and took her fingers in his own, hoping his next words would not cause offence; was she really the one?

"Felicity, sorry, but I need to be at work this morning, half a day at the longest. I hope you understand."

Felicity tightened her grip on Dan's hand momentarily, and replied, "So do I. Our jobs, our work, it's not normal. I never thought I'd find someone who understood, but you do."

"Likewise. So what's next?"

"Well, it's almost nine o'clock, and we need to go to The Furniture Warehouse. It's like a shopping centre, but only for furniture. We must order a bed today, and a three-piece suite."

"Why, why the rush. We can take our time."

"Well, no we can't. You see, Karen needs police housing, and my gaff is it regards Lower Meddlington. I need to be out of there a week come Friday, but get Brownie points for doing it sooner."

Dan stared at her. "You're moving in?"

"It seems to be the best resolution, plus I've opted for police housing here in Norwich. I will end up with an apartment, but one within walking distance of work. It will take some time to come through. The thing is, that this weekend, I need to move out of my present home."

"Ah. Leave that to me, that's boys' work. Consider it done, Ma'am." Dan's cheeky grin elicited a deeper, unspoken sharing.

They left at once, and were two of the few early customers at The Furniture Warehouse. Beds were chosen, as was a lounge suite of composite leather sections, which could be mixed and matched at will. They placed orders for bedding and towels, a magazine rack and coffee table, mainly to Felicity's taste, and Dan's expense. All were to be delivered several weeks later, except for a few specific items, such as their king-size bed.

As they left Felicity said, "That's the basics sorted. You okay with antique furniture? I thought I'd attend some auctions and flea markets."

"Yes, old furniture would suit the house much better. But there's no rush. Maybe we could go together sometime."

They departed for work, and Felicity rang some hours later. "Dan, something came up, and I must deal with it. Sorry."

"Do it. This is your job. I'm with the team, debriefing from yesterday, and there's a lot more I must cover, so I'll be here for what? Say another hour. See you later."

Cathy was showing deliverymen where to put the bed when Dan arrived at the house. She had guessed the right room, and Dan took over. "Thanks Cathy, one bed, a couple of chairs, just the basics so we can live here. We'll wait until the work is complete before delivering, and ordering the rest. Thanks for covering, but why are you here? Your help is much appreciated all the same."

"Kevin called me, and well, you need a woman here to keep tabs on all these tradesmen. I don't need paying, but a posh meal in that pub you live in wouldn't go amiss. Now, the locksmith is due to arrive any minute, so give me some space."

There were floorboards up all over the place, and the electrician had a full team working on rewiring. "We've been thorough and discovered that all the wiring in the kitchen had been done using spare parts from the original owner's boat-building nephew—cloth covered wiring from the 30's and splices galore."

"Nightmare!"

"Just as well you never turned the power on. Poof!"

The plumber was running under floor heating and radiator points. The Aga man was doing gas fittings, one to each coal fire, both upstairs and down, when a local builder tuned up to place detachable front covers to all the fireplaces. They would have the option of real fires, or gas ones. The builder said, "This is illegal nowadays, just so you know. They should be separate flues. I expect no comebacks.

"Understood. I'll say they were already here, but I doubt anyone will notice."

"I cannot complete until the chimneys are swept. Want me to organise that?"

Dan was agog, and gave the go ahead. He was distracted when the locksmith arrived, but they understood one another. All new fittings were of old design. The locksmith said, "These new fangled computer whatchamacallit's, they're dead already, just need to crack the code. Now this beauty I have here, is a piece of art. It would take a thief days to pick the lock. It's treble balanced you know, works like this…"

Dan and Cathy had their hands full. That was until Felicity arrived, and immediately took control. That night, Dan gratified Cathy's obligation, and they had a large meal for all the workers, including Dan's own team, at the village Inn.

The next day proved to be more of the same, and a local farmer turned up to mow the field. He did likewise for next door and Percy's house, but the other occupant of four was out. There were farm gates through to the next property, which the lads cleared with hedge cutter and strimmer.

Dan was watching the mowing, sat on a tree stump, munching upon a freshly picked damson, when Felicity called to him. "Dan. Come. We found a hidden passage."

They hurried into the house, and library, where the electrician was shining a light down a hole in the far wall. A wall panel lay open, as if a secret doorway, but to where?

"We followed the wiring under floor, and we got this." The electrician pointed to the heavy wires running to the edge of the room, and beyond.

He added, "Stokie found the secret lever, here. I ain't going down them steps, mind. There may be dungeons down there. Slavering beasts. So I called the laird of the manor."

Dan looked at the opening, cast a wink aside to Felicity, and drew his gun. People gasped and backed away. "Torch!" he commanded, and one was placed in his hand. He aligned it with his gun sights, and made theatrical incursions into the unknown.

Felicity followed him into the dark, her truncheon in hand, picking up instantly on his sense of theatre, and whispering, "They'll be gossiping about this for months, just wait and see. Lay on MacGyver."

Dan cast her a wry look back, and for an instant, passionately kissed her lips. "To do, or to die, Mi'Lady. Onwards. Excelsior!"

The stone steps, layered with cobwebs from floor to ceiling, and across, went down a long way. Some keystones were treacherous underfoot, but they persevered, acting out the dramatics for those that followed, as much to still their own nerves.

They entered a long room, like a railway tunnel. It had a flat floor and upturned, U-shaped walls and ceiling. There were seats all around, dishevelled, and camp beds that had never been used, but were delaminating.

In the middle were two doors, one to each side. One contained rations from the nineteen forties, and the other, ancient radio equipment, the large communication sets run by valves.

Dan punched the air. "An air raid shelter. Top hole! Now where does the exit lead to?"

They were moving forward, but encountered a mass of thicker than dense cobwebs. Dan used a lighter, but it didn't take out the bulk. Felicity reached into her bag, and sprayed them with hairspray. The effect was dynamic, and they scorched cobwebs upwards, until confronted by a trap door.

Mercer Locke was working in the coach house when he heard banging coming from below. The locksmith had only just breached the old doors, and was attempting to renew security, but with old style fittings. He gathered his senses, and moved towards the sound.

It originated from beneath a section of floor covered by linoleum. Intrigued, he pulled the plastic carpet back, revealing a hatch. It was bolted and padlocked shut. Running fingers over his whiskered chin, he waited for the sound to come again. "There be peoples down there, methinks."

He tapped back to let whoever know he was on the other side, and delved into his tool bag, quickly picking the ancient locks. Tossing them aside, he pulled up the trap door, and saw Dan and Felicity gawking at him. "What you be a'doin' down there then. You'd better come up."

Dan asked, "Where are we?"

"In the coach house. Here, grab my hand."

It was the first time any of them had set foot inside the building, and they hurried to see it all. There were two bays, one with a four-wheeled covered coach, and a second with a two-wheeled open one. Both were well preserved and protectively wrapped. "These would have been drawn by horses. I think we'll find stables on the other side."

The room at the rear had three stables and a tack room, and it faced towards the orchard. The tradesmen were tasked with providing services, water, electricity, and gas for a fire in winter. The builder came down the stairs to the loft and said, "Don't nobody be going up there. The floor's full of woodworm, but it's a decent space. You want me to start on that Ma'am?

"Yes please Sid, quality floorboards and quality work. Get rid of the woodworm, do your best, and we'll see what else needs repairing."

Meanwhile Dan had wandered outside with the plumber. "I know this might not be your thing, but I need a modern septic tank, and could you get the pond working."

"I likes a challenge, so I does. Summut different to be doing. I'll call in experts for the sewage. Best I talks to Sid about it first.

"Get those lads to clear the pond and I'll have a look. I can set up a water feed and aerator unit, and work on an overflow as well. Tell them to be careful with the strange plants, as we'll replant those. I'll ask

Misses Kennedy to drop by and see if there's any rare species. She's into that sort of thing."

"Thanks, I'll have a word with the lads right now."

Cathy provided a buffet lunch at Dan's expense, and afterwards they set about clearing Felicity's house, taking everything to their new home. Percy borrowed Alf's van, and between them, they got her police house cleared by early evening.

Cathy had stayed at Felicity's place, helping them Hoover and clean. Felicity left a kettle and mug with the makings for tea or coffee, and a carton of UHT milk. She also left much of the furniture and cooker, more than had come with the place.

They moved her washing machine, tumble dryer, and dishwasher into the scullery of their new home, leaving a list of jobs for the builder to do in the room. By the time they were done, night had descended, and they were all hungry and tired.

Dan said, "I had hoped to stay here tonight, but we'd find things to do. I propose the same as last night, and sleep at the inn."

Cathy was first to enthuse. "Thanks Dan, that's a big relief for me. Otherwise, I'd be cooking as soon as I got home. Everybody, time to finish up and clear off, Dan's treating us to dinner again tonight."

Chapter 31 ~ Inter-Agency Sharing

Dan was up early on Monday, saw Felicity off, and completed his morning routine. His reports were prepared, but he went to the office for breakfast because he needed a word with Alison and Veronica.

Stella was cooking breakfast, but Veronica relieved her. Trade in the shop was brisk. When she returned, she said, "I'll need a run to the Cash and Carry again Percy, either today or tomorrow. Some items have almost sold out, and others have been requested."

Dan dug into his wallet, pleased with the way the shop appeared to be taking off. "Here's the other six hundred I promised you for stock, and that's your lot. You still refusing to give me discount?"

"You'll pay the full price, just like everybody else. But I only need one hundred of that Dan, thank you. I aim to pay it all back quickly. Mind you, I'll have to pay Cathy for looking after the shop while we're gone."

"Go this morning, Percy, you okay to drive? ... Good, then bring fresh food for buffet lunch. And get an everlasting stew going, it's getting colder, so warm food required. We'll all be here today, I think."

Dan went upstairs and studied the latest developments. "Alison, get me all the information you can regards how Lillyworth Moor operates, especially things like clubs and permits, legal documents and so forth. Do they have a flying club for instance?"

"I'm on it."

"Be quick. I need a hand to play before I report to the Director. Send the results through to me. I'll be at the inn."

Dan received the information, adding it to his report and submitted. The Director came online, as he had expected.

"Dan, they can't just take over an old airbase, get it working again, and run it as a jihad training ground. This is impossible."

"I thought so too, but they've covered all eventualities. Alison has confirmed, just this morning, that they have a licence for a flying club, another for a gun club, and a third for offering dangerous sports. These are all legal, Ma'am.

"The Firearms Act is ostensibly limited to hand weapons, mainly, and their gun club gets around that problem. Did you know there is no law to prevent any of us buying, and using a fully functional tank or howitzer in our back garden? Firing it would be a crime, if any outsider bothered to report it. Out in the wilds of Lincolnshire, I doubt it."

"But this is preposterous. What can we do about it? I need that place shut down immediately."

"No can do Ma'am. We might be able to pursue something regards health and safety, but that's a long shot, and would show our hand. I propose to do nothing, but monitor the place like a hawk. I'll get drones in all over it, and I expect I will need an Arabic translator added to the team, for when I'm not here. I hope you have one ready."

"We will see. Well done with the two girls by the way. You informed Bristol police they are ripping the wrong house apart?"

"I sent a communiqué on Friday, via official channels, to them and the Met, but I have a feeling that will only show up flaws in the system."

"I know your game Dan, and you are correct. The sharing system for inter-agency dissemination of terrorist threats needs fixing. Anything from Bude yet?"

"No Ma'am, and I'm not expecting anything unless they raise a flag, or until they have completed their current investigation. I may pop over to RAF Trimingham, on a personal visit to keep things sweet. I tasked them with monitoring all flights into, and out of Lillyworth Moor. I strongly suggest we get the latest speed cameras on all roads going to the base, but not too close. The Truvelo D-Cam would be ideal."

"Agreed. See to it."

"Ma'am, with the two Bristol suicide bombers, and others Bude will no doubt identify, I think we need to begin working more directly with our main antiterrorist agency."

"That's still the Metropolitan police, and they are trying all ways not to pass responsibilities on to the new National Crime Agency."

"Yes, our formative version of the FBI, except MI5 already have that role. I wish they would all concentrate on the job in hand, and not waste their time building political castles in the air."

"Exactly. Come down here for mid-tomorrow morning, and we'll go and see both of them. No promises how far we'll get mind, but the direction your enquiry is taking means we must begin to include other agencies. I may make a visit to MI5 as well. Until tomorrow, Dan. Ciao."

Dan sat back, wondering what it would take, to get British security forces to react to the obvious, and ominous threat to the entire British way of life. He made a coffee, and returned to his room to think. The only people he perceived to be acting in a way conducive with the threat, were the military, the RAF at least.

He called Bude. "Hello Bernie, how's it going?"

"Ah, Dan. Splendid. We have identified nearly all of those that came into Luton. I need surveillance on that building, everything that comes in, or goes out."

"Consider it done. What about the suspects?"

They talked for some time, Bernie holding back on sending the file until it was complete. Dan knew he was a man that liked to completely finish one project, before beginning the next. Dan came to the reason for his call. "Bernie, did you manage to call a military advisor in?"

"Why, yes I did. That was a great idea. The Colonel will arrive tomorrow morning. You want to meet him?"

"Yes I do, but I have to be in London tomorrow morning, we're meeting the supposed antiterrorist specialists."

"Well, come in the afternoon, he is booked in with us for two days."

"Wonderful, I'll join you mid-afternoon, all being well. Is there anything else you need from us?"

"Not for now, except keep the images coming. You?"

"I'll need more of those latest U.S. drones, set for facial recognition. We plan to blanket cover the British jihad base with them."

"I'll arrange it. Until tomorrow."

Dan smiled, he was warming to working with those who realize the ways of war. His mind turned to the immediate situation, and noticed the hour of the day. He went to the office, where he found the team enjoying early lunch. He was about to tuck in, when Bernie's words came back to haunt him; 'keep the images coming'. The word images reverberated in his mind, until he made a correlation. "Alison, I want you to run all images from the airfields through the best facial recognition software. Those on Bernie's hit list are our main targets, as is tracking them when found. Log and identify all new faces from today, and work backwards to when we began."

"That's one hell of a lot of work. Okay, I can set up a program to run it. I'll need to use GCHQ resources. Who's it for?"

"GCHQ Bude. Liaise with Bernie and Derek.

"I'm on it. Priority?"

"Top priority. Hit this hard and deal with it as quickly as you can, and then continue to update on a daily basis."

Dan looked around the table; "Martin, I want a headshot, body shot, and identification of every single person. I'm relying on you to place drones so every person is accounted for. Interpolate regards niqāb's. If you need more drones, or repositioning, do it, and talk to Alison."

They talked of details and heard the shop bell ringing every few minutes; Stella was being kept busy. She poked her head through to check they were all right, and Dan said, "You have good trade Stella."

"Thank you, I am selling what they want to buy, and I'm a minute's walk from their homes. Told you it'd work. I've also applied to be Postmistress again. It'll save the pensioners going to town."

The bell rang again, and she returned to the shop. Dan hacked off a baton of French bread, split it, buttered it heavily, and pasted a pot of feisty crab spread into the jaw, adding slices of cheddar cheese, coleslaw, and far too much salad dressing. He took a large bite, and coming down from his gustatory high, he noticed others looking intently at him, and his food. "It's delicious, if spirited. Try some," he cut off several slices.

"I'll drive over to Trimingham this afternoon. Percy, Martin, I want you to fly over to Luton and take a selection of drones with you. I need them in the bonded hangar, and on the warehouse, placed for facial recognition as people enter and leave. A bus or van may block the view, unless you can get high enough. Try not to use trees, unless there is no alternative. I remember the yard had floodlights."

Veronica added, "I'll tell Luton when you are due, and arrange a hire car. Let's move upstairs so I can show you on the map."

"Good," said Dan. "Alison, I need speed cameras on all roads in and out of Lillyworth Moor, but not too close. Several miles away would be ideal, just as long as vehicles can't go anywhere else."

"I'll see to it. What type?"

"The Truvelo D-Cam is about the best for our needs, and only we need access. We'll need images of number plates and occupants. If any occupants show up on facial recognition, forward to Bude."

"Martin, plan a drone invasion of Lillyworth Moor. You and Percy will set the drones tomorrow. You'll have to drive there I'm afraid, as I am with the director in London all morning, and at Bude later that day.

"Alison, I would choose to take you with me, and offer your usual digital back-up services. Comment."

"Dan, I would love to go, but I have far too much on. Some of it I will need to show you before you leave. Take Veronica with you, she's fully up to speed, and I'll ensure she has all the information you are likely to need."

"You are with me in the morning, Veronica, and you better print off four sets of the faces we have from Bude."

That afternoon, Dan spent over one hour at RAF Trimingham, without regard his business could have been concluded within minutes, or by phone. His physical appearance led to greater respect and sharing, Dan taking time to understand the operator's problems, and workload.

He also shared with Tom, and they discussed involvement with Bude. Dan mentioned a conference including Bernie and an Army tactical strategist, which Tom found interesting. "Okay. I like the sound of your meeting, and if you give me one day's notice, I'll be there. "

"Great, thank you Tom, but the meeting is set for tomorrow afternoon. You know, when Blighty goes tit's-up, it will be left to the military to respond, and erase the threat of ISIL from our shores."

Tom walked with Dan to his car. Dan said, "Tom, how would you take over a country such as England, given what we know?"

"The same as anywhere, control the skies, the seas, and have an iron grip on communications, the control of information."

"The second phase?"

"Run disruption, like the bombings we have witnessed recently. Tie in emergency services, before the main strike. Cripple infrastructure, including roads, railways, and the internet, but not to the detriment of invasion plans. Where are you going with this, Dan?"

"I'm not sure, Tom. Our recent information indicates they will create small to medium sized Muslin enclaves, which could be protected by forces and artillery from Lillyworth Moor. Whole communities under Sharia law perhaps, but to what ends? This is all conjecture."

"Maybe, but it makes practicable sense. Let me think on it some more. Wait! Dan, I have an old friend, now retired from the SAS. We joined up together. He still lives near Hereford, and was disabled on active duty, but was a Lieutenant Captain when he got plugged. He knows about this stuff, battle tactics, and especially guerrilla warfare strategies. Because of these skills, he has spent most of his career seconded to the Army. I know he still dabbles, and he attends events at Hereford barracks. I'll get in touch with him."

"Thanks Tom, appreciated. I need to put something on the table this week, regards defence of the realm. Everyone seems to be covering their own backsides, and that's not good enough, given the threat we face.

"I worked closely with the SAS, SBS also, in Lebanon, Iraq, and Afghanistan. SEAL's as well. I have, had good friends there. It would be good to meet another that survived."

Tom gave Dan a quizzical look, and wondered what this man had seen and done. Regardless, his smile predominated, and he replied, "In that case I think we should stay overnight, they tend to say more after a beer or two. I'll book us into the Sergeants' Mess. That's the place to find out what's really going on."

Dan shook Tom's hand, then clasped him as a brother. He had short list of the people he could rely upon. Turning abruptly, Dan opened his car door, and never looked back. He had secured more than he came for.

The next morning, the Director, Dan, and Veronica met with the Met's antiterrorist unit. They felt like outsiders, despite their badges and authority. The meeting began badly, and got worse, until Dan reacted. He stood and shouted, "On Thursday, directly due to information my team discovered, we prevented a massacre at a Bristol shopping complex. I spoke to those girls on Friday. Have you?

"They told me something of great interest. Your thugs for colleagues are still tearing number forty-two Acacia Avenue to pieces to no good purpose. That was not where they stayed."

"What? We have witness of them entering that building. How can this be?"

"All I did was treat them as victims, not suspects. I suggest you do the same. They stayed at number fifty-three Salmond Avenue for two nights. Bristol police have been informed via official channels, and so have you. It appears 'official channels' no longer work."

"We have not been informed, which you have a duty to do."

"I suggest you check, sir. Veronica?"

Chapter 31

"Message dispatched at 20:58 hours, Friday, nineteenth of October, precisely, via secure channel communications. I suggest you check your records."

"We have nothing."

"You have not checked, sir."

"Very well ... Apologies, it seems the message was received, but marked junk because the sender, Commander Glover, was unknown."

Dan produced his ID. "I suggest you update your records, sir. Regardless, you were informed, and took no action. This we need to change, and immediately. I remind you, we are supposed to be on the same side, and we are fighting an Islamic invasion of England."

"Your point is noted, Agent."

"Commander. I thought I had just made that plain.

"Now can we move on to the purpose of this meeting, interagency sharing? I have spoken to the owner of the real property the girls stayed in. He is harmless; he believes he helped two runaways. The man behind it was his nephew, Sunil Khan. I suggest you start with him."

At the mention of the name, all eyes turned to look at him, their chief said, "Sunil Khan? We've been after him for months, and he was behind this? That is one good lead, thank you Agent ... Commander.

"I'll see to it that we speak to the girls today, and in the right way. They were kidnapped, raped, made slaves. I can't imagine."

"They chose suicide rather than continue the lives they were forced to endure. They will need to be put in a place of safety, once released. Veronica, a set of photos if you please.

"Gentlemen, these faces we captured entering the country, the two girls are amongst them. Do you know any of these people?"

There was a lot of muttering and pointing. Photographs were grabbed. The chief made a call, and said, "Director, please come with me. The Chief Superintendent wishes to speak with us."

The Director was looking pleased when she reappeared, and they left moments later. Once in the car she said, "That was a brave move Dan, but it worked. We have full co-operation, at least in theory. I think we will be supplying them with information, more than the other way around. But, it is a place to begin."

There next appointment was with MI5, and Commander Miles Cunningham greeted them. The building, its layout and modus operandi, were disturbingly familiar to MI6, as was their hierarchy.

Dan had been expecting this to be a short and barbed visit, but he was pleasantly surprised. The Director opened. "Miles, we have a problem, one we need to share with you. I've just come from the Met, antiterrorism unit, who were less than helpful. Can we speak candidly?"

"Yes Ma'am. We got similar from the Met, yet they are chasing us to identify suicide bombers, and we have little to go on, because they keep all their information internal. They share old news. They are all into their own careers and self-importance as far as I can see."

Dan said, "Miles, can we work together on this, cut through all the interdepartmental bullshit. This threat reaches to the core of our society."

"Yes. I, as Commander, am open to this. We are looking for genuine sharing, but it better be kosher."

"Veronica, please give Miles a copy of my interview tape with the two girls, and the headshots of our latest from GCHQ Bude."

"Thank you Dan, this is marvellous intelligence. True sharing. I'll study the two girls later, when we're done."

Miles began to flip through the images, but stopped and stared at the third, and gawked disbelieving at the next. "This man's one of our most wanted. You know where he is?"

"Yes, Lincolnshire. He's been there for more than one week, running a jihad training camp."

Miles was still searching through the pictures, agog with the information, when he began making calls. Veronica said, "Give me a pen drive … no, no matter, I'll give you one of ours, that way we know we are safe … and zip it is. Here, the files are in digital format."

Dan's Director received an invitation from the MI5 director to join him in his office. She returned some thirty minutes later, and whispered, "It went better than expected. Well done Dan, you rattled them. I think we may just have discovered allies.

"Miles says he will put a small unit together to work with us. Be careful what we feed them with, don't reveal all just yet. Go for the lure … so mix the bait with some good facts. I caution you both, if push comes to shove, we may need them, so think of the bigger picture."

Their last visit, to the National Crime Agency was brief. Turned away they were not, olive branches of future exchange given, and received. The NCA commander was blunt. "I want to help you. We want to be a part of this, but the Met stall us at every juncture. Present me with a good case, which you already have the bones of, and we will open a new file, and department. Until you do, our hands are tied."

Veronica handed Dan the prepared file of headshots, and he said, "Sir, I believe these men and women will feature prominently in the news over the coming weeks. We are trying our best to stop them blowing up towns and cities. You can help us. We need international co-operation, which you can access. We have identified a jihad training camp in Lincolnshire, and five airfields where millions of illegal immigrants are entering this country, each year. I am willing to share what we have, if you set up the new department."

"That would need the sanction of our director, Agent."

"Commander Glover, if you please."

Dan's Director said, "Well let's see her then, Linda I believe. I want this set up as a go before I leave, and we are leaving soon."

The Directors talked alone, before Dan and his opposite number were included in the resultant discussion. A new team would be created once an official brief and operation requirement was received from the MI6 Director.

Pleased with progress, they spoke outside. "Lunch at Saint James', we have to keep our bodies stocked up with nutrients."

"Apologies Ma'am, but we need to be going. I have an appointment in Bude this afternoon, and I must be there."

"Dan, I need a word. Humour me. Let's eat there."

"What, Griggs?"

"No, the side street beyond, it has a great café." They made their way to a table, sat, and ordered.

"Dan, I am being pressured by our budgetary department to reign back spending, especially on your project. Something has to go."

"What's the largest expense?"

"Your plane, by far and away. Not the aircraft itself, which was mothballed. It's the upkeep, parking fees, and servicing it. Norwich airport and the FBO are charging us a small fortune."

"So the options are a small airfield nearby, or my field."

"The latter. I'll pay for the runway, twenty grand. You the hangar."

"Deal. When for?"

"Monday would be good for the books. It must be before the end of the month, which is a week tomorrow."

"It will be as you wish, Ma'am."

He and Veronica departed shortly after, bound for Bude. There, they were presented with the full dossier on all of the illegal immigrants. Many had a long list of flags associated with them.

They were introduced to the Colonel, who was a stiff-upper-lip military type of a bygone era. Regardless, his tactical brain was razor sharp, and with his permission, Dan recorded their briefing. He explained all that he saw in ways they could understand, the elements of defence, attack, regroup, and counter-strike. It all made perfect sense. Dan was offered a full copy of his report, which he gladly accepted.

They spent a little time with Derek, who was already monitoring the new feed Martin had set up at Luton; Bude was happy with progress.

They left a short time later. Dan was ambivalent. "He knows his stuff. But that was battlefield tactics, and extremely good. What we face is guerrilla warfare, and it's not the same. Let's get back. You take the pilot's chair, keep in practice.

Chapter 32 ~ Squaring the Circle

Before work began on Wednesday, Dan called the Sid the builder, and arranged for a contractor to come round and build the airstrip. Dan would need to be there that afternoon to agree on details, payment, and timescale.

He called the plumber, electrician, and gas man, arranging additional services for his to be hangar, and runway lights. He added things Felicity had mentioned, and left them with lists to take care of.

At work, and after breakfast, Dan made a point of putting Alison in contact with their new agency partners, and small exchanges of information occurred. The morning was dedicated to consolidation, review, planning, and monitoring. Alison was working through the latest file from Bude, and left markers for Dan's attention.

Tom rang at midday. "Dan, I just had a word with Lawrence St. John Brown, the Hereford guy I mentioned. He's eager to meet us. I said we'd be there on Thursday afternoon. Does that fit in with you?"

"Yes, that's fine. I'll need to call Hereford, see if they have an airfield or road I can land on."

"Don't bother Dan, I'll make the arrangements. It will be a road with kerbs, so keep the landing tight."

"You need a lift from Trimingham, I should be able to land on your top road."

"Thanks Dan, but no thanks. I plan to leave a little early and have lunch with my daughter in Norwich. You have spoken to her…?"

Later, Dan shared lunch with the team, and headed for his home. He found several teams working on the house, and it was coming along nicely. They had power, water, and would soon have gas to the air raid shelter, accompanied by noxious gas sensors and extractor ducting.

Dan sat in the library, thinking of it as his office, and called London. "Tim, I could do with a private office set-up at my home, one capable of fully interacting with Alison and the team. What you got?"

"You want private use as well? Yes of course. I'll bring two computers down, and put something in place. You'll need secure satellite comm. also. Are you passing through any time soon?"

"Friday late morning, I could pick you up and drop you back."

"Ideal, I'll put your request to one side, and not tell Ma'am, she's going budget bonkers at the moment."

No sooner had the call finished, than Dan was called away. The builder said, "The contract boys have just turned up. I tried to strike a deal with them, but you're from out of town, so they'll want top dollar. Their work is good, without being brilliant, but they are local and have a good name. I suggest you have a word with them."

Chapter 32

Dan greeted Monty Smythe, and they walked the field. Dan was surprised to see a different local farmer turning the grass for drying. As they came close the farmer said, "Should be fair set for bailing on Satday, so long as the weather holds. I don't smell rain, but it'll be close. Ask us months earlier next year. Most of this is only good for silage."

Dan and the construction crew walked the likely path of the runway, and Dan noticed the field was flatter than some he had recently landed upon. It banked gradually, gaining higher ground above the river, but the surface was smooth.

He was having second thoughts when Monty gave him a quotation. It was far too much money to justify the expense. They discussed the matter for a short while. Monty said, "How heavy is the jet?"

"About eight tons, why?"

"You'll never land it safely, it'll sink into the earth, possibly flip over, or tip. What if it rains? Here's the deal. Hardcore, compacted and heavy rollered. Drainage for when it rains. It will need a kerb, but not standing proud, and we'll set it with a channel each side for lights. Twenty grand, and we begin now. Blacktop, another ten grand. Take it or leave it."

Dan realised the man was correct; he would not be able to use the strip if it rained. Dan agreed, and helped them mark out. For an extra tenner, the farmer created a strip of land that was free from drying hay. He said to Monty, "Do your best, and keep it clear, I'll be landing here Friday afternoon. The blacktop better be rollered by then."

"Not a chance. I'll need five grand for a second team, and even then I can't guarantee completion, but it will be close."

Dan agreed, and satisfied wandered back to his new home, the only one he had ever had, and soaked up the tranquil atmosphere. The place had a good feeling about it. The tradesmen were all busy, yet none needed a piece of his time. He returned to the library, and sank into the old leather of his office armchair, such a luxury.

He called Veronica, and the team were fine without him. "Percy and Martin are on their way back. Alison has great coverage and is monitoring Lillyworth Moor in real-time. She's giving me leads to follow up, or forward, usually both.

"Good, so you don't need me there."

"No. Alison has a wedding. She mentioned it to you I believe, so she needs a long weekend away, and she deserves it. I'll cover for her, but want the same the following weekend, catch up with my family, it's my parents pearl wedding anniversary."

"That's fine, great. You all need to rest. Tell Alison to leave Thursday late afternoon, but she'll have to arrange her own transportation. Same regards Martin, but a normal weekend off for him.

I am overnight in Hereford on Thursday: SAS. I'm back late Friday, and will be busy. Even so, I'm only a phone call away."

Veronica pressed her point. "So, this means we get four days off, every two weeks. I can work with that."

Dan's brow creased, and he replied, "I'm not sure that is precisely what I said, Veronica."

"Accepted emergency needs of the job excluded, but this is what we need, and you better sign off on this. Man up Dan, I know you will."

The handset went dead, and Dan stared at the phone for several seconds. Veronica was correct. Dan called Alison and said, "Thank you Alison, for everything you have done. You mentioned a Bridesmaids party on Thursday evening. A Hen Night. Leave when you need to on Thursday, and have a great break."

"Wow! Thanks Dan, you're wonderful. Catch-Yah."

Satisfied he could still man manage, well, woman manage people, he called his prime number expectantly. The call rang out, followed by a brief text message, 'Ten minutes Dan. Meeting.'

Dan used those minutes to speak to the gasman, asking for gas fires. "The nights are growing colder, and winter is approaching."

The man replied, "Sid told me the radiators will be online by Friday morning. I'm already ahead of you regards the fires. Knew you'd ask. I'll install some today. Where do you want them?"

"Big ones in the living room and library, and same in the master bedroom. I'm hoping she will be here tonight, so I want to surprise her."

Dan's phone rang. "Hi Felicity, how's it going?"

"Heavy, and I have too much to do. Tell me something nice."

"The plumber has fitted the new bath, although I still don't understand why we need two dozen jets in it. The gasman is fitting fires, and I was thinking to cook for two. I miss you."

"Me too. Sod this, I do need to clear my mind, but I'll be leaving early in the morning. I'll be with you after six. Stick a leg of lamb in the oven as soon as you can, and I'll be there to help with the trimmings. You are a wonder. Love you, Ciao."

Dan gawked at the phone, mouthing, to himself, she said, "Love you". It was getting serious between them, even if her words were said offhand, flippant. After deliberating on the idea, he welcomed it.

Dan checked the Aga, and went to the butcher's, the farther one that was better for lamb. He returned and put the buttered and herbed joint in the oven on low, and peeled potatoes, leaving them in soak. The builders called an end to their day, and Dan joined them for a pint at the nearest pub.

He did not stay long, but long enough, paying for the next round before he left. He parboiled potatoes for roasting, and set them in the tray of lamb, turning the heat up slightly so they would be done sooner.

He prepped the veg, and took a full glass of Chianti from the refrigerator. It was nicely chilled.

Just after six o'clock, he heard a car in the drive, and poured a second glass, before opening the door and welcoming her into their home. Their kiss was passionate. She went upstairs to run a bath, commenting approval of the gas fires already warming the home.

After dinner, they cuddled up on the settee in front of the fire, listened to music, and chatting casually. Dan had been hoping for a night of passion, but Felicity said, "I should have come on, yesterday. I only had a dribble last month, so I think it's already much too late."

"You're a day late, that's normal."

"No Dan. Do you love me?"

"Yes, of course."

"Then say it. I love you. I mean that."

At that moment Felicity's phone rang. "Work need me to attend the rape and attempted murder of a young girl." She relayed the information as she donned her police jacket and headed for the door.

Dan was immediately wary; commitment scared him. His mind was full of questions and denial of facts. "Filly, how late are you?"

She fixed him like a sharpshooter, and said, "I run a Moon cycle: twenty-eight and one-half days. Period."

She grinned at her pun. "One day, and one month. I've never been more that one day late before. I think we need to choose baby names."

Her speech trailed off in the comfort of knowing she had at last, managed to share her fears with her chosen partner. Dan closed the distance between them. That she could still feel his body, protectively embracing her own in acceptance, allowed her to move on. But she still needed him to fully commit to their relationship, especially with a baby, probably, on the way.

"Dan, we have much to discuss, but tomorrow. I must go. I'll be back. I need you to deal with this … Daddy. Ciao."

Dan's mind somersaulted as he watched her leave. He considered, and then reconsidered the situation and implications. He wanted a drink, but in celebration or commiseration, he did not know.

Thinking back, he knew the moment. Norwich, and accepted full responsibility. Felicity had given him the choice, and he had chosen.

His mind was already made up. He would propose to Felicity, the only indefinite was when. That had just been refined to 'soon'. Coming to a conclusion, he felt a warm glow inside. The word 'Father' resonated through his brain, and he drifted off to sleep on the settee.

Felicity did not return that night, but they talked briefly on the phone. Her case was a bad one, and his heart went out to her.

Dan worked a full morning. After early lunch, he drove Alison to Norwich train station, and met Tom at Norwich airport. They headed off for RAF Hereford. Their arrival was interesting, as the road allotted them for landing was straight, but narrow, with large kerbstones to either side.

Dan made the landing with accomplishment and, following road signs, toured to park outside the Sergeants' Mess. They were greeted by the duty sergeant, who looked at them suspiciously, until Dan recognised the man, and striding over said, "Chuggers, is it you?"

The man's face cracked wide in acknowledgement. "Dan, great to see you again, and looking so good as well. It's been a long time, seven years. How're you doing?"

Dan introduced Tom, and they went inside. They talked about old times, and later, a few others he knew joined them.

Near dinnertime the Commanding Officer popped in to greet Tom and Dan, and offered the Group Captain accommodation in the Officers' Mess, which he accepted. Dan was offered the same, but said, "Thank you sir, but no. I need to spend time here tonight. I know many of the lads from Lebanon, Iraq, and Afghanistan. It would be good to catch up with them, Sir."

"You're here to meet Sinjun, I believe. Great man. Great shame about his injury. He's your friend I believe Group Captain."

"Tom, Sir. Yes, we enlisted and were trained together, more years ago than I care to remember. You'll want to know why we're here."

"I have been informed, but let me take you up to the Officers' Mess. We'll get your room sorted, and then we can have a little chat before dinner. You're the C.O. of RAF Trimingham I understand..."

With Tom taken care of, Dan took the first opportunity to go to his room. He knew the boys would soon be drinking, which was not his thing, and he needed to check in with his team. He spoke to Veronica, who sounded self-assured and in full control. "Alison has already arrived in Brighton. We're fine, but busy. I'm teaching Martin my job, and he is teaching Percy his, so that's fun."

"Good. I'll leave you to it."

Dan stayed in his room, and called Felicity. "Dan, thank you so much for last night, it was wonderful and gave me a terrific boost. The Chief, Karen, and I, all officially move up a rank next Thursday, the first of November, but that's impossible regards the physicality of our jobs.

"The Chief is running through his job, with me, today and tomorrow. I'll have to stay on Friday for a bash they are holding, and doubt I'll be with you before late Saturday morning. They'll expect me to drink like they do, but given the baby. I'll take tonic water, but no gin.

"I'll stay the weekend with you, and train Karen from Monday onwards, until she's comfortable in her new job. There's a lot to being a station commander she has no experience of. That will give us a few evenings together in our home.

Chapter 32

"Dan, she officially moves into my old house a week today as well, but I know she's planning to relocate tomorrow. If you're around, could you drop in on her and check she's Okay?"

"Sure, but it'll be late afternoon before I'm free. I could ask Cathy to come down and help out."

"No, unnecessary. See you soon. Mwah!"

The phone call had just ended when a rap came at the door. "Sinjun has just arrived, Sir."

Dan departed moments later, and met Tom entering the building. They greeted Sinjun, and the old friends caught up, including Dan in their conversation, as often as possible. The meal was a typical mess affair, but it was good and filling. It was almost one hour later, the meal all but complete, when talk turned to the reason for their meeting.

"Dan, Tom tells me you need some assistance with a terrorist plot, guerrilla warfare tactics and countermeasures."

"Yes, that's correct, Sinjun. Let me explain…"

Dan delivered an overall brief of what they were facing. Sinjun almost laughed at times, before realising Dan was deadly serious about the threat of the Islamification of England, major parts of it at least.

Once up to speed, Sinjun was straightforward in approach. "Do you have a video of this supposed jihad training base, Dan?"

"Yes, here on my tablet. This is the feed from two days ago. You can zoom around using these controls, and fast forward or replay. This copy is low resolution, the original hi-def, but it's what we witnessed."

Sinjun smiled at Dan, indulgently at first, before becoming fixated by what he saw. He began to fire arbitrary questions at Dan, and Tom, sometimes speaking aloud as his mind worked. In time he looked up, an extremely worried frown below his furrowed brow. "Dan, this is a nest of vipers. See this here? This is a checkpoint, a roadblock. And here, those are defensive positions. Back here, these are anti-aircraft missiles. They are practising defending territory, towns and cities perhaps.

"I'd need to spend a few days analysing the original feed, but this scares the shit out of me. I thought you were just having me on, but my God, man. I'd like to come over and run a full threat assessment, if that's okay. I still do them for the SAS here, but it's all unofficial nowadays. Sometimes I feel like I've been stuck on the scrap heap, but I am still one of our country's best at this stuff."

"Okay. Come back with us in the morning."

"No, I need to be here this weekend, and prepare on Monday.

"I'll collect you from here, nine a.m. Tuesday, otherwise travelling between here and Norfolk will be a nightmare."

"I greatly appreciate that Dan, until Tuesday."

202

Chapter 33 ~ Tangible Threat

Dan settled into his home office chair late on Friday evening, and sipped from a glass of rum and coke, as he reviewed the week's events. He had just got back from settling Karen Wheeler into Felicity's old house, and she had made a favourable impression.

Dan proceeded to record verbal notes for appending to his log, and sat back satisfied. Apart from Felicity being away, his life appeared to be perfect.

The central heating was on and working, and the jet was parked at the top of the field. He would need to sort out a hangar quickly. The landing had been bumpy, but better than some he had experienced, if because the landing strip was not fully completed. Ma'am in London was extremely happy. Tim had set up a work computer, one for personal use, and had also installed state of the art Wi-Fi, so everything worked together without wires, including his tablet and smartphone.

He wanted to ring Felicity, but knew it was the wrong call. She would be half drunk, and playing police games with her higher ups. He sent a text, and was surprised when she left a voice message a short time later. "Dan. Miss you. Tonight is going well, and not too many drinks. I could probably come home, except I'm over the limit. See you early tomorrow. Love, Filly xxx."

There it was again, the "L" word. Dan downed his measure, and sat back in the glow of a spirit-warmed stomach. He was troubled, so played mind games with his emotions, speaking aloud other associated words, and reflecting upon their significance to his current relationship: "Marriage." "Children." "Baby." "Commitment."

The bottle was half empty, and his torso sprawled across the desk, when the builders arrived the next morning. Dan felt like hell, and sprinted for the nearest toilet. Sid was waiting when he returned, examining the remains of the bottle. "You'd not be a drinking man then. I'll get thee a bacon butty, have thee right as rain in no time. She'll be here soon, so take a shower and change. What brought this about?"

Dan looked up bleary eyed and said, "She said she loved me."

"Ooh, now that's very serious. 'Appens to us all sooner or later. She's a keeper you know, and the perfect partner for you. Not that it's any of my business. Just saying."

Sid watched as Dan ate two hot sandwiches, washed down with a large mug of sweet tea. Sid ushered him upstairs to shower, smiling as he watched Dan depart. He said to the others, "There'll be a wedding soon, mark my words."

Sometime later, Felicity bounced onto the bed, waking Dan out of his slumber. He had only lain down for a moment after his shower. She twisted his chin towards her and said, "Sid tells me you are in love with me."

"Er. I don't know. I've never been in love before, never been loved by anyone. I was adopted remember."

"So, do you think about me often?"

"All the time, except for work."

"And you miss me when I'm not here, right?"

"Yes of course. I love being with you."

"So it's the sex you are after from me then."

"No. Yes, but not exclusively. I like having you around, to cook for, make a home. I don't know how to explain. I would rather be with you anywhere, than be on my own anywhere else. Does that make sense?"

"Perfect. So how would you feel if I wasn't here?"

"I don't know. Lonely I guess."

"Do you love me?"

"I guess so."

"Not good enough, Dan. I'm pregnant with our child! I'm leaving, heading back to Norwich, where I will remain until you decide if you love me, or not. Our relationship has everything a marriage could wish for, except your commitment. Time to man-up, Dan."

Dan watched her rise from the bed, suddenly feeling insecure. She avoided his lunge, and hurried to the door. Turning as she went through it, she said, "Goodbye Dan, forever."

Dan was mortified. His stomach lurched, as he felt the bottom drop out of his world. He stumbled into a pair of trousers, doing them up as he ran barefoot after her. She was closing the car door as he ran towards her. The engine started, but the window wound down, she was waiting for what he had to say: "I think I love you."

"Not good enough. Goodbye."

She began to reverse. Dan flung his torso on the bonnet, his hands gripping the wings to stay with her. She stopped and looked at him, waiting.

"Damn it Felicity, I LOVE YOU!" The last three words were shouted with emphasis.

She smiled and replied, "You'd better hang on while I park."

She drove back up the drive, and into the spot she normally used. Getting out she helped Dan off the bonnet and said, "There, that wasn't so hard, was it. Much better. I love you. Never forget that."

Dan grabbed her waist and kissed her hard on the mouth, the kiss quickly becoming more passionate. Behind them, a cheer rose. All the workmen, and the neighbours next door were watching them intently. Some were clapping, others whistled and cheered. Felicity said, "Looks like we did the right thing. Now, put on some shoes and help me empty the boot. I went shopping this morning."

Dan finished dressing, called to check on Veronica, and carried lamps, small tables, and ornaments into the living room. Felicity had bought several sets of wall lights, and told the electrician where she wanted them.

Three six-wheel lorries arrived in convoy, navigating through the garden. Stunned, Felicity said, "What's going on Dan?"

"Ah, they're for the runway. I better check on progress."

"What runway?" Felicity ran after him. "You landed a jet here? Why?"

"Ah yes. The jet. I'll need to use it for commuting. Work you know."

She gawped at it. Dan said, "Why's it over there?"

A worker said, "We had to get the farmer to tow it out of the way, as you left it in our road."

Dan did not miss the pun, but said, "My road actually. The old bird's sunk into the grass a bit. I'll need a word with Monty. Find him, and I'll go and get Sid. I need a hangar over there."

The outcome of their convoluted conversation was that the hanger would be built side on, allowing entrance one way, and exit the other. Monty would run a depth of hardcore as a loop, allowing the jet to turn around. Once agreed, Sid talked to Dan about the building itself, which was the next priority.

Just before lunchtime, Felicity and Dan paid a visit to Karen, who was busy sorting out her things. While Dan shifted some heavy boxes for her, Felicity leaned in and whispered, "Dan, get her out of this room, and talking about her education. I need to take photos of pictures."

Dan rolled his eyes. He turned and focused, "Karen, please show me exactly where you need this putting."

"On the dresser."

"Yes, but which dresser? There are three of them."

On the way upstairs Dan said, "So how come you ended up in the police force?"

"I could ask the same about you and MI6."

Dan told her. "Your turn."

"Well, I went to Anglia Ruskin University. It's one of the top three Uni's for Forensics, and close to home. I got my Bachelor there, and went on to do Criminology at Masters. I'd hoped for a glamorous job, but the reality was, only the police were interested in me. The pay and conditions, plus the pension were much better in the force, so I signed up. Took me ages to pass the promotion courses though. You have to remember the quotes from law verbatim.

"You weren't tempted to party like most, have a boyfriend?"

"No, I'm all about work and bettering myself. My personal life is my own business."

Chapter 33

"Apologies, I was simply trying to make conversation. We best get back to it. What's next?"

Later, Dan invited the women for lunch. He called in work first, and Veronica said, "I have some flags, and think you should be here. I'm not sure what's going on, and was about to call you. Something is happening. Oh, a secure message just came in from Bude, excuse me. See you soon."

Dan looked at the women, who were watching him intently, and said, "Work. I have to go in right now. Something's up. You can stay here and carry on, or drive up when you're ready. I'll eat at the inn. I must leave now. Sorry."

Dan departed immediately, leaving both women worried. Karen said, "Is this about work, my new job?"

Felicity replied, "Yes. You'll need to catch up quickly, as to what your new posting is all about. Ready when you are."

"Let's go."

Felicity briefed Karen on the way, but she was almost in shock when she realised they were confronting the Islamification of England. Felicity said, "I'll run you through it chronologically, when we get there."

Dan escorted the women into the ops room. "What's happened, Veronica?"

"One of the world's most wanted men, a leader for ISIL, has just been identified by Bude as being in charge of operations at Lillyworth Moor. He came in this morning, accompanied by a ton of weapons and militia. They're about to launch something big. What, and where remain the only questions."

"I'm on it, anything else?"

"Yes, my worry from earlier. Two girls and a woman, who were part of those you first recorded arriving at Luton, are currently in a car travelling towards Leeds. That may not be their final destination, but it is looking more than likely."

"Send me the feed. And ask Percy to come over, I need him on drones."

"Left channel Two."

Dan studied the motorway camera footage. The two women got seats either side of him, and watched events unfold. The car took a road that led to Leeds city centre, and Dan called the Director immediately. "Ma'am, presumed city centre bomb attack in progress, Leeds. Two Boko Haram girl suicide bombers, one controller, and one man driving, presumably controlling her. After last time, they will ensure the girls do not surrender. Which agency should we notify? I prefer the senior Leeds police officer. Time is short. I would like to stop them before they reach the target, save lives."

"Good work Dan, leave it with me. I think we should tell all of them, and gauge their response. I'll speak to the Commander at Leeds first, the Chief Constable, and the others in turn. You are certain about this?"

"Yes Ma'am. There are further details about this threat, and others immanent, on the way to you. You have the live feed?"

"Connecting now. Ciao."

Dan activated two large drones from Sheffield, the nearest to target, and set them on a straight course for Leeds city centre.

He was completing his interim reports for the Director, when Karen left to use the toilet. Percy came in moments later, "Hi Dan, Ma'am thanks for the call, that sister is driving me crazy. I think I need a fishing hut down by the river. What do you need me to do?"

"How good are you with drones?"

"Well, I'm okay with the big ones, and also the little one that detaches. But I need to do them one drone at a time though."

"Good enough. I have two Sheffield drones airborne, and need you to land them in Leeds city centre. Find a large mall in the city centre, and set them one to each side."

Veronica said, "They're on Boar Lane. The largest shopping centre is Trinity."

Percy said, "Adjusting now, yes, drones are close. Dan, I need a city streets overlay map."

Dan said, "Press Control, Alt, and M together."

Veronica said, "They just went underground from Commercial Street, they have a floor underneath."

Percy said, "Almost with you. Large drone parked on the outside, light drone released, following inside. Ooh, the car stopped just inside the ramp. The two girls got out, and the woman is following one of them. You want me to follow them, or the car?"

"Follow the car Percy, I'll pick up on the others with the other drone set. Well done."

The vehicle drove to a central point, a concrete pillar beneath the building, and the driver got out, locking the car with a bleep and flash of lights. He took a suitcase out of the boot, and walked east, before being challenged by security. He shot both guards dead, and walked on.

Dan called the Director at once. "Confirmed Ma'am, this is a terrorist strike. Who have we got on the ground?"

"No one except the local beat bobbies. It's the weekend. There are football matches, plus a protest march, so nobody is available. I have already notified the Home Office. How long till the shit hits the fan up there?"

"Five, maybe ten minutes, and I'm expecting the strike to be in waves, Ma'am. Take out first responders and so forth. I think there are others we have not discovered yet. Sorry, have to go … Damn, Saint

Trinity Church. Call them and tell them to evacuate, our man is heading there with a large suitcase. Ask somebody to break a fire alarm. We need people out of there pronto. Out"

Karen left for the bathroom again, and Percy needed something from his car. He returned a few minutes later, followed shortly by Karen. Eyes turned to look at her. "Sorry, nervous stomach, I couldn't eat breakfast. I think I need to eat something.

Felicity took her to the kitchen, where they hastily assembled a tray of snacks and drinks. They returned just in time to witness the outcome.

The Boko Haram girls had left bombs on timers in many shops, and when the public evacuation was at its peak, blew themselves up at the main exits, taking hundreds of lives with them.

A little later, the car bomb took out the main support pillar. Floors above descended. The building collapsed from the inside out. The destruction accounted for the lives of many survivors of the first blast, and emergency responders.

Meanwhile, the Church had been bombed, and any inside were shot dead. Before setting off the bomb, the terrorist had beheaded the Priest. He then poured petrol around to increase fire damage, and left by the front door. Security lost him going into another shopping complex. They continued searching, but Dan saw it as a distraction from their work.

After the incident, Felicity ran Karen through what they had discovered, showing short clips as required, and the new girl became extremely worried. "Can't you just take them out?"

Dan overheard, and answered. "That is the next stage, which is quickly approaching. Before showing our hand, we need to learn everything about their operation, in Europe as well as UK. These people are not stupid."

Later, they took dinner at the inn, and Percy spoke to Dan aside. "That Karen. You sure about her?"

"Yes, she's kosher. Why?"

"Well, she's been acting a bit strange, and before I came in, I saw her enter the bathroom. As I passed by, I heard the bleep of a modern phone's keypad. I waited, and she was writing something long. I followed her the second time, and it was the same. No noise except the tapping of digital keys. Want me to keep an eye on her? Although it's probably nothing, but just made me wonder."

"Yes Percy, thank you. But be discrete, I know you will be. There could be many reasons for her actions, most of them trivial and normal. She's in a new place, and doesn't know anybody, except for us. She's riding a promotion, as station chief as well to boot. Keep this very low key, but also keep your nose to the ground."

After dinner they went home, and Veronica returned to work. Felicity wanted to slob in front of the TV, but Dan was insistent. "What was all that about earlier. Taking photographs of pictures? Why?"

"Dan, don't. I'm not sure yet."

"Then why take them?"

"You're impossible!"

"Give."

"There was one from fresher's week, I think her second year, and she was an item with a boy. I think I know who he is, the Chief Constable's son."

"Ouch! Have you checked it out?"

"No, not yet. I'm not even certain, but it reminds me of the graduation photo I saw of the young man once. It was a while ago."

"The answer may explain the mystery, as to why her promotion application came from the Chief Constable's Office. You should have told me sooner. I need the image, now."

"But Dan, it is probably nothing."

"I know you well. Yes it is something. Send it to me now, please."

Once received Dan called Veronica. "I need the male in this image identified. I have clues if you need them."

"Not necessary Dan, how urgent?"

"Now would be good."

"Check running … His name is Wilfred Mainwaring, nickname 'Wild Will'. Her name is Karen Wheeler, more coming … it seems they were an item at Ruskin, for the last two years at least. That's it, except that this Karen in now the local chief of police. But you already know that, don't you. She was here today."

"Yes. But I needed independent corroboration. Thank you. It's time you finished for the night."

"Yes, just one more thing, and I'm done. Wild Will is the son of the Chief Constable of Norfolk."

"Thanks." Dan cut the call, and said, "You heard that on speaker?"

"Yes, the all of it. It explains why Karen got the seal of approval from the Big Chief, presuming she kept in good relations with the family. I've no problem there. What about her request in the first place? Why would anyone want to come here? There's more to this."

"When we were upstairs, Karen mentioned doing a Masters at Ruskin. I'll ask Veronica to follow up."

"No Dan. This one's mine, I just have a feeling about it, okay?"

"Just one day. Let her pull any links so you know where to focus. In the meantime, I'll make a pot of coffee, and then I must get to work."

That evening, Dan outlined a profile of Karen Wheeler, and compiled several reports, one concerning the strike on Leeds.

In summary, he made critical remarks about the lack of any tangible support, as even the fire alarm was triggered a long time after he requested it. MI5 had responded with two agents, and one of them broke the fire-glass. But they were in no position to affect the outcome to any great extent. The NCA and MET never appeared, blaming Dan for lack of prior warning.

This led to Dan writing a second report, condemning the fact they had no resources to respond to future threats. He offered suggestions, one being a tie into the military. That was the response they needed, a platoon or two of SAS, ordinary troops for that matter, soldiers on the ground, taking appropriate action, in liaison with Dan's unit.

Dan had just begun a third report when Felicity came in, bringing him a coffee. "Care to share?"

"I'm hoping to get these off to my Director this evening, a present for her morning. You want to run your eyes over what I've done so far, I'll print-off?"

"Sure, it'll keep me in the loop as well. You have mentioned about taking the airfields?"

"No, not yet, that's what this report is about. I think we need to carry on like this for another week or so, as new discoveries are being made daily, especially regards their overall objective, or plan A. But Karen was correct, we do need to take these airfields out sooner rather than later. When we do, I intend to capture as many of their planes as possible. Leaders and personnel also. Put a big dent in their operation.

"Felicity. Sweetheart, no need to run the checks on Karen for her Masters. Veronica found something that worries the shit out of me."

"I got nothing. Gimme."

"The Masters degree she took was a two year course. It was one of the few that put people in jobs. Her closest friend was Benaris Khan."

"What? The same Benaris Khan, as in Inspector at Wymondham police station."

"One and the same. I have photographs of them together, outside school. They appeared to be overly friendly."

"So that's why she requested the promotion here, the real reason."

"It looks that way. I think they had something going on, and it may, or may not have been physical attraction."

"More like mental subversion to the cause of Islam. I'm on this Dan. Thanks to you, and Veronica. At last, I have something to get my teeth into. Now is the time for you to butt out, and let me take this from here."

"Deal. Do I get a kiss for that?"

"No, a kick in the balls. Except, follow me upstairs."

The next morning they were snuggling awake when Dan's mobile rang; "Yes, Director."

"Dan, this latest ball dropped by the MET and NCA is most worrying. I am about to create hell, all the way to the top if needs be. I may need you here today, or on Monday morning. Prepare a full analysis."

"Yes Ma'am. So many innocent lives could have been saved, if only there were a dedicated response team in place. These attacks are becoming frequent, every other day. Now we have a handle on when some may occur, and can track them, we need to react quickly.

"I noted your point about taking over the Muslim controlled airfields, and this is a high priority, but not this week. If this Sinjun fellow is the business, ask him about attacking the bases. We need prisoners, information.

"Now, I need a file, the video of the bombers leaving their base, and I know you now have a direct link with the office. That was naughty of you Dan, but I caught Tim when he returned, and made him tell. I may turn a blind eye, or maybe not. You'd better be on your best behaviour."

"Ma'am. I'll send the file now, anything else you need?"

"No. I should discipline you, but you are the only agent I have that's coming up with the goods. Damn you."

"Ma'am, always a pleasure."

Dan gave Felicity a kiss and headed for his office in his dressing gown and slippers. File sent, he found her in the kitchen ten minutes later, a pot of coffee percolating, and bacon and eggs in the frying pan. He tried to canoodle her back to bed, but the moment was passed.

There were no builders, it being Sunday, so they set about home-making. Evening came quickly, and they dined simply, and tarried before bedtime. The coming week would be hard on both of them.

Seemingly abstract, Dan said, "I love you."

Felicity was reading a magazine, but looked up sharply.

"I know that, now. I didn't yesterday morning."

"I think we should go to bed."

"Are you suggesting you want to make love to me, or make love with me?"

"We don't have to do it you know, but I missed out last night, and this morning."

"Men! You didn't answer my question."

"'With', of course."

"Better. I'll go up now and have a bath. Join me when your drink is done, and if I'm still awake, we'll see what happens."

Monday came with a rush, Felicity engaged with handing over her old domain cleanly to Karen, whilst Dan was gripped within the intrigues of responding physically to the Muslim threat.

Chapter 33

Karen had asked for a moment of the Chief's time, and brought a folder to the desk as they sat down to share. Felicity glanced at the title, upside down: 'Wymondham'. Immediately, Felicity's phone rang, and she was called away as prime officer to oversee a serious incident in Norwich. She departed within moments.

Dan was by then, already headed back to London headquarters regards policy decisions, and the strike back at ISIL on British soil. The Director and he had rehearsed their respective roles before each of several meeting, the last one just below Cabinet level. Dan played his part admirably, was intense, with precise oration, accompanied by relevant facts.

The Director was pleased when they finished, but Dan was not. "We still haven't seen the people in charge, and our instant response team will linger under the thrall of snail-paced bureaucracy."

"What do you suggest?"

"Going to the top. Regards the United Kingdom, Her Majesty the Queen is the head of the Armed Forces, but in name only. The most senior officer is the Chief of Defence Staff, currently Marshal of the Air Force, Sir Jack McBride. I may be able to get to see him."

"It's worth a try Dan. We have nothing to lose, as long as you keep this confidential, which I know you will. Anything else?"

"Yes, we are now facing a tangible threat, and need to respond with full force. Our problem is action by the right people. The military. The handles of power regards the armed services are a bit muddy. The Prime Minister and Defence Minister are actually in charge. We need to see the latter."

"Good point. I'll see if I can arrange a meeting. No promises, but we have to try, at least get the word out, worry people in power. You're here tonight I understand. Dine with me. There are some people I would like you to meet.

"Now, please hone your plans for the scenarios we discussed earlier, and cover the objections we heard today. Come to my office for seven-thirty, and we'll go in my car."

Chapter 34 ~ Ayesha's Escape

Ayesha stood at the sink in Rosie's kitchen, and thought back over the last few months. The old woman had helped her tremendously, finding her a room, and a job nearby with a seamstress, Joyce Smallwood. She had been learning the trade, practicing evenings, and in spare moments between other tasks.

The girl glanced at the sewing she had set aside while she prepared Sunday lunch. After tasting the beef dish, she adjusted the seasoning and took up her needle, as the meal slowly cooked.

She had settled well and quickly into her new life. The large village she lived and worked in was just west of Norwich, and was gradually becoming a commuter town. She was not rich, but was able to pay her way, and put a little savings aside.

Since visiting Rosie on her first Sunday off, Ayesha went round every Sunday morning, and while the old woman was at church, she cooked Sunday lunch. Both were grateful for the meal, Rosie for the company, and Ayesha relished a full stomach, and the safety.

On Monday, Joyce asked Ayesha to run some errands at lunchtime. The trade supplier was late, again, and they desperately needed thread for a rush order. A book of modern wedding dress patterns had also arrived for collection.

There was a short list of other things, as she would have to travel to the nearby shopping centre. This was a regular Monday occurrence, and Ayesha looked forward to the adventure. She bought the supplies for work first, the shop being the farthest away from the entrance, and stopped at the supermarket to buy things on the list. She bought herself some treats as well, keeping the bills separate.

She had looked round a couple of times, feeling she was being followed, but there was never anybody there. She even looked at reflections in stainless steel surfaces, but no one was watching. Her mind was playing tricks on her.

She left the store and was headed for her final destination, a delicatessen Joyce liked, when she heard the voice of her cousin. She dashed into the nearest shop, quickly hiding herself from view.

She watched him walk past. He had three others with him, and she knew those men were enforcers. She realised they were hunting for her. She also knew she must complete her duty. So checking they were out of sight, hurried to the delicatessen, and placed her order. She paid, and was soon making for the main exit, and freedom.

She got outside and glanced furtively around. Two Pakistani men were leaning on a barrier, chatting. One looked up and their eyes met. He said something to the other, and started to chase after Ayesha. The other made a phone call, before joining the pursuit.

Chapter 34

Not knowing where to run for safety, she saw two security guards, and ran full pelt towards them, shouting to get their attention. They turned to look at her, noticing a burly man closing on her, and went to her assistance.

Ayesha blurted out, "They are going to kill me. I ran away from a forced marriage. They will execute me. Please. Do something. Help me."

The guards reacted at once, standing between her and the man. As one of them called for support, the other put his hand out to stop the man, and ask him his business. The Muslim thug advanced on the security guards with menace. Ayesha ran for her life.

The guards soon had the brute in a wristlock. However, his accomplice joined them, and the other guard had his work cut out to try to make an arrest.

They heard shouts and looked up. Others were coming to assist; Ayesha's cousin led them. When they closed the distance, the cousin drew a gun, and told security to back off. They refused, seeing their own help coming in from behind.

The gun fired, narrowly missing Ayesha. He fired three more times, killing both guards, and the brute in the wristlock. They ran off in search of Ayesha, who had disappeared. No passersby had seen her, or were letting on, even with a gun waved in their face.

Sirens could be heard in the distance. The cousin called a retreat, and they headed for their cars. They were almost clear of the car park when a police van rammed into them, and armed police with rifles surrounded the Muslims' cars. They were all taken into custody. Ayesha remained missing.

Meanwhile Ayesha had made it to the car park, and had scurried away from the threat by dodging between vehicles. She saw her pursuers reach their vehicles, and panicked. They would drive round looking for her. She found a Land Rover with an unlocked rear door, and scuttled inside. By the smell, it was a farmer's vehicle.

She poked her head up from time to time, and saw her cousin's car head for the exit, and witnessed them being stopped and arrested. Her heart flooded with relief. She was about to get out, when she heard a noise nearby, and someone unlocking the driver's door with a key.

She hunkered down, the vehicle started, and moved forward. She wanted to escape, but the vehicle was going too quickly, and it left without stopping at the public road.

Ayesha didn't know what to do, except stay put. She worried that if she got out at traffic lights, she would be lost, or others would recognise her. She decided to stay aboard, and sneak away after they arrived at wherever they were going.

After twenty minutes, the last two quite bumpy, the Land Rover stopped in a farmyard. The driver got out, and opened the back door. He stared at her.

Gabbling, she said, "Those men, the shooting. They were after me. Wanted me dead. I had to run. Sorry I am here. Nowhere was safe. Please, just let me go. Where am I?"

The man straightened himself, and looked down on Ayesha, a stern look in his eye. His brow furrowed, and he said, "Why were they wanting to kill you?"

"Sir, I ran away from a forced marriage, mutilation, it is horrific. Had I not done so, I would now be the slave of a man I detest. I would also be his mother's servant. I just want them to leave me alone. I am British, and think like you do. Please, just let me go."

The farmer's expression lightened. "Ah, so thee be a damsel in distress. Come, let's have a cup of tea and sort this out."

He held out his hand to her, and she skipped down from the rear. He insisted on carrying her shopping, saying, "This is man's work. Watch your feet. There's cow shit all over the yard, so don't you be treading in it and walking it into the house.

"Now, where are you from and who were those men?"

"I'm from Luton originally. I escaped, hopped on the first bus that came along, and ended up in Norwich. Those were bad men. My cousin had the gun. They were after me. You do believe me?"

They entered the farmhouse, the door leading straight into the kitchen, and the man said, "Beattie, found a damsel in distress. Being shot at she were, down at that there shopping centre you sent me to. Never knew she was aboard till I got back. Fix us a cuppa, there's a love."

Ayesha settled, the warm tea and buns fresh from the oven warming her stomach and her heart. They talked, and the wife said, "My name is Beatrice, but call me Aunt Beattie, everybody does. Now dear, you can't stay here, you know that don't you. But we need to keep you safe. Fred, have a word with the local bobby, he's sure to know about the shooting. I heard about it on the wireless, and was worried about you. Not that I'd tell you, of course."

Farmer Fred Scully did as his wife suggested, and spoke on the telephone for several minutes. When he returned he said, "They're sending a female policeman out from Norwich, but it may be a while. Here, let's have a fresh pot of tea, this one is getting old. I'll put the kettle on."

Chief Inspector Wigglesworth was attending the mall crime scene, when she received a call from her duty sergeant. "Ma'am, something strange just came in. Old Fred from Hall Farm just rang the local nick, and he says he has the girl at the centre of today's shootings in his kitchen. Apparently, she's on the run from family in Luton, escaping an arranged marriage and FGM. He asked for a WPC. How should we respond?"

"Does she have a name?"

"Ayesha Hussein, Ma'am. "

"Okay. Send Carol out and bring her back to the station … wait. Ayesha Hussein. Luton. I wonder? Give me a minute, Will."

Felicity rang Dan's office, and Veronica answered, "Hi, can you look back through Alison's files re Luton. I remember a girl being mentioned in one of the reports, an Ayesha Hussein, please check this out immediately."

"Searching now … got it. The file is more of a fragment, but Ayesha's brother, Waheed, reported most of our information. It's a missing person report. She was due to be forcefully married to a mister Mohammad. The report says she refused FGM, and I can't blame her. She ran away, and there's been no trace of her since."

"I think I just found her. What are her father's, and her prospective husband's father's, full names?"

After a few moments, Veronica began to speak the names, but stalled. "Oh my God! These are the directors of Mohammad, Hussein, and Ali. I'm checking for mistakes, but this is a plumb bull's eye."

"Confirm as soon as you are certain. I am acting on this now, so be quick. Is Dan there?"

"Sorry Ma'am. He was called to London. Something is going on. Didn't he text you?"

"Maybe. I haven't checked my messages. Too much happening on the ground, but I knew it was likely. Tell me Percy is with you."

"Yes, he's practicing flying drones. Martin is helping him, and he's doing really well."

"Good, put him on."

"Ma'am?"

"Percy, I need you to meet me at Hall Farm, Fred Scully's place. It's just outside of Lower Meddlington's jurisdiction, but we've been there before. I need you to leave at once, this could be most important. Ciao."

She made another call. "Will, cancel Carol, I am going out there in person. I am out of contact, unless of emergency."

Felicity took a moment to flick through her messages. Most were unimportant, but she read Dan's, noticing he signed off with 'love you, Dan xxxxx."

She smiled, knowing her ploy of Saturday morning had moved their relationship forward a great deal. She had been worried about her gambit, but needed him to commit fully to their relationship, especially with a baby on the way.

Her thoughts were interrupted by an Inspector. After giving orders she got in her car and departed for Fred's farm.

When she pulled into the long, dirt track drive, she saw Percy pulled aside, waiting for her. She signalled him to follow, and they avoided the cowpats in the yard on the way to the kitchen door.

After introductions, Felicity spoke to Ayesha in the parlour, where she took an initial statement. There would need to be another, when all the facts were known. Percy chatted to Fred and Beatrice, enjoying oven-hot buns washed down with fresh, sweet tea.

An hour or more elapsed, as Fred and Percy swapped stories of times passed. The women reappeared, and Felicity spoke. "We'll head back to the station, and I'll arrange accommodation for Ayesha. Thank you, Fred, Beatrice, you have been most helpful, and made the correct call. I wish there were more stout-hearted people like yourselves in this world. We won't overstay our welcome. Percy, time to go."

Felicity stopped her car at the end of the long and dusty drive, and spoke to Percy. "I'll find somewhere safe for the girl, she's been through the mill."

"Then take her to the inn, or better still, ask Stella to give her a room. She has enough bedrooms in that house of hers, and it's close enough to keep an eye on, but far enough away from our operation. I dare say she could help out in the shop, as Stella is always having to call on Cathy, and others."

"Under consideration. Thank you Percy. I need you to go to where she has been living. Here's the address. I need all her personal belongings brought out, and the bill for final settlement. I also need you to see the seamstress nearby, who was her employer, and deliver these bags. Tell her Ayesha won't be back, and little else. Make a molehill out of a mountain. I know you can, even it involves a white lie. Needs must."

"Yes Ma'am, I'm on my way. Oh, Inspector Wheeler spoke to me earlier, wanting me back on my old beat."

"Did she now. I'll have a word with her. Percy, consider yourself seconded to whatever I, or Dan, need you working on. I will make an updated, and official requisition in the morning. You work for me only. You are one of the best I have ever known, at dealing with people, their emotions, getting information. And I trust you, a rare commodity nowadays."

"Thank you Ma'am. There's one more thing, and it's probably not important." Percy glanced at his pocketbook. "It's just that Stan said, 'She often comes in to examine my archives, which are almost in order. She has asked some odd questions, as if she has foreknowledge, but never tells me anything. Sometimes I know the files have been tampered with in my absence, as if somebody has been looking at them. Only she and I have a key to the room, well, except for the spare key in the main key press. I'm getting a bit wary of her intentions'."

"That's strange. I'll look into it. Go, I'll see you tomorrow."

Felicity had a dilemma, she needed to keep Ayesha safe at all costs, but thought Stella's house was too close to Dan's operation. If she was a mole … well, there was no need to invite the fox into the henhouse.

On the other hand, the family had tried to kill Ayesha, and most definitely would have done so, if they discovered her whereabouts. The girl was bitter, especially after discovering she was adopted. 'Bought like an animal' were her exact words.

Felicity finished her considerations. She knew of places in Lower and Upper Meddlington that would suit well, but tongues would wag and Ayesha's safety could not be guaranteed. The village was the right place, but working in the shop much too close to home.

They chatted for a few minutes, Felicity ensuring the girl had a modern and Western outlook on life. Once satisfied, she made a call, and drove off, saying, "I may have found just the place for you. I'll take a follow-up statement from you another time, let's get you safe first."

Felicity drove into the village, but parked at the side of the inn. She went inside and spoke to Brian, an agreement was reached. "So, I fix the girl up with a small room, and she helps in the kitchen, or where needs be. I'll see if she can cook a decent curry, been asked for that a time or two I has."

"Thanks Brian, you won't regret this. Let's get her inside and settled in. She's very western in her outlook. I owe you one."

Chapter 35 ~ Pulling Strings

Dan collected Sinjun on Tuesday morning, and later the Brigadier was introduced to the team. He asked for an office, so Dan took him to the dining room, which had all the facilities needed.

Sinjun was soon at work, studying the videos they had on file. He would conference when needs be, and took meals with the team. He worked late, and was otherwise reclusive, except at the bar in the evenings.

Dan popped in to check progress every now and again, but Sinjun had already said, "With this amount of work, and detail missing, which I will need to discover, it will be Friday at the earliest, before I have this plan wrapped up. This must be a cohesive effort, timed precisely at each target, to effectively take them all out. I'm including Lillyworth Moor."

As Sinjun worked, Dan caught up with the team. Alison was back, extremely chirpy, and regaling everyone about her exploits. She was distracting until another face they recognised from Luton, left Lillyworth Moor, and immediately work took focus.

This time Dan called the Director as soon as the car was spotted, the occupants again, two girls, a female, and a male driver. They were headed due west. The Director followed up immediately, and reported back. "Dan, I told all the same people, copying those we met on Monday. It appears somebody gave the Met's anti-terrorist unit a rocket, because they are mobilising and taking notice."

"I'll keep you updated Ma'am."

"Expected. I am bringing up your live feed now."

Alison said, "Dan, the Met's dedicated liaison is asking for our feed as well."

"One moment Ma'am. Give it to them, and also update as we find out more. We need to identify the target."

"At the moment, that is looking like Birmingham, but until they turn off somewhere, it could be anywhere west."

"Understood. You heard that, Director?"

"Yes. I hope the Met are up for this. I'll ask them to fly up to Birmingham, so they are closer to the action, wherever that may be."

"We better warn the Chief Constable trouble is likely headed his way."

"I'll call him now, Dan. Forewarned is forearmed. Ciao."

Time passed as the team monitored progress. Alison said, "Dan, they've just turned off onto the M40, headed south."

"That means the city centre in not the target. Options?"

"Birmingham International airport. Otherwise the National Exhibition centre, possibly Solihull. That's about it, unless they're taking the long route to Oxford, or say Bristol."

Chapter 35

"It has to be the airport. I need the Met ready to intercept."

Moments later Alison looked up concerned. "They're still in London."

"What! Imbeciles. I was informed they were en route to Birmingham airport. This is a disaster. Call the Chief Constable of West Midlands immediately. Let's see if we can limit the damage."

Dan spoke at once with the Director. She called him back moments later, "Apparently they were waiting, ready to go, but would not leave until the target was identified. So, instead of being stationed at Birmingham International Airport, they are one hundred miles south."

Dan shared sharp words with the Director, both of them at a loss to understand the Met's lethargic response.

West Midlands Constabulary had an armed response unit standing by, due to the earlier call. They responded immediately by despatching a team of the best anti-terrorist officers to react to the threat. They had not arrived by the time the car did, but were closing fast.

The Director called Birmingham Airport, and told the Manager to put the entire airport under immediate evacuation. The manager stalled, until his own security reported the car pulling into the airport.

Dan called, and said something odd to the Director. "If you want something done, do it yourself, or choose the right personnel for the job. Without military, I think we should call the Press."

"Good thinking Dan. I have several contacts, and will call them at once. I won't say too much, but just enough to get their feet on the ground. I wish our security services responded as quickly. Ciao."

The outcome was not as bad as Leeds, but the radical Islamic extremists slaughtered twenty-four people, and bombs devastated the terminal.

The Met's forces arrived long after the threat had been dealt with, and mopping up operations were in progress. The Chief Constable, who was on site, told the Met exactly what he thought of their totally inadequate response. He had been briefed by the Director, and was intent on reporting them for gross dereliction of duty. He would take his case as high as he could, threatening court action. He demanded they leave at once.

The outcome was a proposal that Dan had left for the Director's attention on Tuesday evening. Using the guise of the National Crime Agency, they would recruit a quick reaction force, and cut the Met out. They had proved useless on two occasions, and innocent lives had been lost, directly because of their inaction.

Dan was late home, tired and weary. His heart immediately lightened when he saw the lights on, and *her* car parked in its normal place. He went in the back way and grabbed her for a kiss, even though she was cooking.

She gave him a peck on the lips, before saying, "Not now Dan, the sauce will go all lumpy. Shower and change. You look like shit. Rough day?"

"And the rest. We were following the Birmingham atrocity, and should have prevented the massacre, except the Met stayed at base to twiddle their thumbs and toes. We are removing them from our sphere of operations, hopefully, putting real responders in their place. Enough. The rest was as is on the news. What's for dinner, sweetheart?"

Dan nuzzled her neck, until she biffed him with a stirring spoon. "Back off Dan, shower, change, and you'll find out what you are eating in due course. Leave me alone, but do try out the bath, it's amazing."

Dan did as instructed, and took a bath. He played with the jet controls, and loved the massage effect on his tired muscles. It was fitted with a heater, so the water didn't go cold, and he was almost dreaming when Felicity came in and poured cold water over his face. "Time to eat, lover boy. Five minutes, or it will spoil."

When Dan hurried downstairs, the table was laid with a bouquet of flowers, and soldiers of just-toasted bread. Butter and pâté were close by. She joined him, pouring Spanish red wine for both of them, which was moreish, and suited the dish.

Some minutes later, she served steak with Café de Paris style sauce, Dan's medium rare, and hers medium. She had added French fries, raw onion for Dan, butter-fried mushrooms, fresh salad, and coleslaw. Her final addition was a sliver of Stilton cheese, slid into a flap cut on top of the meat for the last minute's cooking. It was delicious.

They finished the meal quickly, Felicity taking a bowl of ice cream, while Dan tucked into cheese and biscuits. Replete, they washed and dried up, and settled hand in hand on the sofa.

Dan said, "I should make my report, but could do it in the morning, I'll be fresher then. The meal was sumptuous, thank you. Tell me about your incident. A shooting so I heard."

"Humph. It would appear to be of little worth. Muslim hoodlums targeting a girl, determined to kill her for insulting their family honour. Those cretins have zero conception of honour, if you ask me. But never mind. I went to see the girl. Percy was there also, and she proved to be most interesting…"

Dan listened intently, becoming alive and engrossed as Felicity reached her bottom line. "The girl is Ayesha Hussein, the daughter of the Hussein we are investigating. She was due to marry Mohammad's son, an alliance. She ran away from the forced marriage, and FGM, and they found her near Norwich.

"She is now at the inn, and working for Brian in the kitchen. We both need to speak to her. I needed her close and safe, but not too close."

Chapter 35

"Good call. I'll make her acquaintance tomorrow evening, maybe stay at the inn for a curry, if she is cooking real Indian curry, and you are not here."

"Pakistani curry actually. Posh people now call that Tandoori. She told me she makes excellent curry, so give it a try. Otherwise, no. Tomorrow I'm in Norwich, and for the rest of this week. I'll be back late on Friday, and it's your turn to cook."

"Ma'am. Beans on toast, my pleasure."

Felicity hit Dan playfully, and somehow during attack and defence, they ended up smooching in embrace. They went to bed early, both shattered, but in loving mood.

The next morning Dan was up well before dawn. He exercised, showered, and started his report in the library. His main intrigues were requests to contact every Chief Constable in the United Kingdom, and Eire, and give them advance warning of what their team were about. He reasoned that in future, should the Director or he wish to speak to any Chief Constable, as a matter of utmost urgency, it would be expected, and not come out of the blue.

Felicity cruised into the room. "I made a fresh pot of coffee. The other was acid. What're you doing?"

"Making the request we contact every Chief Constable in the land, today, so they expect our call."

"Good thinking. Okay, but run it by me first. There are certain keywords that either work for, or against you, regarding Chief Constables. The ones I know of, I can generate more precise input."

"Will do, thanks. Now where's my kiss?"

Felicity gave him a smacker on the lips, but pulled away before his arms enveloped her, she knew where that would lead. Minutes later she read his report, and made subtle changes.

"That should do it for most of them, but key me in on these four, I have prior knowledge that will help you. Here are my notes on them"

She wrote the names and inside information on a pad. "I must go, I need a word with Inspector Wheeler, before I set about my new job in earnest. She's treading on my toes, wants Percy back on his old beat, and I have seconded him, at a higher level than before, for us. Take him with you for the meal tonight. He knows Ayesha. Love you, Ciao."

Dan saw Felicity out, and watched her leave, waving as her car disappeared out of sight. Returning to his desk, he reread the report, and sent it to his Director.

She was on video moments later, furious about the events of the day before. "I have demanded to see the Minister for Defence, and I will not accept 'No' for an answer. This is too pernicious to leave to the fools in Whitehall. You suggestion is bull's-eye, thank you. I'll be contacting all

Chief Constables this morning, and see as many in person as I can. I will need Alison with me, and your plane."

"Why not take Veronica instead, she has a pilot's licence."

"So does Alison. I guess you never asked her."

"No Ma'am, I did not. Are there any more secrets you would care to share?"

"No, not just now. It was in her file, the full file that is, which you did not request. I hear you have a girl who could turn out to be important."

"I believe so, and so does Felicity. I will begin at dinner this evening, and take it slowly. We need to turn her to our side, and she is halfway there already, or so I am told. I need to take this at its own pace, Ma'am."

"Seize the golden egg, not kill the goose before she lays it. Understood. Good luck.

"Oh Dan, I almost forgot to mention. The NCA are seizing their opportunity of a power grab re terrorists, and are pressing ahead. The Met want to send a liaison officer to you. What do you think?"

"Too early. Let's establish a working relationship first, or otherwise they'll be here to milk our information for their own rewards."

"That's how I read it. You could replace me one day, if you stay sharp. I have a message I must take.

Dan heard the dead air of hold, but the Director was back within seconds. "I'm off to see the Minister for Defence tomorrow at ten. I need Alison on backup, so send her to me. This is our golden chance to change things. Toodle-Pip."

That evening Dan finished work late, but interagency communications were beginning to flow, at last. He walked down to the inn with Sinjun. "How's it going?"

"Not bad Dan, but I still need a few more days to put everything together. I have almost done the five airfields, so could give that to you tomorrow morning, except I don't like to work that way. Sometimes, something else comes into the mix that changes things, such as Lillyworth Moor. That is proving to be a big undertaking. I like to deal with the all of it in one fell swoop."

"No problem. So tell me, how did you become an Army Brigadier?"

"Ah, I spent a long time seconded to the Army. The promotion came after the injury that almost killed me. I had friends, and was a Lieutenant Colonel in those days. They needed me off the battlefield, so promoted me to a backwater office job as Colonel. It was boring, but I had always been good at tactics. I volunteered for several courses, vocational ones. I read books as well, watched instructional videos, and learned a great deal. It suited me.

Chapter 35

"I would still be there today, except Bush and Blair decided to invade Iraq, a sovereign country, and without UN sanction. Today's world would be so much safer if they had not. Then imbeciles Cameron with his French counterpart, invaded Libya, and got rid of Gaddafi. We live with the results.

"If they'd gone after Saddam during the first Gulf War, that would have been acceptable, but this was yet another invasion of a sovereign country.

"Do you know the real reason why Saddam invaded Kuwait?"

"To get their oil, and reclaim an area of Basra taken from them in nineteen twenty-two, by the British drawing lines on world maps."

"Not even close, Dan. He invaded Kuwait to eradicate the powerfully rich moguls who were sponsoring terrorism in Iraq. They are still doing so to this very day. Who is the main funder of ISIL? Think about it."

"Qatar."

"Yes, today. The moneymen fled there from Kuwait. To Saudi also."

"That's one hell of a sideswipe, Sinjun! So, what we know of is a smokescreen?"

"Yes. If Saddam had succeeded, the likes of Al Qaeda and ISIL would never have become established. Today, the Middle East would be at peace, and we would not be worrying about ISIL invading Europe."

"Sinjun, I'd write this off as the drink talking, but we haven't reached the pub yet. Yet you became Brigadier?"

"Yes. To answer your next question, I was sent into Afghanistan as a military advisor. The position demanded a promotion, one I did not deserve. I was in the right place at the right time. That's all there is to it. I am extremely good at planning military strategy, all the same."

"Okay. So how does someone in the RAF, end up being and Army General? Did you jump ship?"

"He-he-he. No, it was by chance actually. I was then with the SAS, whom are mainly comprised of Navy Marines by the way, but run as if they are secretive Army teams. The short answer is, I was seconded, and that became permanent. That do for you? We're almost at the pub."

"Yes, time for a beer." Dan stayed at the bar for the first pint, but Sinjun liked a drink, and excusing himself, Dan wandered over to a quiet table with Percy. "We're still working Percy, although in convivial surroundings. I intend to eat curry tonight, one cooked by a girl you know. Care to join me?"

"Err, no Dan. Thanks all the same, but I love the Shepherd's Pie here. You plan to speak to her, here, tonight?"

"No, not so fast. Just lay down good foundations. That is, if she can cook."

224

"Ooh, Brian told me she is one of the best staff he's ever had, he's thinking about paying her, regardless of if her curry takes off."

They ordered one pint later, having shared and caught up. Dan asked Gwen to send the girl to him, as he wanted to order a special dish. She arrived moments later, a flutter of nervous twitches and gesticulations.

"Relax, Ayesha. I want to order a curry tonight, but I would like one to order. Can you cook me a Dacca Chicken?"

"Oh, that's Indian cuisine. I only have the spices provided, so it won't be fully authentic, but close. I need to go shopping."

"Ayesha, after what happened, well, you know you can't leave this village, it's not safe for you."

"Yes, I understand."

"Give Percy or me a list of what you need, and we will get them for you. I presume Raj brand is acceptable, I have seen it locally."

"Yes that's fine, thanks. I know how to do your meal, but may have to look at the recipe book. It is slightly milder than Bombay style, and has a hardboiled egg in it. Yes, my Uncle liked to eat something similar, so I can do it for you. He also liked vegetables in the mix as well, long beans, broad beans, okra, and potatoes."

"That sounds splendid. Set me up for a large uncle meal. I'll need rice, and Chapattis or roti, whatever you call them, four large ones."

The girl scrunched her apron and took a ragged breath. "How do you know my name?"

Percy kicked Dan's foot, and said, "I told him. He's a very good friend of mine. We have no secrets here."

Dan added, "Talking of secrets, the police woman that brought you here is my girlfriend, we live in the nearest town."

Several of the team tried Dan's curry, and soon requests were made for similar, mainly chicken tikka masala and naan bread. "I don't have the ingredients for those yet, but will let you know when I do, a day or so only, hopefully."

The meal Dan ate was gorgeous, and he told Ayesha so, without lying or embellishing. She was an excellent cook. He passed the word to Brian, and told him to put Uncle's curry on the menu.

Dan went up to his room just after nine, leaving Percy to enjoy, or not, drinking with Sinjun. He called Felicity and they chatted for some time, before she said, "I'll need to take a second statement from Ayesha now we have the full facts, how's she settling in?"

"Very well, she cooked a great curry for me this evening, and I will be having another soon. Hold off on the statement until the weekend, and we could see her together, say on Saturday. I'll probably need to spent time in the office. The reason I say, is that I will profile her later tonight, and that will govern the best way to approach her."

Chapter 35

"Okay Dan, I'll leave you to it. Love you, Ciao."

Dan said similar in return, the call ended. He read Ayesha's complete file, and then looked for answers to questions that played on his mind.

He knew Felicity was looking to wrap things up quickly, but that didn't work for Dan. He read the girl differently, and thought there was more to learn from her. But then, he possessed profiler experience his girlfriend did not.

He started a new profile concerning Ayesha, and concentrated, until he got thirsty. He headed for the bottle of rum, and then turned away disgusted with himself. He went down to the inn's kitchen to make a milky drink, and returned with cocoa.

The profile took much longer to complete than he expected, and he was late to bed, the clock broaching midnight before his head hit the pillow.

Chapter 36 ~ Growing Concerns

Thursday came with a rush. Dan only just completed his morning schedule, before breakfast at the office. Alison had already eaten, and was packing a small case. "I need to leave in five-minutes, Dan."

Stella was serving Percy's breakfast, but he said, "You eat this Dan, I can wait for the next one."

Dan gulped down his food, and managed to drink half of his coffee, before Alison appeared, anxious to get going. They arrived at Dan's house, and he showed her the plane and runway. "You cannot be serious Dan, that's far too short."

"You'll be airborne before half way, trust me. You want me to fly?"

"No, I'll manage. See you later."

Dan watched Alison take off, and she made a good job of it, if taking a little more distance than he did. He spoke to the builders next, all that were left. The plumber had moved on, leaving a few final fixes to be made. The electrician said, "This will be my last full day Dan. Everything is sorted, except for the final three jobs, and that should be one day's work."

"Thanks. But four jobs. I need state of the art, lights for landing, activated by the airplane. Like a car garage, but for planes at night."

"Ooh. Interesting. I'll need to buy in resources, a geek maybe. Mobile phone? No, satellite, yes?"

"Correct. Both is fine. I need this soonest. Today would be good."

Sid the builder was busy, but gave a quick review. "We should be out of here by the end of next week. Some of my boys have already moved on to other jobs. I have the hangar to complete, for which the sections of should be delivered tomorrow. The coach house loft has a new floor, but there's about two days work inside."

"So the house is virtually done, except for the attic. Do you also do decorating, as the walls at least need painting?"

"Yes, but for this amount of work, I'll arrange for contractors. Ben Croxton's team are about the best in these parts. Expect them next week.

"Regards the attic, which Madam wants as her own space. That will take one week, as she wants a larger window to the rear, window lights in the roof, and stairs leading up. She wanted a small kitchenette up there, so we'll have to raise the plumbing to a higher level, but the waste is already fitted, as are water pipes leading in."

"Is there room enough for a toilet come shower, if that is possible?"

"I'll see to it. Anything else?"

"Make that French windows, if you can put a balcony on the outside, wide enough for a table and chairs, a small room actually."

"I know what you mean, and it will be done. Dan, sorry to mention this, but cash flow is a bit tight. I could do with an advance for the cost of materials. The hangar was a considerable amount of money, but it will be jet engine proof."

"Okay, I can give you cash now."

"We are talking in the region of twenty-thousand pounds."

"Okay, I'll write you a check, will that do?"

"Admirable. Now, we will press on to complete the job, but skip Saturday, as I am needed elsewhere."

Dan left the builders to their work, satisfied with progress. He was about to return to the office, when he drew Ayesha's shopping list out of his pocket, along with his car keys.

He made a trip to the supermarket, finding everything on her list, and adding items they needed at home. Returning to the village, he stopped at both butchers, and the bakery, buying fresh for lunch, and for home use.

Dan delivered supplies to Ayesha. She was delighted. "I'll make up base sauces in advance. All restaurants either do that, or buy in pre-mix, which is awful."

Dan lingered to chat, working on his profile, but making it fun for the girl, his subject. She moaned. "I'll never be able to live a normal life, or return to college, and I loved my studies. I want to be a scientist. Look at me now, a cook, and afraid to go out of doors."

"You wear western clothes, speak English the way I do, but your hair gives you away immediately. I know it is your tradition, but you need to consider cutting it off. Dying it blonde. I'm not telling you, but think about it."

"But my hair, it is my culture. We never cut our hair."

"Exactly, that is why your people will always recognise you, regardless of what else you do to your appearance. Anyway, that's up to you. Spend the rest of your life living in fear if you wish, when it could all be gone within an hour spent at the hairdressers."

Dan glanced at his phone, pretending a message had come in on vibrate. "Sorry, I need to go, but will see you later. Oh, and ignore what I said, it was just a thought. Bye."

As she watched Dan walk away, Ayesha wondered if he was right about cutting her hair, but she would need to think deeply about that. It was central to her values. An odd thought struck her, one she said aloud. "Huh. What use are the values of my culture, if I will be murdered for being born female, as soon as I return to it."

Dan was also thinking as he left the inn. His ploy appeared to go well. He needed Ayesha to distance herself, as she perceived herself, from the Muslim community. He knew the hair cutting was a big thing, and would wait it out until his, or her next move.

Dan had only just reached his office when the phone rang. It was to be the first call of many that day. "Felicity, what's up?"

"The ceiling."

"No, the sky. I'm outside the office."

"Damn you! Today is my official promotion, along with the Super and Chief Super. Well, I know them well enough, and I'm convinced they're throwing a surprise party this evening. Can you make it?"

"Er, yes, at the moment. Islamic strikes excepted. Say around six-thirty at your office."

"Thanks. I feel great today, knowing it's now official."

Moments later, Veronica was bringing him up to speed with the early morning events, when Alison came over comm. "Veronica, we are about to go in, meet the Minister for Defence. I need dedicated support while we are in this meeting."

"Copy. We are all waiting on you. You'll be fine."

Dan's mobile rang, and he picked up immediately. "Yes Tom, what can I do for you?"

"We found something odd overnight, and I'm not sure what it means. I'm going to send you the feed of our recording, and all I ask of you is to look at it, reach your own conclusions, and come back to me."

"I'll have a look right away. Tom, while we're on the phone, is there any way I could meet the Marshal of the Air Force? I know it's a big ask, but what we are facing is horrendous. We tracked both Birmingham and Leeds strikes, and nobody responded in time. The reason I ask, is that Sir Jack McBride, currently Marshal of the Air Force, is also the Chief of Defence Staff."

There was silence on the other end of the phone. Dan could hear Tom breathing, while he considered the request. In time, Tom replied, "You believe this is a threat to the very fabric of our nation."

"Yes Sir, I do. It is a tangible threat, and one due any day now. I believe a major atrocity will be committed on our soil. I do not as yet know what that could be, but I believe what they have done so far is only the tip of the iceberg."

"I'll see what I can do. Leave it with me. I'll also need reasons, so send me a supporting file, with links to full information. Come over for Sunday lunch, so we can go through it together."

"Thanks Tom, Wilco. Ciao."

Dan began making notes to outline why he needed a personal meeting with the Marshal of the Air Force. He had made good progress when the Director called via secure satellite link. "Dan, I hate politicians!"

"What's up, Ma'am?"

"We laid out a great presentation for the Defence Minister, and do you know what the nit-wit said? 'We'll take this under consideration'.

"I told him straight, 'If there are any more of these atrocities that we have foreknowledge of, then I hold you personally responsible for the innocent, civilian deaths that could have been so easily avoided, if only you'd man-up and face a very real and present danger'."

"You have balls, Ma'am, it appears he does not. Well done."

"We did not stay much longer, and we were politely shown the door. Once I get back to the office, I'll start on the Chief Constables. I'll keep Alison for that as well. You should have her back for tomorrow morning. Thanks for listening, I just needed to let off steam, and you were it.

"Oh, and both Belgium and Luxembourg have general elections today. Keep an eye on the outcome. I have a bad feeling. Ciao."

Dan realised it must be hard at the top, especially when expectations were so needlessly confounded. His thoughts were turning to his proposed meeting with the Marshal of the Air Force, when Veronica said, "I have the Met's liaison on the secure line again. They want to visit us. What do I tell them?"

Dan took a moment, lounging back in his chair, considering carefully the implications. He even profiled the group situation quickly, and made a decision. "Overall, we need the Met fully onboard, and they do not understand us, yet. Tell him to be at Norwich airport for eight tomorrow morning, and that he will return as soon as we are done. I expect that to be before five p.m."

Veronica was a few minutes, as Dan got back to his work in hand. She said, "We've exchanged work mobile numbers, sent to your phone. Do you need me to make the pick up?"

"No, thanks. I am in Norwich tonight. Felicity officially became a Chief Inspector today, and they will have a party. She wants me there. You have an image of the man?"

"Woman. Being sent to you now. Her name is Wendy Colbert, and she has rank of Detective Constable."

"Fine, I'll be there. Why is it women always end up in admin?"

"Perhaps because we're better at it than men. It's all in the details you know. Plus we have better memories."

Dan looked across, his male ego affronted, needing to reply. Veronica had her head down concentrating on work. Dan received a message, and let the moment pass. He also needed to work.

Time passed quickly, Percy perfecting controlling multiple drones, while Martin surveyed Lillyworth Moor in greater detail. He also monitored Luton. When a flight came in, Martin flew a small drone inside to get better footage. On one beam he found electrical wiring, and said, "We have drones that will charge off a cable. We need a couple in Luton, inside the warehouse."

Dan was overly gruff in reply. "See to it."

He finished the sentence he was working on, and apologised. "Martin, I didn't mean to be so abrupt, please do it. This is your operation. Let's do this together, you on controls, and me monitoring. We need to log the installation, camera angles, specific placement."

"Sure Dan, hop aboard. This is what I plan to do…"

After discussing Martin's plan, Dan said, "Good, Martin, I'm impressed. Fly down tomorrow morning, or take the car. The latter would save money, as the Director is on budget watch at the moment. Take four miniature drones, and place them later, when you are able."

"Great, thanks Dan. I'll leave them on the roof, and monitor if needs be. That's as close as can be, but out of sight. Next time the doors are open I'll work to our agreed plan. Oh, and driving down is fine, I hear your runway is rather short."

Dan seldom multi-tasked as regards work projects, but he was viewing Tom's recording, and making notes regards the Marshal of the Air Force sequentially. One or the other would catch his attention, and he would swap interest for the moment.

Dan put his notepad away, so he could focus on the video. Something was nagging him. Because of darkness, it was difficult to define precise detail, but large military type trucks were offloaded from six cargo planes. Tanks and howitzers loaded.

Concerned he said, "Martin, can you enhance these images?"

"Yes, although Alison has the best software."

Veronica chirped in, "Let me have the feed, I'll see what I can do with it."

Martin and Dan discussed what they saw. Veronica sent them her enhanced version some minutes later. The images were much clearer. Martin exclaimed, "Dan, those trucks are carrying SCUD D's. I also make out anti-missile batteries. These are strange weapons to be bringing into our country. Why? They need to defend something?"

"Wrong. SCUD's are offensive weapons. The question is, what are they going to target? These SCUD's have a range of over seven-hundred miles, and deliver a large warhead via operator controlled targeting."

"Look, four of the planes took off again, and landed at the other unofficial airports they use. These must be to protect their airfields."

"Agreed, and the other two?"

"Somewhere else. I'm stumped."

"So am I, but we need answers. Crikey, is that the time. I must call Tom, and then get going for Norwich.

"Tom, I've looked at the video, and it's bad. They landed SCUD D missiles on mobile launchers. Veronica is sending the enhanced video through to you as we speak. I'll run this past Sinjun, see if he can figure out what's going on. I must run. As you know, Felicity was officially promoted today, and they're having a party in Norwich."

"Yea Gads! This is most serious, Dan. Add it to your request, with the enhanced video. It gives me a far stronger hand. Speak later."

Chapter 36

Dan stopped by to have a word with Sinjun, who said, "This changes things." He quickly became absorbed with the enhanced feed.

Dan left for Norwich as soon as he could, knowing he would be late, but Felicity seemed not to mind. The one thing he needed to finish, the request to the Marshal of the Air Force, remained a collection of notes, and that was his most important work. He dictated into his mobile on hands-free, as he drove, covering most of the points needed to put into written format the next day.

The party was not a surprise, but Dan arrived just as things were getting going, and he was not the last to attend. Felicity enjoyed the evening, but they saw a window to escape, and took it. She had a call of duty, a robbery with violence she could attend, or not, and used it as an excuse. They spent twenty-five minutes at the crime scene before heading to her hotel.

"They haven't given you a flat yet?"

"No. The incumbent is being medically retired, and that might take years to come through. I have requested an alternative solution, but know I will be living at home. It's the only viable solution."

As was their habit, they were both early to bed, early to rise, but running late. Felicity manned up to face her first full day as Chief Inspector, and Dan buffed her ego. They departed together.

Later that morning, Felicity was busy. She had received the results of her probe into the histories of Karen and Benaris. She read the memo, then spoke the important parts aloud. "They joined at the same time, and went on the same initial police induction and training course. There are few other notes, other than both had Master's qualifications in police work, and were flagged to be looked on favourably for promotion."

Her thoughts coalesced. "I'll need to contact our training school. No, that might raise flags. Instead, I need to make a phone call."

Felicity called George Lovell, and later spoke to John Stonehouse. "I can get the personnel files and course records for you, on these two, but why? And especially with Inspector Khan being under suspicion."

"Sir, please indulge me. It may be nothing, but I have a coincidence I wish to pursue. Let's just say they knew each other from before joining the force. I need to establish if that interconnection is working today. If it is, it may explain why she volunteered for Lower Meddlington."

"I trust your judgement, and you have no fact of any worth at present. Okay. The files will be with you later today, but keep me in the loop. Do you suspect a fifth column?"

"No Sir, perhaps a honey trap, or Cat's Paw."

"Run with it, but keep me updated. Excuse me, I have to go."

Chapter 37 ~ Ahoy MI5

Dan was early to collect Wendy Colbert from Norwich airport, and they chatted amiably on the way to the office. During the trip, Dan filled her in on what they did. Alison had returned that morning, so they indulged the newcomer, but only up to a point.

They both helped Wendy settle in at a strange computer, and showed her previous attacks. Dan ran through their view of the latest at Birmingham, pointing out what the Met had, and had not done. Wendy said, "It's so obvious when seen from here. They let you down. All those lives could have been saved. Oh my God."

Once Wendy understood how the team worked, Alison helped her bring up secure feed with her operations staff, and settle in to monitor.

Veronica said, "I got another one. Lillyworth Moor headed south. Similar occupants: two girls, one woman, and a male driving, traffic cameras coming up now. This time they're using a white Transit van. I'm not sure why, but there must be a reason. Perhaps to pack more explosives in the back?"

Dan said loudly to Wendy, "This is where you step up. I will need your team ready for takeoff pronto, and see if we can save some lives this, the third time around."

Wendy appeared overawed at first, but settled when Dan, then Veronica, helped her through what was going down.

Alison said, "They are on the M1 headed south. London could be the target."

Dan spoke to Wendy. "I'm glad you are here right now, you will learn what we do, and witness events unfold. Normally at this point, we would call you, and other agencies, to prepare, and hope somebody responds in time. Do you want us to do that now, or relay the information through you?"

"Do as you normally do, in this instance, I'm here to observe how you as a unit function as well."

"I never doubted that for one second, Wendy. Alison, call everybody we would normally contact, but tell Wendy who you are contacting, that's all. I'll brief the Director."

Dan waited as Wendy listened to what was said to each of the Met anti-terrorist unit, MI5, and the NCA. He added, "When we identify the target, we will call the Chief Constable, the person in charge of the target, and initiate pre-emptive response, usually evacuation of premises, that sort of thing.

"At that time, or sooner, we would call for your people to be in the air, closing the distance on the possible targets. Had you done that as we asked regards Birmingham, it would never have happened. Do you understand our concern?"

Chapter 37

"Yes Dan. It's just that they do not trust you yet, which is why I am here today."

"Agreed. Follow what we do, and how this develops."

Alison said, "I'm tracking them on motorway cameras, and they just turned onto the M11. Destinations now are east London, Essex, and Kent."

"Good. Let us know when they turn off. This is how we work Wendy. We will not make another call to your people, or any others, until we have a good idea of what the target may be."

Dan monitored the team for a few minutes, and received confirmation from Martin the new drones were in place at Luton, parked on the target roof. Satisfied the team had things under control, he stood and said, "I have an urgent report to write, and this room is totally distracting. I will have a word with Sinjun, and would normally use that office. I'll be in the front bedroom, so call me the instant you get a whiff of target. Ladies, Percy."

Dan made a coffee, before going up to the room. He worked for thirty minutes, but the end result would be quite short, the planning of what he needed to involve, and especially links to corroborative information, was a huge undertaking.

Dan had the document in draft form, closing on final edit, when Percy knocked the door. "You are needed."

He went to the control room at once. "Yes Alison?"

"Dan, they turned east at Bishop's Stortford, and the only targets I can make out are Braintree, Colchester, and maybe Chelmsford. It doesn't make sense."

"Is this a race day at Braintree?"

"Checking ... No."

"Call Colchester Barracks and have them temporarily upgrade their security level to DEFCON Three. That means armed troops on the gate. I do not think that is the target, but better safe than sorry. Research the local shopping centres, and have working communications in place."

Checking the map he said, "They are at least ten minutes out of Colchester, and they have several shopping centres, which are likely targets. Ask the Met to get airborne, and land at Colchester airport. It won't take them long to get there, if they respond this time. Inform the other agencies as well, but make clear this is a provisional target, one as yet to be confirmed.

"Now, when's the last time any of you had a drink?"

"Breakfast." "Six a.m." "Can't remember." Came the replies.

Dan said, "I'm the tea-boy, we have time. What do you want?"

Percy volunteered, "Put the kettle on Dan, I'll come down with the orders, I'm not actually doing much, except liaising with Martin, and he's driving back."

They returned with hot and cold drinks, biscuits, pork pie, and quiche. Wendy said, "You're allowed to eat, drink at your station?"

Dan eyeballed her and said, "Yes. We are at work, and it is past lunchtime. The job comes first. These are matters of national security. If you blow up the keyboard by spilling your drink, you pay full retail for a new one, which we have replacements for, at cost price, in the store cupboard. Okay?"

"Yes, I like working here."

Alison reported, "They're on the ring road, still headed east, and past the last possible target in Colchester. Where the hell are they going, there's nothing there."

Eyes turned to screens, and targets became fewer. Dan said, "Yes there is, Harwich. A major UK ferry port. They hit an airport last time, so this makes sense. Tell Colchester Barracks to return to normal status. I'll speak to the Chief Constable in a moment.

"Wendy, move your people from Colchester to Harwich."

She sat there, and stared at the screen.

Dan shouted, "What is it? Out with it."

"They are still in London, Sir. I told them to mobilise, just after Alison made the request, and they did nothing."

"Wendy, after last time, you cannot be serious. Are your governors in the pay of these Islamic terrorists? Because from where I stand, it certainly looks that way. I am reporting this as such, immediately. There can be no excuses for such diabolical dereliction of duty."

Wendy began to say, "I agree Sir…" However, by that time Dan had turned away, and was speaking to his Director. "Ma'am, same as before The Met are sitting on their arses doing squat. I want them prosecuted, because I believe they are in the pay of these Islamic terrorists, otherwise would be doing their job…"

The Director was equally disbelieving. She was in a 'take no prisoners' frame of mind, which Dan thought excellent. The call was short.

Dan was about to share with the team, when a thought came to him, and he rushed out of the room, sat on the stairs, and wrote it on his tablet. The final piece of the request he was making of the Marshal of the Air Force, had come to him out of the blue. His words were almost prose, Churchillian in nature, and supported the heart of his proposal.

Dan took time to complete his closing statement, knowing the shorter the work was, the better. He annotated items for deletion, or links, generally abridged his request, and satisfied, returned to his war room. "Status report."

After update, Dan spoke to the Chief Constable of Essex Constabulary, alerting him to the potential strike on Harwich. "And most likely the ferry sir. We are not sure if it will be the terminal, or the ferry itself. I need the direct line for the head of the Border Agency ... what d'you mean, there isn't one ... Damn, so they can just go on board with only cursory checks?"

That call was also briefer than Dan expected, but he said to the team, "The Chief Constable is reacting with a squad of trained men, and firearms units. He was contacted by us this morning, and so was alert to possible strikes. Sorry the Met are not, Wendy.

"Other targets, Alison, Veronica?"

"A few small shopping centres, nothing like the scale we have seen before, and a local gas pipeline. That's it. They are already past the turn off for Clacton-On-Sea, so it has to be Harwich, or Parkeston, the larger nearby town. And yes, I have that covered."

"It has to be the ferry. Focus. I'll update the others. Wendy, see if your misfits can summon the energy to stop an atrocity occurring on British soil. This is their third, and final attempt.

"I am calling MI5 now, and the NCA next. Wendy, the NCA do not as yet have an anti-terrorist team, because that remains the Met's, for today. Tomorrow, the NCA will have a response team, one that will react to national terrorist threats."

Dan was busy on his secure line, but overheard staff talking. Wendy burst into tears. She could see what was happening, and yet her colleagues continued to take no action.

Dan informed MI5 of the new target, and they became most interested. Veronica opened a dedicated channel to liaise with them. Dan updated the NCA, but all knew their hands were tied, for the moment.

Dan looked up, and said, "This may be going down. First and second responders; who have we missed?"

Veronica offered, "The Port Authority?"

Alison replied, "No already dealt with, and they're talking to me. Dan, what about the Navy? If they are after the ship, like a Twin Towers style attack, then we could use a gunboat."

"Excellent Alison. All of you, tell me if you spot anything else we may have missed. I need to speak to the Director, get a destroyer headed there at once.

"Veronica, if this goes to sea, we'll need coastguard and rescue services standing by. Spread the word, but only as standby."

Alison interrupted, "Can we stop the ferry leaving?"

"Call the shipping line immediately."

... "I reached a clerk, who will pass the message on. This is not good. Can we stall them with security?"

"Call the Border Agency. Even though they have no customs there, they may be able to pull a rabbit out of the hat."

Veronica said, "What about bomb disposal? The van is sure to be packed with explosives."

"Good. Get on it. You had better alert Fire and Rescue, and have ambulances standing by. What else?"

Alison said, "Oh. Parkeston and Harwich are the only destinations left. I'm through to the Border Agency, one moment … They've got nobody nearby, but will tell security to raise their threat level."

"That doesn't sound too promising either. We need the van prevented from embarking."

"They have the registration number and details, Sir."

Wendy said, "Our team are on their way, but they need to know where to land?"

"The docks Wendy, on a public road if necessary. Regardless, they will arrive too late again. We need a response team stationed here, under my command. At least we would react. This response is abysmal. I'm going down to ask Sinjun to attend, he may have a perspective we are missing. Excuse me a moment."

Minutes later, Sinjun stated, "You called this correct Dan, from the outset. I can't believe these civilian agencies are so bad, the Met especially. I will report them to the military, as they appear to be working for the terrorists."

Voices joined in chorus. "Dan said the same a minute ago." "Yes, he thinks the Met are working with the terrorists, by not responding." "This is a threat to our nationhood, and the Met are doing as little as they can."

The last person to speak was Wendy. "I mean that. This operation, your previous ones, are being stalled at a high level."

Dan said, "Thank you Wendy. Now you fully understand what we are up against."

Sinjun spoke up. "This is war Dan. Out and out war. How long before they strike at the heart of Blighty? I'd say weeks, not months. What you are chasing here, today, are cells. The real strike is yet to come. With what I am monitoring below, that will be extremely effective, whatever it turns out to be.

"Regards this hit, presuming two girl suicide bombers, one female controller, and one man in command, with a van full of explosives, then the options are few. There is no border control, you said?"

"No, and we're not even signed up to Schengen."

"Yes, feeble. Regards the ferry, there are limited options, and using it as a weapon against another watery target doesn't fit. My best guess, without full consideration, is they will scuttle the ferry in the waterway, rendering further service to the port impossible for many months.

Dan said, "Alison, confirm underwater topography."

"On it ... Yes, a dredged channel. If the ferry goes down, it will blockade the port."

"The vehicle will be below the waterline, get a ship's diagram."

Alison said, "Working on it ...Yes. Got it."

Sinjun continued, "I would expect one girl to take out the terminal, killing as many innocents as possible, and the other to do likewise once the ship is at sea. The van will be below the waterline, and on a timer, thus when it explodes, it will block the channel to port. I would expect the man to take over the Bridge, and the woman and girl setting explosives at exits below. Anything else?"

Dan smiled a curious smile and said, "Then stick around Sinjun and see how this pans out. You may be wrong. Ever consider that?"

Sinjun grinned back. "Yes, I have been wrong a few times in my career, but this is not one of them. So who will take them out?"

"That is our problem. We have nobody responding to our calls for assistance."

"You cannot be serious!"

"Deadly serious. Apart from going in myself, there is zero response, for the third time."

"Dan, let me make a call. Not for this time, the play is all but done. But maybe next time you will have the people on the ground you need."

"Who. Who are you contacting?"

"I cannot say, but he is rather senior."

Dan smiled. "I need to speak to somebody like that, the Marshal of the Air Force precisely. Is that who?"

"I cannot say."

"Oh, so it is the Marshal of the Air Force. Tell him, when you speak to him, that Dan Glover needs a piece of his time. Remind him of our latest intelligence, the SCUD D's."

An argument was brewing, but Alison cut in. "They took the ferry road outside Parkeston. No guesses now the destination."

"Harwich Ferry. Veronica, call all hands to action, the target is confirmed as Harwich Ferry. Wendy, where are your units?"

"En route, Sir. They left as soon as the target was confirmed."

"Not good enough."

Alison said, "The terrorists are in Harwich, but I've no camera coverage, they have old style GATSO's. I'm asking the port authority for live CCTV footage."

Dan's mobile rang, it was MI5. "Dan Glover? MI6 right. Agent Steve Sterling, on the ground at Harwich, what are we doing here?"

Dan pointedly showed his mobile to Wendy, before saying aloud, "I have MI5 on site, and I need to speak to them. Let me know if your lot ever get there."

Dan explained the threat, outlining what, where, and whom. He said, "I'm sending images now, I need you to locate the van, we no longer have visual. They should be entering the port within one minute."

"You need these imbeciles dead or alive?"

"The two girls alive if possible, they will be the easiest to break. Regards the other two, take no extraordinary measures to save their lives. Here's how we think this may go down…"

Dan explained the scenario they had worked out. "But we are profiling unknown individuals in a group situation."

"Guessing then, Dan. At least you have the balls to say so."

"Have you drones with you?"

"Sorry. No drones, but we are armed. I'll put two of our men near the boarding gate, they'll have tickets to board. The other two, one on traffic, and me on the ship.

"I'll call you back Dan, Vince just got eyes on a white van, and two females wearing niqāb's got out of the vehicle, and did something front and rear. I don't know what."

"They probably stuck on new plates, damn."

"We are following on foot, but being seriously slowed by security. There's not much of a queue either, but we'll try to stop the van boarding. What if it's loaded?"

"Follow it. Find out where it's parked, and then follow the occupants. I suspect one will head for the bridge."

"Understood, Dan. Out."

Dan called the Director to update her. She was in a good frame of mind. "So as we expected from the Met. We will not use them again. I am leveraging for our team to work with the NCA, regards whatever you come up with. By the way, I had a working lunch at the Jamaica Inn today, deep inside the catacombs of the City. They call it a Wine House nowadays.

"Samuel Pepys used the place centuries ago. Regardless, I met a dear friend, and journalist. He received a tip-off earlier today, and is already in Harwich with a photographer. The evening press should make interesting reading. I'll update him now."

"Everything now rests with MI5 Ma'am. We're working together to stop this atrocity, but are behind the clock."

"Do your best, I know you will. Ciao."

In the event, both girls surrendered before exploding their suicide vests, but the ferry left dock with the van on board. Dan called Steve, "Ahoy MI5, what's the state of play on the ground?"

"We have eyes on the van, new plates stuck on, known registration below. The back is packed with explosives, and we cannot disarm the bomb. That needs to be done by a professional."

"Bomb disposal are on their way, but will be too late. What about the general situation and bridge?"

"Damage limitation. The van is parked next to the hull, on the lowest level. Confirm, below the water line. Trucks, oil tankers and those carrying chemicals surround it. The fallout will be quite nasty. The bridge has been taken, as you suspected, but we are about to take it back. The man is in control there, but we've lost the woman."

"She may be planting bombs. Check the main exits."

"We are retaking the bridge now, three, two, go." Two shots rang out. "Dan, terrorist taken out, bridge secure."

Dan overheard Steve give the captain orders. "Sir, with respect, Islamic terrorists have a van on board, filled with explosives. This ferry is about to be scuttled and capsize on the left. We need it out of the deepwater channel at once. Their aim is to blockade the port."

The captain responded, "Hard a-port, engines full ahead. Helmsman, steer into the side channel. It's only just wide enough for us, so keep her central and steady as she goes."

The ship was almost fully in the channel when they heard a dull roar from below. The ship lurched to port, and began to slowly keel over.

"Man the lifeboats, all crew to passenger emergency evacuation stations. Take them to starboard, and if necessary, have them sit on the starboard hull, when we hit the water."

Steve's men had found some of the secondary bombs, and hurled them overboard. They did not find them all, but MI5 directed passengers through cleared exits, soon supported by ship's crew. TV crews arrived before the Met's instant response, anti-terrorist unit. Their leader was questioned live on television. Many in power watched the evening news with mounting dread and consternation.

Chapter 38 ~ Calm Before the Storm

The team worked late on Friday evening, Percy took over as tea boy, and when Martin returned, he assisted where he could. Martin managed to get the four drones in and around the Luton warehouse, and Bude were given access to the live feed.

MI5 were deemed heroes of the hour, but they insisted this was a joint operation controlled by MI6. Nevertheless, they received the public plaudits, and Dan did not mind at all. He needed to keep his team and what they did out of the public eye.

Regardless of being publicly shamefaced, the Met tried to take the two girls into custody for interrogation as terrorist suspects. MI5 refused to release the prisoners, and The Chief Constable of Essex Constabulary backed them up when he visited the scene. They were taken to Parkeston police station, and Dan would see them the next day.

Felicity called, "Dan, I am leaving Norwich now, and presume you are still working."

"Yes, it's been one hell of a day. We have several hours work still to do. I think we'll all need a good drink and a meal when this is done."

"Good, I feel a Pernod moment coming on, and want to try Ayesha's chicken tikka masala. I'll stay over and take her statement tomorrow. Anything you need?"

"Just you. Perhaps a kiss."

"Mwah! Ciao."

No sooner had Dan finished the call, than the Director rang. "Dan, best result possible, under the circumstances, well done. The media are crucifying the Met, and so they should. I've had calls from mandarins related to some powerful people. You remember those strings we pulled a few days ago? Well, I am now yanking them hard.

"Something will give way. I am pushing all out for our unit to work exclusively with the newly formed NCA instant response, anti-terrorist support force. I think I'll get it approved by early next week. Our relationship with MI5 has greatly improved. Well done Dan, that's an unforeseen bonus. Hold."

The line went silent as the Director took another call. "Dan, I have just been asked to meet with the Minister for Defence in thirty minutes time. I know the head of the NCA has already been summoned to that meeting. Things look promising. I need your interim report soonest, say within twenty minutes. Get Alison to back up with files and live feeds, we work late tonight.

"Please monitor the election results from Belgium and Luxembourg. I am not expecting any change of the status quo just yet. But I must have the ethnic origins––no, the religious leaning of those elected. That will be key to their power and proof of their intentions."

"Ma'am, consider it done."

Dan finished the call, and made a short speech to the team. He detailed Veronica to follow up the elections, considering them a minor irritation, and said, "Any questions?"

Veronica said, "This is my long weekend off, and I have worked the whole first day of it."

"From now on, days off are a luxury we cannot afford. We are at war. Until this threat is resolved, only special exceptions will be made." Dan added with a wry grin, "And neither are you allowed to be ill."

"Veronica, you said it was your parents wedding anniversary?"

"Yes, their thirtieth. They have planned a big celebration."

"Go now. I need your report this evening, and be back here Monday morning. Hurry before I change my mind. The rest of you, let's get back to work."

Veronica said, "Thanks so much Dan. This means a lot to me, to them, I am their only child. I have the exit poll details as follows; Luxembourg is sixty-three percent Muslim, and Belgium fifty-two percent. Still no overall control. Sound like a takeover to me. Bye."

Dan stared at the figures. He became most worried, and called the Director. It was far worse than they feared. "Dan, this is a nightmare!"

"Yes it is, for when they choose to cross the floor. But when?..."

As the call ended Wendy raised her hand. "This is not a question, but I am totally disgusted with the way my team behaved today. I am seriously considering applying for a transfer. I'd rather be walking the beat, or working in vice, than put up with their bullshit egos, bullying, and gropes. I want to resign. I've had enough."

Dan saw the rest of the team working, and asked Martin and Percy to begin preparing a précis report of the day's main events. The clock was ticking. He pulled up a chair, and sat with Wendy. "I didn't realise it was that tough, sorry."

"Oh, I've learnt to deal with the wandering hands, and unnecessary swearing, but they are bullies, from the top down. Today, everything that is wrong in my life came into focus. I'll be fine, but I am putting in for a transfer. Can I stay tonight and leave tomorrow. I need a beer as much as you do."

Dan chuckled conspiratorially and said, "Yes, we all need a beer, but later. Sure, stay, you fitted in extremely well, and I am impressed with you. Don't do anything rash." He handed her his card and took her private phone number in return.

"Good," Dan continued. "I have the distinct impression that come Monday, the NCA will be recruiting their own anti-terrorist response team, and if that happens, I'll put a good word in for you, especially as you already know how we work. You would remain employed by the Met, but on long-term secondment. How does that sound?"

"Super, thanks so much. Can I help with anything, as my work is virtually done for today. I've just a short report to finish."

"No, go when you are ready. Percy, please show Wendy to the inn, and book her in for the night. Also, introduce her properly to Sinjun, as I'm guessing he will be the first of us in the bar tonight. Now, please excuse me Wendy, I have work to do, and a deadline to meet."

Dan got his tablet, and was pleased with what Martin and Percy had put together. His report was half done, if it needed abridging in some places, and fleshing out in others. His focus was on what the Met did, and did not do. Martin stayed to watch, Dan explaining what he was writing, and why. He found the teaching role gave him an unexpected focus, and his words appeared on screen with ease.

Alison sent him a related file, and after a quick inspection, Dan associated links for the Director. He glanced at his wristwatch. Nineteen minutes, and counting down. He zipped the file and sent it.

A couple of minutes later, his mobile phone rang. "Excellent work Dan, and just in time. I'll need a full report in the morning, but not first thing, you will need to relax and recharge batteries this evening."

"Thank you Ma'am, but, we'll be here for another hour or more regardless. I'm interviewing the two girls tomorrow over in Parkeston, but their Police Chief was on our side. I'll need a translator. The one from last time would be ideal, again with compass and prayer mats."

"She will meet you there, anything else?"

"I also want to keep in touch with Steve Sterling at MI5. They did an outstanding job and almost saved the day."

"Good thinking, we need closer contacts with them, but take it slowly. I'm almost at the meeting. Speak with you later."

Dan dismissed all staff who were not working, which left only Alison at her desk. Taking his brief, and those devised by Martin and Percy, Dan sat down at his desktop computer to compile the full report.

He was putting finishing touches to it, near eight o'clock, when Felicity arrived. She was in a bouncy mood, and totally distracting. They kissed and spoke rapidly about their days. Realising Dan was almost done, she left him with an order. "I expect you to arrive at the pub in five minutes, lover boy."

Alison made a remark Dan did not hear fully, but guessed the intention. "You jealous? You also need a man in your life. Leave soon, finish up, let's be done with today."

It was fifteen minutes before they departed, twenty before they reached the inn, but Dan's report was sent, and Alison's work completed. The pub had a great atmosphere that night, and Dan and his team indulged more than they normally would. Later, most of them ate curry. Ayesha was called for, and complimented on her culinary skills. Brian was well pleased.

Saturday began with sore heads, made worse by Dan's phone ringing. "Well done Dan, your report is acceptable, written last night I note. Your team is good. The Minister was livid, and fully backed our proposal to instigate NCA as our primary response team. We plan to set this up before the politicians change their minds, or they discover who was the leak to the press. A-hem."

"You're a wily old stick, Ma'am. Well played."

"Less of the old if you don't mind. But yes, it worked like a charm. You will need to meet the NCA later today. Your plans?"

"Before, or after I interview the two girls in Parkeston, Ma'am?"

"Better afterwards. I still need to present my own report and tactical assessment. I'll make your appointment for two o'clock, don't be late."

"Ma'am."

Dan reacted by asking for a pot of coffee to be delivered to their room. Gwen brought up a tray with full breakfast, delivered as Dan showered and Felicity came awake.

Dan entered the room dressed in a towel, and thanked Gwen. "Filly, I need to leave ASAP, interview the two girls, then head for the NCA in London. Want to come along?"

"Yes, I'll be in on the interview. But count me out for London, unless I can go shopping instead. I'll interview Ayesha next time."

"Deal. I'll take Wendy with us and drop her back in London, also."

The interview went similar to the one in Bristol. Dan gave them prayer mats and a Mecca locator. Both girls had been enslaved by Boko Haram, and spilled the beans, with subtle prompting from both Felicity and Dan. Maye was again acting as translator. One of them had been a favourite with a leader, and they were able to press her for details, many of which were disquieting. The girl was thirteen years old.

Felicity whispered to Dan, and he said, "We are arranging a secure location for you. You will not be harmed, but treated with respect. You are with friends. Please stay here while arrangements are completed."

They departed for London to meet Linda Snowe, Director of the National Crime Agency. Felicity headed off to one of her favourite shopping haunts, Covent Garden. Dan gave Maye a lift back to central London, but Wendy stayed with him for the duration.

Surprisingly, Linda Snowe was more than amenable. Dan did not need to use most of his prepared material, but left both printed and digital files for her consideration.

They discussed setting up the response team, the target one week from that day. Dan would be required at their headquarters to help set things up, which he agreed to.

Afterwards, names of suitable people were thrown into the mix. Dan took the opportunity, and offered Wendy as chief liaison officer. Linda grilled Wendy for a short while in private, before stating, "She measures up and has worked with you before. I will requisition her on Monday. Now, let's look to the firearms team…"

Dan left with the impression a new anti-terrorist strike force would be operational within the week. He was equally buoyed, but concerned. He dropped a delighted Wendy near an underground station, and met up with Felicity. She was waiting outside a new shopping centre, and eating a cream cake.

"I thought you hated those things, Felicity."

"What, raspberry Mille Feuille. I do, but this was so tempting. Reminds me of Cornwall. Now follow me, I need a new handbag. Come, this will be fun."

Dan shook his head, watching her head off 'girl-shopping', something he detested. They were almost at the entrance to what was nowadays termed 'the mall', when they stopped to look in a window. Dan was bored.

Just then, a car pulled up on double-yellow lines at the kerb, and two females wearing a niqāb got out of the rear. An older female got out of the passenger seat, and he noticed a man driving. Pulling his pistol, he looked back at Felicity and shouted, "RUN!"

He levelled the barrel at the first girl, who dived to the pavement and let her trigger device go. The second girl looked Dan in the eye, and he motioned her to surrender. Her hand moved towards the trigger device, and he shot her between her eyes. There was no explosion.

The woman started to run, but Dan shot her in the back of the head. He turned his weapon on the driver, and fired. His shot missed, as security tackled him to the ground. The boots of a large man appeared in his eye line; "You are under arrest. We don't like murderers of innocent people here."

Dan began to reply, but the other boot hit full force on his jaw. He heard a loud bang, as if a car bomb had exploded, and awoke in hospital.

"Dan, I was so worried about you, are you okay?" Felicity was mopping his brow with a damp cloth, and looking extremely concerned.

He croaked through a dry mouth and the attending nurse offered him a sliver of ice. Felicity took over ministrations until Dan was able to speak, if weakly. He gazed at her and said, "I could do with a kiss."

Female lips planted on his own, but withdrew too soon. "You are incorrigible, Danforth Glover. Just as well you saved my life today, plus many other people's, or I may not have done that."

"You missed me then. You were worried about me?"

"Yes, damn you. How did you know, are you profiling me?"

"No Filly, I almost died saving other people's lives, and feel like shit. Either turn on the compassion or go. I don't need this. Save the petty recriminations for later. How many died today?"

"Three, damn you. The two women you shot dead, and the driver who blew himself and the car, up. Over thirty were injured, including the guard who kicked you. He and five others are in critical condition."

"Serves him right."

"I'm so proud of you, you read the situation perfectly."

"They were Islamic extremist suicide bombers."

"Yes. The car obviously. The woman had remotely activated pipe grenades and worse in her bag. Both girls wore suicide vests.

"I have the remaining girl in my personal custody, but am out of my jurisdiction. I have requested priority control, which I may not get. But the Met are under the Press cosh today, so it may happen."

"Is it still Saturday?"

"Yes, you were out for less than one hour."

"Hand me my phone."

Dan tapped a number. "Director, today at the mall, I need the girl bomber secured, and we will interview her. Can you action this?"

"You are still alive then. That is no surprise. I'm already working on the girl. Felicity called me an hour ago. The Met are determined to charge you with First Degree murder. That's their way of getting back at us for Friday, and it will not happen. Sweet dreams, and speak to you later."

Dan nodded at Felicity, and said, "Disconnect me, I need to go home."

"What! You only just survived a car bomb."

"Yes, and I'm fine, if my hearing's a bit off. I've survived much worse. Give me a hand here, I must leave, be at home, with you. Anyway, yesterday I told the team no one was allowed sick leave. Let's go."

Despite protestations, Dan got dressed and discharged himself from hospital. He had work to do and scores to settle.

Chapter 39 ~ Best Laid Plans

When they got back home, Dan checked in with the team. They were still pouring over data, and analysing feeds. Dan said, "Have a slack day tomorrow, and I'll see you on Monday morning."

Dan was quiet, and Felicity knew he was still hurting, both physically from the boot to his jaw, and mentally from his workload.

She needed to change the environment. "Let's eat out tonight and have a drink somewhere close by. I know this lovely restaurant, so get ready to leave in five. I'll check they have a table. It's Saturday night." She was already on her phone. "Yes, table for two booked. Let's go."

She knew going out was the last thing Dan wanted to do, so did not give him a choice in the matter. He needed spiritual healing, a relaxing drink in convivial company, and dining in a pleasant environment. Her choice turned out to be the recuperative therapy he needed.

As they finished up, she said, "I don't think you're up to going to Mother's tomorrow. Why don't I call them now and invite them down? Lets cook for them for a change."

Dan looked up, his face changing expressions within his thoughts and their implications. As if to seal the deal, Felicity added, "They'll only stay a couple of hours, but it lets them to see the house, and we can relax instead of driving for hours."

"I'm going to say yes, dear. I must speak with your father about work, but it won't take long. I have a request I must finish though, so I will be working first thing, but in the library. I do not believe your mother will be less than three hours, but we'd spend almost that long travelling. Okay, as long as I help prep, and can cook some side dishes."

"Your roast potatoes are better than mine, you blanch them? Never mind, it will be interesting to peek. Have we got any joints in?"

"I bought a lovely looking joint of local beef from the butcher on Thursday, it was too good to pass by. There's New Zealand lamb and chicken in the freezer; I fancy lamb."

"Great! We'll do roast beef with all the trimmings. I'll call them now, and put the joint in when we get back, on extremely low. It's still in the fridge, right?"

"Yes, it's well marbled, and encased in fat. I like the idea. Make the call, but on condition I make the gravy using the meat juices in the roasting pan. It's an art you know."

Felicity ensured Dan did not work when they got home. They slept early, and rose early. Dan took a morning bath, which was most unlike him, but he luxuriated within the ministrations of the massage jets. He seemed back to his usual self over breakfast. His energy had returned, as had his focus on work.

Chapter 39

Dan spent the morning in the library, Felicity preparing most of the meal in advance, and running to the shopping centre for things they needed, or were out of. When she returned Dan was working on the gas cooker. "What are you doing?"

"Opening the oven gas valve up full. It will be as hot as can be. Just one more leverage … there, got it."

"But why?"

"Yorkshire puddings. They need to be treated like the art of tea, everything as hot as can be. These will be eight inches high."

"Impossible. Mine are usually like lumps of fried dough."

"There you go then. What are you doing with that packet? I'll make a fresh mixture, so watch and pay attention. Light and fluffy. I need to impress your mother.

"Oh, and Sid has organised decorators to begin painting tomorrow. I'm for white, unless you have any ideas."

"That's good for most of it, but boring. This place needs picture rails, and coving where the walls meet the ceiling. I'll make some notes. Oh, light blue for the sun room, and wooden ceiling in the attic."

Later they received a call to say her parents were on the way. Dan uncorked a bottle of red, and they sipped as they wandered around the house and into the garden, Felicity remarking on progress.

"This renovation is almost finished, Dan. Your hangar is an eyesore, but out of the way. I'll hide it with plants. Did you get planning permission for it?"

"Erm … No. Technically it's a garden shed."

"Hah! Until you put a plane in it, then it becomes a hangar, and our meadow over there becomes an airfield. The council won't buy it."

"I was thinking to invite the neighbours over for dinner, keep them sweet and onside. The council will only act if they receive a complaint. Regardless, it's only temporary. Once this mission is completed we should be able to use Huntley Spar aerodrome. It also gives us a durable track down to the river."

Felicities eyes were unfocused, her mind scanning future opportunities as Dan continued, "We need a dock by the river, if only for fishing, and a bolthole for Percy; plus boat maybe. It should be deep enough for swimming, if a bit chilly."

"I'll leave that for you and Percy to play with. I'll stick with a swimming pool near the house, a patio for sunbathing and entertaining."

"Agreed. I'll set up the barbeque and outside kitchen when we settle in and know exactly how we want the place to be. We can now use the coach house as a garage for our cars, and I we have winter fuel in, coal and wood."

They walked farther to the orchard, where Felicity turned around, stopped, and gawped. "What the hell is that?"

She had been staring at the back of the house, and noticed the formative balcony under construction. Dan hoped she would like it. She gulped down her drink, handed the empty to Dan, and ran for the back door, beating Dan upstairs as he shepherded her like a playful sheepdog.

He shadowed her tentatively walking up the new staircase to the attic. Dan said, "The steps are fine, just needs painting, or wood dye, or carpet. Go on. I hope you like my surprise."

Felicity briefly scanned the large room, but headed directly for the window, which had been made into doors. Regardless of the tape blocking the exit, she opened the French windows. "They're triple glazed," she remarked.

Her eyes rested on the unfinished balcony. She turned to Dan, her face becoming scrunched up and falling into itself with disbelief. Tears of joy ran freely, but her voice when it came, was high-pitched, squeaky. Her words fractured, becoming husky, were almost indecipherable.

"Dan, I never imagined. Thank you. Amazing! Just what I always dreamed of. It's so big. I could grow plants. Make a roof garden. There's even a retractable awning. I love you."

For the very first time in his entire life, Dan stated with conviction, "I love you, too."

Before they realised, clothes had been dispensed with, and Dan turned Felicity onto her back, in preparation for his next move. He caught a glance at his watch and said, "Shit! They'll be here soon."

Felicity dragged his head down for a kiss, and gasped with a deep voice, almost breathless with lust, "They'll have to wait. Love me."

The heat of the sun caressed them, as they lay dreamily, half-asleep afterwards. Their world was perfect, until Dan's mobile rang. He came instantly awake and said, "Hello, Dan Glover."

Margaret replied, "Felicity is not answering her mobile, and we are in Upper Meddlington. Tom says he knows where he is going, but I do not believe him."

Dan said aside, "They are close, check the meat, and baste it."

"Margaret, Tom is taking a short cut. All he needs to do is go through the village, and follow the main road as it curves right at the end of the main street. We are at the end of that road, a few houses before it meets Lower Meddlington High Street. I'll be out front waiting for you. See you in five minutes."

Downstairs, Felicity withdrew a knife from the joint and said, "I've no idea how, but the meat is perfect. I'm turning the heat up to crisp the fat on top. I took your roast potatoes out, as they are superb, and the veg is on slow simmer. Get the dining table prepared, and we'll swap over."

They rushed out to the road minutes later, and were just ahead of schedule. They waved to the approaching car, and welcomed Felicity's parents to their home.

Chapter 39

Felicity excused herself to work in the kitchen as Dan showed them the coach house and garden. Margaret was picking fruit when Tom said, "Well, I'll be damned. You have your jet parked here. The runway is-- short. That over there will be the hangar I presume, great work. I love this place, and the river down below. The aspect is perfect. Well done."

Felicity called out, and they swapped over, Dan finishing the cooking, and Felicity showing them the rest of the house. Within ten minutes, Dan shouted, "Dishing up now, come and get it."

They asked Tom to carve the joint, which he accomplished with practised ease. Dan returned to the kitchen, bringing out a tray of Yorkshire puddings that had exceeded even his expectations. All were over ten inches high, light and fluffy. They were in great demand, as was his gravy. However, Felicity took the culinary honours for cooking the joint to perfection.

Afterwards the men took tawny port and cheese into the library. Dan presented his request to meet the Marshal of the Air Force, and was told, "It seems Sinjun also recommended the meeting. He is a stout fellow, except late at night in the bar. But with his disability that is forgivable. Show me your request in full."

Dan plugged in a memory stick and said, "This is what we offer. I need that meeting, Tom."

"This is perfect Dan. Everything, all the links work off this pen drive. I'll give this to the Marshal of the Air Force with my personal endorsement."

They talked for a long time, their conversation diverting to the immanent Muslim takeover of Luxembourg and Belgium, through Islamification of other European Countries, to Blighty.

Dan finished, "They will take England by force. The when I do not know, but it will be a week's not months. I've shown you the SCUD's they flew in, howitzers, and antimissile batteries. Why did they do that?"

"Offence, and defence. But we do not know where."

"Correct. I mean to discover which locations they will attack, but time is running out. This will be a concerted move to make Europe an Islamic Governorate. They will call it a Caliphate. Same thing; different ideology. Even with the levers Bude has, interaction with the continent's security services is quasi at best. Sometimes I think that I, and my team, are the only people to truly understand what is about to go down.

"You are not alone. Others are beginning to think the same way. Tell me of your thoughts, misgivings."

"We need to be able to defend ourselves. I would recall all armed forces: Navy, Army, and Air force. All troops back to Blighty, ready to respond immediately to any internal threat."

"You won't get that you know."

"Yes I understand, but I can ask for it. When I am proved correct a lot of people should be sacked. I fear they may already be dead. ISIL do not take prisoners. They punish their own by death for the slightest infringements of their version of Islam. What do you think they plan for us, their sworn enemy? "

"Total extinction of Christianity. Regards Islam, I'm not even sure what that is anymore. They change flavour with the wind. Dan, can I have your word of honour, and I'll tell you something."

"Yes, already given. But I know that you and Sinjun will meet with the Marshal of the Air Force early next week, probably Tuesday. Can I come along for the ride?"

"You are perceptive. Yes, and no. We will need you to pilot the plane. You will remain in the cockpit unless called for. This is military business and you have no jurisdiction."

"It will be so. Thank you."

The door opened and two women entered. "What are you two boys doing in here? Talking shop no doubt. Come, we need to take family photographs and start planning the wedding."

"Mum, don't. We're not ready yet."

"Speak for yourself child, but I know you are ready. And not only for marriage, but for a baby as well. When is it due?"

"Mother, I am not ... How did you? ... Damn! Eight months."

Aside, Felicity mouthed to Dan, "I think."

Tom caught his daughter's unspoken words and grinned. Margaret continued. "Excellent. We could hold the reception here, your field out back is the perfect place for a marquee. We'd need outside caterers..."

It seemed like hours until Margaret left, she wanted to take over an event they had not discussed as a couple and were not ready for.

Once they had the place to themselves, they switched off, and watched a movie on download TV. Felicity got up and made them a milk drink before bedtime.

They parted on the step of their home on Monday morning, and the day seemed to flash by for both of them. Good news came at lunchtime when Wendy called. "Dan, just to let you know, I've been seconded to the NCA immediately and indefinitely. I have this afternoon to clear my desk, and I begin with them in the morning. I'll need to set up with Alison all over again. Will you tell her?"

"Yes, consider it done. Congratulations as well. I feel confident to know we'll be working with you again. I'll see you later this week, not sure when, maybe Thursday. Ciao."

Late that afternoon, Veronica returned, and Sinjun presented his full report, detailing attack and defence capabilities of the five private airfields. His tactical assessment showed areas of strength and weakness, and his assault strategies, two plans for each airfield. "This is how they can be taken with minimum loss of life or resources.

"As you will notice, I have timed each event for capture of the most aircraft, service vehicles, and terrorist personnel. I would also like to present this next plan for taking out their warehouse at Luton, and within the wider scope of the same operation…"

The team were impressed with Sinjun's thoroughness and attention to minute detail. He continued his delivery, outlining strikes against unknown targets, the ones that would be receiving the armoured vehicles, tanks, and howitzers. He confirmed, "This is a little in the air, but so will be the delivery vehicles, so they will land at an airfield. We need to know which one or ones.

"I believe all these targets can be taken out with one, possibly two platoons each. Timing of all strikes will be critical. One enemy phone call, and our element of surprise is gone.

"The final target is Lillyworth Moor, and that gave me many problems. The size of the base is a major problem, and so are the numbers of people there. I estimate thousands of malcontents, any one of whom could pull the trigger of a gun. We would also need air and ground support in full measure.

"As with all the other targets, I have identified offensive and defensive locations, and also strengths and weaknesses. We would not be involved in that operation, except perhaps as advisors. It is too large. A regular Army general will probably take control of the strike force, and they well make their own plan, probably incorporating a lot of the information we given here.

"I'll take any questions, and then head for the bar, and an early night. I understand you are our pilot tomorrow morning, Dan…"

Chapter 40 ~ Rapid Response Force

Sinjun, Alison, and Dan left before seven the following morning, collecting the Group Captain from RAF Trimingham en route. They were granted landing clearance at RAF Coningsby one hour later.

Tom said, "RAF Coningsby is not where the Marshal of the Air Force is based, but it is perhaps not so strange he chose this location. This is one of the main UK air defence stations where interceptor fighters are based. They have Tornados and Typhoons, but few of either due to defence cuts. Ah Dan, park on that apron, and we'll get going."

"Wilco. What, where's the airfield defence? Could they take us out?"

Sinjun muttered, "There is no air or missile defence, disgraceful."

The military men departed, but Dan and Alison were invited to enjoy the Sergeant's Mess for refreshments. Over coffee, they chatted to their RAF companion, who learned they were from MI6. He told them how the base operated, and moaned about the lack of aircraft.

Sometime later a Corporal entered, "Commander Glover, the Marshal of the Air Force has requested your presence. Please come with me now and I will take you to him."

Dan rose, said a humorous goodbye to the Sergeant who had entertained them. He departed with Alison in tow, and a short time later they were shown to a door and the Corporal knocked. "Enter."

Dan went in, stood to attention, and saluted. "Commander Glover, MI6, Sir. This is Agent Porter, intelligence officer. She has information at her fingertips, but I will ask her to leave if you feel she is unwanted."

"No, that's fine, Dan. Come in please, take a seat. But I'm beginning to feel outnumbered. Do I need to call in members of my team?"

Dan replied with a wry grin and sparkle in his eye. "We're all part of your team, Sir. All of us here in this room, have sworn an oath of allegiance to Her Majesty the Queen. I intend to uphold that oath and prevent the destruction of the British way of life, or die trying to prevent UK becoming an Islamic State. Sir"

Dan sat back as the Marshal of the Air Force leaned forward in his chair, and smiled. "Perhaps. I prefer to be addressed as Sir Jack, excepting formal situations. I have read your report, it is thorough and damning, should these events take place. How certain are you we are under threat of direct and immanent attack?"

"One-hundred percent, Sir Jack. It is not a question of if, but when, where, and how bad. You have read Sinjun's tactical report?"

Sinjun said, "No Dan, he has not. I wanted to run through it a final time on the plane, but forgot to load it into my laptop. The wrong pen drive is in my pocket. Perhaps Veronica could forward the right one?"

Alison said, "I'll bring it up now, won't be a second."

"But my computer is secure, password protected."

"Not from me Sinjun, I have the master password. Now which of these files do you want me to work on?"

"Threat Assessment zero-two nineteen B. The entire folder."

"Got it. I'll work at that table over there, this won't take a minute."

Dan took focus, "Let me explain the threat in person, Sir Jack."

As Dan spoke, increasing concern for the cause, Alison finished her review, and called Sinjun over for a final check of his work. He made one small change, before Alison set the nearby photocopier to print. She also saved a copy to a pen drive, and gave it to Sir Jack.

He was staring at the printer, and said, "You did that?"

"Yes Sir. I thought you would like a physical copy as well."

"Well I'll be damned. That is on the secure military net."

"I already have access to that, Sir."

Dan distracted his attention by adding, "She is one of five, maybe six people, in the whole of Europe, that can do that."

Before reply could be made, the desk phone rang. "Yes Ann?"

There was a pause. Sir Jack spoke. "Please excuse me, I must take this call. Refreshments are available in the outer office."

Dan opened his briefcase and handed a folder with pen drive to Sir Jack. "Our assessment of the threat to the stability of European governments. We consider Luxembourg and Belgium to already be Islamic States, it just hasn't been announced yet. Take your time, Sir."

They waited in the anteroom for ten minutes before being called back into the office. Sir Jack looked unsettled, their information lay open before him on the desk, and Dan noted both pen drives in his computer He waved for them to sit down, and roused from his considerations. His words came as a surprise. "Tell me why Dan. Why me?"

"According to the constitution, the Queen is Head of the Armed Forces. Her role is that of figurehead only.

"The person currently in charge of the Navy, Army, and Air Force is the Chief of Defence Staff. You, Sir Jack."

"Yes I am. But that too is as titular head. I have little if any real power, and my only function appears to be attendance of the fine and dandy, that usually includes award ceremonies, a banquet in honour of whom or whatever, and usually both combined. I repeat, I have no real power, so why are you here?"

Dan smiled, but gestured with his arm. "I realise that, Sir Jack. What would be your role if there were no government?"

"What? Are you insane! You are trying my patience, Commander."

"Remember 'nine-eleven'? Our enemy already has tanks, howitzers, anti-aircraft batteries and missiles, not to mention mobile SCUD D missiles, based just up the road at RAF Lillyworth Moor, and probably elsewhere. We need to take them out before they are fired at a target, say a full session of the Houses of Parliament."

There was silence. Several times Sir Jack began to speak, but faltered. In reply to Dan's piercing and questioning look, he gabbled, "In that case, I would be in charge of home defence, and all three services. You cannot be serious!"

"Deadly, Sir Jack. Sinjun, speak of what we discussed when landing here today."

Sinjun replied, "As we were coming in to land, Dan asked me how difficult it would be for the enemy to take out this airfield, but leave the fighters and runway intact.

"That would be easy. There are no anti-missile, anti-aircraft batteries here. I suggest you get some as a matter of greatest urgency. Imagine this base under full control of ISIL. Where would they strike using your aircraft?"

Sir Jack's face turned white. He dismissed them, asking only Tom to remain. As Sinjun rose to leave he said, "Permission to speak, Sir Jack."

"Granted."

"The best aeroplanes we have to combat this threat, apart from those which imbecile Cameron sold to the Yanks as his first act in governance, are the seventy-two or so Harrier GR9A's mothballed at RAF Cottesmore. I strongly suggest they are put back into service, and within days. I consider the threat that deadly. Sir."

Dan added, "That would also be my aircraft of choice, Sir Jack."

Sir Jack was abrupt in reply. "Under consideration. Keep me posted. Daily reports Sinjun, Dan. Dismissed."

As they walked to the mess, Dan said, "He took us seriously, unlike most of the politicians in London. Sinjun, what are your plans for the future? Your work with us is as good as done."

"Well, I could do with a few days back in Hereford, and there is a female I should reacquaint with. But I would like to keep working with you, and that office of yours is a great place for thinking and planning."

"You mean it's right next to the pub. Good, I would like you to work on a new assessment. I want you to don an ISIL leaders hat, and think of all ways this country could be fundamentally destabilised. You heard some suggestions, destroy Parliament, maybe take out the Queen, the RAF here, but use their fighters. Use your imagination, but based in achievable fact. Also, consider their use of nuclear dirty bombs and chemical weapons. As far as I'm concerned, no option is off limits."

"I better stay with the team then. Hereford … she can wait. Thanks Dan, it's good to feel useful once more."

Sinjun lead them to the NAAFI, where he spoke to the manager like a long-lost friend. They bought sandwiches and motorway style coffee from a machine, something similar for Tom, and returned to the plane.

Tom rejoined them after they boarded the jet, and was curiously silent. Feeling eyes on him, Tom looked up and said, "I cannot tell you what was said. I can tell you two things. Sir Jack used to fly Harriers, and so some may be re-commissioned. He seems confident of one or two, but the exact number will be limited."

Dan said, "I love that aircraft. Used to fly them as well. Best jet we ever had for manoeuvrability. I outmanoeuvred a heat seeking missile in Iraq flying one. Awesome things. Sorry Tom, go on."

"The second thing I can tell you is that he was deeply impressed with all of you, and expressly concerned for the future. You may imagine what else we said, but that is all I can relate."

When they got back, Dan called Felicity, hoping for a date that night. "Sorry Dan, I'm up to my eyes with paperwork. The old chief took his best admin with him, and although the new girl is coming up to speed, it is slowly. I'm staying late to break the back of it. What about a date night tomorrow, you could cook for me?"

"I'd love that. Be home around six and we'll have the night all to ourselves. Miss you."

Wednesday became a day for catching up, finishing reports, and planning their next moves. Sinjun had taken to leaving his office door open, and mixed more socially with the team, often popping upstairs for a chat. It was always about work, but he minced socialising and tentative friendship with discussing some of his deliberations as a forum.

Dan made a run to town to buy in food for their lunch, and also meat for home. Sinjun accompanied him and fell in love with what Dan called the Pie Butcher, especially the delicatessen counter.

After lunch, Dan spent time working on his nascent role of setting up the new wing of the NCA. Once his base position was written down, he called the NCA director. "Ah, Dan, I'm so pleased you called. I'll lay out the team members and structure when we meet, but I need to know how we will interact. I take it there has been no insurrection this week."

"No Ma'am, and that's strange. I was thinking to pop down tomorrow, mid-morning, how does that suit you?"

"That's fine Dan, but I am busy-busy first thing, and out of office. Oh, and I'll need you to provide a dedicated member of staff here."

"You have received official sanction then."

"No, but we're going ahead regardless. The Met have had too many chances and blown them all. I need to show you what we can do. I'll also need your advice regards tactical response, an operations appraisal, and how best we can work together. Call it a team-building exercise."

"Ma'am. I'll see you at ten tomorrow."

"Eleven is better for me. Till next time, over and out."

Dan was subdued. He put the phone down and ruminated on his thoughts. He was interrupted when Martin said, "Does that mean we're going to London tomorrow?"

"No," Dan snapped. He looked up and saw the young man's look of disappointment. He quickly realised Martin would make an ideal member of staff there.

"Yes, Martin. How do you fancy spending a few weeks as the dedicated face for our team in London?"

"Wow! Cool Dan. I'll have something to do at weekends."

"I need to take Alison to finish setting Wendy up fully, and maybe have Sinjun join us. They want tactical advice and I think it good they get to know each other. I'll be riding shotgun on what advice he gives, but this sounds like a plan. Ask Sinjun to come up."

Linda had voiced Dan's concerns. Why had there been no suicide strikes that week, at least ones they had prior knowledge of? There had to be a reason, but try as he might, Dan could not fathom the answer.

His disconsolate mood evaporated when Felicity called, "Dan, I'll be down within the hour. I'm now clear of bureaucracy, and must take Ayesha's statement. You want to tag along?"

"Yes, definitely. Am I still cooking tonight?"

"No. I have the urge to eat curry, so we'll dine at the inn. I wished they did takeaway."

"Perhaps they do. Let's ask. See you soon."

Felicity arrived just after four. "Sorry Dan, something came up at the last minute. You ready for this interview?"

"Yes, let's go. I was thinking to do it in her room. She'd feel safer there and there may be some objet d'art that we could use to further elicit conversation. Keep this low key and friendly. But we need to discover as much as we can about her father and his business associates."

The interview concerning the shopping centre incident went well, and was in depth. It covered information since discovered, especially from interviewing the suspects. Dan and Felicity lingered to talk about Ayesha's home life, and her parents, the real reasons why she ran away from home. They were both friendly, encouragingly inclusive, and had helped her so much Ayesha felt obliged to tell them things she would not otherwise have divulged.

Dan said, "We are almost done. Let me recap. Mohammad is the controller in UK, like an Italian Godfather."

"Yes, that is so. He is a vile man. He was one of Osama Bin Laden's first generals. Nowadays he has a high position within ISIL, and other groups, but exactly what I do not know.

"Ali and his greater family are all lawyers and moneymen. They came from the same Pakistani village, a Pashtun clan, as did Mohammad, and my father."

"And your father?"

"I hate him. He is not my real father. Here is my bill of sale as a baby. He is their Enforcer. I know he has killed many people. He is trying to make Waheed, my brother, follow in his footsteps. But he is a good boy, western educated like me, clever. He has a degree in economics and wants to be an economist."

Dan flicked his eyes at Felicity. "Interesting. Ayesha, let's finish here. That is, unless you have anything else you would like to tell us?"

"I could tell you where he keeps his secret papers. There is an office in Luton, part of a complex, but it has a back entrance."

"Give me the details, and then we'll go."

"Thank you, both. This is how to get in…"

When they got downstairs, Dan said, "We'll be having your excellent curry tonight. Do you offer take-away service?"

Brian, who was coming out of the cellar, overheard them "Take away you say. You're the fourth lot this week that have asked for that. All of them curries as well. I'm sorting some of them there Styrofoam boxes, but it'll be Monday before we can offer collection service. Maybe delivery to this village only, but it'll cost more mind."

"No problem, Brian. Next week it is then. We'll dine here tonight, but I need to check back with my office first, Felicity?"

"I'm going home to change and bathe. I'll see you in an hour or so."

Thursday began slowly. There were no terrorists en route to targets, and Felicity was slow to leave. Dan chilled at home until she departed, and then collected the away team. Alison said, "I'll do some shopping in London if there's time."

At the NCA headquarters they met with an assembly of people who did not know each other, and many who were wondering why they were there. Linda was running late and Dan needed to show control. He sent Alison to set Wendy up and turned to the group.

"Hi, I'm Dan Glover, SIS, or MI6 to you. I'll explain why you are here today, but first I want you all to introduce yourselves: name, nickname, regiment or background, skills, why you were seconded to this unit. We all need to get to know one another. I'll begin, I'm Dan…"

Dan noted the group had the credentials required, but were not a unit. They numbered twenty-three and were all specialists: pilots, radio operators, medics, unit or platoon commanders, and computer operators. One was a bomb disposal expert trained in the latest use of suicide vests, car bombs, and IED's used by ISIL.

Dan said, "Good, you will become the backbone of several units. I presume the ground troops will arrive tomorrow."

Dan was interrupted when Linda made her presence known. "Sorry I was delayed, but it was worth it. I have just received provisional approval for this unit to become active, as of this morning. Yes Dan, troops will be joining us over the coming days. Most are firearms officers, but some are ex-military. Dan, please continue."

"Thank you Ma'am. You will be working, at least during the initial phase, with information that our team provide. First I will introduce those of us here, and then I will tell you what we do."

Dan was brief, but thorough. He asked for and answered questions, quickly. "Good, that didn't take long. I will now show you the full threat facing this country. Alison, please set up the projector and run the prepared videos.

"Listen up. This is top-secret information, and what you see here and discuss today, stays in this room. Does everyone understand? You may not speak of this to anyone else in the NCA." Dan waited until each person individually agreed, before proceeding.

After the presentation, which Dan orated, the room was filled with disbelief, and many were speaking. Dan let them continue for a time, before calling order. "Now, I will show you what we have already traced as a result of monitoring enemy strongholds. Alison, if you please. I remind you all, you are here because the Met failed to respond. I'll explain as we go through the videos. They have been kept short."

Dan again orated the videos shown, asking other team members, including Wendy to comment. He finished by saying, "Please note, we only learned of their operational technique at Leeds. Birmingham should have been prevented, but the Met failed to turn up. That is why this unit was created.

"At Harwich, the intention was to blockade the port. We only managed to save as many people as we did because MI5 helped us out. Yes, we work with all services, including the RAF and GCHQ. Had the Met arrived in time, we would also have prevented the ferry disaster, but due to MI5 assistance, the ferry capsized just out of the main channel. We tasked them with damage limitation.

"Wendy can fill you in on the details of the way we work. She witnessed the Harwich Ferry disaster unravel. We rely on real-time satellite, digital speed cameras, and CCTV en route to target. Each of your teams must have at least one person competent with drones, small, multifunctional drones that have portable controls. Martin will ensure you have the knowledge, and Linda, you the drones themselves."

"Thank you Dan. I'll take questions, but remember we will continue with details this afternoon … Good. Time to break for lunch."

During the afternoon, Sinjun offered the NCA team insight into how ISIL operated, their tactics and goals. The director informed them, "The tactical experts won't be here until a week on Monday. Politics."

They finished early and left Martin as the face of the team. Dan reported in person to his Director, allowing Alison a shopping break.

"Well done Dan. This is a good beginning, and at least Martin is in the thick of it, and he will be learning. Now tell me in your own words about your meeting with this Ayesha. Do you think she will be useful to us, or is she a mole?"

It was early evening when the away team landed in Dan's field. He was able to turn on the landing lights using geek wizardry Tim had supplied. He called Veronica. "You're on speaker, thanks for holding the fort. We've just landed at my home, Alison and Sinjun are with me. Have there been any attacks today?"

"No, none at all, for the sixth day in a row. What's going on Dan? Why are they holding back?"

"Good question. I'm certain they have no idea that we are tagging them. There must be another reason. Sinjun, work on that at once. I think they have completed their trial runs and are now waiting for the concerted strikes to begin.

"What those are, we do not know. This may be the main event, or multiple attacks on one day, perhaps the same city, judging how emergency responders react. There is most definitely a mastermind behind how this whole thing is unravelling.

"I need you all to keep working on this until we discover the reason. Bounce your ideas off others. I have the premonition our weekend may be extremely busy, and I doubt the NCA will be up and running by then. Time to put the coffee on, we'll be with you in twenty minutes. Ciao."

As they were leaving Dan's home, his elderly neighbour from next door came over. "Sorry, not the introduction I had foreseen, but well, the wife, she wants to complain about the noise. You have a jet?"

"So sorry, national security. I'll requisition a quiet one, but it may take a few days. You must come round for dinner. My partner will arrange it, and soon. So sorry about the noise and it will be gone soon."

Once in the car, Dan said a curious thing. "What day is tomorrow?"

A chorus of Friday rang out, but Alison thought a little deeper, and said, "Yes, tomorrow is Friday. That is the Muslim holy day. Everyone attends prayers at the mosque--all of the men, and many of the women, but segregated."

Dan said, "If they strike, it will be tomorrow afternoon or evening, perhaps Saturday. I need every station manned, but those that need personal downtime, take it now. I'll leave you to sort it out amongst yourselves. If nothing happens by seven, then finish the day. Tomorrow will most likely be a long haul if I read this right."

There were no attacks on Friday, even insignificant ones. In the late afternoon, Dan said, "This is building for tomorrow. I believe a hurricane of Islamic jihad is about to be unleashed against us. I'll monitor until late. The rest of you should go and get an early night. It may be your last for a long time."

Chapter 41 ~ Triple Whammy

Dan started work early on Saturday. He called the NCA director, "Linda, how's it coming together? … Good. I have a dreadfully bad feeling about today. Are you in position to react if needs be?"

"Oh. Almost. I could put a team together, how sound is your information?"

"This is a gut feeling, Ma'am. But there has been nothing for one week, and after prayer meetings yesterday, I believe the enemy within will have completed plans for insurrection, beginning today."

"I'll get on it Dan, but please know gut feelings don't do much for me. I deal in facts."

"So do I, almost always, but my gut feeling has often saved the day. Please don't dismiss this lightly. Regardless, a strike is imminent."

As the call finished, Dan cursed, he had spoken like a charlatan. His mind wandered, but became distracted by the screen of Lillyworth Moor; a car left. He was immediately alert and called the team to action.

It fitted the attack vehicles precisely. There was a man driving a nondescript vehicle, and three women in the car. He recognised one of them from Luton, and brought up her file.

Dan called Wendy, but she was on a day off. "Dan, I'll be there as soon as I can. We're not set up properly yet, and many staff are off for the weekend. You'd better call Linda."

Dan did just that, told her what he had, and added, "Are you in a position to respond. Yes or No."

"Yes, I need one hour to assemble a team. It seems your gut was correct. You need guns on the ground, right?"

"Correct. And drones. Wendy is on her way in as liaison, I called her direct, sorry. She volunteered. Apologies if I trod on your toes."

"No problem this time, Dan. That is good. She knows you and how you operate. My next move would have been to call her in."

Dan finished the call, as Veronica entered with Alison one step behind. She said, "What is it Dan?"

"I told you this is what would be happening. Look at my screen, this car just left Lillyworth Moor. I have one girl's file open. She's ex-captive of Boko Haram. On this second screen, I have a second car that I picked up moments ago. Your timing is perfect. Follow it please."

They monitored the vehicles for some time. Dan said, "The first car is on the M180, headed west. It's not far from the M18, so we'll see where it goes. I've alerted the NCA, and they are mustering a response. They are not ready yet, but willing and partially able to respond."

"Wow. That's much better than the zero the Met have been giving us. Tracking now. Yes, the second car appears to be headed for the M180. Have you run facial recognition on its occupants yet?"

"No. I only just noticed them. Please follow through."

"Dan, do you think this is one of those double strikes you talked about? They seem to be following one another."

"Perhaps, but it depends upon what the target is. It's too early to speculate. However, I will call the Met as backup, just in case. We have nothing to lose and they have face to save. Regardless, we appear to have two targets. I'll also alert MI5."

Dan's called his Director, explaining the situation and their response to date. "Keep me informed Dan, but not too often, I'm trying to enjoy my first weekend off for ages with the grandchildren. We're at the seaside, and it's bloody freezing. They don't seem to feel the cold, and are having a great time. Ciao."

Dan tried to imagine the Director in a swimming costume on a cold November day, and quickly dismissed the image. Then he remembered about the complaint from next door, and called her back. "Damn you Dan. The only quiet jet we have is mine. I haven't even flow it yet. It's brand new. I had personalised it, but you better have it. I suppose I'll inherit your old one. Don't call me again."

As the call ended his eyes flicked to the Lillyworth camera display. "I've a third car. Alison, this one is yours. As before the car has one male driving, three female occupants. Running facial recognition software now … Match. Both girls landed at Luton on Monday, from Libya."

Veronica voiced her concern. "A triple hit. I don't get this."

"We will soon discover where. Ah, car one on the M18 headed north. I'll update the response teams."

They monitored a strung out procession. Dan said, "Car one now on the M62 headed west."

Veronica added, "Car two on the M18, headed north."

Alison said, "Car three now on the M180, headed west."

They continued to monitor, Wendy joining them on live feed.

Once the first car passed into the Pennines, Dan made his first call. "Wendy, we are a go. Destination as yet unknown. Get your team to Manchester ASAP, they will be in the ballpark. You remember how we narrow the target down. Your team must have drones with them."

Moments after Dan finished the update, Linda came through on a secure channel. "Ah, it works. Martin just set this up for me. Okay Dan, being our first job together I came into the office. Latest update please."

Dan briefed her, and added, "I apologise in advance, but I have also alerted other agencies, including MI5, and the Met. Had this been one vehicle, I would have left it up to you. But we have three cars, three potential targets, and they will be related in some way. You are not up and running yet. The fact that you have already responded does you credit. But, you do not have the resources to handle all three attacks."

"Thank you Dan. Sometimes being blunt works. Don't try me when we are fully functional. What do you think is going down?"

"I'd prefer not to speculate, for now. We have not identified any targets. We will have those when these cars leave the motorways, probably. I'll speak to you later, facial recognition just picked up a hit on the driver of car three, which raised a flag. Ciao."

Dan sat back and stretched his arms above his head, eventually crossing them on his pate. He remained silent, staring at the screen.

"What is it, Dan?"

"I don't know. Something is wrong about the third car. The driver is a top Al Qaeda, operative. He should not be on this trip. He is a general who runs disruption and guerrilla strikes. He does not go on them himself. Shit! I need a drone on this car, now."

Dan called MI5, but they had nothing to offer in the middle of the Pennines. However, they would have eyes on the vehicle once it entered range of Manchester. It was not enough for Dan, but better than nothing.

He called Derek at Bude, who was on a day off. His replacement cover, Ian, said, "I'm on it Dan, and fully up to speed with your operation. Who are you after?"

Dan sent a file with images, and waited for Ian's response.

"We have a file on this guy, an evil sod. I'll get clearance from Bernie, and send it to you. It's not a bedtime story. He's supposed to be in Libya. I'll run fifteen-point facial recognition on your feeds. He must have entered the country recently."

"We don't have a drone, and there's nothing suitable nearby."

"We use the RAF at Waddington, they are the UK drone kings–– long distance flight, and cameras capable of facial recognition. Missiles also. You should introduce yourself to them, but it's too late for today, I fear. Nevertheless, I'll provide live satellite feed down to facial recognition level. Resetting now. This will take a few minutes."

Dan spoke to Tom, then his Director requesting assistance, if in future, from Waddington. He updated with the team some time later.

"Car one now entering Manchester metropolitan region."

"Car two on the M62, headed west."

"Car three just joining the M62, also headed west."

Dan said, "We have a triple strike on our hands. I need to call the Chief Constable of Lancashire Police Force, and forewarn the Chief Constable of Greater Manchester."

Alison said, "I'll update the Met. I now know someone there. Let me try to get them airborne this time. Destination Manchester, I presume."

"Yes, thanks. Manchester airport, or nearby to begin with. Call Wendy first, I need her team in the air immediately."

Dan made a call to MI5, confirming the triple target to be near Manchester, or via it. The controller was not impressed. "Agent Glover, we need precise information before we respond, especially to third-party information. "

"Commander Glover! I thought we sorted all this bullshit out with your director. Respond, or you won't be there in time. Goodbye."

They monitored the procession, as minutes passed by. Dan said, "Car one now on the A57, southbound. Destination confirmed as Manchester city." He repeated the call to MI5, the controller reluctantly forwarding Dan's information.

He spoke to the Chief Constable of Greater Manchester next, who had formed a response unit. "Target confirmed as Manchester central, Sir. Precise targets as yet unknown. Please ready for instant deployment. We will update you in real-time."

Dan's mobile rang and he answered it abruptly. "Yes, Felicity."

"That's no way to greet your girlfriend. Where are you?"

"At work. We have three simultaneous attacks we are dealing with, and there are only three of us here. They appear to be targeting Manchester, but we don't have enough eyes on screens."

"I'll come over, and bring Percy with me. You seem stressed, boyfriend. Mwah. Ciao."

Dan stared at the phone, his thoughts blanked to only one person, as the call ended. He realised he had been sharp with her, and knew he needed to relax. He monitored until the car he was observing changed road. He said, "Car one now on the A57M, heading south."

A few minutes later, Veronica said, "Car two on the A627M. Different destination. It looks like Manchester is the target."

Dan updated the other agencies. The Met were in the air, but the NCA were not. Their director said, "Our paperwork hasn't been approved yet. I am sorting it out, just a few minutes. Sorry Dan, this is the beginning, and the unexpected happens."

Dan was precise in response. "Yes, like unsuspecting civilians being blown to pieces by Islamic head-cases. These deaths are on you, and the bureaucracy that stands in our way. Call me when you eventually get in the air. This time the Met are already on their way. Goodbye."

Alison said, "That was a bit harsh Dan, if justified all the same. You are the best boss I have ever worked with, but please, don't step over into bully-mode. It doesn't suit you, and neither does it work."

Dan had thought of several responses, when the door opened, and Percy showed Felicity inside. "Where do you need us?"

"Thank god. I missed you so much."

Dan hugged Felicity, and broke away to welcome Percy. "Thanks old chum, we are under the cosh here. This is what I need you to do. Percy, can you monitor car three, take over from Alison. I need her skills on reconnaissance. Percy, tell us where the car is going. Filly, I need someone on comm. You up for it?"

"'Felicity', or better, 'Chief' to everyone else here, thank you. Dan, sometimes you are a stupid boy. Who do I contact first?"

Dan knew that they would have coped successfully, but having two competent people dismiss the low level stress was a boon. Alison said, "Percy, before you begin, be a love and bring us hot drinks and some snacks, I'm starving. Percy went down and made drinks for everyone, including Stella, whose shop was busy. Later she brought up a tray of food, but rushed back down as the shop bell sounded.

Percy took over from Alison, but something strange happened. The car went into a tunnel, and did not reappear. "Dan, we have a problem."

"Show me."

Dan hustled over and watched the footage. The car reappeared, but it was missing for fifty seconds longer than it should have been. Then they discovered the driver was not the same person.

Dan ran facial recognition software, but spent most of his time studying the footage. They had swapped driver in the tunnel, and he needed to define the other vehicle.

Others spoke to him, but he replied with a curt word, or usually a hand shooing their words away. There was nothing. He backtracked camera footage before the tunnel, and went farther back.

Dan was about to give up when he noticed a car on the inside lane, flash headlights in the pattern three, one, two, as the target car passed by. He got the number plate, and initiated facial recognition. It was a long shot, but the best they had.

He got a match to the man now driving car three. He jumped in the air and shouted, "Got them! The sneaky bastards."

All eyes turned to him expectantly. "Alison, please find and follow this number plate, sending now. That is car four. This takes precedence over today's operation. I need you solely focused on this. Damn, no drones. Alison, pull the mother drone from Rochdale, it's the closest we have. Follow that car."

The room became quiet. Felicity spoke into the vacuum. "I have the Met and the NCA in the air. MI5 don't know how to respond, want me to have a word with them?"

"Yes, do your best. Tell MI5 not to intercept the car, the man we are after is now in a different vehicle, and we are tracking it. Also update the Chief Constables."

Minutes passed. Dan said, "Car one is leaving the inner ring road, the city centre cannot be the target unless they are avoiding traffic congestion. They are headed west towards Piccadilly. Options?"

Alison said, "The train station, one of the busiest in England."

A few minutes later, Veronica said, "Car two, is now on the M60, headed west. I think I know where they are going. Where's car three?"

Percy replied, "It's on the A56M headed for the West End."

Chapter 41

Felicity said, "I'm updating response teams now."

Dan spoke to the Chief Constable, who transferred him to Detective Superintendent Terry Meads, Officer in Charge. They exchanged numbers, and talked about the three strikes. "If our incomplete information is verified, we have a strike on Piccadilly train station, and possible coach station. Another car is headed for the West End, the shopping district, and my only guess is the third location, Manchester airport. Please dispatch armed teams towards all three locations. I'll liaise with the relevant managers, once all targets are confirmed.

"We work by zooming in on the target destinations, and having appropriate response near enough to be effective.

"Understood. Do we have backup?"

"Yes, the new NCA antiterrorist unit is on its way to Piccadilly. The Met antiterrorist unit are already at Manchester airport, and we hope to have a few MI5 agents near the shopping district. I'll call in bomb squad as well. I have Police Chief Inspector Wigglesworth on comm., so please send all but the most important information via her."

A short time later, the targets were confirmed as Manchester Airport, Piccadilly train station, and the busiest shopping arcade in Manchester. The team took appropriate action.

Alison said in support, "I traced car four Dan, headed into a residential area. Bude are now monitoring it. You still need me on it?"

"Yes. I need you to monitor car four and precisely identify where it goes, who leaves it, and where the occupants go Use the drone to cover the back and sides of buildings, tie it down so there is no way not covered. This will be the most demanding job. Each controller is now dedicated to one car and response team. Chief, please cover any gaps."

" I'll call your Director, she needs updating, you should follow up with MI5, try that number for the agent you know."

The strike on the airport occurred first, as they thought--the farthest away for emergency teams to respond to. The Met were inside and waiting. The car crashed through the main departure foyer, and was met with a hail of bullets. It came to the rest, with three dead, and one unconscious inside. Local police and the Met fought over jurisdiction, Greater Manchester force eventually taking charge.

Piccadilly was a more complex operation, but with the aid of station security and the British Transport Police, all the suspects were taken by surprise, and alive. The car was parked to take out the main entrance, but was deactivated by bomb squad just in time.

Dan said to no one, "You see how they work, disruption outside, then a major hub. That would have used up all spare response capacity, and more. Then they hit the shopping centre. The Met are relocating there, but time is a problem."

Felicity said, "I have MI5 on site at major entrances, and they are in communication with the shopping centre security. Evacuation has been ordered, and people are leaving by all exits. Car three has been waiting in a nearby side street.

"Greater Manchester Constabulary have since surrounded it, and there is a standoff. Wait … shots fired by snipers. The driver and woman controller are dead. The two girls threw their detonators out of the window.

"This is a major result Dan, team, congratulations. We'll celebrate tonight, but there will be a few hours of clearing up, and writing reports first. What can I do to help?"

"I need to speak with everyone that headed, or led teams today, Chief. Congratulate them on our first success, and it is a massive one. I need the words—a script, and then the calls stacked. I also need to apologise to Linda at the NCA, I was out of order, if correct. But I should not have said what I did, aloud at least."

After a rash of calls, Dan rang his Director. She was exceptionally pleased with the result. "Well done Dan. Pass my praise on to the team. This is a great result. My new jet has just been released, so I'll see to it you receive it soon. Ciao."

People set about writing reports. The stress evaporated, and they had their first success. A mood of euphoria was rising, when Sinjun called them to order. "Congratulations team. Excellent result. Please, stop what you are doing, and leave it until tomorrow. You all need to enjoy the moment. Come, it's my round. I'll put it on your tab Dan."

Felicity was first to respond. "I'll take you up on that offer, Sinjun, I feel a Pernod moment coming on."

They all went to the inn, but Dan caught Felicity speaking to Brian. When he asked why, she said, "Oh, everyone is having curry tonight, so I was just warning the kitchen. Cheers everyone. That was a great performance today. My parents are joining us."

Dan needed a word with Ayesha. He was planning to raid Hussein's offices, and wanted a brief update. He caught her before she became too busy, and they spoke aside for a moment. "I'll go in soon. Anything else you can tell me?"

Ayesha was gone for a moment, and on returning, handed him a folder. "I made this file for you. It's all in there. Tuesday early is good, they all go for morning prayers at five a.m."

"That is early. Thanks. I really appreciate this."

Dan rejoined the others, a half-plan forming in his mind. A short time later, Felicity left to greet her parents. Veronica went with her and said, "I'm driving, you may be over the limit. And anyway, I am the only one who hasn't seen this home of yours yet."

Chapter 41

When Veronica pulled into Dan's driveway, she enthused. Felicity gave her a short tour, but it was dark outside, and chilly. When they got to the second bedroom, purposefully the last room they entered, Felicity said, "Help me get this ready, my parents will be staying here tonight."

They were about done when Felicity's phone rang. "I'm five minutes out. Can you put on the landing lights?"

"Yes Ma'am, on my way."

The girls went to the hanger, and flipped various switches before the lights came on. "You stay to greet the Director, I better get back, as my parents should be here by now."

But for the lights, Veronica hardly noticed the plane come in to land. She welcomed the Director, plus two bubbly children who were overtired, and having a ball. "This is great 'Gan-ma'! Where's the air raid shelter?"

"Yes, where is it? You said there are two ways in."

"Not now children. Behave, or I won't bring you again."

The convoy proceeded to the village, and assembled around a large round table, with central Lazy Susan. The evening came to be remembered as the celebration of the first successful strike back at ISIL on British soil.

Before celebrations became overly enthusiastic, Felicity sidled up to Dan and said, "Walk with me."

"Is it about the baby?"

"No. Work. Shut up, and let me give you some news, once we're out of earshot … I've put the pair of them, Karen and Benaris under the microscope, and they both show up clean. The flies in the ointment are circumstantial, and easy to read too much into, or too little I guess. I'm perplexed. Other than have GCHQ trace every phone call, text message, and email between them, I have nothing that makes sense. I hate that."

"Not knowing?"

"Yes. I made a full copy of the file for you to go through. I hate to admit it, but we may need Alison on this. If she's good as you say?"

"No, she's better. What about the Chief Inspector, you dig anything up on him?"

"I never looked, and I doubt anything would show in our records. I'll pull his full file all the same."

"He must have upset somebody to end up there."

"I'll need to check, but I'm sure I read somewhere, he requested it."

"That's odd. Do your worst. I'll ask Alison to ride shotgun for both of them. That must be worth a kiss at least."

"Yes, and a cuddle … Stop it, we are being observed … That's enough Dan, let's get back inside, or no nookie for you tonight."

Chapter 42 ~ Flying in the Face of Destiny

Sunday began quietly, Felicity had put a leg of lamb in the oven on lowest setting overnight, and the smell was already whetting palates.

Meanwhile the Director visited the office, and afterwards drove down to the house in Dan's car, left on purpose for her use. The children were running around like headless chickens, keen to explore everything and everywhere. Dan helped them discover the air raid shelter, and he stopped often to play with them.

Felicity watched him with them and said aside, "He'll make a good father, given a bit more practice."

The Director agreed, "That he will. He has more patience with them than I have. But remember, children should be indulged, but not spoilt."

When Dan passed nearby the Director said, "Good. That will wear them out. I better hand over this plane to you, but I want it back when the replacement for mine is ready. You can customise that for your personal needs. Then I will leave."

Felicity said, "Please stay for Sunday lunch, we're having roast lamb, and there'll be far too much."

"Very well then, thank you. It's been a long time since I enjoyed a family Sunday, but I must be away by two. Dan, let's swap planes now." Tom accompanied them to the field, as Margaret helped in the kitchen.

Dan checked in with Veronica, but she was fine, reports all done, although Alison was busy. He invited them both to share Sunday lunch; "Dan I'd love to, thanks, I'll be there as soon as I've checked my car over, it's leaking water. And I'll drag Alison along with me. Ali, guess what..."

Sunday lunch was a great success, and after the Director departed, Dan told the neighbours that was the last time they would hear the noise. They were surprised to learn another, much quieter jet had landed. Later, Dan tightened a hose and stopped the leak on Veronica's car, and the two women visited until dinner time, before leaving to meet Sinjun in one of the Lower Meddlington pubs.

That evening, when the home was their own again, Dan wrote his reports, and when finished, sat back to think about his life, and his future. Felicity came in. "Penny for your thoughts."

I was thinking about impossible things, like the E word, the M word, and the C word."

Felicity interpreted, just to be sure. "You mean Engagement, Marriage, and Children. More than the one on the way."

"Yes. Not today, but I like having you around."

"So, you plan to entrap me by putting a ring on my finger. Or by getting me pregnant again. That won't work Dan."

"No, silly. My commitment to us as a couple. The future of our relationship, it needs careful consideration, and the timing."

Chapter 42

"Then these three words embody possibilities?"

Dan looked at her, his eyes crinkled. "No, probabilities."

"In that case I better sit on your lap and give you a kiss. I think we should have an early night."

Monday morning became a blizzard of interagency communication. Alison was in the middle of the chaos. Dan kept a watching brief as she and Veronica handled calls, and followed their prescribed response.

Dan called Derek at Bude. "Ah Dan, sorry I missed the action on Saturday. Excellent result by the way. Congratulations.

"Regards the terrorist chief in Manchester, we are monitoring twenty-four seven, and all who enter and leave, including via the rear access. We are also monitoring all nearby houses, just in case there are tunnels or interlinking lofts."

"Good. I have a drone up there that needs to be elsewhere. I'll recall it later today. What else?"

"We have a growing file, but no flags as yet. He is one of the ten most wanted men in the world, so we cannot afford any slip-ups. He uses many names, but in English is known as 'The Executioner'."

"Yes, thanks, I read his full file. Has he broadcast anything yet on the internet?"

"No, but we are monitoring the precise internet address, you will know as soon as we do."

"Good. I am fluent in Arabic, excepting some regional variations, so send me the original files. There will be an English version also, but they may not be the same, or mean the same. I mean no offence."

"Understood Dan. We have found this before. We are monitoring local cell towers and scrutinising all calls, text messages, the works. You have people nearby on the ground?"

"Greater Manchester Police have this in hand, but various agencies are still arguing about who has control. We do. This began as our operation, and remains so. My Director is fighting our corner, and winning. We also have agents who can mix in the area and not be discovered. Two should go in today. We pulled them out of Syria, as the greatest threat is now at home. They will have drones."

The call finished quickly and Dan checked on Percy. "It's going Okay Dan. There are a lot of drones to monitor, but little is happening most of the time. When it does, I watch and enter results in the log.

"Otherwise, I've caught up with everything since Martin left. I'm covering the whole thing except Lillyworth Moor. Alison's on that."

"It's time we took these aerodromes and Lillyworth Moor out. If we don't, we're just creating a bigger problem for ourselves to deal with in the future. Nobody in power seems to understand, or are even interested, so if the Muslims take out Parliament it may be a blessing in disguise. Sir Jack is working on an immediate and brutal response."

Dan called the Director, who had been busy that morning. "Good news Dan, GMP, Greater Manchester Police that is, were most impressed with your operation and are relying on you personally to follow through. They have the captives in a secure police station and want you to interview them. I will join you, say this afternoon?"

"Ma'am, always a pleasure."

"I wished you meant that, but I'll take what's on offer. Collect me from London City Airport at one-thirty, in my jet. Don't you dare put a scratch on it. Ciao"

Later that day, they conducted a series of interviews, the Director doing much of the talking, and Dan profiling. After the last was led out of the room, and knowing they were still being videoed, the Director said, "What do you think?"

"It's pretty clear, Ma'am. Four of the five living, girl suicide bombers are glad to be freed. One is not. I consider her to have been brainwashed. Same with the man and woman. They are hard cases, and will be tough to crack."

The Director said, "I agree Dan, that's the way I read it, although we have something on the man. Came in just before I left the office, and could be a lever. I'll leave it to the locals to play with."

The Director looked up at the camera and raised her voice. "I presume you are still videoing, Police, so send someone senior in here to finish up. Refreshments would be nice as well."

They did not speak again until a man in a suit entered, followed by a uniformed Constable carrying a tray of drinks. "Detective Superintendent Terry Meads," he saluted. "Good interview, Ma'am. Dan, a pleasure to meet you in the flesh."

"Likewise. You heard our comments. Reaction?"

"As we read it Ma'am. Dan, you were taking notes, may I have a look?"

"No, if only because some comments are personal. I'll give you a factual copy before we leave, but I'll need access to a computer."

"Yes, let's get out of here. You can use my office, the Constable will bring your drinks up."

Dan said, "Thanks Terry. You heard our comments on the girl from the airport, what did you make of her?"

"She didn't fit. The others are victims. She's crossed the line."

"Exactly. I think we can turn the man. My Director has something on him. It's worth a try at least. Your team will take over interviewing the hardliners, and they won't be easy to break. MI5 may be able to assist, but in instances like this, they operate on the fringes of the Human Rights Convention, as sometimes do we.

Chapter 42

"What of the four girl victims? Have you anywhere for them to go, as in extremely safe and secure accommodation? Monitored of course."

"Yes we do. Its public face is that of secure housing, but it is more like a hostel come open prison. They have rooms and share the catering and cleaning. Donations provide funds for food, et cetera."

"Good, do you have room for five more? We have other ex-Boko Haram victims that need securely placing, and I'm not happy with their current situation. You say the place is monitored?"

"Yes it is. Full electronic surveillance."

"I'd love a feed of what they say to each other. The secret bits will be in the Hausa language, and you'll need to run whispers by a lip reader. We may have a handle on that. Can we work together, on all these girls?"

"Can't you return them to their homes and families?"

"We'd like to, but no. They would be executed for disgracing family honour––they had sex outside of marriage. To these people, the fact that it was rape is irrelevant. I spoke to several of the girls about this and they all said the same thing. One saw her parents executed."

"In that case, I'd need to pass this one upstairs, but I have no objections and will recommend it. I have found that by getting people under subtle scrutiny to talk to each other, we learn a lot more."

"Exactly, that was my intention. Ma'am?"

"This is a good result, well done the pair of you. Have you finished the report yet Dan, ah yes. I believe we are done here, until next time Detective Superintendent, and thank you."

Dan dropped the Director back at London City airport, and she said, "You better head for RAF Cottesmore, a little bird told me Sir Jack will call you soon. A boys' jolly I believe. Ciao."

Dan had been sideswiped by the Director's last comment, so stopped his plane's taxi to the runway, and called base. "We're fine Dan. Dead as a dormouse here. How'd it go?"

"Remarkably well, I'm sending files now, including the GMP interview recording. I believe it is complete. Otherwise, Manchester has secure housing for all the Boko Haram girls, and we will have video access. Start the ball rolling to move the other girls to Manchester. The Director is seconding a Hausa language expert, but she will remain in London, I think. Excuse me, I must take this call."

Dan switched to his second line, "Sir Jack, my pleasure."

"I read your full file, and you evaded a live heat-seeking missile on tour of duty. I also know you are a Harrier fan. I'm on my way to RAF Cottesmore, they have three ready for flight. Care to join me? I'd like to put the craft through their paces, if only for old time's sake."

"I'm en route, ninety minutes. I'm just leaving London City."

"We'll arrive together. Lock, no load."

"Agreed. A dog-fight it is, Sir."

Sir Jack arrived first, and was chatting with the Station Commander when Dan landed. Their talk was confidential, so Dan spoke to a hastily arranged flight crew and checked over all three aircraft himself.

Sir Jack was dropped off by jeep, and shook Dan's hand. "Good to see you again old boy, and so soon. Walk with me. Oh, and congratulations on the excellent result on Saturday.

"Ah, this should be far enough away. Dan, you are here under false pretences. After due consideration, and considerable research, I have decided to back your plans, at least in principle, to take out these bases. The only problem is, that call is not mine to make, but rests with the Prime Minister, at least, for as long as he remains in office.

"Our current batch of political imbeciles couldn't run a piss-up in a brewery. And as for handing over our sovereign powers to become a vassal state of some European Super-state. Well, it goes against everything I believe in."

"Agreed, Sir. You have a plan, maybe two?"

"You are perceptive as well. Yes, three actually. I've been talking discretely with the other two chiefs, plus our own at the RAF. We have agreed to hold war games, the objective, to take out a base in Libya. We have that coming anyway. We are publicly modelling the attack on Raqqa, but the base we will hit will be a copy of Lillyworth Moor. We need to know what could go wrong."

"Excellent. Much respect, Sir."

"I also had a chat with the Admiral of the Fleet, and he is as upset as I am. He has two aircraft carriers, and no sailors or planes to put on them. Last time he had to borrow fighters from the French."

"Libya. That country would still be stable if the British and French had not decided to remove Gaddafi."

"Precisely, and now look at the state of it. I could say the same for Iraq. I doubt that ISIL, the Afghanistan war, would ever have happened were Saddam still in power. He was barbaric, but knew how to control his people. These are tribal people. Giving them democracy is something they cannot comprehend. They vote for who they are told to vote for, and warlords take over. The machine gun is their ballot box.

"Regardless, the Senior Service has quite a few Sea Harriers, Tornados, and even Jaguars that are almost in serviceable condition. He and I are surreptitiously refurbishing what we can.

The third point is, these three planes today are finished, but the bureaucratic paper trail reads as if restoration is ongoing. Between you and I, the next three fighters are nearly ready. This is not refurbishment, but a far lower standard. 'War Readiness'. That means that they will fly and deliver payload, warts and all."

"This is great news, Sir Jack, but where does it leave us in practicable terms?"

"As Shakespeare penned, 'therein lies the rub'. The military have the power to act, but only if there is no government, and upon command of The Queen. I, we all, are preparing for that moment. The Director informed me it was your considered opinion they would do a nine-eleven. Take out Parliament, maybe Civil Service, and Royalty."

"Yes, Sir. That remains my considered opinion, along with say, the City and financial hub. I believe it will happen within the next week or so. You better hone your battle skills."

"Our false war begins on Thursday, but we can begin today. It's been twelve years or more since I flew one of these things, so I may be a little rusty."

"Four for me, Sir Jack. Dogfight and get lock, game over."

"Precisely. Perhaps a moment to try to break lock, but we will have comm. between us. Let's get to it. Oh, and the Wing Commander is joining us, making the odds one against one, against one."

"Ah, a Mexican Standoff, excellent!"

All three planes were in the air ten minutes later. The pilots familiarised themselves with the aircraft, regaining skills, flying formations, and performing various flight routines. Sir Jack came over comm. "It's just like riding a bike, one never forgets. I'm as ready as I'll ever be. Red wing, break to port, Blue wing, break to starboard, I'll continue and return. Lock, no load."

All three managed to gain lock on the others, but Dan was the only one able to break lock. He used a severe manoeuvre, diving low for air density, before pulling the nose up sharply, and used the thrust of his vertical landing jets to escape the threat. Under excruciating G-Force, he only just managed to pull out in time, his actions pre-planned. He was momentarily unconscious, but slowly came alert.

Regaining full senses, he used the thrusters gently to loop a tight loop, and locked on his aggressor. Feeling weak, he retired, the other two continuing until night encroached.

Chapter 43 ~ Undercover

Dan was in high spirits when he arrived home. He checked in with the office, but they were winding down.

Felicity was already at home when he walked in the back door. "I wasn't expecting to see you for days, what's up?"

"I'm fed up with living out of a suitcase, so decided to come home. I told them I'd take the housing allowance instead. It's worth almost two grand a month. The commute will be a drag, but I can pull local station visits, both here, Wymondham, and others, so it won't be too bad."

Dan rushed to hug her. He was over the moon. "That's fantastic news. I love having you here, it makes this house feel like a home."

"Same here regards you. I didn't hear you land."

"That's the new quiet jet. I'll get my own version in a month or so, but for now, I'm using the Director's, and she's not happy about it."

"Maybe not, but you are. What've you been up to today to put you in such good spirits?"

"Well, I met Sir Jack, and after a most informative discussion, we flew Harriers in simulated dogfight. I was the only one to break missile lock, but cricked my neck. I'll go up for a massage bath."

"What did you do, Dan?"

"Just pulled the nose up, and activated the landing thrusters."

"Did you black out?"

"Yes, but only for a moment. I had already begun to stop the thrust. I pulled four-point eight G. In Iraq it was five-point three."

"Are you mad? Go, I'd better cook tonight. What do you fancy?"

"Fish and chips. I need to keep tonight simple, and I'm early to bed. I leave for Luton at four a.m. to pay Hussein's office a visit."

Very early the following morning, Dan hired a white van at Luton airport, and was in situ ten minutes later, his watch read five o'clock. He exited the side door, dressed in jeans and hoodie, looking like a lost soul on the way back home from a party. He also donned a nondescript backpack and looked at the pavement, as if off on a drugged trip. There was nobody about, but Dan always took precautions. Sometimes there were hidden cameras, or unknown eyes watching.

He sloped into the nearest alley to his target and made a show of stopping to urinate. Undercover, his eyes were alive, and his adrenaline rushing, a feeling he had not experienced for some years.

He had spotted the two cameras he needed to take out, wary of a third Ayesha did not know about. He had a special camera with him, like a Polaroid. It had instant print capabilities, but state of the art. He jumped and scrambled onto the top of the wall the first camera was fixed to, and aligning sight with that of the camera, took an image.

Chapter 43

He cut out the result, and placed it inside a plastic cap, which he then pushed over the lens. Walking atop the wall, he did similar with the second camera, and looked for others. There were none, so he hopped down inside the wall, all senses aware, and made for the door Ayesha had told him about.

It was not the main rear door, but one to the side that looked like it had not been used in years. He was a little out of practice with using skeleton keys, the lock rusty, but he remembered his academy training, and released the catch. He gulped and opened the door, expecting an alarm to sound. The night remained quiet, and he was in.

He mentally followed Ayesha's map, keeping sharp watch for movement detectors, and avoided two. It turned out the building only had cameras outside, and on the main internal thoroughfare.

Upstairs, he slowly nudged the door of Hussein's office open, checking with a wire wand for sensors. There were none. He examined every cupboard and drawer, taking snapshots of anything he found interesting. His mission was reconnaissance, not understanding what he was looking at. That was until he removed a bottom filling cabinet drawer, and found folders of highly sensitive documents beneath.

He went through each one, having worn surgical gloves since picking the lock, carefully replacing each exactly as it had been. When he was done, he zipped and sent his night's research to Alison, his own secure email, and the Director. 'Main mission accomplished'.

Checking the night sky, and his watch, he went through to the adjoining office, and discovered a private diary, which made for revealing reading. He wasn't sure if the person was a plant, and checked for identity. It was Hussein's son, Waheed. It contained a record of the aircraft that had entered UK, and their passenger/cargo list going back several years. He wondered, 'was it for personal use, or insurance?'

There were entries for the coming days, a rise of activity, and then a lull. Dan knew he had the ISIL day of attack down to a half of one day. He started recording at the last entry, and worked backwards.

Daylight was approaching, and he had much information to gather. He leafed through pages as fast as he could with his phone on video. He would unravel the all of it later: having the information was key.

He left sharply when the copy was finished, covering his tracks, and leaving from the far end of the alley. He turned left, the opposite direction from the van, and in a doorway, removed the hoodie. He replaced it with a light jacket, and put his backpack into a carrier bag. Final touches were a cap and spectacles.

He returned to Luton airport and dictated notes once airborne. The flight was short and Dan arrived home in time to catch Felicity leaving. He ran down the drive to her departing car, kissed her lips, and smiled; each relieved the other was okay. It was all either needed to know.

Dan compiled his report, called in work, and then spoke to his Director. He sent a full copy to work, and another to Derek at Bude. He spent most of the day, deciphering, analysing, and cataloguing the information he had discovered. He had almost finished going through the video of the diary when somebody came in the front door.

Going to investigate he called out, "Felicity, is that you? What are you doing back so soon?"

"It's after seven Dan, I worked late. Have you been here all day?"

"Yes, been in the library all the time."

"Jezzz! I bet you didn't eat either. What am I to do with you? Today you broke into somebody's office, and stole private information."

"You should see what I got, the entire plan for the takeover of Blighty. It begins next week. Are you going to arrest me, or kiss me?"

"Neither. You are going to take me out for the night. I need a large Pernod and chicken tikka masala. You have been bragging about eating prawn vindaloo, so tonight you prove it. You are driving, and I'll be ready to leave in thirty minutes."

"Ma'am, it will be as you desire."

Before Felicity could reply, Dan withdrew to the library. He was dedicated to finishing the day's work before they departed.

Later, they joined the others in the bar for a short while, but made their way through to the restaurant. This was their night together. Dan struggled with the vindaloo, and sweat beaded his brow.

Ayesha came to check on them. "Are you enjoying the meal?"

"Yes, it's wonderful, but I think Dan is a little hot. Have you anything to ease that?"

"Well, I didn't pull any punches with the chillies, but yes. Drink milk, not beer, and have a dessert with fresh cream. I can also whistle up a Tarka Dal, without the spices, just lentils, oil, ginger, and garlic. It takes the edge off the heat. The ones that have curry in them don't. I have portions in the freezer, I just need to nuke one. Say five minutes?"

Dan's face was turning redder. Felicity said, "Better bring two. It sounds healthy, so I'd like to try it as well."

Ayesha returned a short time later. Felicity loved it, and Dan became a fan within moments, the heat of the vindaloo being absorbed to the point he began to enjoy the meal again, despite his numb mouth.

Ayesha said, "Felicity, I need a word with you. Both Brian and Dan are hopeless at money. Dan owes Brian a lot, and it's time to settle up."

"Dan, how long since you last paid?"

"I don't know, a few weeks, a month I guess."

"That's for the room, yes? And the tab for bar and restaurant?"

"Yes, that's probably a few thousand by now. Damn, with everything else going on, I completely forgot. Tell Brian I'll pay him immediately, and also pay the tab in advance in future, say one grand."

"I am sorting this out, Dan. I've never met anyone so hopeless with money. I think you should have your wages paid into the joint account, then I can cover all your spending easily."

"And you will pay yours in as well?"

"No. This is the way marriage works Dan, 'What is yours is mine, and what's mine is my own'. Understand?"

"That doesn't seem fair. Are you sure?"

"Positive."

"So, in that case, what will your own wages be spent on?"

"You still don't get this, do you? I will be buying food, probably cooking most of it, buying things for the home, and spending most of the rest on raising the children."

"Yes, about children. We don't have any yet."

"We're not married yet, and you haven't proposed to me."

"Accepted. But ignoring the circumstantial trivia, I think I must be doing something wrong. We still need to practice making babies more often. What do you think?"

"I think you are only after using my body for your personal gratification. I am already pregnant, remember? Practice unnecessary."

"I'm going to have a word with Brian, sort out your tab, and you are sleeping in the spare room tonight."

The next morning, Dan woke as Felicity was stirring beside him. He recalled their banter of the night before, and how it almost became serious, but not quite. They shared a sense of humour, but were both independent people. He realised that their marriage would be good, entertaining, and never boring. He was thinking about popping the question, when his phone rang.

"Dan, I just got a call from Bude. The Executioner has left under heavy disguise, and is in a car headed east. We are both monitoring."

"Alison, I'm on my way in."

"Don't hurry Dan, this has a strange feel about it. They are in an SUV, which I have a drone on. I still need to go through the information you sent in, but I think this is preparatory work. I know you make your reports in the morning, so finish them. I'll call when you are needed."

Instead of making a marriage proposal, Dan offered to make a pot of coffee, and was soon working in the library. His reports sent, he checked in with Alison, who was still monitoring progress.

Dan was making an in-depth report for Sir Jack, when Alison called. "Dan, The Executioner is at the Rochdale airstrip. I have satellite feed, and our drones in place. He is being treated with greatest respect."

"He's setting up the operation for next week. You read the diary. I think we are looking at a long week before they move to take us out. We cannot strike until they do. I find that curious. Keep me updated. Ciao."

Dan sat back to consider what was actually going on. His arbitrarily spoken words were key. 'He is the commander on the ground in Blighty. Visiting all airfields makes sense, but driving does not.'

He called Alison back. "I think The Executioner will visit all the airstrips today, ending up at Lillyworth Moor. Look for him using aeroplanes, and forward any new squawks to Trimingham. Let me know if anything breaks that pattern. I'm currently working on our response to his nine-eleven style strike at the fabric of our nation."

"Get to it, Dan. Sometimes I feel there are only a few of us with Britain's best interests at heart."

"You are correct. Bye."

Dan worked until mid afternoon, and considered calling Sinjun, before realising he needed to support the team with his physical presence. His report for Sir Jack, an appraisal of the forthcoming strike and response had been difficult. It included an assessment of the number of possible targets, ones that Dan had attempted to grade. He needed to speak to the Brigadier about his grading system.

Arriving at the village, Dan checked with the team first. Alison said, "You were correct, he is working through all the airfields in turn, and just left our local one, and we got some high quality images."

"Great work team. Everything else okay?"

The skies were growing prematurely dark, black thunderheads of cumulus nimbus were gathering as Dan made his way downstairs to pick Sinjun's brain.

Dan laid out his plans as a proposal to Sinjun, who took them with great regard. He suggested only a few minor modifications.

"Dan, this is all theoretical, but I have been working along similar lines since we left Sir Jack. Tell me what the EU is?"

"Well, it started as the Common Market, but then became the ECC, and now the EU."

"That is correct for the uneducated, which you are not. What form of financial policy do they practice?"

"Capitalism."

"No. You are quite wrong in that belief. They practice 'Monnetarism', usually re-branded as Monetarism. It's an inside joke the bureaucrats love. The founder of modern Europe is Jean Monnet, and he foresaw a united Europe run by a technocracy, elections and referendums to be avoided at all costs. It's the same political theory Hitler used, except he changed it to being one man in charge. The modern EU has no one in charge, and it is out of control.

"In summary, Capitalism is mostly found in democratic countries, and is focused on trade, often free trade, and subject to market forces. Profit is the key motivation. The will of the people is paramount.

Shareholders, directors, governments even, are held accountable for their actions. Some for the profit return on investment, but also by the general public. A rogue or cheating company will soon go out of business, as will one that ignores ethical trading.

"By contrast, the popular Monetarism is focused solely on money, as the name implies: profit. It pays scant regard to business morals and trading ethically. The only important thing is that the bosses earn as much money as possible. An example: the government prints money to keep the banks and large institutions healthy, while the pensions of ordinary people are raided and continually underfunded. Instead of pumping the money in, they increase the pension age so people have to work into their seventies, so the government save on pension payments. The printed money could go to top that up, or pay for a proper health service, but no. Money for the bosses and investors is their only concern.

"Monnetarism is concerned with the creation of a super state, where nobody is in charge. All trade is regulated, as are the everyday lives of the population. In essence, it is a degree more left wing than Communism. Read Orwell's book. This technocratic system can survive in both communist and capitalist systems, but not in a dictatorship, unless, like Hitler, the leading technocrat takes absolute power."

Thunder rumbled and lightening cracked outside, as Sinjun began pacing the room. "So how does this relate to our current state of affairs?

"Simple. Within the coming week, Luxembourg and Belgium will become Islamic States, and introduce Sharia Law. This means that the social structures and restrictions we have been subject to under Monnetarism, will now be adapted and become new edicts under Sharia Law. The bureaucracy is already in place, as are the EU conduits to make it so."

"Sinjun, this is a nightmare. I had not thought about it so deeply."

"It is the most likely outcome. Dan, I would expect some of the bureaucracy behind the EU project to be dead within twenty-four hours. ISIL will laud over the world, their capture of Europe, now their Caliphate.

"Oh, and to give you the whole picture, the EU is a project of the UN, who want to rule the world using the same doctrine, one Germany conceived before the end of The Great War."

"Sinjun, I already know much of what you just said is true. The United States of ISIL. Caliphate Western Europe. I bet those imbeciles in Brussels never saw that one coming. We need to put the 'Great' back into Britain. It will no doubt fall to us to stop World War Three--which appears to have already begun. I'll catch you next time. Thank you."

Chapter 44 ~ War Games

Dan spent Thursday morning finalising his projections of likely war scenarios, and the afternoon with the Chiefs of Staff, as a guest monitoring their war games. The battle area had been quickly prepared, and wooden constructions marked positions of structures, the full size marked by white lines, representing buildings and places of importance.

Advance troops went in on the ground, and later by helicopter, after all communications had been taken out, including cell relay towers. Whenever a problem became apparent, or things did not go quite to plan, Sir Jack or another, would comment, suggest changes, and ask for military options. Sir Jack concluded by telling the small assembly, "We'll have the Harriers covering some of those problems for the real thing. Other area will require further attention to detail."

Dan had planned to leave shortly after the game was done, but was asked to stay by Sir Jack. They held a full debrief with unit commanders, before top brass retired to the now empty command room.

Sir Jack began, "We now have fifteen Harriers ready for action, with another six on the way. How's it going with the Navy?"

"Very well, Sir Jack. We never actually mothballed two squadrons of Tornados and are having them made ready. They will be serviceable, if nowhere near approved standard. We Chiefs have all moved to 'war ready' status, the lowest category of combat readiness."

"Commendable. Continue."

"We also have two squadrons of the latest Harriers, two of Jaguars, and one of Phantoms that will require more work. We are aiming to get as many planes and ships into the theatre of war as possible. Our recently retired Sea King helicopters are still serviceable, and we have several Chinooks also being readied.

"We are mobilising gunboats. Much of the fleet is also being recalled. I thought to deploy a destroyer or two in the lower reaches of the Thames, and other major cities. They will be of the latest specification, able to take down enemy war planes. We'll call it 'war games' again.

"With your permission, I plan to put our aircraft on three aircraft carriers. The two new ones, plus HMS Illustrious, recently retired from service, but still capable, given a crew. That is my only problem.

"To cover as many bases as possible, we have also re-commissioned the old Trident fleet of submarines, as well as other submarines, and are fitting all with a range of non-nuclear ballistic missiles and torpedoes. The extant nuclear deterrent will not be affected. These will be deployed to take out enemy reinforcements by sea, and supply bases either in this country, or overseas."

"Bravo. And the Army?"

Chapter 44

"We are a skeleton service of what we should be, but we have stopped all premature retirements. We are contacting recently retired men at arms to take up duty again, and have plans in place to bring back as many troops as possible from foreign countries."

Sir Jack said, "This must be kept news dark. If word gets out, either to our own government or the terrorists, we'll be up shit creek without a paddle."

"That is our modus operandi, Sir. I have a teams in place making personal calls and visitations to ex soldiers. I have also upped recall of marines and special forces, so we have enough troops to take out these Islamic airbases. I am counting on backup from the SAS and the SBS.

"There will be great demand for artillery. Again, serviceable vehicles, mainly howitzers and light tanks are being prepared. We also have mobile SCUD units, and are ready to deploy anti aircraft and anti-missile batteries at your command. In brief, all offensive, defensive, transport, and auxiliary units are being put on standby. Some are state of the art, whilst others are at best are 'War serviceable'.

"As a fourth operation, we are mobilising helicopters, especially the Lynx, of which many were put into storage for sale. They will ferry troops, and also field hospitals. We have medics on standby to provide immediate emergency cover in situ. We will need them all, as well as troops, on the streets of England.

"That we cannot manifest until the threat is made real is a major concern, Sir Jack."

"Yes, it is to all of us, but we can do nothing until the government either responds to the threat, or is obliterated. Only then can we act. I will notify the Queen, and the Prime Minister on the morning of the day of attack, which we now know thanks to Commander Glover here. I hope the PM gives permission for us to act, and I know we are all drawing up a secondary plan, should that be the case. I doubt that will happen, nobody in power has believed us so far.

"Thank you Field Marshal. It is good we are all doing the best we can under most trying circumstances. Air Marshal, regards the RAF?"

"In addition to your own preparations, Sir Jack, I'm also bringing some mothballed Tornados back into service, if unofficially. We are readying Jaguars, Phantoms, and anything that will be able to fly in time, and fitting what weapons we can. Because of third party concerns, especially Russia seeking advantage, I have put the Nimrod back into active service, the first should be in the air by tomorrow evening, Sir."

"We have also notified the USAF bases, but they are giving us 'the finger'. Their standard response is that they have appropriate cover. I doubt they do."

Dan spoke for the first time. "So, they are our Achilles heel."

"Dan, you should not be here, but I made an exception because you have been following this from the beginning, and without you and your team's efforts, we would still be in the dark. Have you any comments, something to add?"

"Thank you, Sir Jack. I am aware that years ago the USAF moved many of their aeroplanes to Germany, to counter the Russian threat, but they still maintain several bases in Blighty. What if one or more of those were overrun. Or one on the continent? I agree with you, they have zero idea what is coming. This is our problem, so let me move on.

"The response of all three services is admirable, and I just wish our own civilian security services were as receptive. Were we able to take these fanatics out before they attack, the result would save many thousands of lives. You will all have read my own, and my team's reports, so I won't go over old ground.

"Regards Blighty, not only do we need to take out all centres under Islamic control today, but also those that will be tomorrow. We are expecting many towns, counties, and some cities, to declare for the governorate of ISIL, after, or just before the main attack begins. This will paralyse reaction and emergency services.

"We expect Bristol, and at least one other major airport to be taken out, probably Gatwick because it is the easier target from a military point of view, and closer to the continent. Heathrow is the prime target regards prestige. When in control, they may use the airports to bring in more troops and arms, from anywhere in the world. They will also use our own aircraft against us, think 'nine-eleven'.

"Again, suicide teams might fly incumbent commercial aircraft into other unidentified targets, and not necessarily in UK. I repeat, like in New York, they will use our own resources, our own aircraft, against us.

"And that brings me to my next point. We will have no allies. I expect both Luxembourg and Belgium to be pronounced Caliphates. The EU in Brussels will be liquidated. There will be no survivors, and probably likewise in Strasbourg too. Expect all European Member parliaments to be taken out, along with their civil service. We will stand alone once more.

"Back home, we will need to prepare for the processing and safe keeping of prisoners of war. I noticed none were taken today."

Sir Jack smiled knowingly, "Yes Dan, that is a very good point. The best way of dealing with prisoners is not to have any, or at least, process them in a timely fashion. I am thinking hours and days, but more I cannot discuss at the moment. Please continue"

"Drones, Sir Jack. We need more of them for surveillance, and I believe some can be fitted with weapons. They would be useful for us. I suspect the enemy may already have a stockpile; my question is, can we take them out when airborne for attack or spying?

Chapter 44

Sir Jack looked around and murmuring resulted. With nothing forthcoming Sir Jack replied, "Excellent observation, I guarantee we will be working on it. Is there anything else?"

"There's just one more thing, something that Sinjun came up with that has me deeply concerned. What would be the outcome if the Turkish government were removed and all borders, except to Russia, opened? I will leave you with that disquieting thought."

Sir Jack said, "Thank you, Dan. That was most incisive. I want all of you here to remember these words, because without us standing firm, for the third time in one hundred years, Europe is lost, this time to the tyranny of Islam. 'We are putting the Great back into Britain'."

Everybody stood and shouted the words. A pact had been made. Sir Jack looked at Dan and said, "Is there anything else?"

Dan replied, "No Sir, except to say that my home has a field suitable for landing Harriers and helicopters, if you have need of a forward base. I am also available to fly a Harrier, should you end up with more aircraft than pilots. Good day Sirs, and thank you."

Dan called work before he departed, and caught up with Alison, then rang Felicity. He faced a long flight, and needed to take on fuel before returning home. Later, he discovered Felicity had cooked shepherd's pie, which was keeping warm in the oven. It was delicious, moreish, and he managed two large platefuls, before dozing off in the armchair. She gentled him to bed where he slept like a log.

Chapter 45 ~ ISIL Rebellion Begins

Dan was back on top form in the morning, telling Felicity what he could about his adventures and preparations for war. He also shared his concerns. "We did well last weekend, and starting tomorrow, attacks will increase dramatically. My problem is, we cannot continue to prevent all attacks from Lillyworth Moor. I'm surprised they haven't already smelled a rat."

"Then stick one of your team, or Bude, on identifying other attacks. Ask Tim to create an algorithm to detect possible cars, and run it through traffic cameras via GCHQ. You tell me this is a threat to the very fabric of our nation, so act as if it is."

"Words of wisdom. Thank you. I'll action that in a moment and see how many lives we can save during the coming week. This is going to be hell for ordinary people, and a media frenzy for the press."

In the event, Dan and Alison securely disseminated the nature of the typical attack vehicle to all agencies and police forces. It was marked secret, and to be actioned discretely by those in charge. The brief included short video footage of various strikes they had on file.

Dan kept in close contact with his Director, and the leaders of antiterrorist forces: the NCA, Met, and also with MI5. The strikes began late on Friday afternoon, presumably after religious prayers and meetings concluded. They followed the plan from Manchester. First a strike out of town, drawing out first responders, followed by a second strike, seemingly cutting them off from their base, then a third strike at the heart of the city or primary target.

The police camera operators had some success, as did GCHQ, and one third of strikes were thwarted. To begin with, the strikes appeared to be random, and Dan commented, "I believe they are letting the local teams do what they will. We will pass on forty percent of our information regards threats originating from Lillyworth Moor. To do otherwise would lead to great suspicion and compromise our final play."

Late on Saturday, Dan asked the team to work twenty-four hours; all time off was cancelled. He moved back into the pub and began the first night watch with Veronica. She would continue to cover the night shift until the main threat was realised.

Percy went home, but returned later with Ben. He had answered the call of duty, and would assist Veronica during the night. That evening they taught Ben what to do and look out for. Dan insisted he sleep at the inn in relative luxury.

As it emerged, target cities and infrastructure were hit in a series of blows, mainly between 10:00 and 22:00 hours. Ben became extremely busy in the quiet hours, monitoring aircraft and vehicles that were moving people and equipment into position for the next day's attacks.

Chapter 45

From the diary Dan had photographed, he had expected the attacks to calm down on Wednesday, but they increased. He surmised, "Obviously those plans had not been finalised when I read the entries. In that case, expect everything to get worse."

And it did.

During those days, trust between their team, the NCA, Met, and MI5 increased dramatically, as did their joint collaboration and response. GCHQ became more central in defining terrorist threats, and Dan handed over speed camera monitoring of Lillyworth Moor to them.

The upshot was that during that week, Dan's team became the foremost reporting centre for correlation and dissemination of information about possible terrorist strikes. Much intelligence was provided by GCHQ; the teams role, to provide appropriate response. They were busier than ever, often working with several threats, and police forces concurrently.

Dan realised the team were suffering from information deluge, and occasionally pertinent facts of the moment were not to hand. He acted at once; "Alison, can you set up a feed? Something like a ticker-tape, and send it to the main screen."

Moments later, Alison sent the feed, and said, "Is this what you want? You'll need somebody to add the info, I have too much on."

Dan said, "This is still a mess. I need a box of ticker-tape for each threat we are following, so everybody in this room, at a glance, can see the current state of play."

"I'm on in ... there, that do for you? It is much clearer now."

"Perfect Alison. We do not have enough people. One minute."

Dan went downstairs, and came back with Sinjun. "...As you'll see, we are critically short staffed. I need you to input info into the ticker-tape boxes, and help us follow events. Not what you signed up for, but what is required of you. I need a new info box with breaking news, that of the major kind--things outside of our knowledge or control. Europe."

"No problem, Dan. We are a team and we shall pull together."

Dan spoke to Linda at the NCA, before recalling Martin. He called his Director, who told him to make do with what resources he had.

Dan stated, "Director, with all due respect, we do not have enough people to deal with this. I have recalled Martin, have Ben on nights, and we are still two people short. This country is facing the biggest threat to its sovereignty since ten sixty-six, and you expect me to provide prime service with a skeleton staff. Shame on you!" Dan cut the call.

Early on Thursday morning, the Director walked into Dan's control room and found stressed out people trying to cover too many angles. After a short briefing she said, "I will make available a small team back in London. They will support you as if they were in this room. Alison, please connect with them using your old station access node. You will have a team of three, two on days, one on nights. Dan, are you sure the main strike will be tomorrow?"

"Positive, Ma'am. Today the attacks are of a slightly different pattern, although the suicide contingent seems to be continuing as normal. You will notice how many of these attacks are aimed at isolating Muslim enclaves. They are creating no-go areas and taking over communities. This is becoming widespread across the whole of UK."

Alison spoke up. "They've just hit Bristol council with Sarin, there are few left alive. Attacks in urban areas have increased."

Dan spoke to the Director. "There you have it, Ma'am. By tomorrow, each of these communities will become a Governorate. These districts will conjoin and we will be faced with an impossible choice. Kill the perpetrators, or allow their self-proclaimed caliphate."

"I need to return to London. Good work Dan, I knew I could always rely on you. I have others irons in the fire I must attend. Ciao."

Dan replied, "Me also. Sir Jack needs to be briefed, so I need time away to write a specific report for his eyes only. Tomorrow is the day we run out of governmental dithering options. You will need to prepare to evacuate the MI6 building when I give the word, Ma'am.

"The British intelligence community represents the biggest threat to these Muslim strikes, even more so than America in this instance. They must plan to take out MI5, MI6, and all intelligence centres. Damn! I missed GCHQ."

The Director departed, but Dan did not notice, he was already on secure telephone to Doug Simmons, and minutes later, he spoke of the threat to Sir Jack. "So, we need to install antimissile missiles, and antiaircraft missiles at GCHQ and Bude. I can think of many other critical targets. I'll get on it at once, and also have pairs of interceptors standing ready nearby."

"Thank you, I should not have overlooked this threat, but these are definite targets, as was the Pentagon in USA. Put two Harriers with cannons at GCHQ, readied for immediate takeoff. They are multi-purpose. You'll have my report within the hour, Sir Jack."

Dan returned home mid-afternoon to eat and sleep. He would be on duty again in the small hours and work straight through. This was his last chance to recharge his batteries, for whatever was to come. He slept until four a.m., and was back in the office twenty minutes later.

"Update, Veronica."

"Isolation of Islamic communities is almost complete. We did not foresee riots, which began after dark and are spreading nationwide. This is somewhat dissociated from the Islamic threat I believe, although there appear to be pockets of Muslim agitators. The racial mix is such that I cannot define, more than add, the disenfranchised and troublesome kind of people are taking advantage of the situation.

Chapter 45

"Large numbers of police are on the streets, and looting is rampant. We currently have a sort of stalemate. The police tried water cannons, tear gas, and in two instances, fired rubber bullets. In Muslim held areas, on all occasions they were met with a hail of live machinegun fire."

"Don't the police chiefs have the wit to stand down, leaving a light force. They'll need these officers tomorrow when the real strike begins."

"I already tried that, but the police are a law unto themselves. One commander even swore, told me to go away using only two words."

"'Fakir off' I presume. Unfortunately, they appear to be fakiring themselves. Tough, time for a change of regime."

Veronica's eyes looked up apologetically. "There's more. The ethnic cleansing has already begun. In some towns, non-Muslims, and by that I mean white British people, were allowed to leave. Regards other towns, they only just crossed through the barricades before being gunned down from behind. In some instances, there are reports of bodies lying in the street, the houses taken over in the name of Allah.

"The worst of it is, there are few children leaving with their parents, especially young, pretty girls. I dread to think what fate will befall them."

"Child rape and enforced prostitution, menial and sex slaves. The others, the boys, will become indoctrinated as jihadists. Grim."

"The last thing you may already know. Parliament is due for a full debate on the European crisis today. All MPs have been told to attend."

"The last Parliament. Ben, tell me some good news."

Ben remained silent, until Dan's eyes fixed him. He shrugged apologetically, "There isn't any. The skies have been full of aircraft tonight, and I can't keep track of all of them. It's all recorded."

Dan hopped in the chair beside Ben, and reviewed. What he saw was anything but good. He knew they had underestimated the enemy's capability. He helped Ben get up to date, and then wrote a new report.

As the clock ticked towards six o'clock, he sent a standard version to everyone with interest, including the Minister for Defence. He added further analysis and information for his Director and Sir Jack.

Military and police usually change to morning shift at six a.m., that being the time they are on duty. By then, the team knew that RAF / USAF Lakenheath, and nearby support station, Mildenhall, were under Islamic control. They had old, but deadly F15s. The team did not know what the cargo planes that arrived from Lillyworth Moor were carrying. There were no drones available.

Dan cursed. "I asked the USAF for permission to set drones, and they refused point blank. I should have done so regardless, if nearby, and not technically on U.S. soil.

Dan called Percy, "It has begun and we're under the cosh. Can you ask Charlie to come in and relieve Ben, we need his help, thanks."

Chapter 46 ~ England at War

The morning of Friday, 23rd November, saw an increase of Islamic strikes all across England, some extending to Wales, Scotland, Northern, and even Southern Ireland.

Across England, many Muslim councillors crossed the floor, taking over town, county, and city councils. With the majority vote, Sharia law was introduced. Opponents were shot dead. Those councils that could not be overturned by vote were attacked with traditional or chemical weapons. Bristol had been a warning ignored by the authorities.

Dan called Felicity urgently, and discovered Norwich council was still working as normal. "Put two armed teams in place, and keep safe. They are killing people. You had better do similar for Wymondham if they are not a Muslim council by now. Ciao."

News was slow to filter through to the public at large. The first some knew was when they were being evicted from their homes by Islamic militia, or executed for being Christian. These atrocities occurred in Muslim safe havens, and few incidents reached the attention of the outside world, despite the internet, social media, and cell phones.

Public awareness, and that of the authorities, was diverted by the breaking news that Luxembourg had announced it had become The Caliphate of Luxembourg. The news swamped all media channels, until the same occurred in Belgium.

The media were agog. Normal TV programs were cancelled and the press ran rolling updated news editions. The EU buildings in Brussels were under siege, many having been taken using chemical weapons.

Dan was one of a handful of people Sir Jack kept in close contact with. "I spoke to the Prime Minister, but was told I was overreacting. He was then called away in emergency session. Neither he, nor the Minister for Defence has yet returned my calls.

"I was given polite, if short, shrift by Her Majesty, she informing me my current role may soon come under review. It's like waiting for Damocles' sword to drop."

"Agreed. Alison has just informed me the House of Commons is in full emergency session. Same with the Lords. I doubt we will have to wait long before you are in charge, Sir."

"As soon as I am, we action our counter-strike offensive, which is already being promulgated via secure military channels, to the units concerned. The F15 Strike Eagles are a serious threat that we are working on to take out. Wait … One squadron have just taken off, destination: south."

"London. This is where it begins, Sir Jack. I'll get teams in situ to cover the worst case scenarios: Islamic control of airports."

Chapter 46

Dan called his Director. "Ma'am, you need to evacuate now. Go to the secure bunker at once, and you lead the way. Now! You have minutes only to escape, or you will all die."

Dan spoke similarly to MI5, and tasked Alison with contacting all other key institutions. He issued a series of orders to the team, who responded immediately. They had real-time video of the London controllers on the main screen, so it appeared not all were in motion. Then the feed was cut. They were evacuating.

Alison said, "Martin, can you start a log of major events in UK, and another for Europe. I'll add it as a new box to the main screen."

Dan said, "I'll help set you up."

Alison passed through the first information and Martin gulped. She shrugged her shoulders. Dan looked at the feed, then at Alison, who elucidated, "A public declaration, broadcast on Al Jazeera states, 'Turkey is now a Caliphate of ISIL, and all borders are open. Head for Europe and seek absolute vengeance upon the unbelievers of Allah'."

Reports of other European governments under attack followed, but Bude were tracking eight SCUD missiles. Derek told Dan, "They are already in Greater London airspace. The targets are central."

The information was augmented moments later when Tom called. "RAF Boulmer are tracking eight SCUD missiles, they are seeking a socket to your team."

"I'll arrange this via Alison, thanks Tom. Send her the secure key. Today is going to be rather bad, but tomorrow, things should improve. We should be preventing this atrocity, not waiting for it to occur, so we can finally take the offensive."

Normal military channels were working in enhanced mode, and advised the centre of London be evacuated, they had minutes, nowhere long enough. The SCUD Ds had been monitored, interceptors scrambled, but too late. The missiles were not brought down.

The warheads were guided, and the first landed central in The Houses of Parliament. The towers at either end withstood the blast, Victoria Tower was leaning, and the Elizabeth Tower housing Big Ben appeared critically fractured. The outer wall of Westminster Hall stood for minutes, before collapsing.

Nearby, Westminster Abbey, Downing Street, The Home and Defence Ministries, were destroyed. MI5 and MI6 were also taken out, and the last warhead struck the City. The largest cultural treasure, Saint Paul's Cathedral, had not been targeted.

Alison reported, "Eight more Scud D's en route to London, they must have sixteen launchers, they take ages to reload."

But for the armed forces responding directly to the threat, what remained of power in the United Kingdom appeared to be in Muslim hands. Urban streets and suburbs became guerrilla warfare battlegrounds, and the civilian defence forces had little idea how to react. Few had anything remaining of a chain of command, and what remained of London was under siege.

Then came the F15s. They took out buildings at Gatwick and Heathrow, but left the infrastructure intact. Passenger jets from Lillyworth Moor began to land at each airport, delivering militia, and suicide pilots.

Sir Jack came over secure military comm. "Dan, the Queen just approved military action, almost apologetically I might add. We just began our operation to take out all airbases and Lillyworth Moor. We will also strike at Lakenheath, and the Yanks can protest all they will, but they ignored our warnings. I'm of a mind to operate the base ourselves, at least for the time being.

"Mildenhall will also be struck, but we are low on manpower and resources. Being a supply base, it will be the lowest priority. Two destroyers are now approaching London from Thames east, and should provide a mighty backup. We also have fighters intercepting five of the eight Scud's, and hope to have enough missiles to take them all out.

"I need your team to monitor the country at large, which councils survive, which do not, and a detailed map of all areas under Islamic control. Remain vigilant for aircraft, or other forces."

Dan replied, "We will continue to retake Gatwick and Heathrow. Bristol is for you to overrun, Sir Jack. Most of our tactical forces, and chains of command are still functioning, if from places of greater safety. We may need munitions backup from the Services."

"Someone from the Army will contact Alison. Other matters need my attention, there has been a dire development. Keep up the good work, Dan, and keep me in the loop."

Dan briefly wondered what that could be, but focused on his duty. He called Felicity. "It's as you called it Dan, and I'm now in what remains of the Norwich council chamber. We saved most non-Muslim councillors, and two Muslims who did not cross the floor. The building is secure, and we're responding to riots elsewhere in the city."

Dan spent several minutes informing Felicity of how these riots had proceeded nationwide. "Contain the situation, but do not try to intervene directly. Even after your snipers believe they have taken out all of their snipers and mortar positions. This is regardless of what is happening inside the no-go area. It is a trap to take out police response. I'll send you a file in a moment for promulgation to all commanders in the field. Tell Karen at Lower Meddlington, that we're about to retake Huntley Spa Aerodrome. I'll call her direct when the base is under our control."

"Thanks Dan, this is a nightmare. Will I see you later, it's been so long, and I really miss you."

"Hopefully. I'll see you when the worst of this is over. Once the military publically declare Martial Law, it will be largely out of our hands, and I expect we will return to monitoring and advising."

Dan set about a short, tactical review of what the Muslims were most likely to do in Norwich, or any city or town that was not already under Islamic control. He sent the file as an attachment to Felicity, then forwarded it to Alison. "Please disseminate this to the Chief of Police in each city and town not as yet under Islamic control. You better CC the Chief Constables as well."

Dan had just finished speaking when Sinjun came through the door, accompanied by Stella. "You will need extra pairs of hands, what with London backup out for the time being. Where do you want me?"

"Thanks Sinjun, Stella, that's a big lift. On drones I think. Alison?"

"Martin, show Stella what to do, I need you with me. Sinjun, take Lakenheath and Mildenhall, the Army just gave us live feed for analysis."

"Ahha! Analysis is my forte, Alison. I'll plop down next to Percy."

Minutes later a cheer rang out after Dan announced, "The scuds have been destroyed before reaching target. Five by RAF interceptors and three by navy frigates in the Thames."

After months leading up to the main event, the team were hit with feelings of anticlimax, as others began to take the War For Britain back to the Islamic forces. Streets of the capital flooded with troops, who employed guerrilla warfare tactics.

They slowly reclaimed important areas of the city, and secured what remained under British rule. The attack at Heathrow had not been successful, but the airport was largely unusable.

Passenger aircraft under ISIL control had already taken off from Gatwick. Navy destroyers took out most. Only two got through, and decimated Saint Paul's Cathedral, and the Bank of England. Nearby, the London Stock Exchange was already a pile of rubble.

In other parts of the country, F15s continued to cause damage to critical infrastructure. Dogfights developed over Birmingham, Liverpool, and Portsmouth, amongst others. Tornados and Harriers countered them, the latter proving to be the weapon of choice. They became the first aircraft to take down any F15 during war, seven in total.

In a fluke, a Tornado added one, but the Typhoons, operating from long distance, took out the remainder. England had won the second Battle of Britain, and the mood of defending forces buoyed upon victory.

The next move was to take back the cities under Islamic control. Volunteer ex-military reporting for duty swelled British forces. They had been forcibly retired by a government desperate on saving money, disinterested in any form of defence. They were eager to resume battle. All three services and special forces gained many experienced soldiers.

No one had anticipated the most dramatic moment, when the media became flooded with footage from Buckingham Palace, where the black flag of Muhammad had been raised. The outer gates, which visitors from all over the world loved to visit, were writhing with press. Tanks and howitzers, plus the cargo aircraft that had delivered them, could be seen in the courtyard. Islamic jihadists carrying automatic weapons with live rounds, had replaced uniformed guards wearing bearskin hats, who lay dead and trampled in the dust.

Jeeps with large machine guns to the rear, patrolled the grounds, and menaced the press for effect. To the astonishment of the onlookers, the Coronation Throne was brought out front, central to the building and gates, and deposited on the ground.

Moments later, an old woman wearing royal finery, and carrying the Royal Sceptre and Orb, was dragged to stand before the Throne of her own Coronation. Her legs were kicked from under her, and her symbols of office, followed by herself, hit the ground. The leader dragged her to a kneeling position, and resettled the crown on her head.

To the horror and grief of the on looking press and TV film crews, he drew a long, sharp sword, brandishing it, whilst shouting in Arabic. He drew the sword back, and practiced several blows to the neck of the monarch, drawing blood. The crowd were silent, a few commentating in hushed tones. The militia controlling the palace were chanting in Arabic.

The sword was raised higher than before, and swooping down, cut off the head of Queen Bethany II in one blow. The executioner repeated his previous words in English. "I now declare the Islamic Caliphate of England, and by this act of dethroning, become the supreme ruler of the United Kingdom, and all its dependencies."

Militia played football with the monarch's head, while others rushed to the leader's side, as he sat on the coronation throne, and words were said in Arabic. The Crown was placed upon his head, followed by the sceptre and orb in his hands.

He rose and declared, "I am now the new King of the United Kingdom. All people will bow to Allah, or die. As my titles now include 'Defender of the Faith', I declare the only religion that may be legally practiced is Islam. I instigate full Sharia law immediately. This is Allah's will, as given to me. Go, or be killed."

Many of the press were slow to react, seeking all footage. Two jeeps approached the gates, one from either side, and began firing arbitrarily at the massed press corps. Many reacted too late, but some survived to tell and show the tale. Events were repeated on national TV.

Dan watched stone-faced. "That may, or may not have been the real Queen. We do not know. She uses body doubles.

"The victor was correct. One of her main obligations of office was Defender of the Faith, Protestantism. Her sister became a Catholic, and she did nothing, nor acted to restrict mosques all over the UK. We witness the result. We could run facial recognition, but GCHQ are much better at that than us. I will call them immediately."

Later, Veronica and Ben arrived for nightshift and were briefed. It was emotional for all, and those relieved of duty tarried at their work.

Felicity arrived after eight o'clock that evening. She was stressed, worn out, and needing comfort. Those working late joined them, headed for the pub, a drink, and evening meal.

Dan said, "Felicity, let's get a takeaway and spend the evening at home. One pint is enough for me and I need to rest. You do too."

"No Dan, here is fine. I need a drink to help unwind, and others' company is a boon."

However, talk of work resumed as they relaxed. Dan said, "Alison ran through all available data regards Karen, Benaris, and the Chief. I don't know how she found the time. It's a can of worms. Each could be kosher, or up to no good. It depends upon interpretation of the facts, not the facts themselves, which are lean to the point of being anorexic. Alison, a summary if you please."

Alison said, "Benaris is from a working class background, his father, and father before him, worked at an international car production plant in Dagenham. He was a Trade Union member before he was out of short trousers, and all attended prayers religiously. Pardon the pun.

"When he was sixteen, something odd happened. I discovered he had been accepted for apprenticeship at the car plant, but then he disappeared, and reappeared again at University. It does not add up."

"Thanks Alison, it's clear something happened, and those are defining years for adolescents. I think he ran away. Some would say, that is the act of a coward, while others would praise his spirit of self-determination. His father may have sent him away, of course. Regardless, we'll need to dig a bit deeper."

"Given what we know, or the lack of it, I think we'd better."

"What of the others, Alison?"

"Karen looks clean as a whistle, despite her perceived actions. I discovered something. Not only is she a Christian, but she occasionally, and less often more recently, volunteers at charity events––fund raising for the local church, that sort of thing."

"Nowadays, that is odd, I'm sad to say. What of the Chief?"

"That's still in the wires, I have some roadblocks to get around. That in itself is odd, more than interesting, and I am also checking out the why of it. Anything else?"

"I'll say. Keep at it, and let me know. But tomorrow, Alison, let's leave this for today, and enjoy our drinks and pub meal."

Chapter 47 ~ Restoration of the Monarchy

Sir Jack called first thing. "We took all of the targets, including Mildenhall. Only five of the enemy died, and we got all the big players we were after. We followed Sinjun's tactical strategy, and it was spot-on. Today we'll start on the easier towns, and look for similar success."

"That's great. I'll get in touch with Tom and GCHQ, we'll switch focus to the Governorates, see what air traffic is moving in and out."

That morning, the press led with the beheading of Queen Bethany II. On television, 'experts' pontificated whether it was the Queen or a body double. The consensus being that if the Queen was still alive, she had forsaken her post in time of greatest need. Nothing had been heard from any of her heirs, so to cover the power vacuum, Sir Jack initiated Military Law, until such time, civilian law could be returned.

His speech was almost Churchillian. "...But first, we must confront and dispel the malign influences of Allah, and the fear of Islam from our shores. Evict the all of this evil from this green and pleasant land.

"Fear you not. We will conquer the enemy within, and put them to the sword. We have a patriotic duty to put the 'Great' back into Britain. That is precisely what, together, we will do. We must stand firm, as one to thwart the heinous threat that has already become a cancer in our midst. It must be eradicated. Completely. And in its entirety. I call on every person in this land, to join our crusade to evict the infidel."

Sir Jack made other changes, like replacing the National Anthem with 'Land of Hope and Glory'. People appeared in the street wearing the red cross on white background of Saint George as a Crusading statement. The song Jerusalem was used to introduce the TV news.

Back at base, Dan spoke to the team. "Well done everybody, we will continue to do our job. Veronica, Ben, I'd like you to remain on nights, until the dust settles. I am sure that you both... we all... need time off.

"Martin, after yesterday's successful operations, I need you to take the jet and get our drones back. We'll call ahead, and you'll be able to land at the airfields themselves. They will need to be deployed elsewhere. Alison will update you. This will take you most of the day. So get to it, all except Luton, unless that is reclaimed before you return."

The team's role was evolving, but remained central to the fight. Sinjun was tasked with forming tactics to take out the most difficult targets, like Luton. Stella resumed her role, updating events on the main screen. Overnight, Veronica had made a political map of the entire UK. England was detailed in great depth. Their job was to identify softer targets that could swiftly be returned to British rule.

Sir Jack had been working with the Chiefs of Staff, and later came over all media channels to make an announcement. "In this, our hour of greatest need, the people of this country must stand resolute. Take the good fight back against all who try to oppress them … we are putting the 'Great' back into Britain."

His speech was not long. But it gave the British people an insight into how the forthcoming days would play out, until all of Britain was back under British control. He announced a regular military information channel, which would feed the nation latest news several times per day. His aim was to create a unity of nationhood, encourage patriotism, and largely, it was effective.

Just before midday, news came from Buckingham Palace. TV showed the flag of ISIL being lowered, thrown to the outer courtyard, and burned. In its place rose the Union Jack, and seconds later, the Cross of Saint George. Crowds gathered to cheer, as it became clear ISIL militia had been driven from the palace, or killed.

Some minutes later, a young woman dressed in black approached the gates, holding the hand of a small child; Princess Charmaine. She pulled up her black mesh veil and spoke to the cameras. "My people, there is something terrible I must share with you all. I will be acting as Regent, until our surviving child is of age to become Queen Charmaine.

"Everyone else, so many good people, were executed. The palace corridors are awash with blood. Only we survived. Thank you Sir Jack and the brave men of the SAS who saved us. That was not before the leader and many of his men enforced me to endure repeated, personal violations. I am not good. I feel debased, but I will survive. I live to take up arms against those that dishonoured me, and put them to death.

"I feel humiliated and in the depths of despair, but tell of this to give strength to other women who are unfortunate to find themselves in a similar situation. I will not be cowed. I will not forgive. But I will never think of myself as a victim, as that leads to debilitating self-pity.

"Fortunately, Queen Charmaine was hidden in a secure Monk's Hole, otherwise, she would also be dead. As regent of a country with no parliament, I hereby announce the restoration of the Monarchy. Parliament will be restored, given time. For the next few days, daily power will reside with Sir Jack and his advisors. They report to me.

"I herewith reintroduce the death penalty for crimes of treason, murder, and extreme sexual abuse, especially when based upon ethnic or religious grounds. I abrogate all recent EU laws. They are rescinded as of this moment. The EU no longer exists. A full statement will be forthcoming. It is time to put the Great back into Britain!"

She appeared to shiver slightly, and said, "Excuse me, I have many good people to mourn, and a country to run." She pulled down her veil, her shoulders back, turned, and walked regally back into the Palace.

The nation was silent as the impact of Queen Regent Kathy's words settled amongst the people. Their world had been turned upside down by Muslim extremists. A growing rage of vengeance overpowered many.

Volunteers flooded to recruitment stations to take up arms against the Caliphate of England, and quickly numbers of troops swelled.

The picture was not as encouraging on the continent, where the first to come through Turkey's now open borders were militia and armaments. Germany was under attack at national, city, and town level. ISIL made great inroads as the Chancellor continued to dither, before she, and all other German politicians were publicly executed. The majority of asylum seekers proved to be ISIL operatives under cover. The Caliphate of Germany was declared from the Reichstag in Berlin.

Switzerland, not a member of the EU, was next to fall, the aim being to take over the United Nations, which apart from the figurehead building in the United States of America, was largely based in Geneva. All, but the most useful, or useable UN bureaucrats were killed, replaced by Islamic extremists, who began writing a new set of diktats for the rest of the world to obey.

France had survived better than most northern European countries, and whilst having an Islamic Head of State, the jihadists had not struck as deeply into the mechanisms of government, as they had in UK. Once secure, and with troops and munitions to spare, the British came to the assistance of the French, and war returned to the continent of Europe.

The effort was supported by Portugal, which had been largely left untouched. The country became a safe haven for Spanish and Italian citizens, their military reforming to take the war back to ISIL. For the first time in decades, the British military responded to harassment by Russian planes and submarines, by hunting them and, when found, destroying them. Putinov raised a storm of rhetoric, but backed down, favouring annexation of Finland, Lithuania, and Poland.

Greater Europe may have been in a state of flux, but Britain was fighting back against the terrorist within, and taking back large swathes of the country. Queen Regent Kathy became the public's focus and rock, a heroine, as she took to presenting a daily bulletin.

Meanwhile, Dan's team soldiered on. By Tuesday, they had extra support staff, some on night duty. Regular staff were allowed two days off on rotation. Their work continued to change in focus, but not in nature, they were the main receivers and disseminators of information to all security services, both civilian and military, at home and abroad.

Dan met with Sir Jack on Wednesday, surprised to find Queen Regent Kathy present. He bowed to her, and she spoke first, "Well met Sir Glover. Here, come and kneel before me."

Dan did as instructed, and was surprised when she drew a blade. "With this sword, I dub thee a Knight of the Realm. Arise Sir Danforth Glover of Meddlington."

Dan was abashed, but found the words to say, "Thank you, Your Highness. I do not deserve this honour, but appreciated it all the same."

"Of course you deserve it, otherwise I would not have bestowed it."

"But why, Your Majesty?"

"Were it not for you informing Sir Jack of the imminent threat, the Queen would not have been informed. I was there when the message came in, and I immediately concealed Queen Charmaine. I tried to do the same with my son, but they came swiftly. She is only alive because of you. The British Crown only persists, because of you.

"After the repeated … repeated rapes, I played dead, but found a place of safety. They would have discovered me, but for the SAS reclaiming the Palace. Now, let's get down to business."

Dan had expected his team to be disbanded, but he was overjoyed when it became clear the Queen Regent wanted him to form and head a dedicated antiterrorist agency, one that would supplement their existing intelligence community, and act as liaison between them all, and the military. They also had a brief to include Europe, and later, all matters worldwide that affected the United Kingdom and Commonwealth.

Queen Regent Kathy said, "Dan, you will report directly to me, but in practise, this will be to Sir Jack. Later we will set up new departments, run by military and civilians. Both parliament and the civil service will be reformed, but later, and not as before. This time they will report to me. Your new role has primacy, and you will forge all our intelligence offshoots and specialist units into parts of one cohesive whole. You are the flux ensuring information gets to the right people so they can act."

Before the meeting concluded, Dan was given a second task; to liaise with the French antiterrorist agencies, and also the New French Underground, a term that loosely applied to all disenfranchised citizens dedicated to fighting back against government by Islamic State: France.

Dan welcomed the role, and stood to leave in buoyant mood. The only dark cloud was that the team would have to relocate to London, or a main military city. He was halfway through the door, when he turned back. "Sir Jack, this new role will require me to do a lot of long distance travelling. I will need a super-quiet light jet."

Anxious of overreaching his station, he stood firm, and breathed in, busting his chest out. Queen Regent Kathy said, "They come with the job, don't they."

Sir Jack replied with a quizzical smile. "Apparently. I'll arrange delivery within the next few days."

Dan had the devil in him and said, "Why not deliver it to me in person. We are holding a rather special party on Friday evening, in the village pub. Real food and real ale, Sir."

"You know Dan, I may just do that. No promises mind, but I need a break, and a proper night out in a village pub hits the mark splendidly."

Chapter 48 ~ Proposal

Dan departed to arrange for his special night, and public proposal to Felicity. He worried against worry, she would say 'No', having given Brian his requirements, and a rough idea of numbers and menu options.

Next Dan spoke to the team; "Our job just got bigger. While we will remain part of SIS, for now at least, our role as intelligence collators and dispersers has grown to include all services and special units. In future, nearly all intelligence will flow through us. Nothing will change overnight, but we are expected to recruit new personnel and grow into our future form. This may include moving to a dedicated facility, perhaps London, but nothing will change for the next few weeks. Think of how we can expand, who we can recruit, but for now, let's get on with our jobs. I'll speak to all of you later about this. I'll answer simple questions now, and then I must get home, it's been a long day."

He arrived home to find Felicity was already there, and he helped her cook. He told her about his Knighthood and the new team. Her reply became a papier-mâché of incoherent words. Later, they enjoyed being together, a movie was playing on DVD, but they largely ignored it.

On Thursday afternoon, the team reviewed progress. One week had elapsed since the Islamic revolution. Wales, Scotland, plus Northern and Southern Ireland were not under any form of Islamic control.

Much of England had returned to British rule, but in some towns, entrenched Governorates remained. These were being retaken, but the work was ongoing and would take weeks. Some only held pockets of resistance, but others, like Luton, were a hotbed of Muslim insurgency, and would need to be taken back, street by street. Eastern Birmingham was a no-go area. London had seven small Governorates. Tower Hamlets was due to be taken on Friday morning, during weekly prayers.

Late on Friday afternoon, Dan called Felicity and said he would be dining at the Inn. "I need a few beers and a curry, Filly."

"I don't know. I'm done for. All I want to do is sleep."

"No you don't, one Pernod will set you up. It won't be a late night, I promise. I'll see you at home, six-ish, because I need to change. Ciao."

Felicity was in an almost querulous mood when she arrived home, much in need of a soak in the bath. Dan had already run it, and she was guided upstairs to luxuriate. The long soak and massage jets restored her equilibrium. She was wondering what to wear, when Dan returned. "Filly, get dressed, people are arriving, in our back field."

He was gone before she could reply. Her earlier irritation returned to haunt her perspicacity of the moment. Dressing quickly, she stormed out of the back door, and found Dan parking a plane near the hangar.

Sir Jack stepped out and looked around, quickly grabbing Dan's hand in friendship, saying, "Congratulations."

Chapter 48

Dan whispered, "She doesn't know yet. Shush."

Felicity was slightly flummoxed. Sir Jack said, "Come and inspect your new plane, it's a lot better than that one. Oh, and I'll park a Harrier here soon, just in case we need you. Experienced pilots are hard to come by, and I may yet have a special mission for you: France."

Felicity was about to board, when the low throb of large helicopters grew louder. She was surprised when a light jet landed, and she helped it park, calling on 'the boys' to assist. Dan's Director got out, along with two bubbly children, and Harry McKinnon who had piloted the craft.

Dan said, "I wasn't expecting you tonight Ma'am, but you, Harry, and the children, are most welcome."

"Cut the crap Dan, you must bear in mind, word gets about within the security services. Remember that. I see you have a new plane. Good. I'll be flying mine back tonight."

They all turned, as the throb of helicopters got louder, Sir Jack said, "I wasn't sure she would come, but we have been blessed this eve."

Felicity said, "Who?"

"Wait and see," came the brusque reply.

Outside the main drive, Tom and Margaret were all of a mither. A large Bentley was hogging the drive, and would not let them enter. When Tom got out to complain, several special agents drew weapons on him. "I'm the father of the Fiancée-to-Be."

"Ah." One man talked on his radio, and moments later, Felicity ran down the drive to welcome her parents.

"I have no idea what's going on tonight, but thank you for being here. We better get back, as helicopters are coming in."

Before the first helicopter touched ground, an armed security detail debarked to check the vicinity, working outwards. Once given the all clear, the second helicopter landed carrying Royalty. The doors opened, and Queen Regent Kathy came down the steps, accompanied by Queen Charmaine, who said, "Is this going to be fun, Mummy?"

"A lot more fun than anything we've done recently. These people are our friends. Now, come and play, you will love it."

Queen Regent Kathy was gracious, but relaxed, as she met the others. "I just had to get away. Running the country, and being constantly plagued by well-meaning advisors takes its toll. I needed a break, and this was perfect excuse on our way to Sandringham. I also need time and space to think, without a new drama unfolding, seemingly every few seconds. I've never been allowed to do anything like this before, well, since I was married." She stifled a tear, and walked forward, holding her head high.

Introductions were brief, and Queen Charmaine was introduced to the Director's grandchildren. They were of similar ages, and made friends quickly. Soon they were running off to see the air raid shelter. Bodyguards tried to keep up.

Queen Regent Kathy quickly swept through the downstairs, and was in the library when a panel opened and the children came rushing through. "Dan, you have a secret door, how wonderful. This is turning out just perfect. Now, let us retire to the inn. Charm, come here at once."

They had hardly been a minute inside, and came out the front door as the neighbours arrived to complain about the noise. They fell silent when they saw Royalty in the flesh, and begged forgiveness. Queen Regent Kathy said, "So sorry, the noise will be my helicopters. They will relocate in a moment. The other craft should be gone in a short while. You should join us at the village inn by, way of apology." Dan nodded his head in agreement.

Royalty got into the back of the bullet-proof Bentley, and a convoy of cars sped towards the village. Although Dan was the host, Queen Regent Kathy chose to enter via the bar, and a small sensation ensued. She ordered a half pint of the local ale, and spoke to every patron, if briefly. They continued through to the restaurant, which had a large round table waiting, and Felicity quickly made a seating plan. Queen Regent Kathy toured the lounge en route, and tables of other diners in the restaurant, but hardly stopped to chat. She wanted to make a small impression that everyone mattered to her.

The table was only just large enough. The children misbehaved as they were over-excited and over-tired. Brian brought out a small, low table with child seats, a basket of fries, and the problem was quickly resolved. A Lady in Waiting and bodyguards would watch over them.

Felicity said, "How do you get used to having so many people around you all the time, maids, and the bodyguards?"

"One soon gets accustomed to them. I don't see them anymore..."

Talk was varied and passed around table, until the Director asked, "Why are we here tonight, Dan?"

The table fell silent, and all eyes turned to look at him expectantly. Dan stood and asked Felicity to stand with him. They turned to each other, and he knelt down before her, taking her left hand in his own. "I don't believe this Danforth Glover. How could you do this to me!"

Unwittingly, Felicity had given him the cue he needed. "Because I love you, and I want to spend the rest of my life with you. Felicity Wigglesworth, will you do me the honour of agreeing to become Lady Meddlington? As token of my love, I proffer this ring."

He produced a large diamond ring, and slipped on her finger.

Felicity dragged him to his feet and shouted, "Yes!"

They kissed passionately, if briefly, and she continued, "I would kill you for putting me through that, if I didn't love you more."

Chapter 48

Cheers erupted all around. Focus of the table fell, and remained on Felicity. Her mother and father were the first to congratulate her, Margaret already refining wedding plans.

The meal was a terrific success, and Queen Regent Kathy loved the chicken tikka curry. Later she spoke to Ayesha. It gave her an insight into the lives of modern, British Muslim women, and she wondered how many others, unlike the girl, had not managed to escape.

Her mind remained working, and after Ayesha had finished cooking, she drew the girl aside to chat. That night, in a backwater inn in the middle of nowhere, Norfolk, Queen Regent Kathy learned how she might be able to attack Islamic enclaves from within, via their young women, ones with British values, and loyalty to their country of birth.

As the restaurant emptied, Queen Regent Kathy talked with Sir Jack and Dan. Felicity was included, as soon as the Regent learned she was a ranking police officer who had helped cleanse Islamic parts of Norwich.

She began, "We are starved of information from within these so-called caliphates. No one inside is speaking to us, or getting a message out. One reason why it is taking so long to take back our dominion is not knowing friend from foe. We need a presence on social media used by these young Muslim girls like Ayesha. Thank you Felicity for having the prescience to see the full picture and keep her safe.

"She has given me several websites, and I would like you, Dan, to follow through. Ayesha told me she knows how to make contact with these girls online, so why not let her use a computer in your office?"

Dan said, "Better I arrange for one in her bedroom, it will be secure and non-traceable. Alison will set it up, and we will monitor the feed. We need to maintain our own station security, Your Majesty."

"Overruled, she already knows what you are doing. You need to work with her to generate one or several personas, which she can act out online. I believe in inclusion, and if you still disagree, deal with it."

"Your Majesty, always a pleasure. This presents a great opportunity for us to learn the thinking of modern Muslim women in today's world."

They called Ayesha, and spoke to her about the new job. She was thrilled, and would begin the following afternoon. Brian was content, if not happy, but he knew it was for the greater good.

Sir Jack said, "It is time I departed, I have a plane waiting at the aerodrome, and have an early start tomorrow."

Dan said, "We'll give you a lift, as we will be gone in five minutes."

Their words were interrupted, when an aid whispered to Queen Regent Kathy. She was not impressed and said, "They tell me it is time to leave. This is what my life is like. I have greatly enjoyed mixing with real people again. We are staying. I presume this inn has rooms?"

Dan replied, "I have the best room here, and will vacate immediately. I hardly use it anymore. One moment, Your Majesty."

Brian was a mess of disjointed hyperactivity. His arms waved aimlessly, as his legs took on a dancing gait. His words were short and unintentionally sharp. Dan calmed him, and booked the six free rooms.

He informed Queen Regent Kathy, who said, "That's about enough, the others will have to surf sofas, as I did some years ago. It won't hurt them for one night. Let Brian arrange everything, as my aid will take all night getting things 'just right', which is impossible. Gaelic coffees for nightcap please Brian, and then I need my beauty sleep. Dan, stay a while, we have more to discuss."

"As you wish, Ma'am"

"Meeting Ayesha and getting a personal view of her was a main reason for my stopping by tonight. My advisors and informers were creating all manner of cautions for me to address, so I decided to check her out at first hand. If she comes through this will be a major fillip for us. She passed muster and I also learned more about her situation and that of similar girls, we must put an end to their oppression. Now tell me your next steps…"

" …I think that's all for tonight, Dan. Thank you. If you need anything you tell me or Sir Jack. I'll see you in the morning for breakfast as well brief tour your office. It will be early, I'll give you a call."

Ayesha rose early to help with breakfast. After Royalty departed, she set about making batches of different curries, and putting them in sealed containers, after dating and marking the contents of each. Once cool, she put them in the freezer. Her next task was to prepare chapattis, roti, and naan bread for cooking. She made these in stacks and sealed them in freezer bags.

The under chef had been watching her for some time, and said, "I'm sure I could do some of this for you, and I am keen to learn."

Ayesha smiled, "Thanks. It's quite simple, once you get confident. I'll show you how I make the poppadom mixture now, and then how to cook them. Afterwards I need to make some tarka dal, and then I'll make another batch of chicken tikka masala. It's our most popular dish."

Later, Brian came over and said, "You're teaching Paul the ropes?"

"Yes, and he's doing very well. I'll have him make this himself tomorrow, and then work through the other dishes, if that's okay."

"That's great. You okay with this Paul?"

"Loving it sir."

"What time do you leave, Ayesha?"

"I'll go after lunch, but I'd like to take a nap if I can. I have the feeling I may be working quite late, if not tonight, then in future."

"Go up when you are done here, and no loitering. I'll call you if we have need, but you have made a great stockpile already. I'll need to buy a new freezer, just to keep up with you."

Ayesha woke from her nap at one o'clock and checked the kitchen. Several curries were being prepared but she was not needed. She went to the shop and Stella shouted inside. Sinjun escorted her around back, showing her the usual way in. The team were at lunch, and she took a seat. Dan said, "Tuck in, but these two contain pork."

Her words surprised them. "I sometimes eat it, and I love bacon sandwiches. May I try the pork pie?"

Talk turned to her place within the team. "I think most of my work will be in the evening. I'll begin with chat sites I know, and see where they lead me. I know Luton well, but people come on from all over."

Dan said, "Have you thought about which profiles to use?"

"I was just going to be myself."

"No, you'd cover more ground by being different people, say one an outgoing girl, another who is less certain, and perhaps a boy?"

"Oh, I could do that. All I have to do is imagine Waheed on chat."

"Write down who you are for each character: age, sex, job, school, or vocational training, hobbies even. And whereabouts you live."

Veronica said, "I used to teach this stuff. Come out immediately if you feel something is wrong. Don't lead the conversation, wait for them to disclose information first. I would also have a fourth identity, that being yourself, at least, as much as you can reveal. Don't divulge too much, we don't want them tracing you back here now, do we."

"Okay, this all makes sense. Where do I set up?"

Veronica said, "Dan, I think she should set up next to me, then I can keep an eye on her, help her in case of difficulty."

"Agreed, let's move upstairs."

Ayesha spent the first hour putting her different profiles online. She registered with five websites, including the ones she had used before. Two were in Pashto, two in Arabic, and one in English. She spent time getting the hang of each website. When she felt comfortable, she joined a couple of clubs and chat rooms on each, and waited.

It was Saturday, so the websites were busy, and got busier after five. The evening was busiest of all. Ayesha made contact with some, but she was unknown, an outsider. Usually girls joined as small groups, so they already had friends on the site.

Even more people seemed to be online on Sunday, and again she chatted to some, but most of it was superficial. She logged on for lunchtime on Monday, and the sites were quiet, only becoming popular as the time approached six p.m. From Tuesday, she only worked evenings and weekends, and resumed helping Brian during the day.

Chapter 49 ~ Inside Information

Despite her enthusiasm, Ayesha was becoming downhearted when Friday evening arrived. She had not made any good friends, but she persevered. Her eyes lit up when she saw her closest friend log into a chat room. She changed to her own ID, and made contact. "Hi Fatimah, how are you?"

"Who are you, do I know you?"

"I hope so, I'm Ayesha."

The girls chatted, quickly catching up, but not saying anything that would be flagged, Fatimah had typed, "Be careful, they monitor everything on here."

"You still using the same number?"

"Yes, call me."

Ayesha got out her mobile phone, but Alison said, "Stop. You are ringing into ISIL Luton? You will need a secure phone, one second ... here we are. I've put this phone's number under 'Z', and you can use it like any other. It is highly encrypted, and can't be traced. Make a habit to record all conversations. It sounds like you're doing well."

Once connected, Fatimah told her friend about the horrors of living under the shadow of Daesh.

"We all live in fear of being executed for the smallest mistake. They take the youngest and pretty ones as sex slaves, even very young girls. I wear a full burkha and waddle like an old woman so they can't tell my age. They are evil. I wish I could get out of here, but it's useless. They have the city locked down.

"How could we get in?"

"Are you crazy, keep away?"

"That's not what I meant. I'm working with British security forces, and we need to know their strengths and weaknesses, and how we can take Luton back from Daesh."

"Wow! You've moved up in the world. Okay, it will take me many days, because I have to remain hidden. But I'll find out as much as I can, and be in touch. What's your number? ... Got it. One more thing, there are a gang of girls here trying to subvert the Daesh cause, but we have to be clever."

"Great, can you get them to contact me, either online or by phone."

"I'll do what I can."

"Thanks. We better keep this short. I don't want to get there and find you dead. It's been so long ... see you soon, bye."

Alison said, "That sounds promising."

"It'll be one week or more, but she is thorough. This is a result."

"Are you going to pack up early?"

Chapter 49

"No. Some of my other leads are beginning to show results, so I'll hang around until things go quiet."

Things carried on in similar vein, and although Ayesha did make friends, they were not helpful regards her work for Dan.

During the interim mornings and quiet afternoons, Ayesha taught Paul how to make all the menu dishes. Brian was very happy. One week and more had passed since she had chatted to Fatimah, but there was nothing and Ayesha started to worry about her friend.

She had been given a website to try by one of her new friends, and was visiting for the third night. The room she was in had a strange name, one that could mean several things. She was distracted when her secure phone rang. "Ayesha?"

"Maybe, who are you? How do you know my name?"

"I'm Makaarim, and a close friend, via a friend, of Fatimah. It was because of the information you asked for that I became involved with helping her. You should have the file tomorrow. I advise you not to contact your friend again. Daesh have eyes and ears everywhere."

"Okay, but this is a bit of a shock you know."

"You are on the outside. One of the few to escape. So am I, and most of my team. Whereabouts are you?"

"From Luton, north and east, I'm not close by."

"Good. I'll need to meet you. I'll be in the car park of the Tharp at six p.m. tomorrow. It's the only pub in Chippenham village, just north of Newmarket. See you there. I've got to go. Bye."

The line went dead. Ayesha stared at the phone, and looked for the caller's number. Withheld. She sat back, confused, and ran her fingers through her long hair. She wondered if she should cut it off. Disgusted with herself for even considering doing such a thing, she closed down early, despite it being Saturday night, and went to find the team.

Sinjun was in the bar, but none of the others were visible. She went through to the guest area and knocked on Dan's door. Nobody was in, so she tried Veronica, who answered, and they talked about what was going on. Veronica calmed her by saying, "I need to know the whole story, so start at the beginning and tell me all of it as it happened. If you don't mind I'll record this so we have a verification."

Ayesha said, "That's fine," and was able to virtually repeat her conversation with Makaarim word for word.

When she was finished, Veronica praised her and said, "It is quite easy to misread a situation, or a person's true intentions. But if what you recall is accurate, we have our first contact with those inside a Daesh stronghold. I'll call Dan."

In response, Dan called a team meeting for late on Sunday morning, where Ayesha repeated what she had told Veronica. With Dan's probing she recalled other things like background noises, and that she felt Makaarim was alone and not being pressured when speaking.

Later, Veronica added her insight, and a team discussion took place. Dan said, "We'll have to go in. This has all the hallmarks of a trap, but if it's kosher, we gain friends on the inside. Martin, bring Ayesha to my house for five this afternoon. Alison, you're already busy here, so Veronica, I need you covering on comm. and dedicated to our mission. Can you get me two British vehicles readied at Mildenhall, it's the closest airfield. Sinjun, you need a specially adapted car, so stay here, and I'll ask Felicity to fill the breach."

Later that day, Dan's jet landed at USAF Mildenhall, and they were greeted by the RAF Commander in charge until the USAF resumed operations. He showed them one British car, but the other pool cars were American. Dan said, "I'll take the Chevy 300. That's a man's car."

Dan led the way towards the rendezvous, a journey of five miles but along B class roads. He drove past the pub and pulled over, as Felicity drove into the car park. They waited. Some minutes later, a modern, if non-descript car parked next to Felicity's, and the driver's window wound down. "Ayesha I presume, follow me, it's not far."

"Where to?"

"We've a safe house in Fordham. Come, we have much to discuss."

Dan had Martin call in the registration as a precaution, and they began to follow at a great distance. "Shouldn't we be closer, Dan?"

"No Martin. Now you're learning. I placed at transponder on Felicity's car, Veronica will tell us where it ends up. They won't know a thing at all about us."

A little later, Dan parked in a side street, Felicity's car in plain sight. He called her. "How's it looking?"

"Ayesha's inside and so far so good. What's Veronica got to say?"

"She's got good reception from Ayesha's communicator and thinks they are on the level, but we should go in, make official introductions. Wait for me to check around the back before you go in the front."

Dan headed for the rear of the building, Martin to follow with a ready bag. Entering the alley leading to the rear access road, he spied a man dressed in dark fatigues acting suspiciously, and challenged him. The man drew a gun, but Dan fired his silenced pistol before the enemy could take aim, or sound the alarm. Dan pulled the body aside, took a picture of him and his ID, and hid the body as best he could.

Martin joined him, and Dan sent messages back to Felicity and Veronica. Aware of hostiles, they proceeded with caution, taking out the two occupants of a van parked on the rear access road. Once more, Dan snapped pictures of faces and ID's, then whispered, "Now we take the house, you are the distraction."

Dan peered over the rear fence of the target house and whispered, "There's someone on watch, looks like an ISIL guard."

"Get in position, and I'll distract him at the rear gate."

Martin banged his fist on the solid wooden door, and was met with curses in a foreign tongue from within. Dan went over the fence, took out the guard, and bound the man securely before letting Martin in. Again Dan took photos of the man and his ID, sending both to Veronica.

They hauled the unconscious man to the rear door and relieved him of his Kalashnikov. Dan picked the rear door lock, and they were inside. They ran a cursory search of downstairs, before bursting into the front room, guns drawn.

Three women were talking to Ayesha and sharing a pot of tea. All four screamed and froze. Ayesha waved to Dan and calmed the women, as Dan pointed his weapon away from them and downwards. He indicated silence with his finger, and Martin scanned for bugs. He discovered three; the occupants realised they were compromised. Martin finished and drew his gun.

Dan put away his own gun and beckoned Makaarim to follow him. They went outside, where her anger at their intrusion quickly turned to alarm when she saw the body. "Who the hell's that?"

"That's what we'd like to know, hence our entrance. He's ISIL I'm almost sure. We're checking now. His three buddies are dead," Dan indicated the back alley. "Your team appear genuine, but you are compromised and need to leave right this moment!"

"Why? We are a small, underground group."

"Do you know who Ayesha is?"

"Only that she escaped forced marriage."

"To whom?"

"Erm. A Devout Muslim Man."

"Hmmm. Trust. Okay. You do not trust us, me. Her father is Valinder Jahlide Hussein, and she was supposed to marry Ali Yousef Mohammad. She ran away because of forced marriage and FGM. She is Ayesha Hussein, and was due to marry Mohammad's son, they of Mohammad, Ali, and Hussein."

"But they run Luton, and other towns."

"Exactly."

"Then their enforcers are already on their way here."

"We leave in minutes. Bring everything of value, you can never return here."

Back inside, whispers passed between the occupants, and they quickly cleared the place out. While they were busy, Dan placed his own bugs in likely places, hoping to gain further intelligence. All three cars were quickly loaded, as Dan asked Martin to check their new friend's car for bugs. He found two. Dan held them up and said, "Which of the neighbours cars travels the most, especially at this time of night?"

"The blue Passat, it's an unofficial taxi."

"Good." Dan dropped the bugs into the air grill just below the windscreen, and smiled. "That should distract them. Time to go."

They departed via a longer route, hoping to avoid detection. Dan was driving the ISIL van with three dead and one prisoner inside. At the main junction Martin, leading the convoy, stopped and waited. The reason became clear moments later, when two SUV's sped past, and turned into the direct access road to the house they had just left. As soon as the road was clear, they quickly left the village.

A few minutes later they pulled into Mildenhall, where Dan parked the van in isolation. He spoke to Veronica, who said, "Alison has arranged for an extraction team to remove the prisoner, the bodies, and the van. They are en route and should be with you within half an hour."

"Good work, what about the house?"

"We are monitoring with drones and also recording all conversations inside that your bugs pick up. Wait … they are leaving."

"Send me the conversations … Thanks.

"It's mainly Arabic … they are confused as to what went down and where their men are. They do not know about our involvement, and I'd like to keep it that way. Treat this as intelligence gathering mission and follow the vehicles, plus the passengers when they get out. Find out where they come from, and facial recognition where possible, thanks."

Dan wanted to probe the prisoner, but he remained unconscious. He left Martin on guard, and smiled cheekily at the women; "Time for your interrogation, come with me."

Dan led them to the mess and bought them snacks and drinks, before sitting at a large table; Dan's mobile was recording every word spoken, as usual. A lot of information was exchanged, before Makaarim said, "Okay Dan. Why us? What do you really want from us?"

"I need you to help us take ISIL out of Luton, and any other Governorates you have knowledge of. I need a priority list of targets and routes in for our forces. Mark them on a map, numbered, with a side panel stating what they are, and the best means of taking each out. I'll expect that for early tomorrow morning. Thank you."

"Dan, these are tribal people, they all work for their leader, a Landlord, do what he says, so you need to take the leaders out first."

"Thanks, we had come to the same conclusion. We have a deal?"

"I'm not sure. Let me get this straight, we help you, and you imprison us here. That doesn't sound fair."

"We just saved your lives, and you're free to leave at any time. The question is, have you anywhere safe to go? I could have a word with the Commanding Officer and set you each up with a room at the Sergeant's

Mess. It should be safe for you to leave here once we take out Luton, which will be soon. I need information on local towns like Newmarket, Thetford, and Cambridge, we intend to clear out all the extremists."

"We have been in contact with some resistance groups, but I'll need to work on them. We're all very distrusting."

"And rightly so. Let them know you're helping us free Luton, and try them again once we succeed. We have a deal?"

"Yes, a deal, and thanks Dan. I guess it's expensive here?"

"No, extremely cheap, American tax free, but they only accept U.S. Dollars. There's a change machine on the wall over there."

Outside, Dan waited to hand over the van and its occupants to specialist personnel, before flying back to base.

On the flight back, Ayesha copied the file she had received from Makaarim, and another sent from Fatimah. Dan went through both as soon as he engaged autopilot. The information was extensive, and dovetailed with his expectations, but the devil was in the details that were now open to him.

Once home Felicity said, "I'll stay here and get dinner started. I've some preparation to do for tomorrow, and you won't be long, will you?"

"Less than an hour at the office, let's get moving."

He met with the team when they got back to the village. "That is one excellent result. Well done everyone, and especially you, Ayesha. We would have never got the breakthrough if it was not for you. Will you stand down now?"

"No, not yet, I'll keep in close contact with Makaarim, sometimes it's easier to talk in Pashto. There are others also, and new people Makaarim said may want to talk to me before committing to join us."

"That's excellent, thank you. But you can ease up a lot now that we have a great ally. Alison, you traced our rats to their lair?"

"Yes, several lairs actually, which are now under surveillance."

"Excellent! Alison, if you will follow up, and especially with the van and terrorists we caught."

"I'm on it Dan and you will know as soon as I do."

"Good, let's call it a night as we are back here tomorrow."

It was not long before they all retired to their beds, although Dan did work for one hour at home, before eating and sleeping.

Chapter 50 ~ The Battle for England

Waking after an early night, Felicity left for work, and Dan set to writing several reports. His focus was taking Luton. His first report was sent to Sir Jack, who called him moments later. "Dan, we have almost cleared London and the south, except for a few tough enclaves. This is amazing intelligence you just sent through. We are going in, I'll try to set things up for Wednesday."

"That's excellent. I'd like to blitzkrieg the nearby towns as well, roll from one to the next, leaving behind troops to ensure victory."

"Agreed. That will clear a vast swathe of the country and free up road transportation. I'll need to speak to the army regards numbers of troops, especially the guard force we leave behind. Thursday might be more reasonable to do the all of it."

"What about prisoners of war, Sir?"

"I intend not to have any."

"You're not going to shoot everyone, surely?"

"No, no, quite the opposite. Queen Regent Kathy wants the whole shebang expedited, so instead of due process of law taking months and years, prisoners will appear in court within hours or days. Sentencing will take place immediately, and be harsh. She has already removed by Royal Decree, many of the judiciary, and a new order of Instant Justice is in place. They will act as soon as an ISIL enclave has been liberated."

"That is excellent news, Sir Jack. Regards Sunday..."

RAF Trimingham had been monitoring all flights into, and out of Luton, which no longer functioned as a regular airport. GCHQ Bude had satellite eyes on prime locations and targets, and patterns emerged that military could work to. Sinjun added his tactical perception, and all was set for a series of simultaneous strikes, early on Thursday morning.

Later, Dan called the Mildenhall Station Commander, before he spoke to Makaarim. "You are giving us some great intelligence, keep up the good work."

"Thanks Dan. We're really enjoying it. Are we getting paid for this?"

"I'll cover your living expenses if that helps. Any of you that prove yourselves of worth may be offered a job. How does that suit?"

"Hmmm. It'll do for now."

"I've just asked the Station Commander to provide you with secure computers and internet. I'd like you to expand your operation wherever possible, we'll need to cover all Muslim Governorates in England."

That afternoon, Felicity called Dan. "I have the information regards the Chief Inspector at Wymondham, but need Alison to check some things. I'll need to talk to her direct before I send her information."

"Great. What did you discover?"

Chapter 50

"Later Dan, the file isn't complete, that's why I need Alison's input."

"Okay, sanctioned. I'll call her now. Wait one minute and call her yourself. You coming home tonight?"

"Yes, of course. But let's meet at your office, I want to nail this son-of-a-bitch, and I think we almost have him.

"At least tell me something."

"Okay. He was never fully vetted, hence Alison. Things were different in the days when he joined the force. His past is sketchy, due to limited traceable records, but I discovered that as an adolescent, he was placed in foster care. You'll never guess who to."

"Mohammad, Ali, or Hussein?"

"No, but almost as close: Sylvia Cartwright and Norman Harper."

"Ouch! They run the scam charity and are related to Mohammad."

"Yes. They had one son, Walter Harper. Care to join the dots?"

"No. We both know it. Alison will either prove the connection, or disprove it. Do you have a second theory?"

"No, not really. Not one that would hold water, let alone evidence. I have to go. Work. This is more than a curved ball. Until later, Dan. Ciao."

Much later, Felicity entered the office. She saw Dan and Alison smiling smugly. "What have you got? Out with it."

Alison replied, "You were spot on Ma'am. Chief Inspector Walter Cartwright changed his name by deed pole and used to be known as Walter Harper–Cartwright. He is in fact a mole for Mohammad. Before he joined the police, he was generally known as Walter Harper. There is little digital information relating, as most data was in physical form, but you nailed him."

"How sure are you?"

"As of now, ninety-nine percent certain. By tomorrow, that will be one-hundred percent. I'm tracking his financial details and dealings, bank accounts, offshore dealings, especially with the wrong parts of the world, but most hidden from normal view. I think we got the foster parents as well. I'm following that up also."

Dan asked, "What about direct evidence?"

"It's all in the financial details, which are virtually complete. What I do is not easy. There are large payments from Mohammad to a Walter Harper's account in Panama. That's a forwarder. I went after the usual suspects, and discovered the money ended up in the Cayman Islands, and he's worth a pretty penny, if not quite a millionaire."

There was a break of silence, as each of them absorbed the greater significance of the revelation. The impact of knowing was strong; the means to bring the full force of the law to bear, within reach.

Dan said, "Felicity, Alison, I need you to review this information as it relates to Benaris and Karen. Why are they caught up in this, or at minimum, taking a watching brief? Remember, the question of which side either of them are supporting, as yet remains unresolved.

"Excuse me, I need to write up my reports for tomorrow, and log my ruminations. I'll be in my room at the inn. Knock my door when you get there, and I'll come down to join you ladies for dinner. This is becoming 'The Fifth Column Squared'. Bye for now."

Alison responded, "Ahha! The twenty-fifth column. Byeee."

Luton airport was taken by stealth at five a.m. on Thursday, with little resistance. Mohammad's Pakistani warehouse, and Luton University were locked down.

Dan flew in with Martin and Sinjun, and rendezvoused with one platoon of SAS. Dan and Sinjun knew many of the team, and after greetings, got down to finalise the assault on the offices of Mohammad, Ali, and Hussein. Regular soldiers would support them. They went in following the route Dan had previously used, and deployed troops on ingress, who took up secure and hidden positions.

Meanwhile, a precision paratrooper drop began the main assault against the enemy base in the council chamber of Luton. Thunderflash grenades were followed by elite troops on the ground, and the building secured within minutes. The leader was killed in the strike, while others were subdued and arrested.

The attack spread outwards from the centre, confusing sleepy militia, who were expecting attack from outside. Outer defences had been turned inwards by the time exterior attacks began. Typhoons took out heavy armaments protecting the city approaches. Light tanks sped into the city, taking out sniper positions according to Dan's information.

Meanwhile, Mohammad, Hussein, and Ali had rushed to their office complex. They assembled vital files and digital media for removal, and opened the safe. Dan's forces entered and arrested them all. The information, plus that found hidden under filing cabinets, was removed immediately, as were two brothers Ali, other directors, and their chief officers. Waheed was one of those taken for questioning. Dan took control of his diary, while Martin stayed to run full search.

A military convoy took the prisoners to the nearby airport, the only part of Luton Sir Jack's forces wholly controlled at the time. Later they were moved to a dedicated secure facility for interrogation.

Although Luton was quickly cleansed of militia, many civilian agitators remained, and a roundup of those was underway. Hate-preaching Imams who had avoided deportation by their lawyers misusing the European Human Rights Act were captured as well. They, along with protesting barristers and even magistrates, were sent for immediate trial. Most were found guilty of treason, and refusing to vow allegiance to Queen Charmaine. They were given the choice of execution or deportation, the sentences to be carried out immediately.

Many chose the latter, thinking to buy time to work legal angles. They were surprised to find themselves on crowded airliners, and deposited in different parts of the Middle East. Iraq, Syria, and Afghanistan were popular destinations, with British authorities at least. Large and hastily erected camps were build in friendly areas of Libya to cope with the mass deportations.

The harsh new law had already taken effect as thousands of radical extremist Muslims had already departed England's shores. In Luton, with the main protagonists dealt with, the army went street-by-street, house-by-house, and workplace-by-workplace, asking all to vow allegiance to Queen Charmaine. The emergency courts were exceptionally busy that day, the video evidence irrefutable.

As the cleansing of Luton was effected, advance forces moved onwards, clearing towns such as Newmarket and Thetford. Information provided by Dan's team greatly helped incursion, as support forces followed, and courts of instant justice dispensed sentence. Drawing to the end of a long day, nearly all centres of Islamic power had been removed from western East Anglia, as far south as the M25.

One remained: Wymondham. Dan contacted Sir Jack. "Dan, this has been a remarkable day, and a great success for everybody involved. Once again, your information was spot on, as was Sinjun's tactical analysis. I think we need him back on the payroll. Now, regards expanding your team and their roll, are you resolved to relocate?"

"No, although creating the new team remains a top priority."

"Create it then, but stay where you are. You can begin recruiting. Some names have already been put forward. I'll let you have them later today. You could start training them where you are."

"You're not hassling us to move?"

"No. Her Majesty suggested building a small, secure town to house our intelligence community, including wings from each of the three services. She wants to promote inter-agency trust and sharing. I have a site earmarked near Richmond, which just happens to have a deep and disused section of the Underground running beneath. It's ideal for creating secure bunkers, and offering other routes of escape, entrance and egress. Okay Dan, you can postpone. Now, what can I do for you?"

"We plan to take out Wymondham tomorrow, and Felicity is putting a team together. Her bosses back her to the hilt, and have the goods on the local police hierarchy. We'll take the council chamber, as I need council records to complete our trap to expose Ali and Ali for providing false documents, and regards money laundering."

"You have the evidence ready?"

"Most of it, yes. I just need to relate what actually occurred, to the books of Ali and Ali, and tie in council knowledge aforethought with digital files and hard copy archives. We can support this with the bullying and physical eviction of village inhabitants by Muslim thugs, and we have several fully documented cases lined up for court. Anglo-Asian Holdings were the main players behind this, so a trial of Mohammad, Hussein, and Ali will follow shortly."

"I'll see to it that you have a couple of platoons in support. One of our travelling courts of instant justice will be in Norwich at the beginning of next week. Pencil in Monday. We are having a wholesale clearance of rubbish. Ensure those from the complex you took are there the day before, and you better ask Felicity to clear some cells."

Late that day, Dan received the file of applicants from Sir Jack, and spoke to Alison. She forwarded the list to Veronica, and tasked her to follow up and prepare the recruitment process.

Strikes continued every day, Sheffield falling on Friday morning, and momentum gathering with experience. The army machine rolled through sympathising areas nearby, supported by instant courts that pronounced sentences, which were quickly actioned. The next strikes were against Dewsbury and Rochdale.

Makaarim and her small team, became known as a group which ordinary people could contact for help. Although ISIL interlopers were also present online. Ayesha continued to assist, bringing in her own lines of independent information. As word of freedom spread, so did the amount of information Makaarim was able to supply to Dan.

Volunteers continued to apply for the services, and not all for military positions. Cooks and medics came forward, and training camps became a bustle of fast-track skill set learning. One camp was dedicated to supporting and training European resistance groups, mainly from France, Switzerland, and Poland. They were also supported with the issue of small arms taken from enemy troops.

Elsewhere on Friday morning, the team assembled for breakfast at their office. As Percy joined them, Felicity said, "We take Wymondham today. Percy, what did you discover about Inspector Wheeler?"

"Not much Ma'am. She's well respected by the lads, a bit of an authoritarian, but she's new. I've followed her a few evenings, Stan on most others. She sometimes visits Wymondham, and has been seen out with the Inspector. He said it looked like business, not pleasure. Twice they appeared to be quarrelling, and they always went home alone."

"That's interesting. So we're discounting a sexual relationship. There are other types. Let's keep an open mind. Thanks Percy, Dan?"

"Inspector Khan is a member of a moderate Muslim society, one opposed to terrorism. They counsel those in distress, and act to prevent

British thuggery, like the EDF. They publish leaflets and hold meetings, some at schools, to teach the ways of moderate and integrating Islam.

"Alison did a lot of research and discovered that Karen Wheeler supplies him with information not readily available to the public, or to a police Inspector. She worked for a time as a Superintendent's admin. Alison, with Colin's assistance, traced emails from her, using the Super's authority for release. The few she has on file, were forwarded to Inspector Benaris Khan."

Felicity said, "Good work Dan, Alison. There will indubitably be more for turning up, but I have enough for court."

"There's one thing more. Karen's grandfather was an Indian Muslim. He worked for the British Raj and came to England as a young man, later marrying an English girl, and raising a family. I wonder what tales he told her younger self, when she sat upon his knee?"

"I'll need to interview the pair of them, and will call George now. Otherwise, it's time to move. I'll take Karen into custody first, and tie up that loose end before it becomes a problem."

As she readied to leave, Alison came down and handed her a thin folder. "This just came in, and you'll want to read it before you leave, Ma'am. There's a copy for you Dan, upstairs. Bon voyage."

The file detailed unusual monetary transactions to and from a secret account held by Benaris Khan. Felicity jumped up and shouted, "Got him!"

Dan rose and said, "I'll check what these payments relate to. See you later, but a kiss before you go."

Upstairs Dan said, "Great work Alison. But there has to be more. I need to know why these payments were made."

"Well, I've searched everywhere, even under the bed and mattress. That's it."

"Then check inside the mattress. I don't know — rip up the floorboards, check behind the walls. There's more to this. Run a search for him through our database, and then expand."

"I'm on it, top priority, right?"

Minutes passed as the software ran. Then came a hit, followed moments later by another. "What you got?"

"I got him banged to rites. He's been identified at our local aerodrome, twice. Seems he took a holiday--in Raqqa. I'll fill in the blanks if you leave me alone."

"Brilliant. I'll let Felicity know immediately. She'll need the info as soon as you have it. You found the answer, the twenty-fifth column. Well done!"

Chapter 51 ~ The Twenty-Fifth Column

Later that morning, having already relieved Karen Wheeler of duty, Felicity strode into Wymondham police station. Backed by a team of armed officers, she arrested the police chief and his number two. Thanks to Constable Parfitt, one Sergeant and two Constables were also taken away for questioning. She took charge, immediately recalling all constables not engaged in responding to reported crime. They assembled for briefing, where Felicity explained what was going down and laid out a new plan for the day.

Upstairs, the rooms of the Chief and Inspector were sealed off, to await thorough investigation by internal investigations department. Upon arrest, Inspector Benaris Khan said to Felicity, "I need to speak to the person in charge. This is not what you think."

"Tell me, I am the person in charge. Chief Inspector Wigglesworth."

"Ma'am, there must be some mistake. I have done nothing wrong. I only try to ease the situation, help those in distress."

"No. You allowed innocent people to be evicted from their homes. Aunt Dotty for one. You are a disgrace to the uniform."

Benaris continued to protest his innocence as he was led away.

Meanwhile, Superintendent George Lovell had assigned a Chief Inspector to take over at Wymondham. They arrived together and Lovell's first task was to officially interview the secretaries, and then get to the bottom of what was going on. Felicity would officially act as cover for Lower Meddlington in the interim.

A short time later, the council chamber and building were quickly taken. Felicity lined up all the councillors, and presented each with a copy of the Bible and Quran. She asked them individually, to take the oath of allegiance to Queen Charmaine. "This is not an oath to your faith, it is an oath of loyalty to your country."

All the Christian councillors, and four of the Muslim did so. The others refused and were arrested, to be held at Wymondham police station, as Norwich nick was already bursting at the seams. Felicity said, "This council is formally disbanded until such time new elections can be held. I ask those councillors remaining to continue working in support the local community. You will continue to draw salary and expenses.

"I need to read aloud a Royal Decree, 'From this moment onwards, the practice of Sharia Law is forbidden, upon pain of death. So is forced marriage, and Female Genital Mutilation. All of these crimes carry a sentence up to and including the death penalty.'

"So, an olive branch to true, British Muslims. This implies that moderate Islam will be tolerated, but after recent events, it would be most unwise for any to push the envelope. Deportation is the usual outcome. Or execution. Please spread these words to your communities.

"Percy, Stan, please examine council records. You know what you are looking for, connections to Ali Brothers."

A councillor came forward. "Allow me to assist. I tried to stop it, but they told me to be quiet or my family would be harmed."

"Percy, we'll need this councillor's statement: Identify coercion."

Later, Felicity met with George and they prepared files and evidence before interviewing the three police chiefs, George said, "Top, middle, or bottom?"

Felicity replied, "Bottom. I could do with Karen back at her post, if possible. It may not happen of course."

"We'll approach them like this. Regards Inspector Wheeler…"

Felicity conducted the interview, George watching, appraising both, and occasionally speaking. Talk quickly moved to the matter at hand.

At first, Karen Wheeler was a bit indignant about being arrested, but she was sharp enough to realise she had to play along and tell the truth. She admitted using the Superintendent's clearance to obtain information. "That was years ago, when Benaris was first posted to Wymondham. He called me seeking advice because Muslims were taking over rural villages, and he wanted to stop them, but the Chief overruled, threatening him with disciplinary action if he proceeded.

"I only sent Benaris three emails, and that was a very long time ago. I have no idea how you found out. One contained a file concerning Chief Inspector Cartwright. I could not get that information any other way without serious suspicion."

"So you stole it."

"That's a bit harsh. I was acting for the greater good."

"Tell me what you know about the takeover of these villages."

"Well, at first I did not believe Benaris, because it seemed impossible. But it wasn't. The houses were in tithe to nobody, and a company bought them, installing Muslims as tenants. I knew it was wrong, but it was lawful. What could I do?"

"Tell somebody."

"But who?"

"I found out about it and I acted upon it, you did not. Define your relationship with Benaris. Are you lovers?"

"What? No way."

"Then what, exactly?"

"You won't drop this, will you? It is nothing. We're distant cousins."

"He is Pakistani, and you are English. Try me again."

"Okay. His family used to live in India, before it was partitioned into India, West, and East Pakistan. The latter is nowadays called Bangladesh. They lived west of Jammu, near the Jhelum River, in what is today Kashmir, Pakistan. The area is still disputed territory between the two countries. My grandfather came from Jammu, which although only a few miles distant from his sister's home, was still in India. His sister ended up in Pakistan. She married Benaris' grandfather."

"Accepted, I checked your background. Let's move forward to the day you arrived here. We were in Dan's office and you went to the toilet several times. Why?"

"I told you at the time, I wasn't feeling well."

"But you were fine. You used the washroom convenience to make text messages or emails. Who to?"

"Damn you! I was letting Benaris know about how things were developing nationwide, nothing about the case at hand. I urged him to act against the Chief Inspector."

"That agrees with the print out I have of them. We ran it through GCHQ because had to be sure which side you were on. Regardless Karen, that is correct, and does you credit.

"So tell me, why were you arguing with Inspector Khan, off duty, in Wymondham, twice I believe?"

"You had me followed?"

"Heavens above, no. It was by accident. What was it about?"

"I wanted Benaris to go public, press charges against all, and he refused. He is very loyal, but sometimes to the wrong person. I started making a file, and was intending to make it known myself, but who to? I asked to speak to you privately on your last official visit, and you agreed, but got called away. This is what I wanted to discuss, share with you, and ask your advice about. I was not ready to reveal all. There was information missing, but I was close."

"You could have called round. Or you should have been more persistent. Go on, where is the file?"

"In my office, I intended to show it to you."

"I'll see it later today. Thank you Karen. Excuse us one moment. Refreshments will be brought for you."

Leaving the interview room, Felicity turned to George. "Well?"

George summarised, "She did the wrong thing for all the right reasons. I need her secret file checking. This should be a disciplinary offence, using the Chief Super's authority, but I feel an official warning more suitable, then we won't have staff shortages."

"Yes George, I agree. But it was a long time ago, a misdemeanour at best. Perhaps an unofficial warning, depending upon what I discover when I take her back. We need people like her in the force."

"Under consideration. Let's discuss the other two over lunch, and how this information relates to the way we will interview them."

"I'd rather get this one sorted. I'll take her back now and review the evidence. I'll report, send copies, and we decide her fate at that time. At least she will either be manning the station, or in lockup."

"I'd prefer you waited. Give me a reason."

"Because I need to know what is in that file. It may alter the way we process the Inspector, and the Chief as well. I have new information concerning Khan, with more to follow shortly."

"Hmmm. You're good. Okay, but I need you back here by two."

On her way to Lower Meddlington, Felicity received a call from Alison. "I have it all, and Benaris has been a very naughty boy…"

"Well done, Alison. Ask Martin to drop the file at my old office, as I'm on a tight schedule. I'll need it in both physical and digital form. I'll be there soon, so he better be quick. This is a major breakthrough. Forward anything else you discover to my mobile. Ciao."

A short time later, Felicity entered her old office and Karen showed her the relevant file. It was a good piece of work. She also discovered some information had been gleaned from Stan's evidence, answering that long-standing puzzle. Aunt Dotty and others were noted.

Felicity sent copies to her Superintendent, and later spoke to him in confidence. "Okay Felicity. Give her an unofficial warning, and let's get back to work. This is a minor irritation, but gets one of our own back on the job. That is a bonus when we are so stretched. Two o'clock?"

"I'm leaving in minutes, sir. Ciao."

"Karen, I have to give you an unofficial caution, I'm sorry. This relates to using the Super's computer without authority. It should have been an official caution, but I argued your case. You should have told me before now. We are on the same side you and I. Now let's get on with our jobs."

"Thanks Chief. I was so worried. What about Benaris?"

"That is for me to discover in a few minutes time. Ciao."

Felicity received the new file from Martin, and obtained warrants on the way back. She applied them at once to Khan and the Chief's bank accounts, and came away with bank statements going back four years. These backed up Alison's research and were proof of evidence.

Later, she and George swapped notes. The information Karen had gathered was astonishing for one so new in her position. They also had an interim report from Internal Investigations, mostly confirming what they already knew. George said, "Let's have a word with Inspector Khan, and see how your information compares to what he tells us."

The interview was long. Felicity fired the first question. "How long has your affair with Inspector Karen Wheeler been going on? We know it's been many years. I remind you, you are under caution."

"What? We are very good friends. This has nothing to do with her."

"Yes it does. You see, she volunteered for Lower Meddlington because you were close by. You have been seen out together many times since. We also know she obtained highly confidential and restricted information for you. You have been using her."

"Absolutely not. What makes you think so?"

"Her admission of guilt. She sold you out, Khan. Admit it."

"Yes, but it was in a good cause."

"If so, then please explain the payments I have highlighted? I have here a copy of your bank account records."

"They were private sales. There's nothing unusual about them."

"Oh yes there is. You see, these were transfers made to your account, from Ali Brothers Solicitors. This proves you were taking bribes so as not to follow through with reporting the takeover of people's houses. Is that not the truth?"

George took over at that point. "Inspector, here's the thing. You were in dereliction of your duty for not reporting known crimes. These relate to the harassment and eviction of long-standing tenants, whose villages were taken over by Muslims. That affected the electorate in such a way, that when all Muslim councillors crossed the floor, Islam had control. You are an imbecile for not taking this further.

"But what is most damning, is that you accepted bribes in order to support your religion over those British people who were displaced."

"No. Never, I tried to support them."

"Then why is your signature on this eviction notice? Felicity, the file that you just received."

Felicity handed the file from Alison. "Thank you Chief. Now what have we got here. Ah yes. You joined a militant Islamic group when you were at a Muslim school, and were groomed to become a double agent."

"Impossible. My charitable deeds speak for themselves. I am totally against extremism."

"Really, then why do I have this picture of you, taken a few months ago, in Raqqa? You beheaded a German family. They were Christians working voluntarily for a relief agency. The boy was eight years old."

The Inspector paled, but Felicity struck. "Care to watch the whole video? It is most revealing--you donning black robes, executing the parents and child for no good reason, and celebrating afterwards."

"No! That cannot be me."

"Oh, but it is, Khan. You see, there is no unbroken footage. You are guilty of murdering a child. You took a vacation in Raqqa via a local, private aerodrome, and we now have footage of you leaving, and returning. You are vermin, a snake in the grass."

"Okay. I admit it. But they were Christians. Don't you understand?"

"No, I do not. They were helping Muslim people displaced by ISIL."

The interview concluded shortly afterwards, but others would follow. Afterwards, George said, "Brilliant work Felicity. He is banged to rites. I think he was the controller of the Chief Inspector."

"Yes, it could be, and this is all because of Mohammad, Hussein, and Ali. And money. Religion plays no part in their lives does it, except as lip service. They use it as a smokescreen to cover their atrocities."

"I could say similar about Christianity today, but prefer not to."

"You just did."

"No, I retracted the remark."

"Yes, but after you said it. Let's deal with the all of this today. Come-on George, this won't take a moment with what we now have. I'll assemble the files and meet you at interview."

"No, the canteen. I need caffeine, and we both need something to eat. This will be a long one, you mark my words."

Chief Inspector Walter Harper-Cartwright refused to admit any guilt, or reply to self-incriminating questions. It was the shortest interview of the day, and the outcome remained in doubt until the very end. Felicity hit him with printouts of all his fiscal manoeuvrings. She presented him hard copy evidence, detailing his Panama and Cayman Island holdings. She finished by laying before him, papers detailing the money trail. Everything came directly, or indirectly, from Mohammad.

Cornered, he tried to broker a deal, and got short shrift. He was led away to the cells, to contemplate his selling out of his county of birth, for personal, financial gain. Like most people in power, he considered himself above the law. It turned out he was not.

It was late and they were tired, but took coffee in the canteen. The mood was upbeat, having nailed two of the three. "George, why don't we finish the all of this tonight? It'll only take an hour, and I need these men either disciplined, or back on the job."

"Erm. I guess you're right. I had hoped to be home hours ago, but getting the all of this dealt with while we're here appeals to me. One of them lost evidence, on purpose I believe. The other two made the initial reports, which Khan and the Chief didn't proceed with. There's the little matter of not taking things higher, but what do ordinary people do?"

"Accept the status quo. They keep their heads down, and keep their jobs. There's nothing here, unless we find something. You ready?"

"Yes. I'll call the wife first and then we'll get to it."

The upshot was, the Sergeant and one Constable received an unofficial caution. The other Constable got an official caution for mislaying evidence.

The day had been most productive, but it was almost ten o'clock before the pair departed for their respective homes.

Chapter 52 ~ Hard Choices

Dan and Felicity spent much of the weekend at home, Dan working in the library, and Felicity using her new office in the attic. The decorators were making swift progress. The main rooms were ready for living in, if in need of finishing touches.

Felicity took a break late Sunday afternoon and attended Norwich police station, where Waheed was waiting in an interview room. She spoke briefly with the young man under caution, and opened the door to let Ayesha in. Felicity departed, the official tape still recording.

"Sister you are still alive, and looking so well. I cannot believe it!"

"I would be dead if our cousin had not missed with his one shot at me. Stop, I am fine. You are not. You will soon go on trial, with our supposed father, and most likely will be executed or deported."

"But I had to do what father said. I had no choice."

"Yes you did, you could have escaped like I did."

"You know I could not. They would have found me and killed me."

"Waheed, I know you are a good boy. You did what you did because our father made you do it. I have been told that if you testify against them you may be pardoned, but you must decide now."

"No, I cannot. How can you suggest such a thing?"

"Because it is the right thing to do. How did you like living under thrall of Daesh?"

"It was hell. They are psychopathic animals. They are not Muslims."

"And neither are you if you continue to act like this."

"It is so hard."

"Your diary, in your office, why did you keep that?"

"How do you know about that?"

"We've known about it for weeks, and it is now evidence for the prosecution. Why did you write it?"

"I wanted to keep track of what they were doing."

"Then tell that to the police. Tell them it was your insurance policy. Then tell them what the others were doing."

"I cannot. My family come first"

"You were sold to them, just as I was. They are not your birth parents. I saw the bill of sale. Your father is sterile."

Ayesha walked towards the door. Waheed begged her to stay, but she stated, "Turn Queen's evidence, or you will never see me again. Goodbye brother."

Ayesha was upset and rushed to the waiting car. Looking up, she saw a hairdressers and said, "Martin, I'm going to have my hair cut. I can no longer be two people. Please wait and run me back later."

Meanwhile, Waheed had broken down in tears. He was a wreck of his former self. Felicity waited until his spirit filled with despondency, before entering in a chirpy frame of mind. She sat down opposite with his diary in her hands and said, "What's it to be, Waheed?"

He eyed her like a rodent might a snake, but said nothing. She opened the book and began reading abstract lines. "We used this information to thwart Muslim attacks. I could put in a good word for you, and my testimony carries a lot of weight. Just tell us all you know."

"I don't know. This is so difficult. Please, I am being torn between family duty, being faithful to Allah, and telling the truth. I need advice. Is there a mosque I could attend?"

"No. But there is an Imam nearby whom you could talk to. He is a moderate, not a ranting halfwit preaching fear and loathing for this country. Will you see him?"

"Yes please."

Felicity departed with diary in hand, and some minutes later ushered the Imam into the interview room. The official crime interview tape was still running, although the room was also monitored by superior recording equipment.

"Alayhi al-salām. What is wrong my son? Please tell me."

"Alayhi al-salām. I don't know what to do. My duty lies to Allah, my father, and telling the truth. They do not fit together."

"Ah, I see. You are torn inside, but you must know right from wrong. This is one of the good Lord's teachings, so choose wisely."

"But what do I do--say to them?"

"Is your faith true?"

"Yes. I worship every day, and recant sutra's when needs be."

"Is that lip service, or belief? I ask because there is a great difference, and grave danger if we get confused. I know a little about this case, and I know you are in a difficult situation, so allow me to continue."

"Please, sahib."

"Islam is the true religion of peace. Yet, when I look around, Moslem brothers are blowing other Moslems, or self-perceived enemies to pieces. It is not right. It is against the will of Allah."

"But I must obey my Father's instructions."

"Of course you must. But you can question why. Your father came to this country, and gained citizenship. That was due to the British Commonwealth. You were born here. That is different. So many times have I seen it, young and old. Waheed, where does your allegiance lie?"

"To Allah, to my father, and my greater family. Why do you ask?"

"And what about your allegiance to your country of birth?"

"I am British, and proud of it."

"But yet you support your father and greater family, who are determined to turn this country into a caliphate of Islam. We are guests of Briton. We do not have that right, even you who were born here."

"I disagree. I am a UK citizen, and I have equal rights."

"Yes you do, but no you do not. This is a Christian country, one that follows the words of our great prophet, Jesus. When we turn against our brother, be it in religion, Moslem versus Christian, or Sunni versus Shia, extremists and fanatics with no moral soul come in to cause mayhem and kill. That is the history of Islam. Let me explain about the fourth Caliph, Ali, his battles with Aisha, your sister's namesake, and the Battle of the Camel.." The story was long and familiar to Waheed.

"...And so you see as before, so it repeats today. It never ends, unless we grow to encompass the international community; you must embrace being either British or Pashtun. You can no longer be both. If you are Pashtun, then go to Pakistan. If you are British, then stay and fight for integration, for without it we will be set upon and marginalised.

"Instead, moderate Moslems hide their heads in the sand, as do Imams, and deny any of this is happening, or is their own fault. They do not report extremists, or local mafia, and we live with the results. It becomes like it was back home. By standing up for yourself, your culture, and telling the police what they need to know, you will be doing every moderate Moslem in this country a very great service.

"Tell me, how did you like living under the yoke of Daesh?"

"It was hell. They are animals. They are not Muslims, but bullies and terrorists. We lived under threat of execution for petty offences. One of my friends was beheaded for allowing his wife to wear no head covering at home. She was stoned to death in front of their children. The boys were taken for training, the girls as slaves."

"And what is the lesson to be learned, my son? Maybe their faith, their ideology is twisted by radicals. Perhaps they are badly advised, and avoid contact with moderate Moslems. A few may pretend to be Moslems, but are not. They are thugs and bullies."

"What about my father? He was strict, but very devout. He never missed prayers, and helped in the mosque."

"Yet he was an enforcer. I know of him from Luton, where he controlled the local gangs as if he were still a Pakistani Farm Lord. He was responsible for murdering a good friend of mine..."

They spoke at length, the Imam charting a middle course through troubled seas. He never told Waheed what to do, but counselled the young man on actions and consequences.

Later, they prayed together, and the Imam rose to depart. "Choose wisely my son. These days bring many changes. 'alayhi al-salām'."

The Imam knocked the door to leave, and Felicity thanked him for attending. A constable took him back home, as Felicity returned to her interview. "Waheed, I hope that was helpful for you. We only want to assist you during these trying times. Now is the time to decide. You are either a suspect or a victim. Will you tell us what went on?"

"Yes, okay."

Chapter 52

Felicity could hardly contain her delight, but pulled a straight face and began the interview proper. After serious revelations, she called a short break for refreshments. Seeking to further break the divide, she took him to the police canteen, adopting Dan's ploy of having her mobile phone on voice record, inside her inner top jacket pocket.

The break had a beneficial effect on both, Waheed looking much more comfortable. Felicity said, "Shall we resume—Get this over with?"

It was almost two hours later when she terminated the interview, but Waheed had come across to their side. He freely offered vital information. "Father hides important papers and guns in his bedroom. The bed has a false bottom beneath the mattress. There are two leather cases in the wardrobe, and the keys are behind the dressing table.

"Thank you Waheed. This is great news, and a large plus for your case. I will make my recommendations accordingly, after searching your father's bedroom. However, you must remain here until the trial."

She returned home with interview tapes and diary. Dan ran the recording through his software, Felicity received digital and physical copy, and he kept a copy for the team, saving her hours of transcription.

"That's one hell of a breakthrough, and Ayesha the catalyst once again. She's some girl. It's just gone seven, and I need to check in with the team. You need to break the good news to Ayesha, so let's have a beer and curry at the inn tonight. It's been a while since we did normal."

"No, I can't I have to finish a report, and … Okay."

"Quick shower and change. Ready in ten."

The evening proved great therapy, which was followed by excellent sleep. The feeling of bliss was shattered when Sir Jack called early on Monday morning. "Dan, excepting Birmingham, we take the last major target today, Leicester. They will be expecting us and defend with full force. What's the latest from Makaarim?"

"I'm sending her report through now, together with my report, and Sinjun's revised tactical analysis. He suggests that you do the opposite of 'the butcher of the Somme', whatever that means. His plan is a little bizarre, but should have them completely bamboozled. I'm here as needs be, but need to prepare for a long day in court tomorrow."

"Ah yes, General Haig. Dan, do you know what day this is?"

"Yes of course, Monday."

"Many people also term today Christmas Eve my boy."

"With respect, Sir Jack."

"I suggest we pick this up again, later. Trials in Norwich are rescheduled for Friday. People need a break, and we need to show we are a Christian country. Our main objectives are virtually taken.

"Merry Christmas Dan."

"Likewise, Sir Jack."

Chapter 53 ~ Great Britain

Dan went straight to Felicity, "Do you know what day it is today?"

"Monday silly."

"And when's Christmas Day?"

"Next Tuesday."

"That would be the next Tuesday, as in tomorrow."

She stared at him. "Oh My God!"

Dan pulled her close, taking her weight as she melded her body to his. "Shhh. Sir Jack just told me, otherwise I had not connected the two. I'll need to speak to my team, the trial is rescheduled for Friday."

"That's good news, I need the time to prepare. I'll be in work today, and then on call, first call. Oh Dan, isn't this wonderful, our first Christmas at home. Do you think it will snow?"

"I don't know, but I think I better beat a path to the butcher and buy a turkey, if there are any left."

"Go now, and I'll see you this evening. Invite the team for Christmas lunch, and I'll ask my parents to come over. Love you."

Dan got a big, plump bird, and hoped it would fit in the oven. He checked when he got back, and it did, just. He put it in the pantry, which felt like a walk-in refrigerator. He had collected various stuffings, sausage and bacon rolls, a wheel of ronky stilton, and matured port. He added mince pies, Christmas cake, and Christmas pudding from the bakers, complete with store-bought, 'home-made' brandy sauce. He'd make the bread sauce himself.

Dumping his purchases in the kitchen, pâté and perishables in the fridge, he left at once for the office. He walked into the kitchen, and found Ayesha cooking breakfast. He stared at her auburn, shoulder length hair, before complimenting her.

She smiled back and said, "Now there is no need, I feel free to have my hair as I wish. Meeting Waheed yesterday, it changed my thinking."

Stella hurried in and said, "Watch the shop for a moment, me-dear, I'll finish up here. Full English Dan?"

"Yes please." Dan sat quietly for a moment, soaking up the normality. Percy came in carrying bags from the butchers and baker, followed by Veronica back from an early morning Christmas shopping expedition. He sat and sipped his coffee until Ayesha returned from the shop. All were seated and eyes turned to look at him expectantly.

"I've just discovered something. Not only is today Monday, but it is also Christmas Eve. We need to discuss the festive holidays."

Alison said, "Already sorted, Dan. I'm leaving this morning, taking five days off, and Veronica has the same when I return. This base will always be covered. Martin and Percy have chosen to take longer breaks, the threat being annulled. Sinjun?"

Chapter 53

"I will accompany you this morning, if I may, Alison. I will sojourn in Hereford, and return early in the New Year."

Dan said, "Sir Jack asked me to put you back on the payroll, they have primarily been using your tactical analysis. Today will be key. I'll let you know how that works out. Do you accept the job?"

"Perhaps. I've enjoyed working here, and if we move to London that would suit me greatly. I'll let you know when I return."

"Good. I got the impression there might be a promotion in the offing, a better pension to boot, so make the choice that suits you best. Oh, and keep working on Birmingham, they are saving the biggest cancer for last."

"Ayesha, your work with us is about done. We can always use your skills and teach you new ones. You have a job with us if you want one."

"Thanks Dan. I enjoyed it, but it is not for me. Brian is opening a new restaurant in Lower Meddlington, and he wants me as manageress. I'll keep in touch though, and am always willing to help out."

Dan smiled and said, "Okay, that's perfect. Those of you staying here are invited to my house for Christmas dinner, tomorrow, meaning late lunch."

Talk buzzed the table, before people rose to either work, or leave. Martin offered Alison and Sinjun a lift to central London, which they accepted, and all left to pack. Veronica went up to monitor consoles, Dan stood with Percy, and turned to face him. "Would you consent to being my Best Man?"

Percy spluttered in consternation, "Yes, but why?"

"I was raised an orphan in Malta. I was good at school, but was always moving on. Eventually I ended up in the MI6 academy. They like orphans—no family history, no ties. I've never had a friend, not until you, and I never knew what love was until Felicity showed me. Now, with a wife and child on the way, I have something to personally fight for, to protect. What do you say?"

Dan's eyes crinkled as he smiled at Percy. "I'll be honoured, Dan. Have you any idea of the date? I'll need to organise your stag do..."

Dan interrupted, "Nothing set as yet, and not before this mess is cleared up. Possibly summer, we'll see what the Memsahib says.

Dan's next worry concerned Veronica being alone and bored. He checked and she showed him a mountain of work, and the morning's call list, most if it information requested by military and security services. Once Dan knew she would be busy and was happy, he felt much better. He and Percy stayed to help her process all the immediate tasks before buffet lunch, but left immediately afterwards. A light snow had begun to fall, and Dan cautiously preceded Percy down the road as they made their way home for the duration.

Dan drove on to the shopping centre, where he was lucky to get one of the last, large and realistic, imitation Christmas trees. He bought a selection of lights, baubles, and other Christmas paraphernalia, before purchasing a gold necklace from a jeweller, and perfume from the shop next door, hoping Felicity would like them. He escaped the massing throngs as quickly as possible, and headed home to sort out the house.

By the time Felicity arrived home, he had the turkey ready for stuffing, a coal fire warming the living room, and the Christmas tree set up after a fashion. "Dan, I love it!" They kissed passionately as she stumbled inside. More may have developed if a car had not arrived in the driveway at that moment, bearing Felicity's parents.

The women enthused about Dan's preparations and purchases, and then began on improving things. "I'll leave you to stuff the turkey, Filly." Turning he offered, "Tom, what'll you have?"

"A beer, yes, but let's go to a pub. I fancy relaxing in a friendly environment and to enjoying a bit of normal life for a change."

"Same here, I'll check the girls are okay and we can get on our way."

The women joined them some time later. They ate at another pub, and related anecdotes in front of the home fire before going to bed.

The next day, Veronica, Stella, and Ayesha joined them for Christmas dinner. Ayesha explained, "This is not a Muslim holy day, but Jesus is our revered prophet, so honouring his birthday causes me no problem. Regardless, this is a Christian country."

The meal was a master class of Christmas culinary art, and there was much left over. Ayesha asked if she could take some to the pensioner who first rescued her runaway self and gave her security. An alms basket was put together and Felicity drove, the address and person being closer to her interests. Ayesha also visited her old boss and landlady, giving each a small basket of alms, but did not go inside. They were away for over two hours, but it was time well spent, and their effort was greatly appreciated.

Dan and Felicity enjoyed a quiet Boxing Day together, returning to work mode on Thursday. They had ample time to decipher notes and assemble a mass of verifiable evidence against the accused, which Dan backed up on his laptop. They were set.

Friday saw an extensive and complicated series of interrelated trials take place at Norwich city court. There were three courts in operation, each dealing with different aspects of the interrelated court list. The third court mainly dealt with trials that overlapped.

At times, due process of law appeared haphazard, especially when lawyers representing Mohammad, Hussein, and Ali, proved so divisive and deceitful, they were removed to the dock. They were charged with interfering with evidence, perverting the course of justice, and working for an enemy of the state. They were found guilty of treason, and arrived in Afghanistan five hours later, stripped of their British citizenship.

The case against Anglo-Asian Holdings was proved, and their rights to property disproved. The large farm managers' statements, and personal testimony from Constable Parfitt and 'Aunt Dotty', being enough to secure conviction. It warranted opening a new investigation into all of the company's dealings. Matters relating to Norwich, Newmarket, and Thetford were kept on file. The company effectively ceased trading immediately the verdict was announced.

The lapsed tithe properties without ownership were made Crown settlements with special arrangement. Only longstanding British nationals with proof of occupancy could claim title. The sale price or rent was little by market standards, but set a precedent. The Crown also took legal possession of all tithe property ten years or more out of direct ownership, thus closing the loophole.

Ali Brothers were next, and the trial was short, as related evidence from previous trails remained open to the judges in Court Three. With Dan's analysis of their bookkeeping, and money flowing to offshore accounts, the charge of money laundering was quickly proven. They were shut down immediately, the directors being barred from practicing law. When asked to take an oath of allegiance to Queen Charmaine, they all refused and were sentenced to immediate deportation.

In his summing up, the Judge said, "If you refuse to swear an oath of allegiance, that of loyalty to this Country and our Queen, then you do not deserve to be a part of it. Citizenship revoked!"

V. J. Ali was charged with extortion, smuggling, coercion, and attempted murder. When asked to swear an oath of allegiance, he spat at the bench, and went off on a foul-mouthed tirade. He was sentenced to be executed that day.

The statement Waheed had made went some way to implicate his father, Hussein, although most of the evidence relating to murder, violent behaviour, human trafficking, prostitution, underage prostitution, drug and alcohol racketeering, came from his own records, including those that Waheed tipped Felicity off about. Charges of forced marriage and FGM were added to his file, and Hussein the Father was found guilty on all counts. He refused to take the oath to Queen Charmaine, and was sentenced to death.

Nevertheless, Waheed's evidence had a far more damning effect on Mohammad, who stood stone faced in the dock, and said, "I do not recognise this court, I only recognise the judgement of Allah."

He refused to answer any questions, and looked at people with a menacing glare. When asked to take the oath he tried to attack the Bench. He too was sentenced to immediate execution.

Most of the minor players were dealt with more leniently, and especially those who took the oath to Queen Charmaine. The trials were set to run through the weekend, where councillors and local gang leaders, thugs, smugglers, human traffickers, and child prostitution racketeers, plus enforcers, would be tried. The two ex-senior police officers from Wymondham would be in that group.

Although many were sent to the new regime, harsh prisons, inmate numbers were quickly dropping as foreign offenders were deported, as were many of the newly convicted. To this effect, the Home Office had assembled a fleet of dedicated aircraft, both large and small, to deport those sentenced from the nearest commercial airport. These were supplemented by RAF bases being renovated for the dedicated purpose.

The pattern repeated across England, until the threat of ISIL, and supporters of Muslim extremism, were either sentenced, executed, or deported. University campuses were included, the ringleaders and troublemakers already well know. Similar trials occurred in towns not directly affected by ISIL or Muslim takeover of council.

When Leicester was retaken, only the West Midlands metropolis remained. One quarter of the large city was run by ISIL, and taking back control would be a difficult task because ISIL were deeply and centrally entrenched. Unlike other targets, Birmingham was too large, and ISIL support was scattered throughout the conurbation, making it difficult to tell friend from foe. To gain intelligence, undercover operatives from MI5, MI6, specialist military, and police, infiltrated sympathetic areas.

Makaarim became a part of the expanding new team at Veronica's request. At Dan's insistence, she transferred to the village and was given access to far greater resources than previously available to her team. With renewed enthusiasm and encouragement from office personnel, she came up trumps.

"Veronica, I just found a group opposed to Daesh. They are similar to my team, but are linked with many underground groups. They are based in Sparkhill, the other groups are in Bordesley, Small Heath, Ward End, and Lozells. It's a small and tight-knit community in the heart of the ISIL dominion. They want to work with us. How do you want me to play this?"

"Carefully, they may be ISIL."

"I'm sure they aren't. ISIL/ISIS supporters, they never use the word DAESH: They consider the acronym of 'Dawlat al-Islamiyah f'al-Iraq w Belaad al-Sha', an extreme insult, and kill anyone that uses it. They will be genuine."

"I'll call Dan immediately."

Dan arrived at the office a short time later, and after being fully briefed he enthused, "If this is kosher, it's a massive step forward."

Chapter 53

He called Bude, and later the Director, before speaking to Sir Jack.

"So let me get this straight, Dan. Instead of our planned ground assault, we postpone for a day or so, and undermine from the within?"

"Yes, Sir Jack. We'll insert some of our best agents and ask MI5 for full support, then link up with those of our cells already there and working undercover. I'll also go in, check the new people out personally. If this is for real, we can take them out from the inside. We would need to smuggle arms in, or steal the enemy's. Your siege can then be plan B."

"Yes, a supporting action. I like that. Destabilise the centre first, before we hit. Regular reports, Dan, until we have a plan in place."

With his Director's approval, Dan sent several teams into Birmingham. He liaised with Steve Sterling from MI5, and together with information from other sources, they assembled the framework for a series of subversive operations. When their planning completed, Dan asked, "What's wrong with this, Steve?"

"We don't know these people. You want to go in, check them out?"

"Exactly. It only needs one infiltrator of any of these disparate groups, and we are done for. These are ordinary people, not trained operatives like you or I."

"Agreed. One blabbing mouth and the operation is done for, before it begins. When are you going?"

"Early hours, just before dawn."

"Good. Mind if I tag along, I'm very good at subtle interrogation; most times the subject remains unaware."

"It'll be good to have you along, just the two of us mind. I'll see you at Dudley Port at say, 'O' four hundred hours.

Chapter 54 ~ The Battle for Birmingham

In the predawn of the undercover offensive, Felicity she saw Dan to the door, "Be safe my love and come home to me. I couldn't bear to lose you now."

She was almost teary, until he crushed her to him and soothed, "Shhh now. They haven't gotten me yet, and they won't this time."

Pulling away once she felt stronger and more resolute, she pecked him on the lips and stood back to watch him leave. She waved at his disappearing car, and asked herself, "What am I to do with him? Finally I find a man that I can put up with, and he turns out to be a super-hero."

She answered her own question, "Support him as he does me. Now how can I do that best. I wonder...?"

Later, so early that same morning, Dan and Steve boarded a barge arranged by one of Steve's operatives. They evaded ISIL security checks and headed into the heart of ISIL held Birmingham by using the canals.

One of the bargees moaned to Dan, "It's not right, you know. These airheads have taken over and now I can't work. Been a family business for a hundred years and more, and now I can't shit unless they say so. Many of them weren't even born in this country for Christ's sake!"

The story repeated, often in more colourful language, but to a man or woman, once they realised Dan was intending to free them, they offered barges for moving his troops, and transportation at destination.

Having secured the trust of the bargees, they arrived deep into the heart of the city undiscovered, and were taken to their final destination by resistance fighters. They expected double cross at any moment and were constantly alert, but their fears proved unfounded.

They met their host and Makaarim's contact, Shoaib Azaz, in a backstreet terraced house he used as an operations centre. He was a serious but courteous man who greeted them enthusiastically with a manly hug; "Welcome to my home my new friends. I take it your journey was acceptable. Would you like tea, something to eat?"

After refreshments were served by his sister, he wasted no time in briefing them thoroughly on the current local situation. Steve talked to the man and learned he ran a homeless shelter. In his former life he had been an Army Captain, and because of his experience and local standing among the downtrodden, had become the co-ordinator for the resistance.

When Shoaib was distracted, Steve gave Dan an slight affirmative nod of his head, and Dan winked back in agreement: The man appeared genuine, so they proceeded to discuss objectives and tactics, before Dan said, "Thank you Shoaib, this is excellent. Now we need to meet these other groups and check them out."

Chapter 54

"Of course, it shall be as you wish. I have arranged for my son, Shaheen, to show you around. He should be here quite soon. More tea?"

They continued to discuss incursion plans and avenues of support, before his son, known as 'Shah', arrived to take them to meet with local leaders of their resistance allies.

As the meeting concluded, Shoaib warned, "Be wary of ISIL eavesdropping, both electronically and in person. We are physically secure here, but don't trust your phone or computer, they are hacked."

Steve said, "Impossible!"

Shoaib responded genially, "Better I say intercepted then, copied in transit for later decoding and interpretation."

Dan and Steve nodded to one another. They were well appraised of wire tapping in the digital age and used such devices themselves; a bug on a wire outside of a house, even a fibre optical line, and they secured access to information for a geek to interpolate.

The pair spent two days checking out the various resistance groups with Shah as introducer. They studied prospective targets, firmed plans for incursion, and also met with undercover operatives, before holding private conference on the mission at large.

As they wandered, isolated in a nearby park, Steve said, "Dan, the central players in all of these groups are genuine; they are putting their lives on the line for the cause."

"Freeing themselves from ISIL. Yes, I totally agree. There are some peripheral people who raise concern, but we are both aware of them, and so are their controllers. As it stands, we are good to go."

"Agreed, Dan. We have details of the ISIL weapons stores and local control centres, who is in charge, and we've identified hardliners and agitators who hide in the woodwork. I need to get some highly secure information back to my people, as I'm sure you do."

"Steve, to ensure complete secrecy, one of us needs to go back. I need a short break in 'Free England', as it's now known locally, you want to come along?"

"Yes, but one of us better stay here on the inside to direct action on the ground. I'll give you a secure file for my boss, and no peeking."

"You have my word. I'll need to speak with Sir Jack."

"Rather you than me, he's a bit, what's the word … imposing."

"He's a character all right, but a good man, hand's-on; still flies Harriers, and the bugger almost got me in a sortie.

Dan stopped walking and turned to look his friend in the eye; "Steve, I need good men. You should come across to the new team I'm heading up, I could do with you as my second. Think about it.

"Now, where's the nearest fast barge out of here. I'll be back as soon as I can."

Some hours later, Dan met with the senior officer of their forward command post in Lower Gornal. After introductions, he was shown to an extremely secure portal on the military net, and spoke with Sir Jack. "Sir, we are a go here. What's your position?"

"We are ready and waiting on you, Dan. Your Makaarim came up with something odd. I spoke to Sinjun about it, plus my own advisors of course, and it breaks the rules, but should be highly effective. We will parachute in troops at twenty-two hundred hours, on New Year's Eve. You will need to begin action earlier, but leave zero footprint. Take the enemy arms bases and compromise local cells of resistance. Remove any and all soft targets, but hang fire on ISIL control centres until we strike--That's when you hit those and throw them into total disarray.

"Disruption is the word my good man, get them running around like headless chickens, and then we'll move in for the kill."

"Got it. They won't be expecting that. Good call, Sir. Most will be off guard, and half drunk by then. Islam appears to be a curious religion regards imbibing alcohol.

"We'll need ninja's, Sir. By that I mean our best SAS platoons on the ground to be briefed by me before we strike."

"They will be the SBS, as they're good with water; boats and stuff like that. You mentioned canals. They will need a safe corridor in."

"We have several. The old canals--they aren't monitoring those. Our forces need to come in from the east, south, and the Black Country. We've already prepared the ways in, sending details now."

"Good work. Call me before you go back in, just in case something comes up. We'll be ready to deploy tomorrow evening, New Year's Eve. Excuse me, I need time to prepare reinforcements and back up, people like medics and associated transportation. When the streets are cleared we'll also need some form of civilian authority to prevent looting, et cetera, and gaols. Tally-ho old chap and see you on the inside."

In due course, Dan debriefed with Alison and his Director, before calling other interested parties. He spoke to the MI5, and later handed Steve's digital file over a representative from Norwich, untouched.

Afterwards, he talked at length to Sinjun, who offered to run his eyes over the plan. Once Sinjun was set to work, Dan felt a small relief; if he had missed anything, he knew Sinjun would pick it up.

Finally, Dan called Felicity. At first she greeted his call with enthusiasm, before sounding a little off. "What's up, Filly?"

"Nothing, I'm just being a silly girl--I miss you so much and I wish you were here with me now. Just come home in one piece, OK?"

"Yes, of course I will, I'll be with you soon. Now how's our baby?..."

Having enjoyed talking to Dan, Felicity was aghast when she learned of his plan, but she realised his duty to Country was paramount, as was her own; he would only be gone for one more day after all.

People needed freeing from yoke of ISIL, and she rationalised her personal emotions against the greater good of all.

She knew Dan was going to say more, but she cut the call short by saying, "I love you. Until later then."

She blew him a kiss and was gone. Dan stared at the phone and listened to the dial tone for several moments. He shook his head to clear his thoughts and said, "I miss you too. I love you, bye."

His musings were interrupted when Sinjun rang;, "Dan, this is admirable, have you have been looking over my shoulder? My only concern is to make available backup for the Paras that go in. I've outlined some diversionary tactics you might employ for when and where they are due to land. Nothing sensational but just enough to divert enemy forces for the moment our boys arrive. Sending the file now. Otherwise this should go like clockwork."

For Felicity, time passed slowly.

On the evening of the strike, she turned down offers of New Year celebrations, and joined the team at five-thirty. All except Sinjun were present, and he linked in via videoconference.

Alison said, "Dan and the first wave began at four, sixteen hundred hours. Later, Felicity spoke to him via secure comm.., and he seemed upbeat. She buffed his ego, but afterwards experienced a new feeling, that of impending loss. To calm her fears she kept herself busy making drinks and snacks, before becoming immersed on comm. and speaking often to Dan amongst many others. The hours flew by as the team at the village worked to support operations on the ground.

On his return to Brum, Dan joined Steve, and together they worked with the SBS, conducted drills with different teams of locals to perfect their plan. Targets were assigned to local freedom fighters, with either Dan or Steve working with each group until they were proficient. Late that night they returned to base, and Steve said, "We're a go! Our reconnaissance is complete, both main assault and backup plans are in place."

"Good work, Steve, same here. Let's check this operation over so we associate it into a cohesive whole. The strategy is that if one attack fails, other personnel, other teams nearby provide routes for attack, counter attack, escape and extraction."

"OK, let's get to it. We meet with Azaz in one hour. We better get this right first time., there are no second chances."

And they did. The Allies took out the ISIL control centres and communications first, but after the enemy pursued minor distractions arranged by the resistance; like vehicle accidents, and several alarms were raised to find non-existent infidels.

The paratroopers landed unbeknownst to ISIL commanders, and without control centre communications, the enemy were quickly cornered, killed, or captured. There were few of the latter.

The caliphate were caught completely off guard, and inroads into their infrastructure were quickly made. Pinpointed by Bude, fighter/bombers took out local bases, and as disarray of defending forces mounted, troops began the external invasion.

It was bloody. Many died, including innocent civilians. ISIL used them as human shields, and killed some in desperation of being overrun.

The fighting continued into January, but by the third day, most of Birmingham was again under British control. Isolated pockets remained, to be taken out with regard to preserving innocent life. Resistance fighters secured many British Muslim lives, before buildings housing ISIL warlords were demolished by missiles, aircraft, or drones.

Dan returned to Lower Meddlington office late on Tuesday, the third of January, when the fighting was all but done. He sported new wounds, but was in fine spirits. After debrief at the office, Felicity fell into his arms, her relief palpable for all to see. Once feeling secure, she berated him for being so foolish, and commended him for his bravery. Notwithstanding, admiration for her chosen man soon took precedence, and she took him home to comfort and recuperate.

§

In her New Year's Message to the People, Queen Regent Kathy made a public proclamation. "My people, it is my pleasure to announce the scourge of ISIL been has all but driven from Britain's shores, and will never be allowed to return.

"Some may consider our actions to be extreme, but so were theirs, and we played by their rules. Our aim was to make the roads and byways of Britain, safe for women and children to walk the streets alone at night. We have mostly been successful. This cancer has now, virtually been eradicated.

"We have already deported thousands of thugs and tricksters, con artists, smugglers, thieves, murderers, paedophiles, and people traffickers, back to their home countries in Europe and the Middle East. The vast majority were Muslim extremists.

"Please put aside your personal hatred and bigotry, and welcome into the bosom of our society, those moderate Muslims that remain. Help them integrate and enhance our culture.

"Of those deported to countries now under ISIL rule is not our concern. These people, by their total disrespect for life, human decency, and the laws of this country are guilty of treason. Please report all instances to local police, who will follow up. Our border controls are now some of the toughest in the world. They will not be returning.

"We are undertaking a massive restructuring of government, and later this year hope to hold a General Election to restore Parliament. We are also creating a new, light-weight civil service, and returning core industries and infrastructure to state control. Education, Health, and Power first, followed by implementing a new national police force.

"Please continue to check this channel, and see our official website for latest updates and information. Thank you, may you go in peace."

In the New Year Felicity was given the highest commendation by her force. Her work and results far exceeded expectation. Dan's team regrouped under a new title, and continued to recruit new members. Veronica was tasked with training, and identifying personal skill sets.

The team were still monitoring UK, but the focus tended to be small and specific outposts of Islam. The UK mopping up operation was in full swing, but for the team, their old job was largely done.

Veronica moved on from basic training, to have new teams monitor their past threats out of sequence, where they had to make their own logs, decisions, and calls. It proved an interesting, entertaining, and valuable teaching tool.

Dan spent some time away talking with Sir Jack and other military, plus fledgling government departments. Their first resolve was the security of the British Isles. Some talks included representatives of Eire. Dan made friends with his opposite number in the Irish security services, and they developed a good understanding.

Dan's main obligations for the New Year were, to ensure the continued freedom of Spain and Portugal. Italy appeared to be teetering on the brink, but Dan's number one charge was to liberate France. The team began to work in close association with the Free French, and they largely adopted the British approach.

Dan called Sinjun. "I just finished with Sir Jack, and your work on Leicester was to quote him, 'Brilliant!' well done. They needed the lateral diversions you scripted, to confuse the enemy, and many lives were saved. He gave me his full proposal to pass on. You remain with the new team, for now, and are promoted to Major-General, backdated to when you came to us."

"That is most agreeable Dan. I accept the appointment with relish."

Chapter 55 ~ Last Strike

Time moved on. Felicity held her hen party on a Wednesday, in Norwich. It began with exotic coffee and snacks, followed by shopping. The girls stopped in each bar they came to, and had a great time. They took in a wine bar, a risqué show, finishing in a club. It was late when she fell asleep on a friends couch, but she did make it into work on time the next morning.

Dan also had his stag do the same night, and Percy decided they should have a beer at each pub on the 'square mile', as they called the walk around the roads of Lower and Upper Meddlington. To his party were added Sinjun, Martin, and Alison.

They started in the pub near the police station, dropped in at the pub at the top of the road, and then walked out to the off licence at the shopping centre. Percy called Alf, who gave them a ride to the top of Upper Meddlington high street. He departed saying he'd join them later. They had a pint in each pub, news of what was afoot quickly spreading. Sid the builder and his mate joining them.

The fourth pub in Upper Meddlington, was a little way down the road towards Lower Meddlington, where they topped up and were getting a little drunk. Percy made sure he and Dan ate several rolls, and the half-mile walk back to town seemed to ease their drunkenness. Out of courtesy, they went to the pub that was virtually a restaurant, and had a quick pint there, also spreading the news.

After backtracking to the quietest pub, they went to the nearest from Dan's home, knowing their goal was in sight. Alf joined them, and they stayed for two pints, before heading off to complete the circuit where they started. Many had gathered there to welcome them, local farmers, shopkeepers, and people that knew, or knew of Dan. They held out until last orders, and Percy saw to it that Dan's drink regularly disappeared.

They had had a great night, made a big impression on the people they met. Percy saw Dan home. Dan was asleep as soon as his head hit the couch, and Percy napped in the armchair nearby, waiting for the inevitable. Dan threw up several times during the night, he was not a big drinker. Percy got him to drink isotonic water, and napped.

Sid rapped the door at seven. "I'm going to get the lads bacon butties, do you need any?"

Percy thanked Sid, and ordered four. Dan came out of his drunken slumbers looking bad, but alive, and he revived with hot, sweet tea, and breakfast butties. After a shower, Dan was more like his old self, and thanked Percy for staying. "I had to. Threw up three times so you did, in that bucket right there. You should be as right as rain in a few hours, and you made a good impression with the locals."

"But you drank the same. Why aren't you like me?"

"A secret not to be shared. I did'ne. I drank a little of each glass, and sidled it away, and I also ate a little. Okay, I did enjoy a couple near the end, but for the most part, I was okay to drive. The Best Man's job is to entertain, look after, and look out for the Groom. It was my first time."

Both Dan and Felicity worked on Thursday, and finished their day knowing they had a long week off. They shared a quiet, loving night in, telling tales of their nights out, and talking of what was to come. They were nestling awake on Friday morning, when a rap came to their front door. "Not your mother at this early hour?"

Dan went down and let Margaret in, Tom leaving for work. The morning was dark, cold, spitting with rain. Margaret said, "There's a warm front coming in overnight, tomorrow should be a nice day."

Dan went back to bed, and later, Felicity got morning coffee, as her mother rattled on. "Now you did tell the bridesmaids to come for fitting, didn't you? Who's the chief usher? ... I better get that sorted. Where's the guest list? You see how much there is to do."

Dan and Felicity chuckled. They did not see, and knew everything would be fine. The day became busy, although Dan had little to do, and went into work. That evening the bridesmaids arrived, with their hired dresses, and Margaret checked their fittings until satisfied.

Dan called around seven. "How's it going, Filly?"

"Great, we're almost done. What about you?"

"I'm still at the village, and it's bad luck to see you before the wedding. I'll stay here for the last time tonight, and avoid seeing you in the morning. Percy and your mother can ensure I remain out of sight. I'll prepare in the library, so have my wedding tackle sent there."

"I miss you, but I know you are right. Until tomorrow, then. Mwah."

Dan slept well, completed his morning routine, and ate breakfast with the team. The day was like spring, warm and calm. Percy called at nine. "Time to come home Dan. All is ready and you are expected."

He was being dressed in the library, when the sound of a jet came from the field. He ran out the back, and found Sir Jack parking a Harrier jump jet near the hangar. "Today's the big day. Oh, not a wedding present, but we may still have a little job to do later, and I have a lift back today. Here're the password; read, memorise, and eat."

They walked back, and Dan was ushered once more into the library, where his fitting was almost complete. Several people arrived, including the team, and the house was busy. Cameramen and the local press were in their element. Sir Jack was adjusting Dan's medals, when an aid rushed up. "Sir, Queen's Flight is compromised. The interceptors were drawn off, and there's a new threat."

Dan threw off his jacket and shouted, "Which direction?"

"South," came the reply as Dan ran for the field. The engine was coming up as Sir Jack and a cameraman reached the field. Dan closed the cockpit canopy, saluted with his first two fingers together, and the Harrier rose into the air. Dan activated forward thrust, and pulled up the nose, as the undercarriage was withdrawn. He released vertical thrust as the plane came round, and sped away in the opposite direction. Sir Jack said, "I've never seen that manoeuvre before, we'll need a copy of the recording."

Dan contacted military control. "This is Dan flying Sir Jack's Harrier. I am on my way to assist Queen's Flight in difficulty. Directions to destination and current status."

"Dan, you are the nearest to them. Four fighters drew the interceptors away, and the dogfight is still in progress, if two bogeys down. There is a new threat, an old French aircraft, but it is closing. You should reach QF about the same time. They are approaching a small mountain and will try to dodge behind it."

"How the hell did they get here"

"They came in using civilian squawks from Holland; ex USAF bought on the antique market we think. But they are still a threat."

Dan came closer and saw Queen's Flight nearest him, being hunted. His angle of approach was an advantage. He locked and fired at the enemy plane, taking it out, but not before it released two heat seeking missiles. "Patch me through to QF."

Dan continued to close, taking a route that would put his Harrier between the missiles and the light jet. Closing on position he said, "Queens Flight, this is Dan, I'm in the Harrier in your mirrors. I am going to have the missiles come after me. On my mark, dive, and hope they follow me. Over and out."

Dan positioned himself between the missiles and their target: "Dive."

The missiles were locked on Dan, and he tried to outrun them, drawing both missiles south and further away from Queen's Flight.

He was considering more extreme measures, when his earpiece said, "Harrier pilot, Interceptor one is with you. I cannot lock on the missile, you are too close together. Can you shake it off?"

Dan dived, creating a little more space between him and the missiles, which realigned to target him again. Nearing the ground he said aloud, "Got you now, you bastard."

Dan pulled up the nose sharply, and engaged landing thrusters. He went up and west, the missile down and east. He heard an explosion as he levelled off. "Wow! You broke missile lock. That's some airplane, Dan. One missile downed, one to go."

"I've done it before. It is not nice. I'll try to do it again, but this second missile is very close now. You get Queen's Flight to safety."

The interceptor broke away to shadow Queen's Flight.

Chapter 55

Meanwhile, Dan pulled the nose up until they were climbing almost vertically. The second missile continued to close. He tried to shake it off with normal manoeuvres, but was unsuccessful.

His only chance was to use the landing thrusters, again, to try to avoid contact. He engaged landing thrusters, already preparing to cancel them in case of blackout.

He felt the G-force pressure increase as instantly an explosion rocked the aircraft. Alarms sounded. Shocked, Dan scanned his instrumentation, trying to make sense of what he was seeing,

Dan was in big trouble.

The Harrier was not a glider. It needed power to fly. What little Dan had was focused in the wrong direction; landing thrusters were locked on. Fuel was disappearing at an alarming rate. He had little control over the craft.

Instantly, Dan's mind snapped into survival mode, eyes constantly moving, running checks and options like jumbled ticker tape:

Scanning: body OK, mind clearing.

Distress beacon activated.

Ejector seat... available..

Instruments... a mess of conflicting data; losing fuel, losing height, both too rapidly.

Visibility... useless in the clouds.

Priority: lose height to gain ground visibility.

Chance of landing intact... remote.

Controls, checking all... rudder OK, ailerons limited, Reaction Control System (RCS) damaged, meaning low speed flight difficult, landing compromised.

Landing gear... Deployed.

Scanning... dropping quickly, five thousand feet.

Ground visible... looks close, options...

Scanning visual... houses... trees... a lot of houses, heading slowly around to open farmland. River. Lake... maybe within range, just.

Heading set for lake, fingers crossed

Priority: preservation of life, preservation of property, preservation of Harrier? Preservation of my life? Felicity...

§

Half in her wedding finery, and fully fuelled for battle, Felicity stormed into the Library and shouted, "What the hell is going on?"

Sir Jack was on the phone and waved her quiet, but with a concerned grimace. "Have you the exact location where he went down?

He looked Felicity in the eye and said, "Search and rescue minutes out, understood. Let me know as soon as you have further details.

"Felicity…"

"Sir Jack, where is my husband to be? We're about to be married!"

"Ah, the latest we have is that he either landed or crashed into a lake or field, somewhere adjacent to Helion Bumpstead, just over in, err, Essex."

"I'll give you a hellion if you don't start talking sense!"

Sir Jack moved quickly and held Felicity's shoulders, "Dan went to rescue Queen's Flight who came under missile attack. He saved the day, drawing the missiles away to target his aircraft."

"How is he?"

"We don't know, but the signs so far are good. The Harrier is on the ground and mainly in one piece. Search and rescue will be there shortly, and they will inform me immediately.

"It would appear Queen Regent Kathy was en route between Windsor and Sandringham, and I understand they were likely to arrive here for your wedding."

Reeling from shock after shock, her rage turned to speechless consternation, she let Sir Jack guide her towards Percy, who wrapped an arm around her shoulders and said, "Come, let's find your mother and a nice cup of sweet tea. You know Dan will be fine, he's a survivor. Come along now, chin up… Ah yes, the kitchen, here we are."

The End